"This book is the

depicts the wretched desperation that the police must experience in the face of something as truly awful as people being randomly and brutally killed and being unable to wade through the morass of evidence in time to save lives... [McEvoy] is a fantastic character: far from perfect but never giving up despite provocation…" **Reactions to Reading**

"I for one am a big fan of the police procedural as a genre, and Kitchin gives us an excellent version, emphasizing not the lurid crimes committed by the serial killer but the sometimes plodding pursuit of the killer in the detective's meticulous methodology… The story is tight indeed, moving along at an electric pace that never lets up." **International Noir**

"One of the most unusual crime novels to come out of Ireland in recent times. A gripping thriller with characters that ring true coupled with images and acts that would leave even Hannibal Lecter silent! In particular, the novel portrays hard working, decent Gardai, deeply committed to solving crimes in the community. There are more twists than the red cow roundabout, but you will not lose the plot in this clever and unusual crime novel." **Joe Duffy, RTE**

"Rob Kitchin has shown there is still some life in the serial killer theme if the main investigating officer and the villain can capture your attention. Policeman Colm McEvoy is a sympathetic character who has so many problems to face, both personal and professional, that you feel for him and can identify with the stress he is under. …This was a very promising first crime novel." **Crime Scraps**

"After the first day I was entangled in the web and forgot all about my headache and my runny nose. In the beginning I feared that the combination of serial killer plus male writer might turn into a hard-boiled, graphic story, but in the best traditions of British crime fiction the focus stays with the police work and the increasingly personal battle between McEvoy and the killer. And Colm McEvoy – the very human but frustrated copper and father – is one of those characters you really want to meet again – the sooner the better!" **DJs Krimiblog**

"Kitchin has written a very good police procedural that features a serial killer. …The way the clues are constructed and what the police do with them is clever, unique even, and adds to the enjoyment of the story. Colm McEvoy is a sympathetic and engaging character. …Kitchin has the foundation for a good series and I closed the book wishing that there already was a sequel available." **Mack Captures Crime**

"Two characters lured me deeper and deeper into this book: The Raven, a serial killer who's completely convinced of his own brilliance, and Colm McEvoy… I found the investigation compelling… With the storyline and pacing – and especially with the character of McEvoy – I'm hoping that *The Rule Book* is the first in a series featuring the detective superintendent." **Kittling Books**

"*The Rule Book* puts Rob Kitchin on the Irish Crime map. It's gripping, gruesome, and a hell of a fun puzzle. It shows careful research and digs deep into an interesting character. I was kept guessing until the end, desperately hoping that this novel would not go the crappy Hollywood route. There is a town called Hollywood in Ireland, but this serial killer's spree gives it a wide berth." **Critical Mick**

THE
WHITE GALLOWS

Rob Kitchin

IndePenPress

First published in Great Britain by Indepenpress

All paper used in the printing of this book has been made from
wood grown in managed, sustainable forests.

ISBN 978-1-907499-37-1

Indepenpress is an imprint of Indepenpress Publishing Ltd
25 Eastern Place, Brighton, BN2 1GJ

This is a work of fiction. Names, characters, places, and incidents
either are the product of the author's imagination or are used
fictitiously. Any resemblance to actual persons, living or dead,
events or localities is entirely coincidental.

Printed and bound in the UK

A catalogue record of this book is available from
the British Library

Cover design by Jacqueline Abromeit and Rob Kitchin

This book is dedicated to my parents,
Irene and Mervyn

ABOUT THE AUTHOR

Rob Kitchin is a Professor at the National University of Ireland, Maynooth, where he directs a research institute. *The White Gallows* is his second novel. He writes a regular blog at http://theviewfromthebluehouse.blogspot.com/

SUNDAY

The young man was lying on the gentle slope down to the River Boyne, his head a foot from the shallow water. He'd been badly beaten. Beneath his short black hair his face was bruised and bloody, his lips thick and split, eyes swollen shut. His right arm lay outstretched into a bed of reeds, the hand clutching a blood-stained kitchen knife. His left arm was crooked across his chest, his hand placed over his sternum, fingers dark red. The sleeve of his black jacket was torn at the right shoulder revealing the orange liner beneath, his jeans scuffed at the knees, a streak of mud running down one leg.

Detective Superintendent Colm McEvoy checked his watch – 9.35am – and pushed his six foot three frame up from his haunches. He repositioned his striped tie over a sky-blue shirt, and tugged at the sleeves of a well-tailored suit as he gazed each way along the cinder path hugging the riverbank then across the rapidly moving water to Trim Castle. Dating from 1176, it was the finest Anglo-Norman castle in Ireland – a three storey, crucifix-shaped keep surrounded by a near complete outer wall and moat.

He stared down at the body again, scratched at his thinning hair, and then waved Detective Inspector Jim Whelan over to him. Like McEvoy, Whelan worked for the National Bureau of Criminal Investigation, the branch of the Gardai that investigated the country's most serious crimes, including many murders.

'They didn't make much effort to hide the body,' McEvoy observed.

Whelan nodded his head but stayed silent. In his late forties and bald, except for a thin ring of hair that circled from ear to ear, he was a man of few words.

McEvoy sighed to himself, realising his mistake. There was no point making statements to Whelan – he took them as self-serving. A response required a question.

'Do we have any idea who he is?' he asked, tiredness in his voice.

'No.'

'Nobody's reported anybody missing?'

'No.'

'And there were no reports of any disturbances in the town last night or in the early hours?'

'No.'

'And he was found at 6.25 this morning?'

'Yes.'

'And there've been no reports of any knife wounds at any of the local hospitals?'

'No.'

'For God's sake, Jim,' McEvoy snapped, 'this isn't twenty questions! I need more than yes or no answers.'

'They were yes or no questions,' Whelan answered defensively.

'Are you sure there weren't any reported altercations last night – late night fights or rows? Saturday night blowouts?' McEvoy asked, knowing that the town would have been full of young lads from the estates and farmers from the surrounding area all beered up and oozing testosterone. Whoever Whelan had asked, had probably meant there'd been no more disturbances than usual; that there was nothing beyond general loutishness.

'I'll check again.'

'Who's the local superintendent?' McEvoy said, shaking his head, annoyed at Whelan's non-responsiveness. There was

2

no doubting that the man was a very good detective – brilliant at observing, listening, and joining up the dots – but he could be damn frustrating to work with.

'Tommy Boland.'

'And where the hell is he? Someone's murdered on his doorstep and he feckin' disappears!' When McEvoy had arrived ten minutes ago there had only been three local guards at the scene, along with Whelan and his team.

'He's at the station.'

McEvoy had passed the Garda station on the way to the car park. It was a short distance away on the far side of the castle.

'Well, get him back here! I need to talk to him for God's sake. And get this whole area sealed off properly – I want it locked down from the entrance to the castle car park,' he pointed across the river to where a short row of shops bordered a near empty parking lot, 'down to the road bridge.' He gestured to his left, where a couple of hundred metres away a flat bridge spanned the river.

'You know the routine,' he continued, 'assign one of your DSs to organise a search for evidence and run questionnaires, another to run interviews, and the last to operate an incident room. If the station's too small, find somewhere else suitable.'

'Already done,' Whelan replied, rolling his eyes. 'Your patches not working?'

'What? Yes. I mean no. Look, they're feckin useless.' Of course Whelan had done the basics. And he was right – he hadn't had a cigarette for nearly six months, but that didn't stop the craving; didn't stop him being irritable and short-tempered. The only explanation he could offer was the stress of the job and a lack of a full night's sleep. Nicotine had been a coping drug and now it was gone, but he was still addicted to the thought of what it might do.

He watched Whelan head towards the narrow wooden, pedestrian bridge that led back to the car park, then glanced up to his right. On top of a steep bank, the ruined Yellow Steeple, the only surviving remnant of the thirteenth century St. Mary's

Augustinian Abbey, rose into the overcast sky. A murder of crows launched from the crumbling walls and swept across the river to the castle opposite.

He closed his eyes and massaged his forehead, bringing his fingers down to clasp the bridge of his nose. He really did need a decent night's sleep. A full eight hours comatose. He hadn't slept well since Maggie, his wife of fifteen years, had died of cancer nearly a year before. The killing spree of the Raven six months earlier had only increased his insomnia – nine people had been killed over eight fraught days, ten if the unborn child of one of the victims was counted. McEvoy had been the lead investigator. By any standard the case had been horrific and it was never far from his thoughts, keeping him awake into the early hours. His mobile phone rang.

'McEvoy,' he said flatly.

'Colm, what's the story?' Chief Superintendent Tony Bishop asked without introduction. McEvoy's immediate superior, his management style was a mix of passive and aggressive bullying. Losing faith and patience during the Raven case he'd tried to force McEvoy out of his job and there was still little love lost between the two men.

'I don't know yet. The victim's a young man, probably nineteen or twenty. He's been badly beaten and it look's like stabbed in the chest. My guess is he lost a knife fight.'

'Lithuanian,' Bishop stated with confidence.

'Possibly,' McEvoy conceded. In the previous few years there'd been a number of fatal altercations between Lithuanian migrants to Ireland. The deaths were almost exclusively young men with limited English, working in manual jobs such as construction or agriculture. Since the downturn some had left seeking work elsewhere, but a relatively large number had stayed put, collecting unemployment benefit, aware that things were little better in other parts of the world. On the days when they weren't working the men would often get excessively drunk on cheap vodka, fall into arguments, then fists would be raised or knives drawn. He'd recently read that the murder rate amongst

4

the immigrant group was twice that of their native country. Nobody could explain to him why the phenomenon wasn't occurring amongst the other Eastern European communities such as the Poles and Latvians.

'Well, I have another one for you. Albert Koch, 91, late of Ballyglass, near Athboy. He was found dead this morning by his housekeeper. The local doctor says he died of natural causes, but one of our lot isn't so sure. He thinks there might have been foul play – a fatal blow to the head. Plus his housekeeper thinks that the place has been searched. I want you to get over there and find out how much we need to worry about it.'

'I'm busy here,' McEvoy replied, annoyed. 'And I've already got several other active cases – the Raven, the laundering suicide, Kylie O'Neill. I'm up to my eyeballs.'

'We're *all* up to our eyeballs, Colm,' Bishop snapped. 'We've already passed eighty murders for the year! That's twenty up on last year. And we could be up to ninety by the end of December. We're not getting any more new recruits and it's just us usual suspects at the top, those of us who're left,' he said, referring to the exodus created by the hunt for early retirements in order to cut costs. The recession was biting everywhere, all recruitment and promotion in the public sector suspended, contract staff being laid off as their present terms came to an end, senior staff being encouraged to retire but without replacement, overtime curtailed in all but exceptional circumstances, and a pension levy and income tax hike biting into take home pay. 'Superintendents supervise; just give your DIs their heads.'

McEvoy knew Bishop was right. The Raven had pushed the total up, but so too had the gangland wars between rival families and criminal groups in Limerick and Dublin. There might have been only six recorded cases of manslaughter and murder in 1960, but if things carried on the way they were they'd be investigating over a hundred per annum within a year or two.

'Who's the DI?' McEvoy asked.

'I was just coming to that. If it is a suspicious death, you'll need to run the case; Whelan was the last in the pool. That's everybody now off the Raven case except Barney Plunkett and all leave's been cancelled. Roche is up to his neck in it down in Limerick. Plus Koch wasn't a nobody. He was pretty much a recluse, but apparently he was also one of the richest men in Ireland. He owned Ostara Industries and had substantial stakes in other investments, including a large overseas property portfolio.'

'I thought you just said that superintendents supervise?'

'Only when there are people to supervise! Otherwise they make do. I wouldn't be doing this, Colm, except I've no damn choice. There've been four fatal shootings in West Dublin in the last ten days, and three more in Limerick. Your Lithuanian and Albert Koch make two more. God knows how many open cases we're dealing with at the moment. We're pretty much at breaking point.'

'Look, I'll get over there once I've finished up here,' McEvoy conceded reluctantly. At one point there had been two superintendents, six inspectors, and an army of detective sergeants and gardai working on the Raven investigation. The worst criminal case in the state's history had been reduced to a part-time superintendent, one inspector, two detective sergeants and a handful of detective garda due to resourcing pressures. Bishop wasn't exaggerating when he said they were at breaking point. 'Who do I have to work with?'

'Jesus, Colm,' Bishop said exasperated. 'Find out if there's anything worth investigating. If there is, you can sort out the team for yourself. Pick a couple of sergeants and some competent garda. I'll talk to you later.' The line went dead.

McEvoy stared at the phone for a moment shaking his head then slipped it into his pocket. At least Athboy, a small rural town on the farming plains of Meath, was only ten miles further out from Dublin than Trim. And the laundering suicide was only about thirty minutes drive further north. Only Kylie O'Neill, a young mother found battered to death, was outside of

6

Meath and Cavan, having been found in her home in Tipperary town, a two-hour drive to the south.

He glanced down at the body again and then headed back towards the wooden bridge. He spotted Jim Whelan walking towards him with Tommy Boland and stopped, waiting for them to cross the Boyne.

Boland was broad shouldered and thick set, a concerned look etched on his round face. 'Colm,' he said good naturedly as he neared, holding out a hand.

'Tommy,' McEvoy replied, vaguely recognising Boland from some previous case or course. They shook hands and started to head back to the young man's body. 'Where the hell have you been?' McEvoy asked gruffly, offloading some of his frustration with Bishop and the system. 'And where the hell are your guards?'

'That's what I've been trying to sort out,' Boland replied, instantly becoming annoyed at McEvoy's reception. 'Three of my lot are off playing for the local GAA. I've been trying to draft in replacements from Navan. They'll be here in fifteen minutes.'

'A murder takes precedence over some local game,' McEvoy said sourly.

'Not round here it doesn't,' Boland countered. 'Especially when it's some little gobshite no one's ever heard of.'

'What?' McEvoy said, taken aback at Boland's statement.

'He's probably just some feckin' immigrant who's got too big for his boots. They're always causing some disturbance round the town. The stupid eejits can't hold their drink, then they start looking for a fight. Some nights it can be bedlam round here, especially after they've been paid.'

'What makes you think he's an immigrant?' McEvoy said obstinately, challenging Boland's xenophobic assumption and prejudice.

'The look of him.' Boland glanced down at the victim and shrugged his shoulders. 'Bad haircut. Cheap jacket, jeans and trainers. The knife. The fact I don't recognise him.'

'A town like this must be full of blow-ins; loads of new estates full of commuters to Dublin,' McEvoy observed. 'It could be some young Dublin hood.'

'Yeah, well,' Boland conceded. 'That's where I'd start, that's all I'm saying. Don't worry; the boys from Navan will be here shortly – we can get started then.'

'We'll get started now; here's the technical unit.' McEvoy nodded his head toward where two white vans were parking across the river. 'Do we know when Elaine Jones is likely to arrive?' he asked referring to the state pathologist.

'Ten thirty,' Whelan answered flatly.

McEvoy nodded. He'd wait for her to arrive and give her initial assessment, then he'd head over to Ballyglass to view Albert Koch.

'I want to talk to the poor sod that found him. If he does turn out to be a foreigner you'll need to bring in GNIU,' McEvoy continued, referring to the Garda National Immigration Unit. 'They'll be able to help you contact his relatives and work with the relevant community – organise access, translators and so on.'

Without waiting for an answer he started to head back toward the bridge to meet the new arrivals. Two new cases on the same morning and he was already in a sour mood; though that was nothing unusual these days, he reflected. He seemed to get out of the wrong side of the bed almost every morning.

* * *

Hannah Fallon gathered her auburn hair together and pulled it through a black scrunchy, letting it fall in a pony tail over her luminous yellow coat. In her late thirties, she was in charge of the three-person, technical crime scene team. She opened the rear door of the van and started to unload equipment, passing it to the overweight figure of George Carter, grey-haired and in his late forties. Chloe Pollard, the third member of the team joined them, readjusting the paper suit covering her hour-glass

'Don't worry, Colm, you'll be the first to know. Come on then, Billy, let's get this show on the road.'

* * *

McEvoy passed through a tunnel of tall copper beech trees and turned left into a wide gateway; large stone pillars each supporting a golden eagle taking flight. 'The White Gallows' was etched into the left-hand column. He coasted up the curved gravel driveway, framed each side by a row of lime trees, to the front of a large farmhouse and parked in behind a dark green Audi A4. Three other cars were parked nearby: a silver Mercedes 180, a dark blue Mercedes 320 and a marked garda car.

The farmhouse was a two-storey structure covered in Boston Ivy that had recently lost its bright red leaves. Three steps led up to a Georgian door, a semi-circle of clear glass above it. There were two Georgian sash windows to the left of the door, one to the right. A single-storey structure continued past the house to the right, interrupted along its length by a high archway. From McEvoy's experience it almost certainly led into a farmyard that would be framed all the way round by outbuildings. It was a modest house for someone reputed to be one of the richest men in Ireland.

He exited the car, climbed the steps to the front door and clunked down the large, brass knocker.

A few seconds later it was opened by a flustered looking man in his late twenties. 'Yes?'

'Detective Superintendent McEvoy. I believe you're expecting me?'

'What? Yes, yes, join the party!' the man said sarcastically, standing to one side and ushering McEvoy into a cold, wood-panelled hallway. A broad staircase rose on the right-hand side, a narrow, stain-glass window on the landing above letting in weak light.

'I really don't think all this attention is necessary,' the man said to McEvoy's back. 'The doctor said he died of heart failure.'

'Who is it?' a shrill female voice asked from an adjoining room.

'Another guard,' the man answered as if McEvoy wasn't there.

'Can't you get rid of him? I thought we'd got this awful mess sorted out?'

McEvoy headed towards the woman's voice, pushed open the door and entered a simply decorated living room. It was occupied by a woman and man sitting together on a mid-blue sofa. They appeared to be in their late fifties and dressed smartly: the woman in casual, tan trousers with a pale blue cashmere cardigan over a white blouse; the man in dark blue suit over a cream shirt with gold cuff-links and no tie. The woman's shoulder-length hair was dyed blonde, though her grey roots were just starting to show, and her make-up was subtly applied. A fire was blazing in the grate, warming the chill air.

'I'm afraid the answer to that is no,' McEvoy stated flatly. 'I'm Detective Superintendent McEvoy. I'm in charge of the case, if there is a case. First, let me offer my condolences on the death of Mr Koch. He was…?' He let the question hang.

'My father. He was my father.' The woman raised a white cotton handkerchief to her left eye, but left the impression of crying crocodile tears. 'I'm sorry, superintendent, but I think you might have had a wasted trip. The doctor says he died of natural causes.'

'Look… er… You have my deepest sympathy, Mrs… Koch?'

'D'Arcy.'

'Mrs D'Arcy. And I'm sure the last thing you need right now is the guards intruding at such a difficult moment, but one of the officers who responded to the emergency call feels there might be more to it.'

'And your officers are qualified doctors, are they?' Mrs D'Arcy asked facetiously.

'No, but they're trained to observe for signs that might indicate foul play. The state pathologist is presently in Trim and

14

since she's so close, if I agree with the officer, I'll be asking her to come and take a look to clear up any misunderstanding.'

'I don't think that's necessary,' the man stated. 'He was an old man; in his nineties. He died in his sleep.'

'And you are?' McEvoy asked curtly.

'James Kinneally,' the man replied rising to his feet. 'I'm the CEO of Ostara Industries, the company Dr Koch founded.' He held out his hand which McEvoy shook firmly.

'With all due respect, Mr Kinneally, we have to investigate all suspicious deaths even if that suspicion turns out to be groundless.'

'But the only person that has that suspicion is one of your officers,' Kinneally protested.

'Look, I know you're both upset by the death of Dr Koch, but it will only take a minute to verify if there's anything worth investigating. If there isn't, we'll be out of your hair shortly and you can get on with your arrangements. If there is, then I'm sure you will want to bring the perpetrator to justice.'

'This is ridiculous,' Marion D'Arcy muttered to no one in particular.

* * *

McEvoy and the local sergeant, Tom McManus, were standing next to the double bed on which lay the body of Albert Koch. The cadaver was covered by a pure white duvet, only his head showing, propped up on a pillow. His face was gaunt, the skin pulled tight to the bones, a full head of grey hair messily arranged.

The man who had opened the front door hovered nearby. McEvoy had discovered he was Kevin Boyle, a former journalist, now employed as a PR person for Ostara Industries. He was there to handle the press or any other parties interested in Koch's death, including the gardai. He'd made it clear to McEvoy that Ostara and Koch had a public image that had to be managed scrupulously.

'I'm sorry, but can you leave us alone please,' McEvoy stated gruffly, his earlier tetchiness surfacing again.

'I… I was just…' Boyle trailed off, unsure whether to stay or go.

'This is an official investigation; don't worry, we're not going to steal anything,' McEvoy said sarcastically.

'Er… right.' Boyle backed out of the bedroom.

McEvoy turned to Tom McManus, a thick-set man, almost bursting out of his dark blue uniform, with short black hair and stubble in need of a shave.

'Okay then, you better show me what set off the alarm bells.'

'Well, I… I'm not too sure… I mean…'

'Look, don't worry about what the doctor said or the rest of them,' McEvoy reassured. 'Plenty of doctors make mistakes.'

'Well,' McManus took a step forward, 'there seems to have been a blow to the head, here.' He pointed to a spot on the top of Koch's head. 'And he appears to have some bruising on his legs.'

He moved back to let McEvoy occupy his position.

'Also the way he's lying on the bed,' McManus continued. 'It's like he's slightly twisted, as if he'd been thrown on. I mean, you couldn't sleep like that – well, not for long anyway.'

McEvoy leaned in close to Koch's scalp. It was possible to see slight traces of blood near the roots.

'You think he was killed elsewhere?' McEvoy asked, pulling back the duvet.

'I'm not saying anything. It just doesn't feel right.'

McEvoy moved down the bed, lifted up the quilt and tugged up the left trouser leg of Koch's pyjamas. There was evidence of fresh bruising on the calf.

'And the reason for these?' he asked, pointing.

'Somebody dragged him up the stairs? I don't know.'

McEvoy nodded his head in agreement. 'And what did the doctor say?' he asked.

'That he'd most probably died of heart failure. Simply old age.'

'And the wound on the head? The legs?'

'Nothing much. Maybe he'd fallen out of bed or had a fit and knocked it on the bedside locker. Either way, he doesn't think it would have been enough to kill him.'

McEvoy glanced at the spotless locker. 'I've heard that before. Jesus,' he muttered to himself. 'I'm going to need to make a phone call. Can you make sure that eejit isn't listening at the door? And clear everybody out of the house; this is a murder scene until I'm convinced otherwise.'

'They're not going to like that.'

'I don't care what they like,' McEvoy snapped, his temper fraying again. 'And while you're at it, you'd better get hold of your superintendent and get him out here.'

'He'll probably be halfway round the golf course at this stage of the morning,' the sergeant replied, glancing at his watch. 'He won't want to be disturbed.'

'As I've already said, I don't care. I want him out here. Tell him that if he's not out here in half an hour I'll start shaking the tree.'

'As long as he knows I'm only the messenger.' McManus shook his head and left the room, closing the door behind him.

McEvoy pulled his mobile phone from his pocket. He scrolled through the names in the address book and pressed connect. The phone was answered after three rings.

'Colm?' Elaine Jones said brightly.

'I think you better come up to Athboy once you've finished there,' McEvoy replied flatly.

'You don't think it was a natural death then?'

'No. It look's like his head's been bashed and the body moved. Can you also ask Hannah to follow you out?'

'I think she's about to head back into town; she's in court tomorrow.'

'Yeah, I know, but I'm only ten miles down the road and it'll save me getting a new team out. That'll take an age to or-ganise. If they need to come back tomorrow, George and Chloe can work the site without her.'

'I'll let her know, but she won't be happy.'

'None of us are happy, Elaine,' McEvoy said without rancour. 'I'd sooner be watching Man United versus Chelsea, but instead I'm traipsing around the country looking at dead bodies and trying to work out how and why they died.'

'There are worse things in life to be doing,' the pathologist observed.

'Such as?'

'Such as being the dead body. I'll be there shortly.' She ended the call.

McEvoy stared at the phone and then turned back to look at Albert Koch. Two bodies in one morning; things really were starting to get out of hand. He patted his pockets, instinctively searching for a pack of cigarettes, then shook his head at his own lameness. 'For feck's sake,' he muttered to himself.

The door to the bedroom was flung open.

'What the *hell* do you think you are doing?' Koch's daughter shouted. 'Have you *no* respect for the dead?'

McEvoy turned slowly.

She was standing in the doorway, a tumbler of whiskey in one hand, swaying slightly. It hadn't occurred to him that she'd been drunk when he'd spoken to her downstairs. Standing behind her were James Kinneally and Kevin Boyle, both looking anxious.

'I have every respect for the dead,' he said flatly. 'However, from my observations I'd say there's more to your father's death than simply heart failure. I've called the pathologist and she's on her way. Until she confirms things one way or another this is a crime scene and I want the house vacated to preserve whatever evidence might be left. So, if you'd leave the building, I'd be very grateful.'

'My father was *not* murdered,' Mrs D'Arcy slurred. 'He died in his sleep. Anyone can see that! You're just doing this to embarrass us. I want you to leave. Now! Go on fuck off!'

'Marion,' Kinneally warned. 'He's just doing his job.'

'The doctor said he died of natural causes! He was my father's doctor for over forty years. He should know. They just want to throw their weight around, get a few headlines and blacken the family name. I want you out of here now! You hear, now!'

'I'm sorry, Mrs D'Arcy, but we're not going anywhere. I know you're upset by the death of your father—'

'Upset!' she interrupted. 'You have no fuckin' idea what I'm feeling!'

'Well, I'm afraid you're wrong there,' McEvoy said solemnly. 'My wife died a year ago this Friday. I know all about losing someone you love. Now, can you please leave the house. If not, I'm sorry, but I will have to have you escorted off the premises.'

'Don't you threaten me!' Marion D'Arcy screamed, ignoring McEvoy's admission, spilling her whiskey. 'This is my home! I know my rights. I'm a lawyer.'

'Clearly not criminal law,' McEvoy muttered with little sympathy.

'Come on, Marion,' Kinneally said, grasping her shoulder. 'If they're wrong we can sue them later.'

She tried to hold McEvoy's stare then gave up. Reluctantly she turned on her low heels and left the bedroom.

Tom McManus poked his head round the door frame. 'Sorry about that,' he said sheepishly.

'Don't worry about it. Try and get them off site; I don't want them messing up anything more than they have already.' He pulled his mobile phone from his pocket yet again. He needed reinforcements.

* * *

Elaine Jones parted Koch's hair with gloved fingers and peered at the skull. 'Well, there's definitely been a serious impact here.' She traced the scalp with her fingertips and applied a little pressure. 'Can you get out of the way of the light, Billy?'

'Sorry,' her assistant mumbled and lurched to one side.

'I'd say he has a depressed skull fracture. I'll only know for sure once I perform a full autopsy.'

'It was enough to kill him?' McEvoy asked.

'Possibly.'

'But he did die of a heart attack?'

'Again I'll only know when I do the autopsy, but it may well be the case. The head injury might have led to severe internal haemorrhaging and clotting. It could have triggered a cardiac arrest.'

'So the local doctor could have been right?'

'Technically, yes. But discounting the head wound so quickly verges on negligence. He must have known it could have been a significant factor in his death.'

'Unless he had a reason to pronounce a natural death,' McEvoy hypothesized.

'That kind of speculation is your territory, Colm, not mine. All I know is that I smell a stinky fish.'

'What about his posture and the bruising on his legs?'

'I think the local sergeant is right. I'd say the body was moved. Most probably dragged up the stairs and thrown on the bed. He must hardly weigh a thing; it shouldn't have been too difficult.'

'Difficult enough though,' McEvoy observed. 'He'd be a dead weight.'

'I don't know. With the adrenaline of the attack I think even I could have pulled him up. Might have been a struggle, but doable. I'd say he only weighs about 50 kilos or so.'

'What's that in old money?' McEvoy asked, still unsure of metric conversions.

'About eight or nine stone. Given the lividity, my professional opinion is he died in the bed or very shortly beforehand. I'd say somewhere between midnight and 4 am. I'll be able to tell you more later.'

'So he was killed in the vicinity?' McEvoy surmised.

'Almost certainly.' She stepped back from the body and her assistant took a couple of photographs of Koch's head and shoulders.

'Well, that might help,' McEvoy stated flatly.

'Chin up, Colm. It could be worse,' the pathologist said brightly, her tired eyes sparkling above her face mask.

'It could be a damn sight better as well. Any idea what he might have been hit with?'

'I think that's my job, isn't it?' Hannah Fallon said from the doorway. 'Good to see that you got suited up, Colm.'

'Didn't seem much point at this stage,' McEvoy said, shrugging his shoulders, but nonetheless feeling guilty at his laxity.

'Well, I'm glad the example setting starts at the top. I take it they're not your footprints on that white rug?'

McEvoy looked at the rug, at his feet and back at the rug, unsure of his guilt. 'I, er, well…'

'So what have we got,' Fallon said, not waiting for a full reply, and breaking the seal on a paper suit.

'A blow to the head,' McEvoy said hesitantly, thrown off guard by Fallon's abrasiveness. 'It looks as if the body's been moved; probably dragged up the stairs.'

'And do we know where he was killed? I suppose you've trampled all over that as well, have you?'

'I, er, look, Hannah, I…'

'Look, I'm sorry,' Fallon stated, pulling the paper suit up over her trousers. 'I'm just a bit wound up about tomorrow. Having to process two sites today is not exactly ideal preparation. I've left Chloe in Trim to finish things off. George will be up in a minute. Do we know who he is?'

'Albert Koch,' McEvoy replied, ignoring her excuse, 'supposedly one of the richest men in Ireland. He lives here alone with his Polish housekeeper. According to the local sergeant she was out all night, staying with her boyfriend in Athboy, and discovered the body when she returned. She called the guards, who called the local doctor.'

'So what did he do to get rich then?' Fallon said, tugging on a pair of rubber gloves.

'He founded Ostara Industries. I'm not sure what they do exactly, but Ostara Pharmacies is part of the group.'

'I take it he's not Irish? Albert Koch sounds... German, I guess.'

'Sorry, Hannah, I know as much about him as you do. I don't think he was one for the limelight. I'll leave you to it, okay?' McEvoy said, heading for the door. 'I'll be on my mobile if you need me, Elaine.'

'As soon as Hannah's finished, we'll take him over to Navan Hospital and get started on him and the young Lithuanian,' the pathologist replied cheerily.

'I just hope this isn't going to drag on into the evening,' Fallon said distractedly. 'I need to get my head ready for tomorrow.'

'We're all in the same boat, Hannah,' McEvoy said descending the stairs.

'Well, it's sinking,' she called after him.

* * *

The sky was shades of light grey, elongated low clouds drifting across from the west threatening drizzle. McEvoy switched his attention to the old, gnarled branches of the leafless trees, wondering where his reinforcements were. He reached in through his shirt, pulled the nicotine patch from his upper arm and scrunched it up. He didn't know why he bothered with the things; they made practically no difference to his craving.

Tom McManus rounded the end of the building and approached.

'Well?' McEvoy asked as he neared.

'Mrs D'Arcy, James Kinneally and Kevin Boyle are holed up in her place. It's a couple of miles down the road. Roza, Koch's housekeeper, is with her boyfriend in Athboy. She's still pretty upset.'

'No sign of your superintendent?'

'Not yet. A couple of local lads have turned up. I've put one on the front gate, the other at the back entrance.'

'Good. So what do you know about Koch?'

'He's something of a local folk hero. Practically anything

of any significance within a ten-mile radius has been funded by Ostara. They're also the biggest employer for miles around. Anyone not working for them directly is taking their employees' wages over the counter.'

'So general, all-round good guy?'

'I wouldn't go that far,' McManus said cautiously. 'From what I've heard he was a cantankerous old bastard. He could be as difficult as hell to deal with and anyone who crossed him knew about it. And the old folk say he was ruthless when he was building his empire.'

'Then why so generous with the local amenities?'

'He mellowed?' McManus hazarded.

'So who would want to kill him? Any enemies?'

'I thought this was a burglary gone wrong?'

'Then what was taken?' McEvoy asked. 'If it was a burglary then they were after something specific because they seem to have left what few valuables there were. And why take the body back upstairs? Why not just leave it where it was? That blow to the head wasn't going to fool anybody.'

'Fooled the doctor,' McManus stated flatly.

'I'll need to talk to him later. He has some explaining to do.'

'So you don't think it was a burglar then?'

'It could have been,' McEvoy shrugged his shoulders. 'I've an open mind at this stage. It just doesn't seem to hang right, that's all.'

'I guess,' McManus didn't look convinced.

'So what about enemies?' McEvoy prompted.

'I don't know,' McManus shrugged. 'You'd have to ask the family, but you can't get to be as rich as Koch without rubbing a few people up the wrong way.'

'So why hasn't he got any security then? You could just walk into this place. Not exactly Fort Knox.'

'He used to employ a private security company for a while – you can still see bits of their kit around the place,' McManus pointed to a small surveillance camera hidden in a tree, 'but he discontinued their services a couple of years ago.'

'If he could afford it, why discontinue it? If he thought he was a target then, he was a target now.'

'Perhaps he felt safe enough?' McManus speculated. 'Or felt he could look after himself?'

'Perhaps,' McEvoy said, watching a red Volvo throw dust up as it sped up the drive.

'Here we go,' McManus muttered.

The car ground to a halt a few feet away. The driver's door flew open and a tall, dark-haired man in his late-forties levered himself out from behind the wheel. 'This better be important,' he growled as a greeting, rounding the car, still dressed in his golfing gear – pink pullover and pale blue trousers.

'And you are?' McEvoy demanded.

'Superintendent Cathal Galligan. And you?'

'Detective Superintendent Colm McEvoy, NBCI. I'm glad you could finally join us given that one of most important people in the area's been murdered.'

'Murdered!' Galligan exclaimed. 'I was told he died in his sleep.'

McManus shifted uncomfortably signalling that this wasn't entirely the case.

'He may well have done,' McEvoy said evenly, 'but he was still murdered.'

'Well, that's your territory, isn't it,' Galligan said, still trying to make an excuse for his absence. 'Whatever resources you need, just ask and we'll do our best to help. Tom here can be your liaison. How's that sound?' He started to back away towards his car, seemingly anxious to get back to his game of golf.

'I want to co-opt him into my investigative team; I only have one available DS and he knows the area and the people. You'll be doing the media work. As soon as they find out that Koch has been murdered they'll be all over this story.'

'I'll be doing the media work?' Galligan repeated.

'Yes. That's the policy. I have other things to be getting on with, like solving a murder. My suggestion is you better start taking an interest in things.'

'I… I should go and get changed,' Galligan said, looking down at his attire.

'That's up to you. Personally, I'd get up to speed on the case and contact the press liaison office.'

'I… er, yes, right.' Galligan rounded the car. 'Tom, er, you better get some people out here to help Superintendent McEvoy with the investigation. I'll… I'll be back in fifteen minutes or so.' He slipped in behind the wheel of the Volvo, reversed back quickly and sped down the tree-lined drive to the front gate.

'It'll be more like an hour,' McManus muttered, 'probably longer.'

* * *

'Colm. There you are!' Fallon stated loudly. 'I've been looking for you.'

McEvoy was leaning against a fence, looking down the length of a field to a small lake. The field was ringed by a hawthorn and ash hedge and the landscape was dotted with clumps of oak and beech trees. To his right was a large hayshed half-filled with large round bales. He glanced back at Fallon as she approached. Several nearby cows looked up then settled back to chewing the cud.

'What are you doing out here?' Fallon asked.

'Just having a look around while I wait for the others to arrive; it's a pretty modest place for a multi-millionaire – just the farmhouse, the farmyard and the hayshed. And it's all basic stuff; nothing expensive or flash; no fancy equipment or appliances. It's as if the house is frozen in the 1960s.'

'Perhaps that was all he needed?'

'Perhaps,' McEvoy repeated, continuing to gaze at the field.

'I came to tell you that we think we've found where Koch was attacked. There's a tiny amount of blood on the floor and a couple of shards from a vase just inside the door to his study.'

'And the rest of the vase?' McEvoy asked, turning towards her.

'Missing.'

'I'd better take a look,' McEvoy said without enthusiasm, setting off back toward the house.

They entered through the front door and turned right. The room was four metres or so square; book shelves ran floor to ceiling round all four walls, the only gaps being two doorways, the window and a fireplace. Lined along the shelves were thousands of books, intermittently divided by various ornaments and knick-knacks. Several other piles of books were scattered across the floor and stacked up on an old mahogany desk inlaid with green leather. Tucked up against the desk was an ancient wooden, swivel chair. The door opposite the window led through to the back of the house.

Fallon crouched down and pointed to a couple of spots barely visible on the dark floorboards.

'They're recent enough?' McEvoy said, lowering himself to join her, the boards creaking under his feet.

'Last day or so. There's a shard here.' She pointed to a piece of white porcelain, one edge stained blue, nestled in against the spines of two books on the nearest shelf. 'There's another one at the bottom of this pile.' She pointed to one side.

'So he was killed in here and then carried upstairs?'

'Attacked in here at least, perhaps. He might have died later on.' She shrugged her shoulders.

Their conversation was disturbed by the noise of two cars crunching up the driveway. McEvoy eased himself up and headed for the front door.

Detective Sergeant John Joyce and Detective Garda Kelly Stringer clamoured out of their respective cars and approached McEvoy. Round faced and boyish looking, Joyce was dressed in a scruffy grey suit, his thin hair shaved close to his head. He'd attained a doctorate in Sociology from Trinity College Dublin before changing career track and joining the gardai. He was still viewed with suspicion by a few colleagues, some of whom felt threatened by his obvious intellect, some of whom suspected they were part of an ongoing ethnographic study.

Just over six feet tall, Stringer was conservatively dressed in a two-piece, dark blue trouser suit over a plain white blouse buttoned to her neck that made her look ten years older than her twenty-nine years. Her dark-brown hair was twisted round and pinned up.

'You took your time,' McEvoy stated flatly.

'We had a few problems finding this place,' Joyce explained. 'Are we the first to arrive?'

'You'll be the only ones to arrive; we're fully stretched. I've recruited a local sergeant, Tom McManus, to help with the questionnaires and searches. John, I want you to work closely with me, okay. You're the dogsbody. If I get called away on other cases, you'll be in charge. That alright?'

'No bother.'

'Kelly, you're to set up the incident room.'

'I'm to what?' she said, surprised, aware that it was a job usually reserved for somebody more senior.

'I said, set up the incident room. I hope I'm not going to have to repeat everything. Hannah Fallon and George Carter are inside,' he continued without waiting for a reply. 'We need to organise a search of the farm, start the interviews, and talk to the locals. Things are moving too slowly.'

* * *

Roza Ptaszek was a short, thin woman in her late twenties, with shoulder-length black hair tied back in a short ponytail. Her face was pale, her blue eyes rimmed red. Her boyfriend's apartment, which he shared with two others, was a mess; a scattering of clothes, food wrappers and old newspapers strewn everywhere. She was sitting on the edge of a red sofa, her tall, stocky boyfriend standing behind her looking concerned.

'Will I be able to collect my things soon?' she asked with a light, East European accent.

'Not for a couple of days,' McEvoy replied neutrally. 'We need to look for clues as to what happened to Dr Koch.'

'It was terrible,' she repeated for the fifth time. 'Terrible.' Her boyfriend squeezed her shoulder, offering sympathy.

'What time did you leave the farm last night?'

'About ten o'clock. We watched television and then we came into town and meet with some friends,' she said in slightly broken English.

'And there were no visitors?'

'I left Dr Koch by himself. I always go out on Saturday night.'

'And when did you go back?'

'This morning. I got back to the house at about eight o'clock to make the breakfast. Dr Koch did not came downstairs so I went up to see why. He was always at his desk by eight o'clock. I know straight away he was dead. Somebody killed him, so I called the police.'

'What made you think he'd been attacked?'

'He'd been hit on the head. He was old, but he was… how you say… well. He was very strong.'

'Do you have any ideas as to who might have attacked Dr Koch?'

'I don't… I don't know. He was a very important man. Very wealthy.'

'Have there been any visitors recently? Anyone Dr Koch argued with perhaps?'

'His daughter was there yesterday; Mrs D'Arcy. They argue all the time. Mr Kinneally also visited yesterday. He works for Dr Koch, running one of his companies.'

'What did he argue with his daughter about?'

'I don't know. They always have the door closed. She is not happy person, Mrs D'Arcy. She drinks… how do you say, like a… fish?' She raised her eyebrows quizzically.

McEvoy nodded his head. He doubted that Roza didn't know why Koch and his daughter argued, but he didn't want to press the issue; he'd ask Marion D'Arcy himself. 'Who else worked at the house? Were you the only one?'

'No, no. Mr Farrell is the farm manager. He sometimes has helpers. Mr Freel is his business manager. Janek helps with gardens two evenings a week,' she patted her boyfriend's hand. 'Sometimes at weekends.'

'And were any of them there yesterday?'

'Mr Farrell was there all day. He left at about six o'clock. Mr Freel was there in the afternoon. He was working with Dr Koch. They were always working.'

'And when did Mr Freel leave?'

'I don't know. Before eight o'clock. Dr Koch ate on his own.'

'How about anybody else?'

'I don't think so.'

'What was Dr Koch like to work for?' McEvoy asked.

'He was... He was a clever man. He worked hard.' Roza stopped, looking embarrassed.

'He could be difficult?' McEvoy hazarded.

She nodded her head. 'He liked things the way he liked them.'

'Did you get on well with him?'

'I... we got on well. He was an interesting person. He know all about Polish history.'

'Did you work for him for long?'

'Three years. Do you... I no longer have a job?'

'I don't know,' McEvoy said truthfully. 'You told one of my colleagues that you thought someone had searched the house?'

'Yes. Many things had been moved. Only a little, but I could tell. They searched everywhere. You think it was a thief?'

'I don't know. Possibly.' McEvoy shrugged. Thieves were rarely so careful as to try and erase all trace of their presence.

* * *

The sun had long set and it was dark outside, given the absence of the moon and stars and any ambient light of street lamps. He found the quiet and stillness unsettling. One could drift through this landscape, the farmland, ditches, hedges and mature trees, and no one would be any the wiser. Whoever killed Albert Koch hadn't needed to worry about witnesses beyond the cattle in the adjacent fields and the local fox.

He kicked a small, gravel pebble from the top of the steps out onto the driveway and checked his watch – 5.32. He needed to call home and let his sister and Gemma know what he was doing and then check-in with his inspectors to see how their cases were progressing. He pulled his mobile phone from a pocket and started to pace, uneasy in the silent gloom.

The call was answered after four rings.

'Hello?'

'It's me. I'm sorry, but I'm going to be tied up until late.'

'Don't worry about it,' McEvoy's sister, Caroline, said calmly. 'As soon as I heard the news on the radio I knew you'd be calling. We've got in a DVD. There's no problem with her staying over – the room's set up as usual. Do you want a word with her?'

'In a minute,' he answered. Given the hours of his job, and the fact that he could be investigating a case anywhere in the country, his daughter often stayed over with his sister. It was an arrangement that McEvoy was both thankful for and embarrassed by, but there was little choice unless he looked for another line of work, and that wasn't really an option, especially in the short term. 'How're you feeling?' he asked.

'Fine. I feel a bit like a sumo, and it's only five months, but I'm grand otherwise.'

Once the baby arrived McEvoy wasn't really sure what would happen with the babysitting. Maybe Gemma could help out. As twelve-year-olds go she was sensible and responsible. Whilst still often childlike, she'd become old beyond her years since the death of her mother. Somehow she was morphing into her. It was strange to witness.

'If you feel like a sumo now, just wait a couple of months.' He winced as he said it.

'Oh, God, don't! I always remember what mam said to you once – "giving birth to you was like passing a ten pin bowling ball through a ten pence slot." It put me off starting a family for years!' she laughed. 'I'm hoping it's going to be more like a marble. At the most a tennis ball. But, I doubt it somehow. I just hope that when I scream for the drugs, they give them to me! Look, Gemma's hovering. Here you go.'

'Hello, Dad?' Gemma said cheerily.

'Hiya, pumpkin. How're things?'

'They're okay. We're going to watch a DVD. You're not getting back until late?'

'I'm sorry. I'm not sure what time I'll be there to pick you up. I imagine you'll be asleep.'

'Don't worry, I'll be fine. Who are you investigating – the Lithuanian or the billionaire?'

'Both of them; we're short staffed.'

'So you're going to be away for a while then?'

'No, no. I'll be coming home each night, but I'm going to be busy. You'll be okay at Caroline's?'

'Yeah, yeah, half my stuff's here now.'

'Just make sure it's tidy, okay. Not like your room at home.' He glanced at his watch again. 'Look, Gemma, I'm sorry, but I have to go.' It was always a pleasure to hear his daughter's voice whilst he was working, but it constantly jarred with the mood of the investigation – a rarefied chink of innocence creeping into a dark world. 'I'll see you later, okay?' he muttered regretfully.

'Remember to drink and eat,' she warned. 'You know what you're like!'

'I will, I will,' he said, realising that he hadn't eaten since breakfast and had barely had anything to drink either. He got so wrapped up in things he simply forgot to sustain himself. 'I love you, okay. I'll see you later,' he repeated and ended the call.

He pinched the bridge of his nose and breathed out slowly. After a moment he pulled up Jim Whelan's phone number and pressed call.

'Whelan.'

'Jim, how's it going?'

'Nowhere.'

'Do you know who he is yet?'

'No.'

'How about piecing together what happened last night? Who he was with? Where he went?'

'Nothing.'

'And forensics?'

'Hopeless.'

McEvoy rolled his eyes and stared out at the lime tree silhouettes, frustrated at Whelan's one word answers. 'Ring me if you hear anything, okay,' he snapped and ended the call immediately pulling up Johnny Cronin's number, the inspector in charge of the laundering suicide.

'Yeah?' Cronin answered distractedly.

'Johnny, it's Colm.'

'What? No, no, over there. There. Sorry, hello?'

'It's Colm. How's it going?'

'Usual shite with the locals, but otherwise okay. It's the same guy – same description and pick-up routine. He talks to someone at the bar, pump primes them for information about themselves and the other people in the pub. Then he heads over to the one he thinks is the best bet with a little proposition for them – "you scratch my back, I'll scratch yours; it's not exactly above board, but it's easy money and no one gets hurt. What do you think?" It looks as if the guy knows the person at the bar, he certainly knows all about them, so he seems pretty kosher.

'He took the old man for thirty grand. He'd borrowed almost all of it from two of his brothers. He's a bachelor farmer in his sixties; one of the last of the old school. Lives in a shit heap of a cottage on forty acres of bog with two dogs, a few cows and some sheep for company. He has a few debts and no way to pay them other than to sell the land. He'd sooner die than do that so he was suckered in.'

'Poor bastard. Any leads on your man?'

'Same as before. Big guy, Ulster accent, dark brown hair, dressed in a smart suit, driving a black Mercedes with Monaghan plates.'

'Get that description circulated and prepare a press conference, we need to let people know he's struck again and to be
on the look out for him.'

'The family don't want any publicity.'

'All you need to say is that another scam has taken place,
you don't need to name the victim.'

'I'll get on it.'

'Okay, let me know if you have any luck. Otherwise I'll
talk to you tomorrow.' McEvoy ended the call and immediately rang DI Jenny Flanagan for an update on Kylie O'Neill's
murder in Tipperary. After four rings he was transferred to her
answer service. He left her a message asking her to ring him
back when she had a moment.

Next up was Elaine Jones.

'Colm?' Elaine answered.

'Have you got any news for me yet, Elaine?' McEvoy asked
business-like.

'The young man from Trim was pretty badly beaten. My
feeling is that it was by more than one person. Either that or
someone lost control. He was killed by a single stab wound
just to the right of his sternum. The knife slid between two ribs
and pierced the lower half of his heart and collapsed one of
his lungs. He died of a fatal heart attack and internal bleeding.
I wouldn't be surprised if the knife he was holding was the
murder weapon – it was about the right length of blade; twelve
centimetres. I'd say time of death was sometime between three
and five in the morning. He was five and half times over the
limit. Probably near paralytic when he died.'

'And Albert Koch?' McEvoy asked as the front door opened
behind him and Tom McManus stepped out. McEvoy acknowl-
edged him with a nod of his head.

'Just as I said earlier; depressed fracture of the skull. He
was hit with some force. The blow—'

'Would a vase have been strong enough?' McEvoy
interrupted.

'Possibly. It would depend on the vase. It would've had to

have been pretty sturdy. Is that what you think; he was hit with a vase?'

'They found a couple of shards along with some drops of blood in his study.'

'All the real bleeding was internal,' the pathologist continued. 'He had a subarachnoid haemorrhage – bleeding in the layer around the brain – and we found two large blood clots in the parietal lobe. Effectively he had a stroke, the clots stopped oxygen circulating.'

'So what you're saying is that he was killed by the blow to the head?' McEvoy asked.

'In short, yes.'

'Well, he didn't do that to himself while lying in bed.'

'No. And the bruising on the legs is consistent with the idea he was dragged up the stairs. My opinion is that he died sometime between one and three in the morning.'

'Right, okay. Thanks, Elaine. I'd better be getting on.' McEvoy ended the call and turned towards Tom McManus. 'I hope this is going to be good news, sergeant.'

'Depends on what you think is good news.'

* * *

They stood in the gloom at the base of a large oak tree, Colm McEvoy, John Joyce, Tom McManus and a local guard, staring up at the heavy rope hanging from a thick branch, its end coiled into a noose high up in the canopy.

'Well, this puts a different complexion on things,' McEvoy said, moving his torch beam across the branches. 'He was either killed deliberately or this is to try and head us off down a false trail.'

'Why wasn't he hung out here?' Joyce asked. 'If you're going to kill him as a statement you might as well make the statement.'

'Maybe they got disturbed or they panicked,' McManus hypothesised.

'In that case, why not just leave him in his study?' McEvoy asked. 'Why carry him back up the stairs and put him back into bed?'

'Perhaps they thought whoever found him would think he'd died naturally?' McManus offered.

'Nearly did,' Joyce said.

'Perhaps it was too much work for one person to carry him out here and hoist him up,' McManus suggested. 'Or maybe the blow was just to stun or subdue him; get him to walk out here? Only the blow was too much and he died?'

'Perhaps.' McEvoy nodded. 'Or maybe he wasn't dead when they took him back upstairs. They might have thought that he'd just been knocked unconscious. The noose was meant as a message for when he came round. We'll need to see if we can find out anything from that rope. John, get George Carter to take a look tomorrow morning when it's light.'

'No bother.'

The local guard shifted uneasily, signalling his discomfort at being in the presence of a group to which he didn't feel he belonged.

'This is Carl Mannion,' McManus said, introducing him. 'We've drafted him in from Delvin. He's a bit of a history buff. He's been telling me... look, why don't you tell them yourself, Carl,' McManus suggested.

'Well, I... I mean... I'm no expert, you understand.' Mannion paused, but no one intervened. 'Just over here,' he pointed to a spot a few metres from the tree near to a laneway, 'was the site of the gallows. The white gallows, that is, you know, like the house name. This lane used to be the main route to Athboy before the present road became the preferred choice. All the locals would have had to pass the unfortunate bastards hung here.'

'So what you're saying is that this rope is no coincidence,' McEvoy said, stating the obvious.

'I wouldn't think so,' Mannion concurred. 'Somebody knew their local history. Back in the nineteenth century this house was occupied by Lord Kilchester's land agent. Kilchester was gentry but he was also a major industrialist. Like Albert Koch he was a chemist; made a fortune creating and manufacturing dyes, soaps, and the like and exporting them round the world. He inherited the Kilchester Demesne from his father, but rarely travelled to Ireland. He just came over for a few weeks each year and left the running of the estate to the land agent,' he said, warming to the subject.

'In the early 1870s one of the agent's men was killed in a dispute, probably over rent or the conditions of tenancy. The agent organised the local police and rounded up three local men and accused them of murder. They might well have been guilty but no one knows for sure. The agent then set up a kangaroo court and persuaded a local judge to convict them. They were forced to build their own gallows, facing out on to the laneway, which they were made to whitewash. The men were hung the following evening.

'Once the London media heard of the men's fate it was branded the Kilchester scandal. It even caused angry scenes in Parliament. The agent fled to America, Lord Kilchester's business suffered a terrible backlash and he ended up selling his interests in Ireland. The agent's house and outbuildings then fell into disrepair until the farm was bought by George Byrne, a wealthy Dublin merchant in the late 1880s. For whatever reason, he renamed the place after the incident. I'm not sure when Albert Koch bought it, but it was certainly over forty years ago. The Big House was burned down in 1922. It was about a mile down the road there.' He pointed to his right. 'It was probably the finest Palladian mansion in Ireland.'

He stopped and stared at the ground, feeling he had rambled on for too long.

'And what about Koch?' McEvoy asked. 'What's his local history?'

'I don't really know,' Mannion said. 'I'm more interested in the late eighteenth and nineteenth century – 1798 to independence. Plenty of rumours though.'

'Such as?'

'That he was a Nazi war criminal who fled here after the war or he was a prisoner of war who stayed on. That he wasn't averse to ignoring a few rules and laws; a few brown envelopes here and there. That he could be like that land agent – a real terror to work for and deal with. There are plenty of people who held him a grudge round here. Some people still do. Plenty of people who also thought he was a great fella.'

'Would someone hold enough of a grudge to kill him?' McEvoy asked.

'It wouldn't be the first time a grudge led to murder,' McManus observed.

'He was rich and powerful, and a cantankerous old bastard; no surer way of making enemies,' Mannion said.

McEvoy's mobile phone rang. 'Yes?' he answered, distracted.

'What the hell are you up to, Colm?' Chief Superintendent Tony Bishop snapped. 'I've just had Paul Cassidy, TD for North Meath, on the phone complaining about how you're handling Albert Koch's death. His daughter's on the war path. She claims she's being treated with malice and disrespect and that her father died of natural causes.'

McEvoy wandered away from the other guards. 'Well, the last bit's rubbish; talk to Elaine Jones. Albert Koch was killed by a blow to the head. She's just flexing her political muscles; letting us know how well connected she is.'

'So Koch was murdered?'

'Yes, unless he hit himself on the head.'

'Just tread carefully round her,' Bishop said calming down. 'She's clearly hysterical and she could cause us some grief.'

'As long as she doesn't try to hinder our investigation.'

'If she becomes a problem, pass her onto me, okay? The last thing we need is another media relations disaster after last time,' he said, referring to the Raven case in which the gardai were severely criticised during and after the killing spree.

'With pleasure. Does that mean I get more people to help?'

'Don't push your luck, Colm.'

* * *

The incident room had been set up in Ballyglass GAA club, a long, single-storey structure located in front of a large pitch surrounded by a low griselinia hedge and ash trees. At the far end of the hall was a shuttered bar, in front of which had been positioned a clean whiteboard and a notice board on which had been tacked a large-scale map of the area. Along the right-hand wall were a row of three computers placed on bar tables, followed by a table carrying a hot water urn and a stack of styrofoam cups, and two more empty notice boards. Windows ran the length of the left-hand wall giving a view out across the pristine pitch. Several tables were scattered across the hall, each surrounded by a cluster of red upholstered chairs.

Kelly Stringer and a couple of local, plain clothes detective gardai were standing near to one of the windows deep in conversation. Tom McManus and John Joyce were busy at the water urn making cups of tea. Cathal Galligan hovered nearby in an immaculately pressed uniform, staring into space, looking lost. George Carter and Chloe Pollard were sitting off to one side, silently nursing cups of coffee and trying to stay awake. Hannah Fallon had travelled back to Dublin a couple of hours earlier.

McEvoy turned away from the white board, which he'd just wiped clean. 'Right, okay, let's make a start,' he instructed. 'Come on, take a seat.'

He waited until they settled.

'Well, let's start with what we know. Albert Koch, aged 91, killed by a blow to the head, probably by a vase, somewhere between one and three in the morning. He was seemingly attacked in the downstairs study and then carried upstairs to his bed. Whoever attacked him left a noose hanging at the site of the old white gallows.

'Koch was reputedly the third richest person in Ireland, the founder of Ostara Industries. He had extensive business interests in Ireland and abroad. It seems he was a difficult person to deal with, was a ruthless businessman, and wasn't short of enemies or rumours. Whoever killed him was almost certainly searching the house for something and they knew the history of the place. Have we got anything back from the questionnaires?' McEvoy asked.

'Nothing concrete,' Joyce replied. 'We've been surveying all of the houses along the approach roads. Nobody saw or heard anything suspicious other than usual late night traffic; people crawling home from the pubs. Koch had been receiving some unwanted attention though. A few months ago a young, East European couple were hanging around the area asking questions about his past. A week or so ago they reappeared.'

'Do we have any idea who they are?'

'Not yet, we're working on it.'

'And what were they asking about?'

'Maybe you're better answering this, Tom,' Joyce said.

'When he turned up in the area?' McManus said. 'If people knew who he really was? When did he start his company? When did he start a family? That kind of thing.'

'Right, well, we need to track that couple down as a priority,' McEvoy observed. 'Anything else?'

'Nobody seems to have known him that well, but he was a bit of a folk hero round here,' McManus continued. 'That said, the same kind of nasty rumours keep coming up – that he'd fled Germany after the war, that he was a Nazi war criminal, that he'd a criminal past, that he'd helped the IRA on occasion back in the 1950s, possibly since. It also seems as if he'd been in a long-standing dispute with one of his neighbours about ownership of a small strip of land. I guess the general impression is that people thought he was a terrible firebrand and crook, but he was their firebrand and the area had benefited from what he had given back. This clubhouse was paid for by a donation from Ostara.'

'Do we know who the neighbour is?'

'Martin O'Coffey. He has a farm bordering Koch's land; lives on it with his grandson, Peter and his family.'

'We'll need to interview the pair of them. Kelly, can you try and set that up for tomorrow.'

'No problem,' Stringer replied.

'As for the other rumours, we need to get a full picture of Koch and his business dealings. I want to know everything about him and his companies. Everything,' he repeated.

'We also need to identify everyone who was in contact with him in the last two weeks. I want a full timeline of his movements and meetings and I want all of them interviewed. I'll deal with the family, okay. Nobody else. They've already complained about their treatment through a local TD. John, you concentrate on the foreign couple.

'We also need to find the missing vase shards if we can. Widen the search; drag the small lake if necessary. George, Chloe, keep searching for any forensic evidence. And keep an eye out for whatever the person was searching for – and yes, I know you don't know what that was – or if anything obvious is missing. Whatever it was, it's the key to all of this. Also, we need to find out what we can about that rope. Right, okay then, does anyone have any questions?'

Galligan raised his hand. 'I'm getting hassled by the media. What can I tell them other than he was found with a fatal blow to the head? Can I say anything about the vase or the noose?'

'Say as little as you can,' McEvoy replied. 'Tell them we're following an active line of enquiry and that we don't want to say anymore than that at present. If they press you on the issue, tell them that we hope to issue a fuller statement in the next forty-eight hours. We can worry about that later.'

Galligan nodded his head, but didn't look convinced. It seemed to him that he had to take all the crap from the media without having any say in the investigation. He was just a mouthpiece.

'Anybody else?'

Everybody stayed silent.

'Right, well I guess we can wrap it up for today. We'll make a fresh start in the morning.'

* * *

The hall had emptied leaving only McEvoy, Kelly Stringer and one garda still sitting in front of a computer screen at the far end of the room.

McEvoy was staring at a map of the area pinned to the notice board, getting a feel for how The White Gallows fitted into the wider landscape. Out of the corner of his eye he caught Stringer pulling a face and shaking a clawed hand up and down. 'Are you okay?' he asked, turning towards her.

'It's just classic symptoms of mobile phone madness,' she said laughing, though clearly frustrated. The phone beeped several times. 'Every time I enter a number into this damn thing it disappears!'

'Do you want me to have look?' McEvoy offered.

'No, no, I'll get it sorted. Oh, sugar!' She stabbed at the phone, then tipped back her head and pulled at her hair in mock anger. 'I'm just flustered at the minute.'

'You're not going to go to pieces on me are you?' McEvoy joked. 'I'm relying on you to run the engine room.'

'Don't worry about me, I'll get everything shipshape; get my sea legs.'

'Not that your legs...' McEvoy stopped, realising that he was potentially heading into dangerous territory. He wasn't sure how any perceived flirting would be received, or how he felt about it. Kelly Stringer was thirteen years his junior. He'd been married for the same amount of time. And, if he was honest with himself, it would be a long time before he would be ready to try another relationship.

He shook his head. He'd gone from sea legs to near marriage in two seconds. 'I guess I'd better be heading home. It's been a long day,' he said, changing the subject, feeling like an old fool. 'I suggest you do the same.'

Stringer glanced at her watch. 'I'll make a move in a bit. I just need to get this sorted. The cat's probably dragged something in for dinner at this stage in any case. It's a good job he can look after himself.'

'I wish I could say the same for daughters,' McEvoy

muttered. 'She must wonder why this stranger occasionally turns up to say hello.'

Stringer pulled a tight smile of sympathy. 'I'm sure she knows it's not easy.'

'It's not exactly fair though, is it?' McEvoy said wistfully. 'God, listen to me. Look, I know running the incident room's a step up, but I'm sure you'll do a good job.'

'I'm glad you think I'm up to it.'

'I wouldn't have picked you otherwise. I know you've much more to offer than a good looking pair of sea-legs. Not that…' McEvoy trailed off, instantly regretting his words, feeling his face flush – so much for good intentions.

'Thanks!' Stringer laughed. 'I should hope not.'

'Right, well, I'll be going then,' McEvoy said embarrassed. 'Safe home, okay.'

'And you.' Stringer turned her attention back to her phone as McEvoy shuffled towards the door. She glanced up coyly as he pulled it open and exited.

* * *

The drive towards Dublin was quiet, the road almost deserted of traffic. As he approach Dunslaughlin his phone rang.

'McEvoy.'

'It's Jenny. You rang earlier?'

'Yeah. I was just seeing how're you're getting on?' The last time McEvoy had travelled down to Tipperary to catch up on the case had been two days ago.

'We're not. We all know it was the husband, but we've got nothing but intuition and poor circumstantial evidence. He's as cool as cucumber. He knows we've got sod all.'

'Just keep working the angles. Something will turn up. What about his alibi? Did you check that out again?'

'His mobile phone records confirm that he was in the Bansha area that morning. He made five calls and received nine between eight and eleven thirty all using the Bansha mast.

There wasn't a large enough gap between calls for him to get home, commit the murder and get back there.'

'Perhaps you're chasing the wrong suspect?'

'Or he gave his phone to a friend or accomplice,' Flanagan countered.

'As I said, keep working the angles. Just so you know, I'm not going to be able to come down for a few days as I'm heading up two new cases in Meath. If there's anything important, give me a call; otherwise just use your own judgement. Perhaps we could meet in Dublin sometime this week?'

'Yeah, no bother. I could do with a trip home; the digs here are a kip. I feel like I'm a student again.'

'If only we were all still that young. I'll talk to you tomorrow, okay?' He ended the call.

Things were going from bad to worse. People were killing each other faster than they could be investigated and the killers were becoming cleverer, learning from the media's obsession with crime. To add to their woes, court cases were taking longer and becoming more complex. Officers were being pulled between more difficult cases at the same time as being tied up in red tape. They needed more skilled staff and quickly.

He stabbed at the stereo, flipping between channels until he found something he recognised – Dancing in the Dark by Bruce Springsteen. It was only a couple of years since Maggie and himself had seen The Boss at the RDS. He started to mumble along.

* * *

It had just gone eleven thirty. All of his cases had been reported on the news bulletin along with another killing in Limerick, four fatal car crashes in which nine people had died, and over two hundred and fifty dead in an earthquake in Peru.

He turned the stereo off and sat in the dark and quiet. He massaged his tired eyes before pushing open the car door and stepping out into the damp night air. Off to his left the engines of an approaching aircraft were droning, one of the last planes flying into Dublin that evening. He headed towards the locked gates of Collinstown Cemetery.

As he levered himself up and over the black railings, the plane screamed overhead only a couple of hundred feet above him. He made his way to Maggie's grave, crouching down on the damp sod to clear autumn leaves away, feeling guilty that he hadn't visited for a couple of days. He still couldn't believe that she was gone; that lung cancer had eaten her from the inside out before taking her from him and Gemma. She'd barely made it past her fortieth birthday.

He stayed for a few minutes, talking to her headstone, before reluctantly heading back to his car. He set off to pick Gemma up from his sister.

MONDAY

There was a loud knock at the door. Hannah Fallon glanced at her watch – 8.06 – stuffed the last of a slice of toast into her mouth and headed out of the kitchen, dressed in a smart business suit. As she neared the front door – the shape of a person visible through the frosted glass – a long, black metal pipe was pushed through the letter box. The person dashed to one side, the pipe clattering to the floor.

It took a moment before she realised what was happening. The pipe bomb exploded as she dived left through the living room doorway. The blast blew the glass out of the front door and shrapnel cut through her lower legs, twisting her body as she fell and slamming her into the door frame and wall. She landed awkwardly on the arm of a two-seater sofa, tumbling backwards onto the wooden floor.

Instinctively she tried to pull herself further into the room, afraid that her attacker would enter the house to finish her off. The pain from her legs was excruciating, her head pounding, ears ringing. She felt herself slipping towards unconsciousness as a figure appeared in the doorway.

'Jesus Christ!' her next door neighbour snapped, recoiling at the sight of the bloody stump that had been Fallon's lower right leg, the other a mess of deep cuts, a portion of snapped bone sticking out through the skin. 'Hannah? Hannah, are you alive?' She moved forward to try and help. 'Call an ambulance!' she shouted over her shoulder.

'Is she okay?' a male voice asked.

'No, she's not fuckin' okay. There's blood everywhere.'

'Fuck. Yeah, ambulance,' the man said, turning away.

'And tell them to hurry. She's bleeding to death.' The woman knelt down on the floor, leaning over Fallon's torso. 'Hannah? Are you okay, love?'

'Don't touch anything, okay,' Fallon mumbled, feeling nauseous, drifting on the edge of darkness. 'I don't want any evidence fucked up.'

* * *

After checking in on Gemma, McEvoy had reluctantly left her sleeping at his sister's knowing that he would be leaving home early the next morning. He'd left the house shortly before seven o'clock and had made good time.

He turned right through a metal archway into the Ballyglass GAA car park, passing a couple of early birds from the media, and parked next to a van from the Garda Technical Unit. His plan for the day was to interview Koch's children, his business manager, Stefan Freel, and Martin O'Coffey, the farmer with whom Koch was in dispute, and to deal with whatever else turned up.

He levered himself out of the Mondeo and headed for the main door. The day had barely started and already his eyes ached and he felt washed out. As he reached the building his phone rang. He dug it from his pocket.

'Barney?'

'Have you heard?' Barney Plunkett, the last remaining detective inspector on the Raven case, said excitedly.

'Heard what?' McEvoy said, not sure whether he should be feeling buoyant or down, but hoping that Plunkett had good news.

'Someone shoved a pipe bomb through Hannah Fallon's front door. It blew off one of her legs.'

'Someone tried to kill Hannah?' McEvoy said slowly, doubt in his voice.

'She was just getting ready to leave for court.'

'For fuck's sake!' McEvoy spat, the news finally sinking in, jogging back to his car. 'Is she okay?'

'She'll live, but apparently there's nothing they can do about the leg. I don't know the full story, but it seems that two men wearing motorcycle helmets arrived at the house on a motorbike. They shoved a pipe bomb through the letter box. The only reason she's alive is because she dived through a doorway. They've taken her to Connolly Hospital.'

McEvoy started the car, reversed quickly and drove through the gateway, speeding along the potholed road towards Athboy. 'I told Bishop this would happen! You get rid of Hannah and you get rid of the main forensic witness in a dozen or more cases. Charlie Clarke obviously didn't fancy taking his chances with her.'

'Is that who you think it was?' Plunkett asked.

'His trial starts today. It'll be a couple of his boys or hired help. Clarke would kill his own mother if he needed to. Who's in charge of the case?'

'I don't know. I've only just found out the news. Harcourt Street is buzzing,' Plunkett said referring to the headquarters of NBCI.

'Well, if you find out anything else, let me know. I'm on my way there now.' McEvoy ended the call and pressed the accelerator down as far as he dared.

As he left Athboy his mobile phone rang. 'McEvoy.'

'Colm, it's—'

'I told you this would happen!' McEvoy snapped, interrupting Bishop. 'We left her too exposed.'

'Don't tell me what we should and shouldn't have done, Colm,' Bishop said, angrily. 'We'd no god damn choice! What else could we have done?'

'Shifted the work around more people,' McEvoy said, not backing down. 'Hannah's worked practically every Dublin gangland killing for the last six months!'

'Look, Colm, stop before you say anything you'll regret,' Bishop warned.

'We need to bring in Charlie Clarke's gang,' McEvoy continued. 'They'll be holed up in West Finglas somewhere. And you'd better call in armed response; they'll probably try and fight their way out.'

'I'm ahead of you already. You stay with Koch and your other cases; I'll worry about Charlie Clarke.'

'Who have you assigned to it?' McEvoy asked, swerving round a tractor and cutting back in quickly, narrowly avoiding an oncoming lorry.

'I'm dealing with it personally.'

'You?' McEvoy said in disbelief.

'I was a detective superintendent for six years before taking on this job,' Bishop snapped. 'And a DI for ten years before that. I know how to investigate a case. You look after yours and I'll deal with Charlie feckin' Clarke.' Bishop ended the call.

McEvoy continued for another mile or so, raging at the attack on Hannah. Along with everything else, they were now coming under personal attack. The situation with gangs in Dublin and Limerick was spiralling out of control; if a check wasn't put in place it would disintegrate into chaos. It would be open warfare with the guards meekly caught in the middle. Eventually he slowed and turned around, heading back to Ballyglass, his anger still simmering.

* * *

There was nothing modest about Marion D'Arcy's house. Barely two miles from her father's, it was a wide, white, two-storey structure with a central portico of four Ionic columns rising to the height of the roof, surrounded by well-tended gardens. In the fields on either side several horses watched the car's progress up the wide drive. Off to the right, thirty yards from the house and screened by a row of rowan trees was a small square paddock of twelve stables.

McEvoy pulled to a halt at the front of the house, levered

himself out his car and stared up at the classic columns before striding to the door.

After a short wait it was opened by James Kinneally.

'Superintendent,' Kinneally stated without opening the door fully.

'I'd like a word with Mrs D'Arcy, please,' McEvoy said puzzled by Kinneally's presence.

'I'm afraid she's in bed under sedation. She's not taken the news of her father's death at all well. Perhaps tomorrow would be better?' Kinneally offered.

'Perhaps,' McEvoy conceded. Marion D'Arcy was probably suffering the mother of all hangovers. 'I need to build up a picture of her father and any enemies he might have had. You must have known him well, being the CEO of Ostara Industries?'

'I thought Dr Koch was killed by a thief he'd disturbed?' Kinneally replied, deflecting McEvoy's query.

'That's one possible scenario, but there might be more to it than that. Can I come in, please?'

Kinneally hesitated and then stood back, holding the wide door open.

McEvoy entered into a large hallway with a white marble floor. A marble staircase rose in front of him, twisting back on itself. Hanging on the landing halfway-up was a large classical painting – a Roman market scene set in a large plaza.

'Are you here alone with Mrs D'Arcy?' McEvoy asked, turning to face Kinneally.

'No, no,' Kinneally replied defensively, heading through a doorway into an opulent living room. 'Her brother's here as well. He's out riding. Her husband is on business in France. He's flying back later today. I'm… I'm a friend of the family. I'm just… well I'm trying to help out, given the tragic death of Dr Koch.' He sat down and pointed to a seat.

McEvoy lowered himself down. 'So how long have you worked for Ostara Industries?'

'Thirty-five years next September. I started straight after graduating from Trinity and worked my way up.'

'Dr Koch was a good employer?'

'He knew how to run and expand a business and how to reward people who shared his ambitions.'

'But he was a difficult man personally?'

'He… He wanted things… Look, I don't see what this has got to do with anything.'

'I want to know what Albert Koch was like as a person; get a sense of the man. How would you describe him?'

'Driven. He was determined to make Ostara all it could be, but on his terms. He didn't want shareholders messing him about.'

'And yet he lived quite modestly,' McEvoy observed.

'He wasn't really interested in material wealth. He wanted to create a legacy; a great company. With the exception of the farm, he hardly spent any money on himself; just the bare necessities. And the farm pays for itself as a going concern.'

'Not like his daughter,' McEvoy motioned at the room. 'She likes the finer things in life.'

'And why not?' Kinneally asked. 'She can afford them. She's built up a very successful law company. And without her father's help.'

'He didn't share his wealth around then?' McEvoy asked.

'Not exactly, no. Dr Koch believed that everyone should make their own way in the world. He gave them a good education; after that it was up to them.'

'So neither of his children work for Ostara?'

'No, no. If they proved themselves elsewhere, then they could apply to join the company like everyone else. Marion went into law; Charles into academia. He's a professor of chemistry at NUI Galway.'

'Chemistry runs in the family?'

'To an extent,' Kinneally stated, 'but I've always had the impression that Charles was a little bit of a disappointment. I think Dr Koch was expecting Oxford or Harvard and Nobel prizes. Instead there was a slow journey through a small, provincial university.'

'So he didn't see fit to pass the business on to either of them when he retired?'

'Dr Koch never really retired,' Kinneally smiled wanly. 'He simply devolved some of his power to a board of executives while at the same time diversifying his interests. He started to invest in property and shares. He must own half of London at this stage, plus he has significant property and business interests in Ireland, Germany, the US, and the Far East.'

'And Ostara was wholly owned by Dr Koch?'

'Yes. We have significant borrowings from a variety of investment banks, but Dr Koch never floated the company or brought in other partners. With no shareholders he was free to run the business as he saw fit. Everyone in the company was on a salary, including himself, though certain key individuals could obtain modest profit bonuses.'

'So he liked to keep a tight rein on power?'

Kinneally shrugged. 'You could say that.'

'So who will take over now then? His son and daughter?'

'I've no idea. He never revealed to me, and I'm sure to nobody else either, what he intended for the company once he died.'

'He didn't tell anyone? Could he do that? Surely there had to be a contingency plan in place?'

'I did try to broach the subject with him several times, but he was adamant. He just said it's all in his will. I imagine that the majority shareholding will pass on to either Marion or Charles, or to one of his grandchildren. Mark D'Arcy is a rising star in the company.'

'And yourself?'

'I'm happy enough to continue as CEO. I'm well paid and I'll be retiring in a few years' time in any case.'

'So you've no idea who has most to benefit from Dr Koch's death?'

'You think he was killed for his wealth; for control of the company?'

'I've no idea,' McEvoy mumbled neutrally. 'At the moment, all I know is that Dr Koch is dead and his house has been searched. Somebody was looking for something. So far I have no motive and no suspect. I'm trawling for possible leads,' he said, keeping the information about the hanging rope to himself.

'Well, I'd start with the housekeeper, if I were you,' Kinneally offered. 'She strikes me as a bit of a gold-digger.'

'Roza?' McEvoy said sceptically.

'Don't judge a book by its cover, Superintendent. She acts like butter wouldn't melt in her mouth, but she's not as angelic as she looks. My guess is she's been angling for a slice of the pie for taking good care of him.'

'You think she's been putting on an act to secure a big payoff?'

'Wouldn't you? She's looking after one of the richest men in Ireland. Even if she only got a tiny proportion of his wealth it would set her up nicely. Perhaps she got tired of waiting?'

McEvoy let the statement hang in the air for a moment, a doubtful look on his face. 'She could search the house when he was out; why do it in the middle of the night?'

'I've no idea,' Kinneally shrugged. 'I was just telling you where I would start, that's all.'

'Just for the record, where were you on Saturday night?' McEvoy asked, turning the tables on Kinneally, tired of his bitter answers.

'Me?' Kinneally replied indignantly.

McEvoy nodded.

'I… I was in my apartment in Dublin.'

'And can anybody confirm that?'

'Am I a suspect, Superintendent?'

'Everybody's a suspect at this stage until we can eliminate them from our inquiries.'

'Jesus! Well if you must know I was there by myself. My wife was in our house in Kells. I was… we're… we're separating,' Kinneally said, flushing with embarrassment.

'I'm sorry to hear that,' McEvoy said disingenuously.

'Not as sorry as me, she's taking me to the cleaners,' Kinneally said rising, indicating that he'd had enough of the questions. 'I really need to be getting on, Superintendent. I need to head in to work; the place will no doubt be in turmoil.'

McEvoy nodded his head, standing. 'Perhaps I could have a word with Dr Koch's son before I leave?'

'If you can find him,' Kinneally said, opening the front door for McEvoy. 'He'll no doubt be down the fields somewhere. You'd be better off arranging to meet him later; God knows how long he'll be. I'll leave a note for him if you like.'

'Thanks.' McEvoy held out a business card. 'If you think of anything useful, then please get in touch.'

'I will, I will,' Kinneally said, shutting over the door.

McEvoy turned and shielded his eyes from the low angled sun. A shotgun fired in the distance and a horse brayed loudly.

* * *

The stables appeared deserted except for four horses staring out over their half doors. They watched McEvoy's progress impassively as he glanced round the small yard.

Marion D'Arcy was clearly not short of money despite the tight pockets of her father. These weren't hobby horses, but thoroughbreds. Through the far side of the yard he could see three more horses in a lush field accompanied by a young girl with tied-back, blonde hair, wearing dirty cream jodhpurs and a green wax jacket.

He heard the trotting horse before he saw it. A chestnut brown mare wheeled into the yard, its tail swishing, its neck covered in sweat, nostrils flaring for air. On its back sat a man in his late fifties, wearing a plain black riding hat, dark blue jacket over faded jeans, and black boots. He was the image of Albert Koch; the same gaunt face and thin frame. He pulled the mare to a halt and swung his right leg over her back, dropping to the ground.

'You're either a guard or a journalist,' Charles Koch stated flatly, tugging at the horse's saddle.

'Guard,' McEvoy replied. 'Detective Superintendent Colm McEvoy. I'm in charge of the investigation of your father's death.'

Koch said nothing, continuing to work on the saddle.

'I'm trying to get a picture of your father and to work out why someone might have killed him.'

'I was led to believe that he was killed by a thief,' Koch stated flatly.

'We think there might be more to it than that.'

'You do? Why?'

'I'm afraid I can't say more than that just now,' McEvoy said weakly. 'You're a chemist, like your father?'

'Not quite like my father. I'm a very ordinary chemist at a small, Irish university. My father was a brilliant chemist, but he chose the path of business.'

'You weren't interested in following your father's footsteps?'

'I was never presented with the opportunity. It was expected that I would become a great chemist; follow the path that he would have liked to have trodden. My father might have licensed and sold my discoveries, should I have had any, but I was to walk the hallowed halls of academia.'

'But that's not what you wanted?'

'That's exactly what I wanted, but the truth is I'm no Carl Bosch. I do solid work, but I was never destined to win a Nobel Prize. The only way I would be appointed to the faculty at one of the major universities was if my father offered them an enormous donation or an endowed chair. And to be honest, even if he had, I would have preferred to stay in Galway. I would have felt like a fraud.'

'And what now? You'll take over from your father? Run Ostara Industries?'

'I doubt it.' Koch slid the saddle from the horse's back, steam rising from the dampness underneath, and draped it over a stable door. 'I imagine that it'll be passed over to the Board of Directors or something. I've no idea how these things work.'

'But surely ownership passes to you and your sister?'

'We'll see, but I'm not holding my breath. My father had his own way of doing things.'

'But who else would he pass it on to?'

'That's a good question. I don't know. Perhaps we will inherit, but even if we do, I doubt we'll be in charge of the business. He'll have wanted someone who knows what they're doing in order to keep his legacy going.'

'James Kinneally?'

'Perhaps. I don't know. I'm happy doing what I'm doing. I'm not rich, but I'm not poor either. Whatever happens, I've no plans to change anything.' Koch started to lead the horse towards McEvoy, who was forced to step backwards. 'I'll be retiring in a couple of...'

'Ah, shit!' McEvoy spat, interrupting Koch. He stared down to where his right foot and the hem of his suit sat square in a fresh pile of horse dung.

'It'll wash off, Superintendent; occupational hazard of hanging around stables.' Koch led the horse into a stall and started to remove the bridle.

McEvoy eased his foot free and squelched to the stable door, trying to shake the dung free. It was his best suit, picked out with his daughter at the end of the Raven case.

'And what about your sister, will she be happy at that?'

'Marion? She'll be livid. She's always resented being frozen out of things.'

'Is that why they argued?'

'Amongst other things. Marion argues about everything. It's in her nature. She always thinks that she knows best.' Koch hung the bridle on the door and started to rub down the horse with a handful of straw.

'Is that why your father blocked her working for Ostara? She was too combative?'

'I've no idea, Superintendent. And I can't see what it's got to do with my father's death either. Marion is a lot of things, but murder isn't her style. Not unless she got a cast-iron guarantee that we inherit Ostara, with her at the helm.'

'And you don't think she has?'

'I seriously doubt it. My father was fit and well. The only documents he signed are ones that made him more money.' He dropped the straw on the ground and patted the horse on the neck.

'But if you do inherit, that would give her a lot of say in things.'

'She didn't kill him, Superintendent. Why risk it? He was an old man. She'd inherit in time in any case.'

McEvoy let the statement hang in the air. As reasons for murder went, financial power was a pretty potent force. 'Any ideas as to what the killer might have been searching for?' he asked eventually.

'No. My father was surrounded by rumours. When I was a child, he'd started his business using stolen Nazi gold and he still had some hidden in the house for emergencies. Or it was looted Jewish treasures, or money stored in mattresses, or old American bonds. My father was German, he arrived in Ireland after the war and started a successful business. He attracted wild speculation.'

'But there was no truth in the rumours?'

'My father arrived in 1948 with a small cardboard suitcase to join his brother. The case could barely carry his few clothes let alone gold bars. He worked extremely hard for four years to get enough money together to buy a failing fertilizer plant and to start Ostara. He was shrewd, clever and determined to succeed. He didn't need gold bars or treasure.'

'How about enemies? Can you think of anybody—' McEvoy was interrupted by the horse braying at his mobile phone's ringtone. He held up a hand in apology and backed away from the stall. 'McEvoy.'

'It's John Joyce. The gossip in the area is that the Lithuanian found dead in Trim worked on Koch's farm.'

'What?'

'I said—'

'I heard what you said. Have you spoken to Jim Whelan?'

'Yeah, he's on his way up.'

'And did Koch employ any Lithuanians?'

'Occasionally the farm manager took a couple on for seasonal work, though he says there are none working for him right now. A few work in the factory in Athboy and some others over in Kells.'

'Okay, I'll be back shortly.' McEvoy ended the call and headed back to where Koch was pulling the saddle from the stable door. 'Look, thanks for your time, I've got to head off. I'm very sorry about your father's death. I'll be in contact over the next few days as we work on the case.'

Koch nodded his head but said nothing.

'I'm afraid I have to ask this, but where were you on Saturday night?'

'At the races at Navan.'

'And after that?'

'I have a holiday cottage near Oldcastle, close to Loughcrew.'

'Can anyone confirm that?'

'No. Like my father I'm a widower. My wife died six years ago of breast cancer; same as my mother. The children all left home years ago. I live by myself.'

McEvoy nodded his head. He wanted to share his grief for Maggie, but kept his feelings to himself. 'I'm sorry,' he said lamely. 'Just one other thing; you said your father came to Ireland to join his brother. Why was he here?'

'He was a Luftwaffe pilot. He got shot up over Belfast and crashed into Carlingford Lough. He spent most of the war interned in the Curragh and working on local farms. When the war ended he was shipped off to an internment camp in Britain. When he was released he headed back to Ireland to marry a local girl; my aunt. My father followed shortly afterwards, escaping the ruins of Europe.'

McEvoy turned at the sound of a new horse arriving, a grey stallion snorting air through its nostrils, ridden by a man in his late thirties who bore an uncanny resemblance to Albert and Charles Koch. He wasn't wearing a helmet and his face was flushed from the ride, his hair sticking up at odd angles.

He swung off the horse before it had come to a halt. 'This boy can really fly,' he announced, patting the horse on the neck, ignoring McEvoy. 'Marion must be delighted. A couple of months training and he'll be winning races.'

'My son, Francis,' Koch said to McEvoy. 'Francie, this is Detective Superintendent McEvoy. He's investigating the death of your grandfather.'

'I thought he died of natural causes,' Francis Koch said. 'My father said you thought… but Marion seemed so convinced…' he trailed off.

'Your grandfather died as the result of a blow to the head.'

'So the doctor got it wrong?'

'I'm afraid so.'

'Stupid old fecker. He never should have—'

'Francis!' Charles Koch interrupted. 'He was your grandfather's physician for over forty years. He had no reason to—'

'How can you miss a blow to the head?' Francis interrupted. He eased the saddle from the horse's steaming back and carried it to a stable door. 'Somebody killed him and if it had been left to the old fool they'd have gotten away with it.'

'That's enough,' Koch senior said firmly. 'I don't want to discuss this any further.'

'I'm afraid I have to ask you this,' McEvoy continued, noting Charles Koch's tone but ignoring his request, 'but where were you late on Saturday night?'

'I was at Navan races with my father.'

'And after that?'

'I went to the Darley Lodge in Athboy. I'd had a successful day. Three winners; one of them at 20/1.' Koch junior turned his attention back to the horse. 'I'd won over three thousand euro. Not a bad day's work.'

'And then?'

'Then I went home.'

'And can anyone confirm that?'

'Everyone in the hotel bar. I probably made an idiot of myself, buying everyone drinks. The evening's a little hazy. The pints and whiskey were flowing.'

'And after the bar?'

Francis Koch wheeled round to face McEvoy, his face creased in anxiety. 'Why are you asking me these questions? Am I a suspect?'

'We're asking everyone who knew Dr Koch the same questions,' McEvoy replied neutrally. 'We're trying to account for everybody's movements so we can eliminate them from the inquiry.'

'After the bar, I went to the chipper and then I walked home to my big empty house.'

'You're separated?'

'Never married. I've never understood its appeal; being bound to one person for the rest of your life. It would be too claustrophobic; too… predictable.'

McEvoy reflected that Francis Koch made it sound like a life sentence. For him, being married to Maggie had given him a sense of security and stability. He liked the routine and predictability, the feelings of familiarity. Marriage wasn't a prison he'd been looking to escape from; it was something he was glad of, that he'd embraced. He'd lost that and yet it was something that Francis Koch was not even interested in attaining. Perhaps if he was more like him, McEvoy reflected, some of the pain might disappear, though it would be a shallow and banal life.

* * *

The incident room buzzed with the activity of a new case. Several uniformed guards were working at different tables.

Kelly Stringer and John Joyce were standing next to the whiteboard still displaying his notes from the previous day.

Stringer was dressed in a smart, two-piece, grey suit, over a pale blue blouse. She'd undone the top two buttons on her blouse and her hair was down rather than pinned up. The change was quite striking, taking years off her appearance. Somehow it made McEvoy feel his age.

'Any sign of Jim Whelan?' he asked as he approached.

'Not yet. He's on his way,' Joyce replied, staring down at McEvoy's stained trousers, immediately spotting the source of the foul smell.

'How about identifying this Lithuanian?'

'Nothing.'

'Any news on Hannah? Is she going to be okay?'

'She's in surgery at the minute,' Stringer replied, backing away and scrunching up her nose. 'She's definitely going to lose the one leg from the knee down. They're trying to save the other. It sounds like she was lucky. If she hadn't dived through the door...' she trailed off.

'Charlie Clarke isn't going to know what hit him,' McEvoy predicted, unaware of the stench emanating from his suit and shoe. 'If he thought this was going to scare us off, he's made a bad mistake.'

'Bishop's on the warpath,' Joyce said. 'He's called in armed response; the works. O'Reilly's all over the radio,' he said, referring to the Minister for Justice

'About feckin' time. Things have got out of control. Trying to kill Hannah's the last straw.'

'Have you been to Koch's farm?' Joyce asked, changing the subject.

'No. Should I have been?'

'No, no. It's just... it's just that you smell like you've... y'know.'

'It's that bad is it?' McEvoy said concerned, looking down. 'For God's sake!'

'It's a bit ripe,' Stringer joked, waving her hand in front of her nose.

'Well, I haven't got a spare pair, so people will just have to put up with it.'

'You could try washing them out,' Stringer suggested. 'There're changing rooms out the back. If you wring them out they should dry quite quickly.'

'I'll do it after. Do you have anything to report?'

'Nothing much beyond yesterday afternoon. The farm manager has confirmed that the rope is one of his. It was taken from a shed. We've arranged for Roza, the housekeeper, to look round the house with George and Chloe; see if anything's missing. She's up there now.'

'Good idea, though I've been warned about Roza. James Kinneally has her down as a gold-digger. He reckons that she gave Koch extra special care in the hope of a payoff when he dies.'

'You think Roza is a suspect?' Joyce said doubtfully.

'I think everyone is a suspect until proven otherwise.' McEvoy turned, sensing a presence behind him. 'The silent one has arrived,' he said to Jim Whelan.

'Horse shit,' Whelan replied.

'That's no way to describe Kelly's perfume,' McEvoy said, instantly regretting it.

'I, er...' Stringer stammered.

'Chanel 5,' Whelan said.

Stringer nodded her head, amazed that Whelan recognised it.

'I take it that's better than horseshit?' McEvoy asked.

'No contest,' Whelan replied.

'Fair enough. Did you bring a photo of the victim?'

Whelan nodded his head.

Stringer's mobile phone rang and she stepped to one side.

'Show it to Koch's farm manager, around Ostara's factories, and the town,' McEvoy instructed. 'If he's from around here, someone will recognise him.'

Whelan nodded again.

'Call me the minute you get a positive ID. I'll get Tom McManus, the local sergeant, to give you a hand. Any joy tracking down the couple asking questions?' McEvoy asked Joyce, waving his hand at the whiteboard.

'Not yet. We're ringing round the local hotels and B&Bs.'

'Sir,' Stringer interrupted, her finger placed over the mouth-piece on the phone.

'Yes.'

'It's George Carter. The housekeeper says that the only thing that seems to be missing is a handgun that Koch had hidden in the back of his wardrobe.'

'A handgun?' McEvoy repeated.

* * *

He carefully opened the small door at the back of the wardrobe, admiring the craftsmanship of the clever design. 'And he definitely kept a gun in here?' he asked without looking over his shoulder.

'Yes. A small gun,' Roza replied. 'Very old.'

'How did you know about it?' McEvoy pulled back out of the confined space.

Roza Ptaszek was standing a couple of feet away, wearing a dark blue cardigan over a light blue summer dress with black leggings underneath that stopped just short of her thin ankles. She was a good foot shorter than McEvoy. Her face had regained some of its colour, though her eyes were still bloodshot, her stance wary. 'I found it while cleaning,' she said defensively.

'He never told you about it?'

'No, why should he? It was for, how do you say, protection. He was an important man.'

'And it was there before he was killed?'

'I don't know. I found it and I left it there. I didn't check on it.'

McEvoy nodded. If Koch had heard a burglar downstairs he'd probably taken the gun with him while he investigated.

After he'd been attacked the thief had probably taken it as a precaution or souvenir.

'And there's nothing else missing?'

'No, I don't think so.'

'Do you have any idea what they might have been searching for?'

'Money?' Roza shrugged. 'Dr Koch was very wealthy. Perhaps someone thought that he might have money here?'

'And did he?'

'No, no. He kept his money in the bank.'

'And were you after his money?' McEvoy asked.

'Me?' Roza asked, confused.

'Were you hoping that Dr Koch would make you wealthy?'

'Why would he do that?'

'Because you were taking such good care of him.'

'I was taking such good…' Roza said uncertainly. 'You think I was sleeping with Dr Koch?' she said with disgust, realising McEvoy's insinuation. 'I look after the house and cook the meals. I am not a prostitute! I never…'

'Whoa, whoa, look, I didn't mean that,' McEvoy said trying to defuse the situation. 'I didn't say you were sleeping with him. I was trying to see why you were doing the job.'

'Because he offered it to me,' she said indignantly. 'He placed advert in newspaper, I answered it. I come here to work for good money.'

'Dr Koch paid well?'

'He pay average, but he also provided somewhere to stay.'

'He was a good employer?'

'He was… okay,' she finished lamely.

'And how about his family or people who visited the house, what were they like?'

'Okay.'

'Just okay?'

Roza nodded her head meekly.

'Yesterday you told me who had visited on Saturday. There

was Marion D'Arcy, James Kinneally and his business manager, Mr…'

'Freel.'

'Mr Freel,' McEvoy repeated. 'Anybody else?'

'Dr Koch's son, Charles, was also here in the morning with his son, Francis; Dr Koch's grandson. They only stayed for half an hour. They went to the horse racing.'

'Is that it?'

'Yes. Dr Koch has very few visitors. Mostly his brother and Mr Freel. Sometimes Mr Kinneally.'

'His brother's still alive?' McEvoy asked surprised. Since Charles Koch hadn't proffered that information, he'd assumed that the brother had passed away.

'Yes. He lives nearby with his wife. He is very old, but quite well. He visited every week, one or two evenings. They listened to old music and speak to each other in German.'

'Do you know where—'

There was a knock at the door. George Carter poked his head round the frame. 'Sorry to interrupt but you'd better come and have a look at this.'

'Can it wait?'

'Not really. One of Koch's neighbours is trying to take back what he says is his land.'

'Mr O'Coffey,' Roza said rolling her eyes. 'Him and Dr Koch were always fighting.'

* * *

Whichever way he looked at it he was going to have to wade through thick mud laced with cowpats. He looked up from the sodden ground and stared down the field to where a local guard was remonstrating with a man in his late thirties dressed in a check shirt, a dirty pair of jeans and green wellington boots. Behind him was an old, red, Massey Ferguson tractor, an elderly man behind the wheel looking nonplussed. Several posts and rolls of fencing wire lay on the ground. The cows in the field continued to chew the cud whilst keeping a careful eye on proceedings.

He took a deep breath and stepped forward, his shoe sinking into the mud, water edging over into his socks. His suit was already a mess – if he was in for a penny, he might as well be in for a pound. He squelched his way down the field.

'What's the problem?' he asked the guard as he neared.

'They're saying that this land rightfully belongs to them and they're taking it back.'

'That true?' McEvoy asked the man in the check shirt.

'And who the fuck are you?'

'Detective Superintendent Colm McEvoy. I'm in charge of the investigation into the murder of Albert Koch. And you are?'

'Peter. Peter O'Coffey,' the man said, calming a little. 'This is our land.'

'This is a murder site,' McEvoy replied tartly. 'I don't care if you think it is your land, I want you off it until we've completed our searches.'

'All we're doing is putting up a fence,' O'Coffey protested.

'I don't care. And from what I hear this is still an open dispute.'

'All the maps show that this strip of land is part of our farm. We're just taking back what belongs to us.'

'What's the problem, Peter?' the elderly man shouted from the tractor.

'They want us to leave,' O'Coffey shouted back. 'This is a murder site.'

The old man shook his head dissonantly and stared away across the field.

'You've been fighting over this land for long?' McEvoy asked.

'Since before I was born and this is when it ends.'

'I doubt it. You put this fence up and it'll end in court.'

'Nothing new there then. They can employ all the fancy lawyers they want, but this is still our land.'

'Worth killing over?'

'Are you accusing me of killing the old bastard?' O'Coffey said, bristling, squaring up to McEvoy.

'I'm seeing whether it's a possibility,' McEvoy hedged.

'I didn't kill him, Superintendent; nor did my grandfather.' He nodded his head towards the tractor, his mouth set firm.

'You can account for your movements on Saturday night?'

'I was at home with the wife and kids. We live on the farm with the old man.'

'Did you see anyone hanging around the area at all? Perhaps acting suspiciously?'

'No. I'm up early and I'm to bed early.'

'Right,' McEvoy said deciding not to push things. 'You'd better pack up your stuff and move off. You can have this argument another day.'

'It *is* our land.'

'I'm not saying it's not, but I *am* telling you to leave. Either you do so of your own accord, or I'll have to have you escorted off.'

* * *

He stared down at his mud-stained trousers. He had tried to wash them in the farmyard with freezing water from an outside tap, but they were still a mess. At least his shoes were clean. He straightened his jacket and knocked on the bright red door of an old, cut-stone bungalow surrounded by well-tended, mature gardens with an immaculately cut lawn.

After a few seconds it was opened by an elderly man with a full head of grey hair, dressed in dark trousers and a tweed jacket over a plain white shirt buttoned at the neck.

'Yes?' the man said with a slight accent, staring down at McEvoy's suit.

'Detective Superintendent Colm McEvoy.' He held out a hand. 'I'm investigating the death of Albert Koch. You're his brother?'

'Yes. Frank. Frank Koch.'

McEvoy was surprised at the strength of Koch's handshake.

'I'm very sorry about your brother's death.'

Koch shrugged and stood back to allow McEvoy to enter. 'He was an old man,' he said to McEvoy's back, 'and he led a full life. Please, come in here.' He indicated a doorway.

McEvoy entered a large sitting room with a floral carpet, a glass cabinet full of figurines, two bookcases crammed full, and a worn, green three-piece suite. Sat in one of the armchairs was an elderly lady, her dark grey hair cropped short.

'This is the detective investigating Albert's death,' Frank Koch said to the woman. 'Superintendent McEvoy. This is my wife, Mary,' he said to McEvoy.

'It was terrible what happened to Bertie,' Mary said. 'Terrible.'

'My wife has arthritis,' Koch said. 'Some days are better than others. I walk everyday to keep fit, but Mary's... she's not so good.'

'I manage!' Mary said defiantly. 'What do you expect? I'm ninety-two. He's ninety-three. We're not bad for our age, hey? Sit, sit. Would you like a drink? Tea? Coffee? Fruit juice?'

'I'm fine, thanks,' McEvoy said, not wanting to create any work.

'It's no bother, we'll be making one for ourselves,' Koch said, heading for the door. 'I'll put the kettle on. What do you want?'

'Tea. Tea would be great. White, no sugar.'

'White, no sugar,' Koch repeated disappearing from view.

McEvoy sat down on the three-seater sofa. Out of nowhere a black and white cat landed on his lap.

'Casper!' Mary snapped. 'Come on, get down. Down!'

'It's okay,' McEvoy said, stroking the cat. 'He's a nice cat.'

'He's spoilt,' Mary replied.

'Aren't all pets?'

McEvoy and Mary Koch swapped small talk for a couple of minutes, the cat purring loudly on McEvoy's lap, until Frank

Koch re-entered the room carrying a tray loaded with a teapot, a small jug of milk, three china cups on saucers, and a plate of biscuits. He placed the tray down on a coffee table and started to pour, handing the first cup and saucer to McEvoy, the second to Mary, before taking the final cup and sitting on the free armchair.

'So, Superintendent, how can we help you?'

'I'm trying to get a sense of your brother. He came to Ireland after the war?'

'Yes,' Koch said warily.

'He followed you here?'

'I asked him here. It was better here than in Germany.'

'You met Mary during the war?'

'What has this got to do with my brother's death?' Koch asked, his brow furrowing.

'Whoever killed your brother left a message. It might be something to do with his past.'

'What kind of message?' Koch asked.

'I'm afraid I can't tell you that just yet. Let's just say that it casts doubt on the idea that your brother was killed by an ordinary thief.'

'He was killed by somebody he knew?'

'Or somebody who knew about him,' McEvoy hazarded.

Koch snorted derision. 'That could be any number of people. My brother was very well known, especially around here.'

'He was also surrounded by all kinds of rumours. Maybe the killing is related to one of them?'

'Successful people are always surrounded by rumours,' Koch said dismissively. 'Others get jealous. My brother worked hard all his life. He never stopped working. And he funded many things for the local community.'

'He was a very generous man,' Mary added.

'Did you work for Ostara as well, Mr Koch?'

'For the first couple of years. I then set up my own business selling cars – Volkswagens. I had eight garages by the time I retired,' Koch said proudly. 'There are now twelve. My sons also sell Mercedes. I can get you a good deal if you're interested? Much better than a Ford!'

'You're talking to the wrong man, I'm afraid. It's a garda car. I just drive what I'm given,' McEvoy said and took a sip of his tea.

'And your own car?'

'That's my only car.'

'Well, let me know if you change your mind. Mercedes is a good, safe car. Very reliable. And very classy, y'know; good for your image.'

'Always a salesman, Superintendent,' Mary said, smiling. 'He can't help himself.'

'Unfortunately I'm always a policeman,' McEvoy said, trying to get the conversation back on track. 'Do you have any idea of who might have killed your brother?'

'No. It could be anybody.'

'Somebody searched the house, do you know what they might have been looking for?'

'Money?' Koch speculated. 'Something they could sell? Many people have lost their jobs. They are struggling to make ends meet.'

'Nothing specific?'

'I don't know. Mary?'

'I… I don't know. Bertie was a very private person. He led a simple life.'

McEvoy wondered whether it was possible to lead a simple life when running a billion euro suite of companies. The cat stretched on his lap and then curled up in a ball, settling in for a short nap. 'The only thing that seems to be missing is a handgun. Did you know about the gun?'

'It was an old gun. He brought it over after the war. It was for protecting himself. I doubt it still works.'

'He employed a security company until recently. Surely they would have protected him. Why keep the gun?'

'You can never be too careful. He got rid of the security

company – he thought they cost too much and they were more trouble than they were worth.'

'Perhaps he accidentally opened the way for someone with a vendetta to get close to him? Without a security patrol it would have been easy to break into the house.' As far as he knew they'd been no sign of a break-in, but he'd check again with Joyce and McManus.

Koch nodded his head but said nothing.

'Has anybody been taking an unhealthy interest in your brother recently? Anything out of the ordinary?'

'No, no. I don't think so.'

'Nobody been asking questions about his past?'

'No,' Koch said firmly.

McEvoy looked over at Mary who glanced away, staring over at the glass cabinet. He took another sip of his tea.

'He never said anything to you about any threats at all?'

'No.'

'And you saw him regularly?'

'Two or three times a week. The last time I saw him was Friday – Friday morning – and he seemed fine. His usual self.'

'He didn't mention anything out of the ordinary?'

'No.'

McEvoy took another sip of the tea. 'At the moment I think that whoever killed your brother knew him well, Mr Koch. If you were me, who would you put under the microscope?'

Koch stayed silent for a moment and then said, 'Stefan Freel. I've never felt comfortable around him. He's too ambitious and arrogant.'

'But why would he be searching your brother's house in the middle of the night?'

'I don't know. Papers? Stefan Freel is greedy, pushy and ruthless. That's why my brother liked him. He was good for business.'

Freel sounded like a mirror-image of Koch himself. Perhaps he was being groomed as a successor; someone to take over the helm of Ostara Industries when Koch passed away. McEvoy took a slurp of tea and reached for a biscuit.

* * *

McEvoy wandered across the incident room glancing down at stacks of paper on the tables. Next to the coffee canteens were three platters of sandwiches and a plate of digestive biscuits. He selected a ham sandwich, aware that beyond the biscuit at Frank Koch's house he hadn't eaten since early that morning. He took a large bite and wandered over towards where Kelly Stringer was standing, her back to him.

'Anything to report?' he asked, mumbling through the half-eaten bread, catching himself staring at the curve of her calves.

She turned to face him. 'Not a lot. The stories about Koch continue to grow – he'd come to Ireland via Argentina; he was personal friends with Charles Haughey; he'd been involved in covering up an accident at one of his factories in Africa where several people had died; he started his company using money from bank robberies; he was secretly funding research into genetically modified crops and growing them in Irish fields. It seems he attracted all kinds of speculation and accusations.'

'No doubt most of it rubbish,' McEvoy said dismissively. 'Do you have anyone checking them out?'

'Some of them; it's difficult to know where to start. I have someone checking out the bank robbery angle and also trying to track down immigration files.' She brushed some hair off her face, tucking it behind an ear. 'Someone else is doing a newspaper archive search for any stories related to Koch or Ostara Industries.'

'Good. I feel like I'm investigating a ghost here,' McEvoy said shifting nervously. Now the mud had masked the horses-hit on his trousers he could smell Stringer's perfume and she was looking at him somehow differently; straight into his eyes. 'No one seems prepared to say very much about him.'

'He still commands respect,' Stringer offered.

'Or fear. Any word about Hannah?'

'Nothing. If I hear anything I'll let you know. I'm sure she's okay.'

'Charlie Clarke better hope so,' McEvoy said, turning away to the coffee table. 'Coffee?' he asked, placing a styrofoam cup under the canteen. He needed to get away from Stringer, yet he felt compelled to stay. He wasn't sure how he felt, just kind of torn in an odd kind of way.

'No, no, I'm already gently buzzing,' Stringer laughed. 'If you wired me up you could probably jumpstart a motorbike.'

'If you hooked me up, I'd drain its battery flat,' McEvoy said neutrally then took a sip of the steaming brew.

'Not feeling the best?'

'The joys of being an insomniac; you're constantly tired. If they could bottle sleep I'd probably be an addict.'

'Better than cigarettes,' Stringer replied, immediately blushing, remembering McEvoy's patches and Maggie's cancer. 'Not that… I mean…'

'That's the truth,' McEvoy said solemnly.

'I'd say those trousers have had it,' Stringer said, looking down, trying to change the subject. 'You're never going to get them clean. You should have rolled them up.'

'Hindsight's a wonderful thing. I'm going to need to talk to Stefan Freel, Koch's business manager,' McEvoy said becoming more businesslike. 'Can you track him down for me?'

'No bother. I'll get on it now.'

'Thanks. I'm going to talk to George Carter.' Surely he was too old to be feeling like a teenager, he thought to himself. He was still grieving for Maggie, for God's sake.

* * *

Carter was walking across the mucky, cobbled farmyard carrying a battered leather case when McEvoy appeared, heading towards him.

'Any news on Hannah?' Carter asked as he approached.

'I was going to ask you the same thing,' McEvoy replied.

'It's like a black hole; no one seems to know what the fuck's going on,' Carter stated, frustration in his voice. 'All I know is she seems to have lost a leg and they're trying to save the other. Don't bother arresting the fucker who did it, Colm, just fuckin' shoot them. He was trying to kill her; she's bloody lucky they didn't.'

'Like that's going to solve anything,' McEvoy reproached. 'We'll get them, don't worry, George. They might accidentally fall down some stairs but that'll be it, then a long stretch in Mountjoy.'

'That could have been any of us,' Carter continued. 'We're all at risk. We've been telling you for years that you're putting us in danger by making us critical to cases. It's not been a question of if, but rather when. We're lucky she's still alive. If she wasn't, the Commissioner would be out of a job.'

'I know, I know. I've been saying the same thing.'

'Well nothing's fuckin' changed, has it? It better do now, that's all I can say. We'll be getting the union involved. I don't mind taking the risks associated with the job, but not if the risks are going to be increased due to poor management. My wife's through the roof – she wants to know whether she should take the children out of school and go to her mother's.'

'I'm sure we can arrange some protection if you're worried,' McEvoy said, trying to placate Carter.

'I don't want any protection! I want to be able to do my job as safely as possible without psychos like Charlie Clarke thinking I'm the answer to his problems.'

'Look, there'll be a full review. We'll get it sorted.'

'We don't need a full review! We know what the problem is. What we need is a change in procedures, more people, and better labs and equipment. We're running to standstill.'

'You're preaching to the converted, George. I'm on your side.'

'Then get it sorted!'

'I'll do the best I can. Have you found anything useful,' he asked, trying to change the subject.

'We've just taken some casts of footprints we found near to the noose. We've also got some good fingerprints and hairs from the rooms in the house but the place is littered with them.'

'Great,' McEvoy said sarcastically. 'And no sign of a break-in?'

'No.'

'So perhaps whoever it was had a key?' McEvoy speculated.

'Or the place wasn't locked up properly.'

'Unlikely; he seemed pretty security conscious.'

'Might have been a professional. If you knew what you were doing it wouldn't be too difficult to let yourself in. Sixty seconds tops. Stupid fecker had the alarm turned off.'

'How about the gun?'

'Dr John's got a couple of teams out combing the fields. He's talking about getting the divers in to search the lake.'

'Right, okay, well I'm off,' McEvoy said. 'We need to find out who has keys for this place. If you hear about Hannah, let me know, okay? I'm sure she'll pull through just fine.'

'She'll pull through alright, but whether she'll be the same person, who knows.'

* * *

Stefan Freel was tall, thin and prematurely bald, with a prominent nose and intelligent eyes. He was dressed in a smartly tailored, dark blue, pinstripe suit, salmon pink shirt, blue tie and highly polished black shoes. He glanced up and down at McEvoy's muddy suit, a wry smile curving up the edge of his thin lips, and held out a manicured hand.

His handshake was firm and confident. Still smiling he sat back down behind his large desk and closed the lid of his laptop. 'Well, Superintendent, what do you want to know?'

'You were Albert Koch's business manager?'

'I'm not sure business manager is quite the right title, but yes, I worked with him closely for the past seven years.'

'So what is the right title then?'

'I don't really have one. My job was simply to make what he wanted happen. I acted as a liaison between Dr Koch and his various companies – he didn't leave the house that often.'

'So you work for Ostara Industries then?' McEvoy said hesitantly.

'That's technically who employs me, but I only answered to Dr Koch, not one of the various divisions or companies.'

'They're not all part of Ostara?'

'They all had the Ostara branding, but were not necessarily part of the larger group. How each was established and run was mainly to do with tax issues or eligibility for grants or financing and so on.'

'So you report to James Kinneally then?'

'He kind of reports to me, to be honest. I told him what Dr Koch wanted and he reported back any news from head office. I liaised with all the heads of Dr Koch's interests.'

'A powerful job then?'

'You could say that,' Freel shrugged nonchalantly. 'Dr Koch was an extraordinary man. Even in his nineties he was a brilliant businessman. He could spot grains of gold on a beach of sand, then hoover them all up to make a full bar.'

'I've been told he was ruthless when conducting business; he must have made a lot of enemies?'

'There's no love in business, Superintendent; he would do what he needed to do. Sometimes there are casualties, but then what do you expect? He always said there are winners and losers, but never take prisoners; they bring nothing but trouble. People go in knowing what the rules and risks are and if you swim with sharks you'd better be a shark.'

'So he tended to steamroll over people?'

'He bought, sold and invested wisely,' Freel pulled a sly smile. 'He always drove a hard bargain. He never threatened physical harm or tried to intimidate people; he was too canny for that. He could spot a trend and he moved in and made it his own. He was always in at the ground level.'

'And where were you Saturday night?'

'In London, closing a deal. I flew over Friday evening, returned yesterday.'

'So who should I be investigating then? Anybody hold a grudge? Maybe threatened him?'

'If I were you, I'd start with his children, Marion and Charles. They've been pressuring him for years to let them take over the business.'

'I didn't think Charles was interested,' McEvoy said, his brow furrowing. 'He has his own career.'

'Don't believe everything you hear, Superintendent. In fact, take everything Marion and Charles Koch say with a large pinch of salt. They're both a pair of schemers. Charles has been trying to persuade his father to invest in one of his hair-brained schemes for years. The stupid thing would cost millions and have very little commercial value. He's also been pushing for his son, Francis, to be employed on a fast-track management scheme. He was worried that Mark D'Arcy would be in a prime position to take over Ostara, cutting out his children.'

'And will he?'

'Probably not. Mark's not stupid, but he's not got his grandfather's vision. He's plenty of his mother's arrogance though. He's probably already trying to use his family status to re-position himself in the company given his grandfather's death. Dr Koch, however, could see right through him. He wanted Ostara to be run for the benefit of Ostara, not for the ego and gain of his family.'

'And that means you?'

'I've no idea. Perhaps,' Freel shrugged.

'You don't seem too bothered.'

'I'm still in shock to be honest. It's a little disrespectful at this stage to be thinking about the future, don't you think?' Freel said disingenuously. 'I spent fifty hours plus a week working with Dr Koch; he was a close friend.'

76

'I get the impression he didn't really have friends, just people who circulated around him.'

'Well, you're wrong there, I'm afraid. He had a small coterie of very close friends; people he kept in contact with regularly.'

'Such as?'

'His brother. Myself. Martin O'Coffey. Maurice Coakley.'

'Who's Maurice Coakley?'

'He heads up Ostara Pharmacies. Koch and Coakley go way back.'

'And Martin O'Coffey? I thought they were at war with each other over a piece of land?'

'They were still friends. They used to take a drink together every Friday evening. It's the grandson that's got a chip on his shoulder. As I understand it they're barely hanging on. The country might have had a boom but not all boats went up on the tide. The rural economy has long been in freefall. God knows how they're surviving now.'

'Do you think O'Coffey or his grandson could have killed Koch?'

'It's a possibility,' Freel shrugged. 'The grandson definitely seems to be teetering on the edge. He was up at the house again last week ranting, threatening legal action. Land and money are a potent combination. Who knows, maybe he cracked?'

'And how did Dr Koch react to the threats?'

'He just tried to calm him down and reason with him. He knew him well from when he was a child.'

'And what did he do?'

'Eventually he stormed off saying he was just going to take it back. We did what we always did – sent Simon Farrell, the farm manager, down to keep an eye on the place.'

'Why didn't he just give him the land if it's only a narrow strip? A few feet was hardly going to make a difference given how many other properties he owned.'

'It's the principle. Dr Koch owned that piece of land, despite what the O'Coffeys thought. Once you give one concession, you're on a slippery slope. It'll then be another bit and then another.'

'You said earlier that his son and daughter were trying to gain control of Ostara,' McEvoy said, changing tack. 'Were they working together?'

'Not from what I could tell. Marion D'Arcy seems to have become increasingly obsessed with making sure Ostara stays within the family. The fact that her father wouldn't tell anyone his intentions concerning what would happen when he passed away clearly worried her a lot. Probably with good reason. If I were him I would have lined up alternative successors. She might have built up a mediocre law firm, but she's not up to running something as large and complex as Ostara. She knows absolute nothing about the sectors it works in and she's a loose cannon. She has rubbing people up the wrong way down to an art form. Everything would be in disarray within a few weeks.'

'And Charles? Did he want more than his son taken on?'

'He just wanted his share. I think he was more worried about Marion. If she was to take over Ostara she'd have no problem freezing him and his side of the family out. All she's interested in is herself. Ostara would give her serious political and celebrity clout. It would almost certainly make her the richest woman in Ireland. She'd revel in that title and all it would bring.'

'Surely she's already moving in all the right circles? Opening nights, gala charity events, the VIP paddocks?'

'But this would make her the queen bee and also put her on the world map. Until now she's been the daughter of a billionaire recluse with no access to his money. If she inherits his fortune she'll move up into the super-rich.'

'And do you think she'll inherit his fortune?'

'I've no idea. As I said, none of us do. He kept it to himself.' Freel made a point of glancing down at his watch. 'Look, Superintendent, I need to get on. I have a lot of things to get sorted.'

'Right. Right, yes. One last thing. Can you think of anyone else who I should be taking an interest in? Anyone hanging round? Perhaps threatening him?'

Freel stared up at the ceiling for a moment. 'There were a couple of East Europeans that called out a few times. He always seemed pretty agitated whenever they turned up. Other than that, no, not really.'

'Have you any idea what they saw him about?'

'He never said. It wasn't business though; he'd have told me if it was. He just wanted them to go away. They certainly got to him, whatever it was; he was always a little distant afterwards.'

'How many times did they call?'

'I don't know; four or five times when I was there?'

'And when was the last time they called?'

'Hmm… the Saturday before last?'

'And do you think they might have been responsible for his death? Were they looking for something?'

'I've no idea, Superintendent. Look, surely that's your job? I need to get on.' Freel stood and walked around the desk.

'Yes, sorry,' McEvoy pushed himself up out of his chair. 'Look, perhaps I can talk to you again sometime? I need to get a better idea about Dr Koch and Ostara; get some sense of how everything's organised.'

'That shouldn't be a problem. How about tomorrow lunch time? We'll get some lunch on the company tab.'

'I'd have thought that Dr Koch would have run a tight ship with respect to expenses,' McEvoy stated.

'Always feed the animals well before taking them to the market, you'll get better prices,' Freel smiled and opened the door.

* * *

As McEvoy neared the door to Ballyglass GAA club it opened and John Joyce exited.

'You better be wearing a hard hat if you're going in there,' Joyce warned, 'Galligan's on the war path. He feels he's being frozen out of the investigation.'

'He was never *in* the investigation,' McEvoy said, agitated. 'How're you getting on in any case? Have you found that missing gun yet?'

'No. We're going to get the lake dragged.'

'And do we know what the killer was searching for?'

'No. Roza, the housekeeper, has been through the whole place, but she can't see anything obvious missing.'

'I'm guessing there's nothing from the questionnaires?'

'Not that I'm aware of. You'd need to talk to Tom McManus. I did hear one interesting thing though. Marion D'Arcy is not Dr Koch's natural daughter. He adopted her when he married her mother in the early 1950s. Somehow her family managed to keep her out of a Mother and Baby home; she'd have been a prime target. Marrying Koch gave them some level of respectability.'

'Jesus.'

'It gets better. Her mother was an O'Coffey. The neighbour he was fighting with over that piece of land was his brother-in-law!'

'Well, that explains a few things,' McEvoy mumbled.

'Like what?'

'Like why Koch and O'Coffey used to meet every Friday night for a drink; they were family – blood thicker than water and all that.'

'Then why fight over a small strip of land?'

'The principle; they both thought they were right. Somehow they managed not to conflate the personal with the professional, something I'm guessing the grandson wasn't able to do. I'd better go and have a chat with Martin and Peter O'Coffey.' McEvoy turned to head back to his car.

'What about Galligan?'

'For God's sake!' McEvoy wheeled round on his heels. 'I'll talk to you later, okay.'

The hum of conversation filled the incident room. Galligan had cornered Kelly Stringer between the coffee table and the white board. Even from the far side of the room McEvoy could see he was giving her a hard time.

'You were looking for me?' he asked, interrupting the local superintendent.

Stringer gave a weak smile.

'What?' Galligan wheeled round, his face red.

'I said, you were looking for me?'

'I… yes,' Galligan muttered, momentarily knocked off track. 'This murder happened on my patch. Given it's my resources you're using, I should be much more centrally involved in the case. Instead I'm being treated like a pariah!'

'Look,' McEvoy tried to say calmly, 'no disrespect intended, but NBCI is running this investigation. We work closely with the local division and we try to involve them as much as we can, but we run the show. As the local superintendent, we ask that you deal with the media so we can concentrate on trying to catch the killer. That's it.'

'I… well… to deal with the media I need to know what the hell's going on!' Galligan said forcibly, his face bright red.

'We're telling you all you *need* to know. I don't want any important information given to the media that might accidentally jeopardise the case. We operate the same way in all cases. If you don't want to do the job, that's fine, I'll find someone else.'

'No, no. There's no way you're pulling that trick on me. I'll continue dealing with the media, but I need full access to the case.'

'Well you're not getting full access; you'll get what you're given.'

'What I'm given?' Galligan snapped. 'I'm not some little school child, McEvoy. This is a murder investigation in my divisional area. I'm going further up the chain; this is ridiculous.'

'I wouldn't do that if I were you,' McEvoy warned. 'Senior management are not in a good mood at the minute given the attempt to blow-up one of their officers this morning. They'll ungraciously put you back in your place and also mark your card.'

'Is that a threat?'

'That's advice. If you want a threat, then I'll ring them up and tell them that you're wilfully hindering my investigation.'

'You'll do what? You can try and throw your weight around, McEvoy, but just remember that it's my resources you're reliant on. Without me, you'll grind to a halt.'

'My suggestion is that you leave right now,' McEvoy said, losing his cool. 'As of now I'm reassigning the media spokesperson.'

'You're doing what? No fuckin' way!' Galligan spat. 'If you want a war, then you've got one.'

'Whatever,' McEvoy said dismissively. He turned to Stringer, trying to hide his rage.

Galligan stared at him angrily for a moment and then stormed to the door, slamming it behind him.

'I take it he's left then?' McEvoy said, smiling apologetically.

Stringer nodded. 'Talk about butting stags.'

'He's a stupid gombeen. He was giving you a hard time?'

'Nothing too serious in a chauvinistic, threatening kind of a way,' she smiled.

'Well, I don't know what you're smiling for; you're the new media spokesperson.'

'I'm the what?' Stringer said, instinctively patting down her hair.

McEvoy's phone rang. 'You heard. Yes?'

'Colm, it's Jenny. Do you have a minute?'

'Yeah, fire away,' McEvoy said, taking a step away from Stringer.

'I think we might finally be getting somewhere. We have a witness who saw the husband's car on the road from Bansha to Galbally on the morning that Kylie O'Neill was killed. He remembered it because of the sticker on the back window. "Honk if you're honkytonk." I doubt there are many of those around.'

82

'And he definitely saw it on the right day?'

'He thinks so.'

'He thinks?'

'He's pretty certain.'

'Jesus, Jenny, the case will last two seconds.'

'He killed her,' Flanagan said defensively. 'We all know he did. Do you want to come down if we interview him again?'

'Look, I'm sorry, but I can't, I'm up to my eyeballs here. I'll give you a ring later, okay? I know you think he did it, but tread carefully; you don't want to make problems for yourself later on. See if you can find anyone else who might have seen that car that morning.'

'Shit,' Flanagan said, disappointment in her voice. 'Any news on Hannah Fallon?'

'Hang on a second.' McEvoy turned to Stringer. 'Kelly, any news on Hannah?'

'She's out of surgery and she's doing okay. They managed to save the second leg but she'll be in hospital for at least a couple of weeks.'

'Did you get that?' he asked Flanagan.

'Yeah, thanks. I hope they string the bastards up.'

'I think "throw away the key" is the phrase you're looking for.'

* * *

Martin O'Coffey motioned towards an old wooden chair placed in under a Formica-topped table. The kitchen reminded McEvoy of his childhood – fake wooden laminate over chipboard with cheap plastic handles, an old electric cooker with spiral elements, a large, off-white Hotpoint fridge, and a Belfast sink. Set against one wall was an ancient Aga, pumping out a low heat.

'Do you live here on your own?' McEvoy asked, pulling the chair out and sitting down.

'Aye,' O'Coffey took a drag on his cigarette and flicked the ash onto the brown lino floor. He was wearing an old, light grey suit jacket over a dirty white shirt, and dark flannel trousers.

'You're a widower?' McEvoy asked, trying to ignore the tantalising smell of O'Coffey's smoke.

'Eleven years.'

'And your grandson?'

'Next door.' O'Coffey pointed over McEvoy's shoulder and moved towards a kettle. 'Tea?'

'Thanks. You were Albert Koch's brother-in-law?'

He trickled water into the kettle. 'Aye.'

'So you knew him a long time?'

Another lengthy pause. 'Aye.'

'He married your sister and adopted her daughter?'

'Aye.'

McEvoy rolled his eyes. It was like interviewing Jim Whelan, only slower. 'So Albert Koch was not Marion's natural father?'

'No.' The old man shuffled to a kitchen cabinet and took out a packet of Rich Tea biscuits, the top twisted tight.

'But he always treated her as such?'

O'Coffey placed the packet carefully in front of McEvoy, avoiding his eyes. 'Aye.'

'So who was her father?'

'Don't know.'

'How long had you been arguing with Albert Koch over the strip of land?'

'Fifty years.' The kettle was coming near to the boil. 'Milk?'

'Please. And you couldn't come to an agreement in fifty years?' McEvoy said reproachfully.

'No.' O'Coffey shook his head sadly.

'So why didn't you just forget about it?'

'Because it's our land,' the old man stated determinedly.

'So you argued about it?'

'Sometimes,' O'Coffey shrugged and pulled open the fridge door.

From where he was sitting, McEvoy could see that all that the large fridge contained was a joint of ham, a carton of milk, and a small lump of cheese.

'But you still met each other every Friday?'

The kettle clicked off. 'No reason not to.' O'Coffey poured the steaming water into two mugs.

'So you didn't hold a grudge?' McEvoy asked as gently as he could, trying to coax the old man along.

'No.'

'But your grandson did?'

O'Coffey shrugged and placed an unwashed mug full of milky tea in front of McEvoy.

'Your grandson argued with him over the land?' McEvoy pressed.

O'Coffey stayed silent, pulled out a chair and sat down opposite him. A cat that McEvoy hadn't noticed leapt into the old man's lap. The old man ignored the cat and its purring and reached across the table to the biscuits. He slowly untwisted the plastic wrapping and forced a biscuit up through the opening, tipping the packet towards McEvoy.

McEvoy plucked the biscuit free. 'Thanks. Your grandson?'

O'Coffey pulled his arm back and freed a biscuit for himself. He dunked it in his milky brew and took a bite before the soggy mass broke free. 'Once or twice,' he conceded as he chewed.

'Did he ever threaten him?'

'No.'

McEvoy's phone rang. 'I'm sorry,' he said as he pulled it from his pocket. He glanced at the screen, deciding whether to answer it. 'Yes?'

'What the hell are you playing at, Colm?' Tony Bishop snapped. 'Some stupid gobshite named Galligan's on the warpath. I've just had the Assistant Commissioner warm my ear. I don't care who he is or what he's done, but you better start re-building some bridges.'

'I... er...'

'Just do it, okay? I don't have time to be clearing up after you.' Bishop ended the call.

McEvoy stared down at the phone and inwardly cursed Galligan. He was obviously better connected than McEvoy had anticipated. He'd have to reappoint him as the media spokesperson. He glanced up at O'Coffey and pulled an apologetic smile, trying to get his mind back on the case. 'Sorry about that. Do you still see much of your niece?'

'Marion?'

'Yes.'

'No.'

'She doesn't have time for her family?'

O'Coffey stayed silent and stared out of the window into the farmyard.

McEvoy took a bite of the biscuit and followed his gaze. The light was fast fading. Two Belgium Blue cattle stared back at them from a shed roofed in red corrugated iron.

'Mr O'Coffey?'

'Sorry?' O'Coffey turned his gaze back to McEvoy.

'Your niece, Marion D'Arcy?'

'Yes?'

'She doesn't have a lot of time for you?'

'No.' He took a loud slurp from his tea and stared down at the table.

McEvoy sighed to himself. He wasn't going to get much more from the old man. And what little he would get would take hours.

* * *

It was barely past four thirty and it was already nearly dark, his headlights dancing on the rough and patched tarmac. He was heading back to Ballyglass GAA club, trying to decide how to deal with Cathal Galligan. His mobile phone rang.

'McEvoy.'

'Dad?' Gemma asked cautiously.

'Hiya, pumpkin,' he replied less gruffly. 'How're things?'

'We've just heard the news. They said that a bomb had exploded at Hannah's house and that she'd lost a leg. Is she okay?' she asked concerned. Gemma had come to know Hannah Fallon over the years. She was one of his few work colleagues that she liked, mainly because Hannah treated her as an equal rather than a child. For a twelve year old there was nothing worse than being patronised by an ingratiating adult.

'She's going to be fine. She'll be in hospital for a while, but she'll be okay.'

'Are you going to go and visit her?'

'I was thinking I might pop in on the way home. She's probably not allowed any visitors but I thought I'd stop by in any case; see how she is.'

'Can I come too?'

'I'm not sure that's a good idea, Gemma. She's been operated on for most of the day. I doubt anybody will be able to see her.'

'But you're going,' Gemma pleaded. 'If you're going, I want to go. She was my friend as well.'

'Look, Gemma, I know you like Hannah, but you barely know her. You've only met her a few times when she came round for dinner,' McEvoy said, referring to when he and Maggie used to invite colleagues round for a meal and a few drinks. Maggie and Hannah seemed to hit it off and they occasionally met by themselves for coffee and a chat. 'I'm sure she's got lots of people wanting to visit her. Perhaps we could both go tomorrow night when she's going to be feeling a bit better?'

'I met her loads of times with Mam,' Gemma replied. 'I won't cause any trouble and I'll get to see you as well. If you go on your own you won't be home until late and I'll have already gone to bed.'

McEvoy rolled his eyes. 'I'll pick you up from Caroline's, okay?' he conceded, feeling guilty for not spending enough time with his daughter.

'Thanks, Dad! You're the best,' Gemma said excitedly. 'I'll go and get some flowers and chocolates.'

'We might not get to see her,' McEvoy warned, not wanting her to be disappointed later. 'She'll be very tired after the operation.'

'What time do you think you'll pick me up? We don't want to be too late; visiting hours are over at eight.' Gemma was more than familiar with how hospitals worked. Her father had been taking her in and out of them for a few months before Maggie had finally lost her battle with cancer.

'I'll be there as soon as I can, okay; definitely not later than 7.15 – hopefully by seven.' He glanced at his watch. He'd organise a team meeting then delegate things to John Joyce. He'd need to leave Ballyglass by six o'clock to be back in Dublin in time. That only left just under an hour and half to try and wrap things up for the day.

'I'll see you at seven then,' Gemma said. 'Don't be late. We'll also have some dinner ready for you.'

'I'll be fine, don't worry about dinner.'

'You've got to eat. You're no use to anybody ill. I'll see you at seven.' Gemma ended the call before he could reply.

'For God's sake,' McEvoy muttered to himself as he turned into the GAA car park. He was going to have to drive past James Connolly Hospital into Dublin to pick up Gemma to drive back out again.

* * *

The room was a buzz of activity and whispered conversations. McEvoy and Jim Whelan were standing near to the notice board, both nursing lukewarm and stale coffee in styrofoam cups.

'So you've still got no idea who the victim is?' McEvoy asked.

'No.'

'And he's definitely not one of Ostara's employees?'

'No.'

'Is that a no he isn't, or no he is?'

'He's not.'

'So you have no definite lines of inquiry?'

'No.'

'And no one recognised him in the pubs in Trim?'

'No.'

'Jesus, Jim! That's five no's in a row,' McEvoy said frustrated.

'They were the answers.'

'At last, a sentence! Maybe we could move towards having a conversation?'

Whelan didn't reply, staring down into his coffee.

'For God's sake! Well, it doesn't look like the two cases are linked if he didn't work for Ostara. I suggest you get back to Trim and see if you can generate some kind of a lead. Trawl round the pubs again; canvas the surrounding villages; see if you can get his picture into the papers. I don't care. Someone must know who the hell he is.'

Whelan nodded in agreement.

'Call me if you find anything, okay?'

'No bother,' Whelan muttered and lumbered across the room towards the door.

McEvoy closed his eyes and held the bridge of his nose, silently counting to ten. His shoulders were stiff, knotted with anxiety and stress, and he gently rolled them, seeking relief.

He smelt Kelly Stringer's perfume a few moments before she spoke.

'What you need is a good massage,' she said from behind him, clasping his shoulders and digging her thumbs deep into his shoulder blades and gently rotating them.

He felt his head tip back in relief before he thought about what was happening and managed to squirm himself free. He twisted round and gave Stringer a tight smile before glancing round the room trying to assess how many people had seen the little moment of intimacy between them.

'What I need is a week's holiday,' he replied, his eyes still avoiding hers.

'Do you have somewhere in mind?' Stringer asked, smiling.

'Bed.' The word was out of his mouth before he realised what he was saying. 'Not that…' he trailed off, knowing that he was just going to dig the hole a little deeper.

'Not a bad place to spend a week,' Stringer replied, arcing her eyebrows.

'I guess we better get started,' McEvoy said, trying to change the subject. Whatever was going on with Stringer he needed to work out how to nip it in the bud without offending her. 'I need to get out of here; I want to visit Hannah Fallon before visiting time is over.'

'Make sure you pass on my best wishes,' Stringer replied. 'I just hope she's going to be okay. I can't imagine what it was like.'

'I hope neither us ever find out. Come on, let's get started.' McEvoy glanced round the room. John Joyce and Tom McManus were standing by the hot water urn deep in conversation. George Carter was sitting by himself, rubbing his tired face with the heel of his hand. Half a dozen local detective garda were sat in two groups of three chatting amiably. Galligan was at the back of the room, perched on the edge of a table, leaning back, held up by his outstretched arms, a smug look on his face. Barry Traynor from the press liaison office hovered nearby looking lost, like the uninvited guest at a house party.

'Right, okay, let's make a start,' he said loudly. 'Come on, quieten down.'

Stringer moved away and sat down next to John Joyce.

For the next fifteen minutes they worked their way through what each team member had found and mapped out a plan of action for the following day.

McEvoy started to wrap things up. 'So, has anyone else got anything they want to add?' he asked.

He was greeted with tired faces and silence.

'Well, let's get back to it. Superintendent Galligan, if I can have a word please. DS Joyce, if you can stay behind as well.'

Galligan wandered through the others to get to McEvoy, a sly smile painted on his face.

'If it were up to me, you wouldn't be here,' McEvoy said quietly so no one could overhear, 'but it isn't, so you are. You're to work closely with press liaison who will be taking a more active role. I've arranged for one of their staff to work with you on this full time. Everything is to be run past me before being released.'

'If this is my job, then I'm going to do it my way,' Galligan said defiantly.

'I'm in charge of this investigation,' McEvoy pressed. 'Your position on the team is still answerable to me whether you like it or not. If you want a second round on this, fine; this time I'll do it the right way and you won't be able to go squealing to your friend in high places.'

Galligan's smile disappeared and he looked ready to explode. 'You're still on my patch, McEvoy. We've been cooperative up until now, but you've just dispensed with whatever good will there was left. We'll still help out, but well...' he let the sentence hang. 'And you better start looking for a new sergeant as I'm reassigning Tom McManus.'

'And have you asked him what he wants?'

'It doesn't matter what he wants. I say jump, he feckin' jumps.'

'I wonder what Ostara Industries and the hundreds of local people who work for them will make of your attitude? I don't imagine they'll want this case given a low priority. They'll want the killer of Albert Koch brought to justice.'

'Well, that's your problem, isn't it?'

'Small town, small mind, small man. Just leave, okay,' McEvoy said rolling his eyes.

'What did you say?' Galligan demanded.

'I said you'd better leave. I believe there's another press conference at seven o'clock.'

'You might think you're the big man, McEvoy, with your high flying job and your girlfriend running the incident room, but you're just a second chancer. If it was up to me, I'd have kicked you into some backwater six months ago. You fucked up the Raven case, and you'll no doubt fuck this up as well.'

'A backwater being somewhere like here?' McEvoy said facetiously.

'Fuck you.' Galligan turned on his heels and stormed to the door, once again banging it shut. Barry Traynor raised his eyebrows quizzically at McEvoy before turning and trailing after him.

John Joyce drifted over to where McEvoy was standing with his head tipped back, his eyes closed. 'What was that about?' he asked.

'Building bridges,' McEvoy said, rocking his head forward, still seething.

'You've a long way to go until you meet in the middle.'

'Maybe,' McEvoy conceded. 'I seem to have a talent for rubbing people up the wrong way at the minute.'

'Too much stress,' Joyce observed.

'And not enough nicotine. I'm going to head off. I'm going to drop in on Hannah Fallon and see how she's getting on. You're in charge for now. Don't stay too late and if you need me, I'll be on the mobile.'

'No bother. Give my best to Hannah. I hope she's going to be alright.'

'She'll be fine. She's as tough as old boots. Look, I better be going. Ring me if anything major occurs.' McEvoy went to move off and then stopped. 'Oh, yeah. Galligan wants to take Tom McManus off the case. Have a word with him, will you. Tell him I'll get it sorted out. In the meantime tell him it's up to him what he does. I want him working for us. He's doing okay, isn't he?' he asked as an after-thought.

'Yeah, yeah, he's grand. Why does Galligan...' Joyce trailed off.

'Because he's an idiot. He thinks that because this is his patch, he should be running things. Ring me, okay?'

* * *

He pulled to a halt outside of a plain semi-detached house, red brick at the bottom, white rendering above. As he pushed open the car door, the front door flew open and Gemma spilled out and raced down the path carrying a bunch of flowers and a plain white, plastic bag.

His sister's growing frame filled the doorway. She waved at him and he gestured back.

Gemma yanked open the passenger door and clambered in. 'You're late!' she snapped. She dropped the bag between her feet, placed the flowers on her lap, and tugged the seat belt across her. 'They'll be shut by the time we get there.'

'Five minutes late,' McEvoy replied. 'It'll only take ten or fifteen minutes if we take the motorway.' He pulled off, waving again to his sister.

'And you stink!' Gemma said wafting her hand in front of her face.

'I've been on a farm.'

'What did you do, take a bath in a pig's sty?'

'No, I stood in a pile of horse dung and waded through a field of cowpats and mud.'

'Phewy! Open the windows,' she demanded. 'Come on, I'm being gassed to death.'

'It's not that bad.'

'It's not that bad? You absolutely stink! It's worse than Niamh Giles' farts and, believe me, they're the worst.'

McEvoy cracked open a couple of windows and wondered whether he should have changed before heading back out to Blanchardstown. 'So, how was school?' he asked, trying to play the fatherly role.

'It was okay; same as usual.'

McEvoy sighed. An entire day summed up in six words.

'Nothing exciting?'

'No. It's school.'

'And your friends?'

'They're okay.

McEvoy rolled his eyes at her reluctance to divulge her day. 'So what's in the bag?' he persisted in an effort to have some kind of conversation.

'A card, some Chez Emily chocolates, and your dinner in a plastic container; you'll have to re-warm it when we get home. It's chilli con carne.'

'And you got the flowers in the village?'

'At the florist. You owe Aunt Caroline ten euros. I bought the chocolates.'

'I'll pay you both back later, don't worry.'

'Do I look worried?' She arched her eyebrows. 'I'd say the Bank of Dad is good for its debts.'

'You cheeky monkey. The Bank of Dad! Where did you get that? One of your friends?'

'I saw it on a T-shirt. I was going to buy it for you for Christmas.'

'Don't you dare! You've done your homework?'

'Maths, French and Irish. Finished it straight after tea.'

They continued to swap stilted small talk, catching up on each other's lives for the past two days as the orange street lights flashed by overhead, the frigid air from the open windows swirling around them.

* * *

It took five minutes of driving round aimlessly to find a parking place. He waited for the elderly gentleman to reverse out and then eased the car into the slot and glanced at the clock – 7.50. 'Come on, we should just make it.' He levered himself out of the door, twisting in the narrow gap between his own and the neighbouring car.

'Jesus, Dad, look at the state of you! Your trousers are covered in mud.'

McEvoy glanced down as they walked. Even in the pale glow of the car park's street lighting, he could see his suit trousers were filthy from the knees down. 'It'll wash out,' he mumbled.

'It's a wool suit. It's ruined! I doubt they're going to let you in.'

'It'll be fine. People come into here from accidents covered in all sorts.'

'Not onto the wards they don't.'

'Don't worry about it. I'll use my badge. I guess we go to casualty and see if they know where she is.'

They entered the brightly lit foyer to the Casualty Department, and hurried through a set of double doors into the noise of the main waiting room. There was a short queue to a desk where two hassled looking women were fielding queries. After a couple of minutes, they reached the front of the queue.

'I'm looking for Hannah Fallon,' McEvoy said.

'Another one,' she replied nonplussed. 'And you are?'

'I work with her. Detective Superintendent Colm McEvoy.' He held out his ID.

'The only people allowed onto the wards are family,' she said as if repeating it for the hundredth time.

'I'm a close personal friend. I've worked with her for years and she was a friend of my late wife. We've bought her flowers.'

Gemma held up the bouquet.

'I'm sorry, sir.'

'We'll only be five minutes. I just want to see how she is. She was working on my case when she was attacked.'

'Five minutes max,' the woman said, folding. 'She's on Ward 21. She's probably asleep in any case.'

'Thanks.' McEvoy turned, took Gemma's hand and started to head towards the far end of the room. He'd only got a few yards when the woman called out to him.

'Whoa! Whoa. Hang on. Stop!'

Several people glanced over at the commotion, wary that an incident was about to burst into life.

The woman came from behind the desk and trotted over to them.

'You can't go up like that. Look at the state of you. And the smell,' she said as if noticing it for the first time above the stench of disinfectant. 'What have you been doing?'

'Hunting round farmland for a murderer.'

'Couldn't you have got changed first?'

'I'm working sixteen to eighteen hours a day on four different murder cases. It's a miracle I found enough time to get here, let alone get home and get changed first.'

'Well, you can't go up like that.'

* * *

He felt like an idiot. He was wearing a green surgery gown over his suit jacket and a black, plastic bin bag over each leg, taped to his thighs to keep them up.

'I wish I had a camera,' Gemma said, still giggling five minutes after he emerged from an ante room.

'We all agree I look ridiculous,' McEvoy said as they approached Hannah Fallon's private room. 'Five minutes then we're out of here, okay. She'll be tired after the surgery.'

There was a uniformed guard that McEvoy didn't recognise sitting outside of the room. Stacked to one side of him was a pile of flowers and presents. 'How is she?' McEvoy asked.

'And you are?' the guard said defensively, staring at McEvoy's attire.

'Detective Superintendent Colm McEvoy, NBCI. I work with DS Fallon. This is my daughter, Gemma, and this is a long story,' he said holding out the gown.

'She's doing okay,' the guard said, seemingly satisfied with McEvoy's identity. 'Well, as okay as someone who's had a bomb pushed through her front door. Her sister's in with her.'

'Do you think it's alright to pop my head in?'

'I've been told not to disturb her. There's been a procession of people coming up.' He pointed down to the pile of flowers. 'I think she's tired of all the attention.'

'Right,' McEvoy said, regret in his voice. 'Fair enough. Can you tell her we came by? That we're thinking of her.' McEvoy clutched Gemma to his side, knowing that she would be disappointed after her efforts to get them there.

'Of course. No bother.' The guard reached out to take the flowers and plastic bag from Gemma.

As he took them the door opened and Hannah's sister stepped out holding an empty disposable cup. 'Colm?' she asked, her hand flying up to her mouth, stifling a laugh.

'Hi, Catherine. How's she doing?'

'Jesus, she has to see this! What the hell are you wearing?' Hannah's sister took hold of McEvoy's elbow and pulled him into the small, darkened room. 'More visitors,' she announced. 'One of them in fancy dress.'

'What?' Hannah mumbled from the bed. Her legs were slightly elevated, the bed clothes draped across them. Her hair was tousled and, even in the low light, her face pale.

'Hi, Hannah.'

'Colm?' she asked groggily.

'And Gemma. At least you won't be going to court this week.'

'I wondered what the silver lining was,' she tried to joke. 'Why are you dressed for surgery?' She closed her eyes.

'They didn't want me contaminating the place; I've come straight from Koch's farm. I'm wearing bin liners over my trousers.'

'I wish you'd do the same when you examine crime scenes.'

'We bought you some flowers and chocolates.' He nudged Gemma, who placed them on a chair next to Hannah's bed.

'Thanks.'

'We're all thinking of you. Anything you want, just ask.'

'Make sure that scumbag Charlie Clarke rots in hell,' she whispered without opening her eyes.

'Bishop's already working on it. Come on, Gemma, let's leave Hannah to sleep.'

McEvoy and Gemma left the room, followed by Hannah's sister who closed the door over quietly.

'She's still groggy after the surgery,' she said, 'I don't think it's really hit her yet. They've removed her right leg from below the knee. The other one is still a bit of a mess. They think they've saved it, but it's going to need additional surgery.'

'Jesus,' McEvoy muttered. 'Just let me know if you need me to do anything. Anything, okay?' He started to walk away, Gemma's hand grasped firmly in his own, the bags on his legs swishing together.

Seeing Hannah had rattled him, stirring memories of Maggie's time in hospital. Suddenly he wanted to leave the hospital, to go and find a quiet spot and sink a few drams; if the truth be known to drink to oblivion. He knew that wasn't an option; that he'd go home, re-heat his dinner, make sure Gemma got to bed, take a shower, and then stare at the bedroom ceiling for a few hours. He'd pay good money for a cigarette right now. Instead he sucked in a lungful of fresh air, letting the breath out slowly.

TUESDAY

Bishop glanced at his watch and looked up anxiously at the dimly lit street. His breath steamed in front of him. It would be another couple of hours until the sun rose above the horizon.

A team of four armed guards were crouch-walking behind a garden hedge approaching a red-brick, mid-terrace house located on the edge of a social housing estate in Mulhuddart where over half the residences were now in private ownership. A similar team were making their way to the rear of the house.

He glanced at his watch again. A voice in his ear whispered, 'Team one, ready.' A second later, 'Team two, ready.'

Bishop took one last glance around the silent street. 'Go, go, go,' he said quietly but urgently.

The four figures rose from behind the hedge and rushed toward the door. Dressed in dark blue, with bulletproof vests and black helmets with visors they moved confidently, assured by their training. The lead man took up a position flat against the wall next to the door. The second swung a battering ram into the area of the lock. The sound reverberated down the street. He repeated his action and the door popped open. The first man swung round into the doorway and stepped into the hall.

The first bullet hit him dead centre of his chest, stopping him in his tracks. He staggered back a step, his head tipping up, exposing his chin. The second bullet smashed through his jaw, penetrating his neck and exited his back, narrowly missing his spine. One of his colleagues grabbed hold of him and dragged him out backwards through the doorway, another returned fire to the top of the stairs where the waiting gunman continued to shoot.

There was a loud noise from the rear of the property as the second team smashed through the back door. As they cautiously entered the hallway, hugging the wall out of view of the gunman, the shooting stopped. One of the guards, his pistol firmly grasped in two hands, his arms outstretched, tentatively made his way up the stairs, his colleagues covering his progress. He swung onto the landing to find it empty, a step ladder rising through into the loft space. He motioned the next person up.

'They're in the roof space,' he stated loudly into his radio mic heading for the ladder. He started to climb the ladder. 'Armed response! You're surrounded! Drop your weapons!'

From outside he heard the dull noise of a motorbike engine kicking into life, revving loudly, and then roaring off; then the voice of Chief Superintendent Tony Bishop, 'Shit!'

* * *

His hand hunted round the bedside locker trying to find the mobile phone. He finally located it and pulled it under the duvet. 'McEvoy.'

'Have you heard the news?'

'Barney? What's the time?'

'Nearly half past six. There's been a gun fight in Mulhuddart. One of the armed response guys – Gavin Reddan – got shot through the neck. He's on the critical list; could be touch or go.'

'What?' McEvoy said, still trying to wake up after only a few hours' sleep.

'I said, there's been a gun fight...'

'I got that bit,' McEvoy interrupted. 'A gun fight over what?'

'Bishop organised a raid of the house that two of Charlie Clarke's gang were holed up in; the two that tried to blow up

Hannah Fallon. Only when they broke down the door they were ready for them. They shot Reddan three times; once in the neck, twice in the vest. They also wounded another of our lot. Shot through the hand. When they finally got in they discovered they'd gone up into the roof space. There was a passageway all the way along the terrace. They got out the end house and away on a motorbike.'

'For God's sake.' McEvoy pushed himself upright. 'They got away?'

'Disappeared into thin air.'

'Jesus Christ. Whereabouts in Mulhuddart?'

* * *

He rode the Mondeo up onto a kerb and clambered out into the frigid morning air, his breath steaming from his nose and mouth. He'd roused Gemma from her slumber, bundled some of her clothes into a bag and driven her over to Caroline's house. His sister's partner Jimmy was pretty nonplussed at being dragged from his bed so early. He'd simply opened the door, let Gemma pass beneath his arm and closed it again without waiting for an explanation. McEvoy had lost count of the number of pints he owed him.

The road ahead was chaos. Blue swirling lights, blue and white tape draped across the street, locals standing around in pyjamas and dressing gowns, kids running and shouting, and guards in luminous jackets trying to bring some kind of order to things. He turned to see an RTE van pulling in twenty yards behind him.

He set off towards the tape, flashing his identification to a hassled looking guard, and ducking underneath. He found Bishop standing alone by a broken doorway, the ground at his feet flecked dark brown.

Bishop's face was flushed red, matching his short red hair. 'What the hell are you doing here?' he snapped as McEvoy approached. 'If you came to gloat you can leave now.'

'I came to see if you needed a hand?' McEvoy replied defensively.

'What I need is for you to look after your cases, I'll deal with this one.'

'They got away?' McEvoy asked, ignoring Bishop's bile.

'Through the roof space. Clarke and his cronies own the whole damn row. Rents them out and turns a tidy profit. One of them is injured; we found blood at the top of the stairs and in the attic. If he turns up at a GP or hospital we'll get him.'

'Somehow I doubt he will. Somebody tipped them off?'

'Somebody must have – if I find out who, they're a dead man. I'm going to need Jim Whelan; you'll have to take over his cases.'

'You're joking?'

'Do I sound like I'm joking?'

'Well, can I take Barney Plunkett off the Raven case? Just for a week or so to help out?'

'No way,' Bishop snapped. 'We do that and the media will go crazy. It's going to be bad enough as it is. There's no way we can let that case go cold, even for a week. You know that.'

'So how am I meant to investigate all these cases at once?'

'Clone yourself,' Bishop said facetiously. 'I don't care; this takes priority. Charlie Clarke has declared war on the Gardai. We need to shut his gang down and send out a signal to everybody else that we mean business. If we let them start to push us about we'll totally lose control, and then the whole thing becomes a real maelstrom.'

A uniformed guard approached. 'Sir?'

Bishop glanced over at him. 'What?'

'RTE want to know if we have a statement.'

'I bet they do. I'll be there in two minutes.' He turned back to McEvoy. 'I have to go and face the music. Have a word with Whelan and get back up to Meath or wherever it is you're meant to be. If the shit hits the fan up there, I don't want to know.' Bishop started up the path without waiting for a reply.

McEvoy glanced around and then followed him, heading for his car. Bishop was right. If the situation with the Dublin gangs got even more out of control than it already was then it would be pandemonium. It would take forever to regain the initiative and longer still the confidence of the public. In the meantime, whole swathes of the city would be run by criminal gangs. If they thought things were bad now, they were on the cusp of it becoming a whole lot worse.

* * *

The inbound traffic was already heavy on the N3, commuters making their way into Dublin. He called up Jim Whelan.

'Hello?'

'Jim, it's Colm, have you heard the news?'

'No.'

'Bishop had a house raided in Mulhuddart. It was a disaster. Two of our lot shot, one of whom is fighting for his life – Gavin Reddan, do you know him?'

'Vaguely.'

'The two occupants escaped through the roof space and got away on a motorbike. Bishop wants you to transfer onto his team, ASAP; I'm to take over as investigative officer on your case.'

'Okay,' Whelan reply neutrally.

'I need to know where you're at.'

'Same as last night.'

McEvoy shook his head. He'd almost managed to get Whelan to say a whole sentence. 'Look, tell your team I'll meet them at eleven, okay? I have some other things to do before then. They're working out of Trim station, right?' After that he'd have to rush off to meet Stefan Freel.

'Right.'

'You'd better get yourself back to Mulhuddart,' McEvoy said and ended the call.

There was no point meeting Whelan; he wasn't going to get any more useful information out of him. That wasn't simply a function of Whelan's stubborn silence; there genuinely seemed to be no firm lines of enquiry. And losing Whelan, however recalcitrant he was, posed a serious problem. He was inheriting a case that was going nowhere and the best he would be able to do was direct it from a distance. The Koch case had to take priority – it was higher profile and there was a greater chance of solving it.

* * *

McEvoy had visited briefly the incident room for an update before driving out to Marion D'Arcy's house. Thankfully Stringer had been deep in conversation with a local guard so he was spared talking to her. He hadn't yet worked out what he was going to say. No doubt it would be something inane like, 'You're really nice, and I really like you, but...'

He turned into D'Arcy's driveway and drove up to the front door, parking in the shadow of the out-of-place portico. The horses in the neighbouring field stared balefully at him as he clambered out of the car, then lowered their heads back to the lush grass.

He was kept waiting at the front door for a minute or so until it was opened by James Kinneally.

'Superintendent?' Kinneally said, feigning surprise and blocking access to the hall.

'Seems like this is your second home,' McEvoy stated. 'I'm here to see Marion D'Arcy.'

'I was just seeing whether Marion was okay,' Kinneally replied testily. 'Unsurprisingly she hasn't taken the death of her father at all well.'

'So you've been consoling her?'

'I've been... helping out. Did you make an appointment?'

'I told you yesterday I'd be back today and I believe one of my officers rang to arrange a time. Are you going to let me in and inform Mrs D'Arcy I'm here?'

'I'm not sure she's taking visitors. Perhaps you might call back?'

'And perhaps you'd better go and check,' McEvoy said, losing patience. 'It's either that or I'll hold down the horn on my car until she appears. I'm sure the horses wouldn't really appreciate that.'

'I'll be back in a minute.' Kinneally closed over the door leaving McEvoy standing on the steps.

After a short while it was opened by Marion D'Arcy. She was dressed in a smart cream business suit with a blue pipe trim. The dress stopped just short of her knees and she was wearing matching cream slingbacks. Her make-up had been carefully applied, but it couldn't hide the tiredness in her eyes. 'Superintendent?'

'I need to talk to you about your father,' McEvoy explained.

'I'm getting ready to go into work. I need to travel up to Dublin.'

'Don't worry, this won't take long. You did agree to meet me at nine this morning.'

'Ten minutes, is that okay?' she said firmly, implying that McEvoy's presence was an imposition she was prepared to tolerate but little more. She opened the door wide so he could pass into the hall. 'I need to catch up on yesterday. One day away and it starts to pile up.'

'As I said, it shouldn't take too long,' McEvoy tried to reply neutrally. Her father had been murdered and yet she couldn't find time for the person investigating his death.

She opened the door into the same room in which he had spoken to James Kinneally the previous day. She perched on the edge of the sofa, her knees closed tight and pointing to one side, and indicated to McEvoy to take a seat on an armchair.

'So, how are things going?' she asked, pulling a tight smile.

'Slowly. It seems your father was surrounded by rumours and we're still trying to piece together the last couple of days before his death and get a picture of his life. You were close to him?'

'I used to see him at least once a week, sometimes almost every day. It depended on his work schedule and mine.'

'And you'd class your relationship as good?'

'As good as anyone else's,' she replied defensively.

'But you argued a lot?'

'No more than any other father and daughter. I wanted him to take better care of himself; slow down and enjoy his retirement.'

'You wanted to take over Ostara Industries?' McEvoy speculated, finding it difficult to warm to her.

'I wanted him to relax,' she replied firmly. 'Take some holidays. Enjoy some of his wealth. When my mother was alive he would barely take a break. After she died, he never took one. He was a work-alcoholic.'

'And you would take over to make his life easier.'

'I offered to help,' Marion conceded, unsure about how much McEvoy knew of her battles with her father. No doubt Roza would have overheard some of them and her father could easily have confided in Stefan Freel.

'Perhaps now you'll take his place? Now that he's,' McEvoy paused trying to find the right word, 'gone.'

'Are you implying that I'm a suspect?' Marion said testily.

'I'm exploring why you argued with your father.'

'We always argued! We argued about everything. That's what we did. If you think that I murdered him, you clearly have a screw loose. I was trying to prolong his life – make him take it easy – not kill him!'

'Perhaps it was his work that kept him going?' McEvoy hypothesised. 'Did it frustrate you that he wouldn't let you help? That he blocked you from working for Ostara?'

'No! I have my own successful business. He did me a favour by making me stand on my own two feet.'

'You didn't resent it?'

'No, why should I?'

'Because you could have been at the helm of one of the biggest businesses in Ireland.'

'I still might be, Superintendent,' she said smartly.

'And how about your son, Mark?'

'What about him?'

'I thought you were grooming him to take over from your father.'

'He doesn't need grooming. He's doing exceptionally well by himself. Even if he wasn't my father's grandson he would be where he is today.'

'And what about James Kinneally? Or Stefan Freel?'

'What about them?'

'I would have thought that they would be at the head of the queue for taking over Ostara Industries. Plenty of experience and they're already doing the right kind of job, aren't they?'

'Stefan Freel will take over Ostara over my dead body. He's a scheming, little...' she trailed off, aware of her bile.

'I take it you don't like Stefan Freel?'

'I... he's... he wouldn't have been my choice as an assistant.'

'I think he was a little more than an assistant,' McEvoy said. 'He seemed to be your father's hatchet man, running round doing deals here, there and everywhere.'

'Well, I wouldn't trust him as far as I could throw him. If I were you, that's where I would focus my attention.'

'Why?'

'Because he would kill his own grandmother if he thought he could make money from it.'

'Sounds suspiciously like your father. Surely killing your father would be like killing the golden goose?'

'Not if you think you're the golden goose in waiting. Are we done yet? I need to be getting on.'

'I believe you also argued about your father's will,' McEvoy persisted.

'Who told you that?'

'It doesn't matter. But if you were arguing about his will then it sounds like you weren't happy with it.'

'What is it you're trying to say?'

'Perhaps you decided to try and find his will to check it? You aren't, after all, Dr Koch's natural daughter.'

'You... what?' Marion D'Arcy replied, temporarily flummoxed. 'How dare you... You've no right to pry into my affairs!'

'I'm investigating the murder of your father and exploring *his* affairs. As his daughter you're part of that. He adopted you when he married your mother?'

'So what!' Marion snapped, her forehead creasing in anger. 'I... I don't believe you're... Albert Koch was as much my father as he was Charles'! He never said or acted otherwise. We were always treated the same. Do you hear, the same!' She stood up and started towards the door.

'Mrs D'Arcy?' McEvoy said, standing, realising that he'd pushed her too hard. 'I'm sorry. I know this is very difficult, but it's my job to ask these questions.'

She stopped and turned back to face him. 'It's your job to find my father's killer – if there was a killer – not to make wild accusations. You're implying that because I was adopted I had a motive to murder my father! That I was searching the house for his will. Why would I be searching the house in the middle of the night when I could look for it anytime? Besides, his will is held by his solicitor,' she said angrily. 'I've never been... You seem to forget that I'm a lawyer,' she said, regaining some composure.

'I might not have studied or practised criminal law for years, but I have many friends who do,' she continued. 'If there is one thing you can be sure of, Superintendent, it's that I'll be getting the very best legal advice. And I won't be speaking to you again unless my lawyer is present.' She paused, challenging McEvoy to say something. 'And speaking of legal matters and the will, when are we going to find out what my father's will says? His stupid, old fool of a solicitor says he wants to wait until the killer is caught before he'll make it public, but we need to start making plans.'

'Plans for what?'

Marion D'Arcy's desire to know the contents of her father's will troubled McEvoy. It would detail the redistribution of billions of euros of assets. People had been killed for much, much less. And when that kind of money was on offer, others could be drawn into the conspiracy or contract thieves or killers hired. Koch's daughter might not have killed her father directly, but she could still have been the main agent of his death.

'Plans for the future of Ostara. Our own plans. Just plans!' she snapped.

'What's the rush?' McEvoy asked as neutrally as he could. 'A few weeks isn't going to make a big difference, is it?'

'Because we need to know,' Marion stated firmly. 'If it's not released in the next day or so I'll be seeking legal action.'

McEvoy decided not to pursue the issue. He'd already pressured Marion D'Arcy more than he should have. And now, no doubt, he was going to have to deal with lawyers much more accomplished than those he usually dealt with. Needling her hadn't been a clever move. No surprise there. His handling of the investigation so far had been haphazard and poorly executed. He was too tired and stressed and it made him antagonistic and impetuous. His mobile phone rang.

He pulled it from a pocket and checked the screen. 'I'm sorry,' he muttered, 'I should take this. I won't be a second. McEvoy.'

Marion D'Arcy rolled her eyes and stormed from the room, pulling the door closed behind her.

'We've found the East European couple who'd been asking questions about Koch,' Joyce said. 'They're staying in Navan. They claim they didn't come forward because they were worried we'd think they'd killed him.'

'Why would we think that?'

'Revenge. The woman says Koch killed her grandfather.' Joyce paused. 'In Monowitz; a satellite camp of Auschwitz.'

'Auschwitz?' McEvoy repeated. 'Oh, Jesus. I'm on my way. Don't let them go anywhere.' He headed for the door, massaging his tired scalp.

James Kinneally was waiting for McEvoy in the hall. 'What the hell did you say to Mari... Mrs D'Arcy?' he snapped. 'She's furious.'

'She didn't like being questioned,' McEvoy said unsympathetically. 'Unfortunately I have to question everyone, including the deceased's daughter. I'll be back to interview you further as well.' He opened the front door and stepped out into the chill morning air. He stopped and turned. 'And if you see Charles Koch, tell him I'll need to talk to him again.'

* * *

'How did you find them?' McEvoy asked.

'Persistence and luck.' Joyce paused. 'And a tip off.' He smiled coyly.

They were in Navan, a bustling market town 30 miles to the northwest of Dublin, standing on the steps of a well-maintained bed and breakfast, the genteel ambience somewhat dissipated by the heavy traffic on the road just beyond the gate.

'And what do you make of them?'

'They're driven and they tell a hell of a story. They have a strong motive, but also an alibi. They were here on Saturday night.'

'And the owners can verify that?'

'Well, they were definitely here for some of it, but there's nothing to say that they didn't sneak out to take a look round Koch's place, things went wrong, they killed him, and they crept back here to lay low.'

'Nothing either to say that they did,' McEvoy observed.

'True,' Joyce conceded. 'I think they're more motivated by justice than revenge.'

'Right, okay, let's go and talk to them then. Their English is good?'

'Pretty much perfect; there's no need for any translators.'

'Good.' McEvoy followed Joyce into the house. He glimpsed a nervous looking face at the end of the hall, probably the owner, and turned right into the front room.

The waiting couple rose from a floral patterned sofa, both wearing worried frowns. The woman had an oval face framed by long brown hair that was starting to turn prematurely grey, and sad brown eyes. She was wearing dark blue jeans and a sky blue jumper with a patterned, blue silk scarf wrapped around her neck and tucked into the neckline. It was difficult to judge her age, but McEvoy guessed she was probably in her late thirties or early forties. She was clutching a large, plain brown envelope. The man appeared slightly younger, with short brown hair with a side parting, and clear blue eyes behind small, round glasses. He wore a brown corduroy jacket over a pale blue shirt and faded blue jeans.

'I'm Detective Superintendent Colm McEvoy.' He held out his hand. 'I'm in charge of the investigation into Albert Koch's death.' He shook their hands in turn.

'Adolf Kucken,' the woman said firmly with the trace of an eastern European accent.

'I'm sorry?' McEvoy asked puzzled, indicating that they should sit down again.

The couple dropped back down onto the sofa, but both perched on the edge of the cushions. McEvoy sat on the arm of an armchair and Joyce continued to stand by the door.

'Adolf Kucken,' she repeated. 'That was Albert Koch's real name before he changed it. He was a Nazi war criminal.' She removed a photograph from the envelope and handed it to McEvoy.

The photograph showed a head shot of a young man who clearly resembled Albert Koch. The man was wearing the black uniform of the SS, his officer's cap, with its distinctive skull badge below an eagle and swastika, tugged rakishly to one side. His eyes were dark, staring fiercely into the lens.

'Kucken was a member of the SS and a chemist at the Buna factory at Auschwitz,' the woman continued, 'and he almost certainly took part in the infamous Jewish Skeleton Project.'

'The Jewish Skeleton Project?' McEvoy repeated slowly, aware that the case was taking on a whole new aspect.

'One of Heinrich Himmler's pet projects. The aim was to create a collection of Jewish skeletons for supposedly "scientific" purposes; that of identifying Jews through their pathology, such as their skulls' shape and size. The project was part of the Institute of Military Scientific Research, a branch of the Abnenebre. That was a research organisation founded by Himmler to prove the superiority of the so-called Aryan race,' she explained in what seemed to be a well-rehearsed speech.

'The process was simple – you take many measurements of a person's head and body while they are alive, then you kill them, take away the flesh and measure their bones.' She pursed her lips and shook her head sadly. 'Of course, to make sure it is properly scientific you need Jews from different places and you need a lot of them to have a sufficient sample. A good place for that was somewhere like Auschwitz, where millions of people from all over Europe were sent to be murdered.

'The only problem with Auschwitz was that Silesia was a long way from the laboratory of August Hirt, the scientist responsible for the experiments, and the journey would be un-refrigerated so the bodies would decay. The solution was to ship the intended victims to the Natzweiler concentration camp in the Vosges Mountains near to the Anatomical Institute at the Strassburg Reich University then kill them there. Bruno Beger, an SS researcher, visited Auschwitz in 1943 to select suitable victims, to take initial measurements, and send them on to Natzweiler.

'Natzweiler had a specialist medical laboratory for the lunatic, Hirt, where he performed very cruel experiments with mustard gas and he tested methods of sterilisation such as injecting testicles with various poisons. In order to kill the new prisoners they built a gas chamber. However, getting cleaned skeletons was not so easy. Once dead the problem is to remove all the flesh. The traditional process was to first put the bodies in lime chloride to dissolve the soft tissues. Then they put them in gasoline to get rid of the fat. The whole process takes weeks. As a skilled chemist and enthusiastic member of the

SS, Kucken was consulted about how to more efficiently strip the flesh from the bones of those Jews murdered at Natzweiler. We think Kucken was temporarily moved from Auschwitz to Strassburg to help Hirt carry out the task.'

'You think?' McEvoy said, his mind trying to process the horrific story.

'We're almost certain,' the man said, his voice weak and reedy. 'We have many boxes of evidence – documents and witness statements. We know that Kucken was on leave from Monowitz and in Strassburg at the right time. The prisoners were shipped there in early August 1943. Eighty-six of them were killed from the eleventh onwards and the corpses shipped to the Anatomical Institute within a few hours of death. Kucken was there from the ninth to the nineteenth; at the Institute. He had no other reason to be there. His family were in Freiberg.'

'And Monowitz was?'

'The forced labour camp built to house the slave workers used in constructing the buna factory; it produced artificial rubber for the German war machine,' the woman answered, handing McEvoy four more photos. One was of a large factory with four tall chimneys, two wide stacks, and a plethora of buildings and exposed pipework. The second was row after row of barracks surrounded by barbed wire and watch towers. The final two photos were of emaciated men in striped rags staring forlornly at the camera.

'Auschwitz was a complex of many camps and works. Many of the workers at the factory were foreign, "volunteer" labourers or ethnic Germans, but twenty to thirty per cent were concentration camp prisoners who were systematically worked to death. Somewhere in the region of thirty-five thousand unfortunates passed through Monowitz between 1943 and 1944. The number of *confirmed* deaths was twenty-three thousand. People were forced to work eleven or twelve hour days carrying heavy loads in all weathers with pitiful clothing and the minimum of food. And these were the people fit enough that they weren't sent straight to the gas chambers as they climbed off the trains.'

'Jesus,' McEvoy muttered.

'Have you heard of Primo Levi?' the man asked.

McEvoy shook his head no.

'He was an Italian chemist who survived Monowitz. Everyone should read his books.'

McEvoy nodded his head, unsure what to say. If true, then Ireland had not only been sheltering a war criminal for nearly sixty years, it had enabled him to live a very successful life.

'Kucken was the star chemistry student of his generation at Heidelberg University,' the woman continued. 'Heidelberg had produced a number of Nobel Prize winners, including Carl Bosch, one of the founders of IG Farben, and it was felt that Kucken had the potential to follow in their footsteps. In 1941 at the age of twenty-three he was already near to completing his doctorate and he'd secured a post with IG, then the largest chemical conglomerate in Germany. An early member of the Hitler Youth he was recruited by the SS and encouraged to continue his career. When IG started to build the buna plant near to Auschwitz, given his interests and his SS involvement, Kucken was an obvious candidate to go there and help run it.

'He was a brutal man who we know from personal testaments killed at least five people in cold blood; probably several more. We have a picture of him standing next to a gallows from which several people are hanging. He certainly attacked and maimed many people. And we have strong evidence that he knew about and took part in the Jewish Skeleton Project. Through his SS contacts we know he also came into contact with the infamous Josef Mengele – the Angel of Death – and that he also met Bruno Beger when he visited Auschwitz.'

'And what evidence do you have that Albert Koch was Adolf Kucken?' McEvoy asked trying to equate their story with the ashen corpse he'd inspected a couple of days ago. It was hard to see the frail, old man as a mass murderer, despite the fact that he knew murderers had no typical recognisable traits.

'You've seen the photograph, Superintendent. Even after sixty years he looked the same. Besides, his brother also changed his name. Franz Kucken became Frank Koch. If you check the internment records for the Curragh camp during the war there is no record for Frank Koch. But there is for Franz Kucken – Adolf Kucken's brother. Adolf Kucken laid low after the war, then somehow found a way to Ireland. Once here he persuaded his brother to slightly modify his name and started a new life, keeping his past hidden.'

McEvoy realised that he'd let the couple say their piece without actually finding out anything about them. 'And you're here to expose his past?' he asked.

'We're here for justice,' the woman said firmly. 'One of the people he killed in cold blood was my grandfather on my mother's side. He shot him in the head in January 1944 for not working fast enough. We've been trying to persuade Kucken to confess to his crimes.'

'And you are?' McEvoy asked, taking the opportunity to wrestle back the initiative.

'I am Ewa Chojnacki from Krakow in Poland. This is Tomas Prochazka, he is from Slovakia. We both belong to an organisation called Yellow Star. We try to track down the last of the war criminals before they die to capture their confessions and to make sure the world does not forget the evil they committed. Adolf Kucken lived a very good life. He became very rich and very powerful. He destroyed thousands of lives and yet he did not suffer for his crimes. Instead it appears that he was rewarded.'

'And would taking his life be a suitable revenge?'

'If you are asking whether we killed Adolf Kucken, then the answer is no. We wanted Kucken to confess; to admit to his crimes and face prosecution. A quick death was too good for him.'

'And what did Dr Koch say to your accusations?'

'He refused to talk to us. We tried to persuade him; we threatened to take a case against him unless he confessed.'

'And what did he say to that?'

'He told us his lawyers would wrap us in legal tape to silence us. We tried talking to his brother, but he just got angry and wouldn't answer our questions. We also tried to talk to his housekeeper, Roza, but she didn't want to know. She lost several family members during the war, including a grand-uncle that died on a death march from Auschwitz towards Germany as the Russians approached the complex. This is our third trip here to try and persuade him.'

'Does Roza know about her great-uncle?' McEvoy asked.

'Possibly. We don't know. We haven't told her yet.'

'And what were you doing late on Saturday night?'

'We were here in the guest house.'

'And can anyone confirm this?'

'Only each other, and perhaps the landlady. We did not kill him. We wanted him alive so that he could suffer the humiliation of being exposed for who he really was.'

McEvoy nodded his head. If what the couple were saying was true then Koch's reputation would soon be in tatters.

'If you didn't kill him then why didn't you come forward straight away?'

'We wanted to see if the real killer was caught quickly. Given our interest in Adolf Kucken we are seen as suspects, yes?'

'I'm afraid so. Koch's, or if you are right Kucken's, house had been searched when he was killed. You were after information about him. Did you break into his house?'

'No. We have all the evidence we need from the German, Polish and Irish archives. We were after a confession, nothing more.'

'But you did visit his farm on Saturday?'

'We went to the house in the morning, but he would not talk to us. His son and grandson were there. We left and did not go back.'

'You needed evidence that Koch was Kucken.'

'We *knew* he was Kucken. You've seen the photo. His history fits.' She shrugged as if to say, 'what more do I need to say to prove it?'

116

'We're going to need to verify your story. You said you have boxes of evidence?'

'We only have a little of it here. Most of it is at our headquarters in Israel.'

'Israel?'

'It is the safest place for it. Many people would like our files to disappear, Superintendent. Much of the original sources are still in their proper archives, but our files are carefully catalogued and cross-referenced to reveal patterns of association and guilt. Adolf Kucken was a billionaire. He could have tried to use his wealth to destroy our evidence, so we protected it well.'

'And what about yourselves?'

'What about us?'

'Perhaps he could have tried to make you disappear?' McEvoy suggested.

'He could have tried, but he would be making a bigger problem for himself. If we disappeared, then Yellow Star would mobilise fully against Kucken and Ostara Industries. We are a small organisation but we have very influential friends and funders. It would quickly turn into an international incident.'

McEvoy nodded his head, unsure what to say.

'I can arrange for copies of the evidence to be sent to you,' Ewa continued, 'though the documents are mainly in German. The witness statements are in Polish, Hungarian, Russian, Hebrew, Italian, French and other languages. Very little has been translated into English.'

'We'll take anything you have,' McEvoy said, unsure of how they would be able to fully analyse the material without lengthy and expensive translation and transcription. 'Particularly anything that proves your claims as to Koch's identity and his guilt of war crimes. We'll also want to know where the original sources are so we can make sure they're genuine. I'll arrange for someone to collect the material you have here. Is that okay?'

'Yes,' the woman nodded. 'We have copies.'

'I'll also need you to provide full statements as to your movements over the past few days and especially on Saturday and Sunday.'

'That's not a problem.'

'Right, okay. I think that's it for now. What will you do now that Koch is dead?'

'Once we are no longer considered suspects, we will tell the world his story. Just because he's dead does not mean that the crimes he committed die with him. People should know what he did. Do you know what Ostara means, Superintendent?'

'No.'

'Ostara was the pagan god of rebirth and new life; new beginnings. In some places she was known as Eostre. It's where the word Easter comes from; the time when things re-emerge after a dark winter and start to grow again. Kucken saw Ireland as a place where he could forget his past and start over afresh. We're going to expose that past and why he needed to start again.'

'And what about the people who work for Ostara Industries,' McEvoy said, starting to think through the ramifications of their story. 'They might lose their jobs if the company gets in trouble.'

'If history is anything to go by, they might experience a slight downturn, then grow back. Look at all the big German companies today. Many of them served the Nazi war machine and now they are thriving. The uniform Kucken wears in this photo,' she held it up again, 'was tailored by Hugo Boss. People forget and forgive corporations quickly. But they will not forgive Adolf Kucken.'

McEvoy nodded his head in agreement and pushed himself to his feet. 'I'm afraid that I must request that you do not leave the country until further notice.'

Ewa and Tomas levered themselves standing.

'We understand,' Tomas said.

'Somebody will come to collect your material and statements.' He shook their hands and left the room.

McEvoy exited the bed and breakfast and waited on the steps leading down to the gate, shielding his eyes from the low sun. He felt strangely calm. All of his frustration and stress seemingly dissipated. The couple's story was otherworldly. If true, then the search was no longer for the killer of a rich, but innocent, old man. Rather they were seeking someone who had killed a murderer, a monster who had been an active contributor to genocide. A monster who had not only evaded justice, but had prospered seemingly without guilt or shame. The front door closed behind him.

'Well?' John Joyce asked.

'They had a strong motive for searching Koch's house,' McEvoy said neutrally. 'Perhaps they disturbed him, he came downstairs and they got into a fight? Koch almost certainly had a gun. They could have been defending themselves?'

'Perhaps,' Joyce said unconvinced.

'And the hanging rope would make sense as a statement.'

'Or that's what someone wanted us to think,' Joyce speculated.

'Well, we have two definite lines of enquiry for now – Marion D'Arcy and her strong desire to see her father's will and our two friends in there.' McEvoy gestured over his shoulder. 'Marion D'Arcy might not have been snooping round the house, but that's not to say that someone else wasn't doing it on her behalf. I want you to get hold of the doctor who pronounced Koch's death and find out if Mrs D'Arcy placed pressure on him to declare a natural death. Also track down Koch's solicitor. I'll want to talk to him. And get Kelly Stringer to organize the collection of whatever evidence those two have, to take full statements from them about their movements, and to talk to the landlady to corroborate their story.'

'I'll talk to the landlady again before I leave,' Joyce said.

'And ask Kelly to check with military records about Frank Koch's internment in the Curragh,' McEvoy continued. 'I'm going to talk to him again.'

He glanced at his watch. 'Jesus,' he whispered to himself. He was late for his meeting in Trim about the dead Lithuanian.

He was going to have to delay it for now and also rearrange his meeting with Stefan Freel.

* * *

Frank Koch opened the door before McEvoy had a chance to press the bell. 'Superintendent?'

'I'm afraid I need to ask you some more questions. Can I come in?'

'Yes, yes,' Koch said smiling, 'please. It's good weather for a change, no?'

'Anything's better than rain,' McEvoy said, following Koch into the living room.

Mary Koch was sitting in the same chair, a newspaper in her lap. 'You look better than yesterday,' she observed. 'More colour in your cheeks. Do you want a cup of tea? Frank, will you put the kettle on?'

'No, no, I'm fine,' McEvoy muttered. 'I need to ask you both some more questions though, if that's okay.'

'Sit, sit,' Mary demanded.

McEvoy and Koch sat in the same places as they had the day before.

'Are you making any progress?' Mary continued. 'It's terrible about Bertie. I still can't believe it's happened; to attack an old man like that.' She shook her head in disbelief. 'We've been told we can't bury him yet, so everything's all up in the air. And I haven't slept right since for worry. What if he tries to break into our house in the middle of the night? My Frank isn't as strong as he used to be.'

Frank Koch pulled a tight smile, but stayed silent.

'We're making some progress,' McEvoy replied, 'and hopefully we'll catch whoever's responsible for Dr Koch's death soon.'

'I hope so, I really do.'

'I'd like to ask about when your brother moved to Ireland,' McEvoy said to Koch. 'His son, Charles, said he moved here in 1948.'

120

'Yes,' Koch replied warily.

'He came from Germany to join you in Athboy?'

'Newbridge,' Mary answered. 'We were living in Newbridge. That's where I met Frank. We moved to Athboy in 1952 when they bought the factory.'

McEvoy nodded. The Curragh internment camp was a couple of miles from Newbridge in County Kildare, about forty miles to the south of Athboy. 'The factory?' he prompted.

'We bought a fertiliser factory that had just gone out of business,' Koch stated flatly.

'The two of you?'

'Yes. We worked very hard for four years to save enough to buy it. It took us three months to get it operational again. We lived in the factory to save money.'

'All of you? I mean, both of your families?'

'Yes. We couldn't afford anything else.'

'So Albert was now married?'

'Oh, yes,' Mary said. 'He'd married Maura in 1950. She died in 1987 of breast cancer. It hit Bertie hard.'

'And both his children had been born?'

'Yes,' Mary answered. 'Charles was born just a couple of months before we all moved. It was not easy living in the factory with young children. We had two of our own at that stage and I was pregnant with Karl. The place was filthy and there were mice and rats everywhere, but we coped.'

'And did anyone else move with you from Newbridge to Athboy?'

'Why are you asking these questions?' Frank Koch said, his voice hardening.

'I'm trying to get as full as picture of Dr Koch as I can. When he married Maura, he also took on her daughter as well, didn't he?'

'If you already know the answers why are you asking these questions?'

'Because I don't know all the answers. I have some bits of

information, which may or may not be true, that I want to piece together into a full story.'

'Maura O'Coffey was my best friend, Superintendent,' Mary said. 'She went to Britain in 1943 to work as a nurse in Liverpool. She stayed on there after the war for a couple of years and returned to Ireland not long before Bertie arrived. When she finally travelled home she had a four-month-old daughter. She told her family and friends that she had married a local man, but that he had died a couple of weeks previously whilst clearing a bomb site – a wall had fallen and crushed him to death. With a young child and no breadwinner she decided to come home.'

'And was she married?'

'No. But this was 1940s Ireland, Superintendent. Mothers without husbands were sent to Mother and Baby Homes. The child might have been taken away for adoption. The family would lose face with their neighbours. It was easier for everyone to pretend that she had been married. And then Bertie came along.'

'He rescued her?'

'They fell in love. They were close from the minute he arrived. They were both determined to make a better life for themselves.'

'So it wasn't a marriage of convenience then?'

'What has this got to do with anything?' Frank Koch demanded. 'He was killed by a thief.'

'It's to do with understanding Albert Koch's family tree,' McEvoy replied, ignoring Koch's assertion. 'In 1948 your brother arrived in Ireland. He met Maura O'Coffey – Martin O'Coffey's sister – married her and took on responsibility for her daughter. They then had a son a couple of years later. Martin O'Coffey, Albert's warring neighbour was his brother-in-law, and Marion and Charles' uncle. I'm assuming Martin O'Coffey moved here with you in 1952?'

'You can't possibly suspect Martin,' Mary said. 'There's not a bad bone in his body.'

'I never said Martin O'Coffey was a suspect, Mrs Koch.'

'Martin helped at the factory,' Frank Koch said. 'He was our first employee.'

'Doing what?'

'Just helping out. He left after a few years to run his farm. I left to open my first garage. Albert was the chemist, I wanted to be a car salesman, not a fertiliser salesman.'

'There must be a lot of money in just helping out to be able to buy a farm,' McEvoy noted.

'We all worked hard and we all shared the rewards of that work. Land was not that expensive at the time.'

'Albert didn't resent the fact that Marion was not his natural daughter?'

'Bertie loved Marion and Charles equally,' Mary replied.

'But they argued all the time,' McEvoy stated.

'Marion is like her mother. And her father,' she added. 'Headstrong. Albert loved Maura and he loved Marion.'

McEvoy decided not to push the issue any further, instead changing tack. 'When I spoke to you yesterday you said that nobody had been asking about Dr Koch, but we have had several reports of a couple going round trying to talk to people about him. We've managed to track the couple down and we've spoken to them. They say they'd tried to talk to you.'

'Pah!' Koch spat, waving his hand.

'They have some very strong accusations about your brother,' McEvoy said evenly. 'Did you speak to them?'

'They were crazy. I sent them away.'

'They say they have evidence that your brother was a war criminal.'

'That's nonsense! He worked as a chemist during the war. I do not want to talk about this. It is lies and it makes me angry.'

'Frank?' Mary asked, her brow furrowing.

'They were crazy,' Koch said to his wife. 'They were saying crazy things. Did you ask them whether they killed him?' he asked McEvoy. 'Hey? They kept going to his house.'

'We did ask them and it appears they have an alibi. We are checking it at the moment. So, you think there's no truth in what they said?' McEvoy asked, aware that he needed to talk to Frank Koch alone since his wife clearly didn't know anything about the accusations being levelled against her brother-in-law.

'There is absolutely no truth. It is all lies. My brother was a good man.'

'Right. Right, okay,' McEvoy said, nodding his head and rising to his feet. 'Well, I think that will do for now. Thank you for answering my questions.' McEvoy didn't move towards the door, waiting for Koch to show him out.

Eventually the old man rose and headed from the room, McEvoy trailing after him.

McEvoy paused at the front door. 'If there is any truth in their accusations, it will all come out. And if it is true, then your brother will be remembered as a monster.'

'We'll fight any slander on our family name.'

'Which name is that,' McEvoy said, 'Koch or Kucken?'

'Koch,' Frank Koch said firmly. 'I do not want you to come here anymore. If you want to speak to me again I will come to the police station. I do not want my wife upset for no reason.'

'We're already checking the military records. If there's a Franz Kucken but no Frank Koch registered for the Curragh camp, I'll be back to talk to you again.' McEvoy turned and set off for his car.

Koch stayed on the doorstep until McEvoy was out of sight, then slowly closed the door.

* * *

He was driving from Athboy to Trim, winding his way through low lying, gently rolling farmland and a procession of odd-matched, one-off housing, when his mobile phone rang.

'McEvoy.'

124

'Superintendent, my name is Mark D'Arcy, Marion D'Arcy's son,' the voice said evenly. 'Can I speak to you please?'

'I'm driving, but yes, okay. I have you on the hands-free.'

'I want to protest to you in the strongest possible terms,' D'Arcy said calmly, 'as to how my mother is being treated by you and your investigation. She is extremely upset by your visit this morning. She feels she's being treated as a suspect in my grandfather's death. As a result, she's already consulted some of her lawyer friends. I am sure this is all a misunderstanding and I want to stop things spiralling out of control. The gardai and the family should be working together to catch my grandfather's killer, not falling out unnecessarily.'

'I… I know your mother was upset, but I am only doing my job, Mr D'Arcy,' McEvoy said uncertainly. 'Unfortunately that means I have to ask people, including your mother, questions that they might feel are upsetting or inappropriate. That's especially the case when there are no definite lines of inquiry or suspects.'

'I understand that, Superintendent, but my mother is extremely upset at the death of my grandfather. I can't possibly see how she could be a suspect. What would she have to gain?'

'Your grandfather was extremely wealthy, Mr D'Arcy. With wealth comes power. Your mother is potentially about to inherit a fortune. Whether she's guilty or innocent that makes her a suspect, even if she is not the prime suspect. And I'm afraid the whole family are suspects until either we have solid alibis or we get a positive lead. That might not seem fair, but that's the way it has to be.'

'I understand that, but my mother has a solid alibi. She was at home.'

'But she doesn't have anybody who can corroborate that.'

'But that's…' D'Arcy said as if he was going to correct McEvoy before trailing off.

'That's what?' McEvoy prompted.

'That's preposterous,' D'Arcy managed to catch himself, his calmness starting to fray. 'My mother has built up a very successful business of her own and my grandfather was very old. She's already independently wealthy and would inherit shortly in any case. Why would she risk doing anything stupid?'

'Perhaps because she's not set to inherit? I don't know. It could be for any number of reasons. I'm not saying your mother did kill her father. I'm saying I can't simply rule people out without substantive evidence.'

'This is ridiculous!' D'Arcy snapped. 'My mother might be all kinds of things, but she is not a murderer!'

'I haven't said that she is,' McEvoy tried to say patiently. 'All I'm saying is that I can't yet eliminate her as a suspect.'

'The family want to make an appeal for witnesses,' D'Arcy said, changing tack. 'And Ostara Industries is willing to put up a fifty thousand euro reward for information leading to the capture of my grandfather's killer.'

'Perhaps we could start with the appeal for witnesses?' McEvoy suggested cautiously. 'The money will bring out every crank on the island. All the rubbish they'll give us will just slow the case down.'

'And buried in the rubbish could be the truth,' D'Arcy said pointedly.

'There's no point burying it when it could be on the surface. Let's try appealing for witnesses, offering the reward in a couple of days if we don't get anywhere?'

'Okay,' D'Arcy conceded reluctantly. 'How do we go about doing that?'

'You need to talk to our media relations team. Are you ringing on a mobile?'

'Yes.'

'I'll forward your number to them once I've parked up and they'll call you shortly. That okay?'

'That's grand. Look, Superintendent, my mother really isn't responsible for my grandfather's death,' D'Arcy said, returning to his original theme. 'She's very delicate at the moment. She might act all tough and businesslike, carrying on regardless, but it's all an act – putting up appearances. She's an emotional wreck. I'd appreciate it if you could tread lightly around her, even if she is one of the thousands of potential suspects,' he added, slight sarcasm in his voice.

'We'll try our best,' McEvoy conceded. 'How about you? Did someone take your statement?'

'Yes. A Detective Sergeant Joyce. I was in Galway at a concert with my wife and some of her family. I spent the night at my in-laws. Believe me, if I was going to kill any of my family, that's where I'd start. Not that I'd ever…' D'Arcy trailed off.

'It never seems like a joke once you say it, does it?' McEvoy said flatly. 'The media relations people will be in contact shortly. Perhaps we could meet sometime in the next couple of days to discuss Ostara Industries? I want to try and get a better handle on your grandfather's business interests.'

'You think his death might be related to Ostara?'

'Somebody was searching the house for a reason. The reason might have been related to his business dealings. If we can determine the reason, we narrow down potential lines of inquiry.'

'I'm not sure I'm going to be able to help you much,' D'Arcy said cautiously. 'You'd be better off talking to James Kinneally or Stefan Freel. They would have a much better knowledge of the company and anyone who might hold a grudge or who might want to steal company secrets.'

'I thought you were the rising star of Ostara?' McEvoy pressed.

'I'm just working my way up the same as everyone else,' D'Arcy muttered defensively, clearly used to people thinking his promotions were due to family connections rather than business acumen.

'Nevertheless, I think it would be useful to meet. I'll get someone to call to arrange a meeting.' McEvoy ended the conversation. Mark D'Arcy had started assuredly then drifted towards caution, and he was holding something back. The best way to try and prise whatever it was out of him would be face-to-face when McEvoy could get a better sense of the man – gauge his body language and read his eyes.

His mobile phone beeped telling him he had a message. He sighed to himself and dialled his answering service.

'You have one new message,' the automated voice said. A moment later his sister-in-law started to speak. 'Colm, it's Ciara. I know you're probably busy but we need to talk about Friday. I think I've got most things sorted but I wanted to check in with you. Give me a call, later, okay? Okay, bye for now.'

He ended the call. He'd try and remember to ring her later; he couldn't face talking about Maggie and her memorial service right now. If truth be known, he really wasn't looking forward to the day. Ciara wanted it to be a day of reflection, remembrance and celebration. As far as McEvoy could see it would be a whole day of re-living the past, of wallowing in grief; a day of re-stoking his anger, sorrow and guilt at her death.

* * *

The room contained more than a dozen men. McEvoy recognised only four of them – two of Jim Whelan's sergeants, Mickie Brehan and Colin Vickers, Tommy Boland the local superintendent, and Kenny Clarke from the Garda National Immigration Bureau – all of whom he had just spoken to for updates. The others were local detective constables and others assigned to the case.

None of the team's reports had done anything to improve his sour mood. Tommy Boland had been courteous but cold after their last encounter. He'd made it clear he was determined to try and help solve any murder on his patch, but he wasn't going to put up with much grief from outsiders either. Whelan's sergeants were as downbeat as their boss. They were a couple of days into the investigation and they had no leads and no ideas. Kenny Clarke wasn't any more hopeful either. All they could think to do was show the picture of the young victim to various immigrant groups, try and keep the case in the national press, and seek some coverage in the Lithuanian media, assuming he was Lithuanian. Unfortunately, Koch's death and the attack on Hannah Fallon had pushed the story deep into the inner pages of the papers and to a twenty second slot late on in the television news.

'Right, okay, let's get started,' McEvoy shouted, trying to settle the room. 'Come on, pipe down!'

The room slowly quietened to a few murmured conversations as people took seats or sat on the edge of desks.

'Well, so far it looks like this case is going nowhere fast. Our dead man's identity is still a mystery. No one knows anything about him. The rumour that he worked for Ostara and therefore might have had a connection to Albert Koch's death has proved to be false so far. Beyond hoping that his picture in the papers jogs someone's memory we need to widen the search. I want all places of work within a twenty mile radius of Trim that employs manual labour surveyed in the next couple of days.'

A loud groan rumbled round the room, accompanied by harsh mutterings.

'I know, I know,' McEvoy sympathised. 'Don't worry, I'm sure you'll get the usual overtime, but we *need* to find out who the victim is. Once we have that, we can work on catching his killers. It might not matter to you, but it'll matter to his family and friends. You'd better add pubs and fast food shops to that list,' he said as an afterthought. 'Any questions?'

His audience stared down at their desks or feet, or rolled their eyes at one another.

'Right, okay. Well, let's get to it then. I want every survey logged. And no shortcuts. Colin, Mickie, Kenny, can you stay behind, please?'

The rest of the team filed out the door, swapping snide remarks and quips.

Whelan's two sergeants remained sitting behind desks, Kenny Clarke perched on the edge of a table.

'Colin, I want you to carry on running the incident room,' McEvoy continued. 'Log and cross-reference all of the survey data. Mickie, I want you to coordinate those surveys. Make sure the whole thing is done as systematically as possible. Somebody must recognise him from something. He didn't get drunk and land here from Mars. Kenny, see if you can get the appeal for information translated into as many East European languages as possible for that lot to take round with them. And get back on to the media and see if you can get them to give the case a bit more profile. Offer to do interviews; whatever it takes.'

'Surely that's Superintendent Boland's job,' Clarke said unenthusiastically.

'I don't care which one of you ends up with the theatrical make-up on if it moves things forward. Just do the best you can.'

'I doubt it's going to do much good,' Clarke said disconsolately. 'He's going to be buried a John Doe.'

'That might be the case, but we're going to do our best to make sure that doesn't happen, aren't we?'

Clarke remained silent.

'Aren't we?' McEvoy repeated, feeling like a school teacher.

'Sir,' Clarke mumbled without conviction.

'Right, well, I'll let you get on with it. If you need me I'm on my mobile. I'm heading back up to Athboy. I'll pop back in on my way home tonight; see how you're getting on.'

'I'm not going to be here past six thirty,' Vickers said. 'My daughter's appearing in a play. I promised I'd be there. Sorry.'

'I promised the wife I'd help her brother knock through an internal wall,' Brehan added defensively. 'He wants to make the kitchen and dining room into one. I've already clocked up several hours of overtime this week.'

'Whatever,' McEvoy said, waving his hand and heading for the door. 'Just make sure that the survey is carried out properly. I'll talk to you later.'

The door clicked closed behind him and he descended the stairs, rolling his shoulders trying to ease out the knots of stress. It was obvious that the rest of Whelan's team were going to be just as awkward to deal with as their boss. The only thing he could do was to try and keep the pressure up. The case was probably as hopeless as they were expressing, but that was no excuse to not even try.

* * *

Stefan Freel held the front door of The White Gallows wide open allowing McEvoy to pass into the hallway. The building had a stillness that was unsettling; the air cold and damp.

'I'm sorry you couldn't make lunch, Superintendent. Are you sure it's okay to meet here?' Freel asked closing the door and drifting past him, heading for the back of the house. He was dressed in smart black boots hidden under pressed, dark blue jeans, a black polo-neck shirt and a black jacket. 'Your men are finished here?'

'They've done all the preliminary work. They'll keep drifting back for additional tests and searches.' He rubbed his hands and followed Freel into the back office. The room contained a desk pressed up against a wall and several filing cabinets.

'Roza hasn't lit the fires since Dr Koch's death,' Freel explained, sitting on an office chair and pointing to another. 'She's been avoiding the house. She feels it's haunted.'

'But she is here?' McEvoy said sitting, wanting to meet her after Freel.

'Yeah, she's across the yard in her quarters. She's deciding what to do. Marion D'Arcy's asked her to move out now that she's no longer needed to care for her father.'

'Jesus Christ! He's only been dead a couple of days. She's going back to Poland?'

'I don't think so. She's moving in with her boyfriend. I've offered her work as my personal assistant. She wanted to think about it.'

'What's there to think about?'

'Her future? She's very shaken by Dr Koch's death. Perhaps working for me would remind her of him?'

'Maybe she's concerned that she's not qualified for such a post. Or perhaps she's suspicious of your motives?' McEvoy knew he would be – there was something oddly disturbing and unsettling about Stefan Freel, but he couldn't quite put his finger on it.

'My motive is simple – to make money. She might not be qualified in business terms, but she's very good at organising things. Dr Koch often had her arrange meetings. Running his house was not simply a case of doing a bit of dusting and turning down the beds at night. I'm sure she'll do an excellent job if she wants it. And if she's got a bit of sense she could do very well from it.'

'As you've done?'

'Exactly. If someone like Albert Koch thought that buying gold was a good investment, then I've found it was prudent to follow suit.'

'So what are you doing out here?' McEvoy said, swinging his arm round the room.

'Tidying up the files and catching up on business. Just because Dr Koch's been tragically murdered doesn't mean that business grinds to a halt. We had a number of deals in progress that need to be completed.'

'On your behalf or Ostara's?'

'Both. We can't afford for people to think that they can take advantage of the situation. We need to press ahead.'

'Money doesn't grieve,' McEvoy observed, feeling that Freel would sell seats at the funeral if he could get away with it.

'One way of putting it,' Freel said, pulling an ugly smile. 'It's a good job we're not a publicly listed company or the shares would be tumbling. Investors would be worried about what would happen now that the company's biggest asset is gone. We need to tell people it's business as usual.'

'Which means you taking over at the helm?'

'It means I continue to do my job. James Kinneally is still the CEO of Ostara until I hear otherwise.'

'But you still pull the strings,' McEvoy stated. 'You're expecting him to be replaced?'

'I'm not expecting anything. I have as much knowledge as to what happens next as you do. I assume it's all in his will. Until that's announced, it's in all of our interests to carry on regardless.'

The way Freel was speaking, it seemed to McEvoy that he was quite confident about how things would turn out. 'There are those that seem to think that you've most to benefit from Dr Koch's death,' he prompted, 'That you're best placed to take over his empire.'

'By those, I'm assuming you mean Marion D'Arcy and James Kinneally. Both of whom would kill their own...' Freel trailed off, smiling. 'Sorry, bad choice of metaphor. Marion D'Arcy has long been jealous of my position as her father's right-hand man. She would have loved to have been in that role. She would have been disastrous in it, not that she would admit as much, but she'd have also revelled in it. As I've said to you before, I didn't kill Dr Koch. I had no reason to and I could have searched the house anytime I wished. I spend most days here.'

'And nothing seems to be missing to you?' McEvoy asked, wondering how wise it had been to agree to meet Freel here and to let him get back to business using Koch's files.

'Not that I can see. Your officers have not been the greatest at putting everything back as it should be, but nothing appears to have been taken. Certainly no worse than after one of Marion's fishing expeditions.'

'You're saying that Mrs D'Arcy had searched through the files?'

'It was either her or Roza and I think Roza would have been more careful to cover her tracks.'

'When was this?'

'It's happened a couple of times, the last time two or three weeks ago. I think she was just trying to get a handle on things;

understand what's going on; how much she'd be worth if she inherited. She really is obsessed with her father's business. She rooted through pretty much everything. There didn't seem much rhyme or reason to it.'

McEvoy nodded slowly. Marion D'Arcy appeared to be a control freak with little control. Pushed away by her father, she'd tried to stay in touch and muscle in on his business by searching his personal effects. And there was clearly no love lost between her and Stefan Freel.

'She's not the only one,' Freel continued. 'I've also caught her brother snooping around as well. Claimed he was trying to find a hotel receipt he'd accidentally left behind when visiting so he could claim it back through university expenses.'

'You didn't believe him?'

'If he'd left it in the living room as he said he did then Roza would have found it and rung him. It wouldn't have ended up in here.'

'So what's in here?' McEvoy said, pointing to the three filing cabinets.

'Mostly it's open projects; deals that we're presently working on. In the main it's property or land deals or stocks and shares. Markets might have collapsed but we were still trading. In fact, buying in a fallen market is the time to invest – plenty of growth when it does rise. We shuttle the files back and forth to a safe store as needed. Most of what they were looking through would no longer be here; they would be back in Blanchardstown.'

'And the files are kept by Ostara Industries?'

'No, they were filed in a data store on behalf of Ostara Investments, a division of Ostara Industries.'

'So, they're not accessible to the rest of Ostara?'

'Each division keeps their own files. Dr Koch would have access to all of them and technically the Executive Management Board, but each division is effectively run as a separate company. Ostara Investments is the one Dr Koch ran personally after he officially retired from Ostara Industries as a whole.'

'And were there others searching through the files?'

'I don't know. It's possible. I wasn't always here when his family were visiting. I usually went back to the office or home. The information here is interesting, but I'm not sure what they would do with it.'

'Perhaps they were searching for something else,' McEvoy offered. 'Such as Dr Koch's will.'

'He doesn't keep a copy here. That's kept by his solicitor. He wasn't prepared to discuss it with anyone.'

'Not even you?'

'Not even me.'

'So tell me about Ostara Industries,' McEvoy said, changing tack.

'Such as?'

'Let's start with some history. Koch and his brother, Frank, started Ostara in 1952 after buying an old fertiliser factory. What happens next?'

'They manage to make a go of it. Dr Koch knows his chemistry and his brother's a natural salesman. The 1950s is a tough time in Ireland; lots of people getting the boat to England, some to America. Thousands are leaving agriculture given the weak economy and farm mechanization, but Ostara manages to catch the first wave of farming intensification selling specialist fertiliser depending on soil or crops. In the late fifties, his brother left to set up his own business and Ostara diversified into pharmacies.'

'With Maurice Coakley,' McEvoy said, remembering the previous day's conversation.

Freel nodded. 'In the sixties the company diversified again into cement, concrete and oil refining. The seventies saw a move into dyes and paints and a modest expansion of all the other divisions. Where we really start to hit the big time is in the early eighties' London property boom, followed by our own Celtic Tiger.'

'Yet, Ostara are hardly in the public conscience and Koch is barely a public figure.'

'That's not entirely true. Ostara Pharmacies are on the main streets of pretty much every town in Ireland, and anyone in agriculture or construction would have heard of us. As for Dr Koch, well, he liked to keep a low profile. He knew all the major players in any sector, but he didn't seek any publicity. He didn't need to and he didn't want to.'

'And the company is sound? It's not about to collapse in a debt ridden heap?'

'The company is thriving despite the recession. Certainly some of the divisions are under pressure – paints and dyes, for example. The property portfolio is down a fair bit, along with construction supplies. It'll bounce back again, eventually.'

'You think?'

'I know. Property always rises over the long term. As long as you can ride out the negative equity and pay back the loans you're fine.'

'And you can?'

'Nearly all of our property is owned outright. He hated paying interest to the banks.'

McEvoy nodded his head and rose to his feet. 'Well, thanks for your time,' he muttered.

'That's it?'

'I need to get on.'

'You think it was one of the family?'

'What makes you say that?'

'The searched files and the fact that there is no sign of a break-in. Someone let themselves in.'

'Or they were a professional,' McEvoy said, heading for the door. 'Wouldn't have taken more than thirty seconds if you knew what you were doing. And more than the family had keys – yourself, Roza, the farm manager. Perhaps even his good friends, Martin O'Coffey and Maurice Coakley.'

* * *

Roza's quarters consisted of a large living room-cum-kitchen, a bedroom and a bathroom. The space was several degrees warmer than the old house, heated by a wood burning stove that also pumped hot water to a set of radiators. The living room had a contemporary feel – varnished pine roof with spotlights, granite breakfast counter, a silver extraction fan above a gas cooker, and a large abstract painting above the stove.

Roza hadn't looked pleased to see McEvoy as she opened the door, though she had invited him in, given him a cup of coffee and offered a plate of sliced cake and chocolate biscuits. Her complexion was still pale, her eyes rimmed red.

'Mr Freel said that you don't like going into Dr Koch's house,' McEvoy said with a mouthful of cake. He was sitting on a red, two-seater sofa, Roza to one side on a wooden rocking chair, her feet tucked up, her hands warming on her mug.

'It does not feel right. He is haunting it. It makes my back shiver.'

'But you don't need to worry about that much longer; Mrs D'Arcy has asked you to leave?'

Roza shrugged as if it didn't matter. 'Without Dr Koch there's no job. I can't stay here. There are ghosts here – Dr Koch and others. I can feel them.'

McEvoy nodded. Even if Roza didn't know the story of The White Gallows and the men murdered within fifty yards of her rooms, the place had a haunted feel in the pale afternoon light.

'You'll go back to Poland?'

'I'll get another job. Here in Ireland. I like it here. Pay is good.'

'Given the economic crisis there are no jobs.'

'I'll find something.'

'Mr Freel said he's offered you a job as his personal assistant.'

'I don't want to work for a snake.' She pulled a weak smile. 'I might get rich, but I might also get bitten.'

'You don't like Mr Freel?'

'He is interested only in himself and money. He looks at you as if you are the next course in a dinner.'

'You think he'll treat you like dessert?'

'I think he thinks that I would be a good fuck.' She

137

immediately blushed. 'Sorry, I should not say such things. Maybe he would be okay.'

'And maybe you're right,' McEvoy said. 'Do you think he could have killed Dr Koch?'

'Yes. But they were good friends.'

'You think he'd be happy to get rid of anybody or anything that got in his way?'

'In *their* way, yes. He liked working for Dr Koch. He respected him. Not like some. Some people think that all old people are senile or past it; that they should let younger people do everything. Mr Freel does not think that way. He liked Dr Koch.'

'And Dr Koch liked him?'

'They were like father and son. They were very close. They both liked making money. They liked doing business.'

'The files in Dr Koch's study, have you ever looked through them?' McEvoy asked trying to steer the conversation in a new direction.

'No. They were his personal things.'

'Not even once?'

She nodded her head slightly, conceding her guilt. 'I once took a quick look but I could not understand them. They were all numbers and funny words. I left them alone after that.'

'Dr Koch never asked you to file material or tidy it up?'

'Never.'

'Did anyone else ever take a look at them?'

'Mr Freel looks at them all the time – sometimes with Dr Koch, sometimes on his own.'

'Anyone else?'

'I once saw Mark D'Arcy looking at them. I disturbed him while I was cleaning.'

'And Mrs D'Arcy?'

'No, but I know she was in the room on her own. She left things out of place.'

'And Dr Koch's son, Charles?'

138

'No, but I think his son, Francis, used to look round the house. I once found him in Dr Koch's bedroom looking under the bed.'

McEvoy nodded. Most of Koch's family seemed to be searching for something. 'What did he say?'

'He told me he thought he had heard mice upstairs.'

'But you didn't think so?'

'I don't know what I thought. I don't like him – another man who undresses women with his eyes. They are everywhere,' she said distastefully.

McEvoy stared at his near empty mug, not wanting to meet her eyes, worried that he might do the same. 'I need to ask you about an East European couple who called to the house to talk to Dr Koch. They said that they spoke to you as well?'

'They say all kinds of lies,' she said angrily. 'I don't know why they do this! Dr Koch was not an easy man, but he was not a war criminal.'

'How do you know? He was an old man; what they said happened took place a long time ago.'

'I do not work for war criminal,' Roza stated firmly.

'How do you know he wasn't a war criminal?'

'I would have been able to tell. Many of my family died in the war, some murdered by the Nazis, others by the Russians. I could not work for a war criminal,' she said as if saying it would make it true. 'Perhaps they killed him, they were crazy; always coming to the house.'

'They were here on Saturday?'

'I don't know. I did not see them. Dr Koch always told them to go away. He never got angry with them, despite their lies. He just sent them away. If he were guilty he would have argued with them. Instead he was patient. He always listened to them and then asked them to leave. They are damaged people looking for... looking for people to blame for things that happened a long time ago. Dr Koch was German. That does not make him a war criminal. And despite Hitler there were some good Germans.'

'What if they are right? What if he was a war criminal?'

'You believe them?' Roza said aghast.

'I need to see their evidence before making a decision, but you have never come across anything to suggest he was a Nazi?'

'No!' Her hand was covering her nose and mouth, her eyes blazing concern, worried that her hands had been bloodied; that she'd been serving a man who might have had a hand in the killing of her family.

* * *

Twilight was already closing in, though it was only late afternoon. Rakes of red-orange leaves were blowing across the road. Charles Koch exited the small church, made his way down to the old wooden gate, framed by ancient yew trees, and slipped into the passenger seat of McEvoy's car. Ahead of them was a dramatic view across lush, green farm fields framed by whitethorn hedges interspersed with ash and oak trees.

'Thanks for meeting me,' McEvoy said.

'It's no trouble. I've not been sleeping well since his death. I don't know why I feel so drawn to the church. I haven't been in years. I think I like the peace and quiet, the space to reflect and mull things over. It feels like a sanctuary.'

McEvoy nodded. He'd spent many hours in the silence of his local church after Maggie's death. It was another-worldly space; somewhere to just sit and contemplate. It didn't matter that he wasn't a believer.

'I still can't believe he's gone,' Koch continued. 'He seemed so invincible. I half believed I would die before him.'

'He did a lot with his life,' McEvoy observed.

'He made mine seem quite trite,' Koch stated. 'A run-of-the-mill chemist; hardly Carl Bosch.'

'You led your own life. Nothing more you could have done.'

'I could have tried harder.' Koch paused. 'But it wouldn't have made any difference. Even if I'd emulated Bosch he wouldn't have been happy. He wanted me to be better than he was, and yet he intimidated me and stifled my ambition.'

'Sounds like you've spent a lot of time thinking about this,' McEvoy observed.

'Years. I think we all know our shortcomings, Superintendent, and we know why they exist. We're much worse at admitting them to ourselves. I'm a journeyman academic. I've had a few insignificant ideas, I've taught generations of mediocre students, and I'll soon retire to obscurity.'

'That sounds a bit harsh.'

'The truth is painfully bleak. So, what can I do for you?' Koch said, more upbeat, trying to redirect the conversation.

'Information I've received suggests you were more interested in your father's affairs than you first intimated. You wanted your father to invest in some of your ideas, but he refused.'

'He knew they had little commercial value,' Koch laughed. 'He wasn't stupid.'

'And yet you still asked him to invest.'

'I had to do something; give some indication I was trying.'

'Why?'

'Because that's what was expected. Call it duty.'

'You also wanted your son fast-tracked into a management post,' McEvoy prompted.

'I wanted him to have the same opportunities afforded to other members of the family.'

'You mean Mark D'Arcy?'

'Yes. Marion has been pushing strongly in Mark's favour. I reciprocated for Francis. I was trying to be a good father.'

'You were worried that your father's fortune would all end up on Marion's side of the family?'

'I was worried that Francis would get overlooked. Look, Superintendent, being part of the Koch family is not easy. Everyone is so damn competitive. My father owned several businesses. Marion has a successful law company. Uncle Frank's children seem to own half the car showrooms in Ireland. I had a duty to fight our corner.'

McEvoy nodded, noting the second use of duty by Koch. 'Did that extend to spying on your father's work?'

'What?' Koch said irritably.

'You used to look through your father's files.'

'Is that what Roza said? No, no, I bet it was that weasel, Freel. The man who thinks he's the son my father never had. If I was going to look anywhere for a prime suspect that's where I'd start.'

'Are you denying that you ever looked through his things?' McEvoy said, ignoring Koch's accusation.

'No. Every child on the planet has sneaked a look through their parent's belongings.'

'Usually when they were a child, not when they are approaching retirement. What were you looking for?'

'Evidence as to who he might promote – Mark or Francis. I'm not proud of what I did, Superintendent. I did it for Francis. And, as it happens, I didn't find anything.'

'You were at the house on Saturday? You met an East European couple?'

'They were talking nonsense. They were trying to persuade us that my father was a war criminal. They've been at it for weeks. The whole thing is a fantasy. You should be questioning them. They had motive and seemed the type to break-in and search the place.'

'We are questioning them,' McEvoy admitted. 'They have a pretty convincing story about your father's activities during the war.'

'The key word there is story. Yes, my father was a chemist during the war. Yes, he worked for IG Farben, but no he did not work at Auschwitz. He was based in Austria working at one of their subsidiary companies. They're mud slingers after a pay day.'

'They claim to have evidence that your father was a war criminal.'

'Most of the files from that period were destroyed. God knows what evidence they've concocted. None of it's true.

None of it!' Koch hissed. 'If this allegation leaks out through the guards, I'll be speaking to our lawyers. It's bad enough that you seem to be taking this nonsense seriously, but my father's not around to defend himself.' He pushed open the passenger door. 'You should think carefully about how you're conducting this investigation. Ostara is a powerful organisation.'

'Is that a threat, Professor Koch?' McEvoy said evenly.

'It's free advice.' Koch slipped out of the car. 'I might not have been as successful as my father, but I am his son. I will fight any slander on this family.' He slammed shut the car door.

'Shit,' McEvoy muttered. Another interview that had not gone as planned.

* * *

Athboy's main street was traffic chaos, cars parked seemingly at random in any available space. The town had managed to keep its small town feel, lots of small, locally owned shops, with an odd assortment of frontages, and no chain stores beyond a couple of corner shop franchises. Further down the street and on the opposite side to where McEvoy was parked were the three units of McElhinney's department store – an old-style clothing emporium.

He glanced at his watch – 5.15 – and cursed John Joyce. They'd been due to meet Koch's solicitor at five o'clock, though McEvoy had only just arrived himself and he'd been fortunate to grab a space across the road from the Darley Lodge Hotel. His mobile phone rang and he checked the screen before answering.

'Kelly?'

'Do you have a minute?'

'Yeah, go on. I'm just waiting for Dr John to turn up.'

'Well, I've just got off the phone with Marie Hines; she looks after the old military records held at the Cathal Brugha Barracks in Rathmines. She can find no record of a Frank

Koch or Franz Kucken in the Curragh records. She recognises the name, okay, and she knows Frank Kock personally – he's visited the unit a number of times trying to track down old colleagues – but the records are missing.'

'What a surprise,' McEvoy muttered. 'Jesus Christ.'

'She can't remember whether the original record was Koch or Kucken, but she assumes it must have been Koch. She says there are other files missing as well – eight of them. There were only fifty-five German internees, so the gaps are easy to spot. She thinks they all relate to the same hut, but she needs to check that out. And she doesn't think there are copies elsewhere unless one of the historians working on the files took down the details – there've been a number of students in doing theses on the Emergency. It seems that there's a mini-boom of writing about Ireland during the Second World War at the moment.'

'Any idea as to how long they've been missing?'

'She's not certain – could be any time in the last year maybe.'

'Since our East European friends turned up,' McEvoy observed. 'They claim to have copies; you'd better check that out.'

'I'll get on it right away. Do you think Albert Koch was a war criminal?' Stringer asked sceptically.

There was a knock on McEvoy's passenger window and John Joyce's round face peered in.

'I've no idea,' McEvoy continued, holding up his index finger to Joyce. 'We need someone to go through whatever evidence that couple's got and to try to make sense of it. Look, I'd better go, Dr John's finally turned up.'

McEvoy ended the call and levered himself out of his car. 'Where the hell have you been?'

'I couldn't find anywhere to park. The place is a nightmare. I ended up in behind the back of McElhinney's. You should go in there by the way. I managed to pick up...'

'What did the doctor say?' McEvoy interrupted.

'He kept me waiting and then talked nonsense. He's threatened to sue us for harassment.'

'We'll counter-sue for negligence,' McEvoy spat frustrated, dashing across the busy road. 'Is he living on the same planet as the rest of us?'

'Living on his own, more like. I think he's a wily old bastard. He knew exactly what he was doing – a natural death, a quiet funeral and plaudits all round.'

'At Marion D'Arcy's behest?'

'At Albert Koch's is my guess.'

'So she didn't pressure him into trying to hush the whole thing up?'

'He claims not, but that doesn't mean she wasn't glad of the verdict.'

'For God's sake! Right, let's see what his solicitor's got to say. If anything.'

* * *

Henry Collier looked to be well past retirement age. He was a short, portly man, bursting out of his green tweed suit, his grey hair combed over a large bald spot. Introductions over, he pointed at two wooden chairs with green leather seats and slid behind a huge mahogany desk free of clutter.

'So, gentlemen, what can I do for you?' Collier asked, glancing between McEvoy and Joyce.

McEvoy cleared his throat. 'Well, it's clear from our investigation into Dr Koch's death that someone was searching the premises for something valuable. We think it might have been his will. We were hoping we might be able to see a copy.'

'I'm afraid not,' Collier said gravely, shaking his head. 'The will can only be read after the murder investigation is concluded and a conviction secured. Until then it remains confidential.'

'It might contain important clues as to who the killer might be,' McEvoy suggested, trying to keep his frustration out of his voice.

'The killer may have been searching for the will,' Collier said evenly, 'but they did not – could not have – found it. I possess the only copies, both lodged in safe deposit boxes. Only myself and Dr Koch knew its contents. What the will contains then is unlikely to be the reason for murder, though finding it might have been the motive. As a result there's no need for you to view it. Indeed, the contents of the will might prejudice any inquiry into his death and therefore, the outcome of any trial. As such, I'm not prepared to divulge its contents until the case is solved and a conviction secured.'

McEvoy nodded wondering why things were never as simple as they could be. 'Nonetheless,' he pressed, 'the will could help us identify potential suspects. It would, of course, be treated in full confidence and it doesn't need to leave this office, if necessary.'

'With all due respect, Superintendent,' Collier said smiling weakly, 'Dr Koch's estate is worth billions of euro. I am not, at present, prepared to share its contents with anyone connected with your investigation. If the murderer was to offer you just a tiny fraction of the estate in exchange for burying evidence you would retire a very, very rich man. As it stands, you wouldn't know whether any offer has substance or not.'

'And what if we don't catch his killer?'

'Then the estate will remain frozen for the next five years to be released at my discretion.'

'So you'll have effective control over Ostara Industries in the meantime?'

'No, no. Ostara will continue to operate as normal through its Executive Management Board. Only substantial deviations in its business practices will have to be ratified by me, although I will manage the rest of the estate. After five years that estate will pass to his beneficiaries.'

'At your discretion,' McEvoy said.

'Yes, at my discretion,' Collier repeated, a smug smile spread across his face.

'From where I'm sitting that gives you a strong motive to kill Dr Koch. Assuming you weren't caught, you'd gain control of his estate, able to transfer assets for your own ends during the five-year window.'

'I'd be careful what you say, Superintendent,' Collier warned. 'You don't want to be rash in your accusations. I've been Dr Koch's personal solicitor for over forty years. We were good friends. Believe me, if you do solve the case, which I sincerely hope you do, I will be handsomely rewarded for my service. And I'll have much more ready access to those funds. It's in my interest as well that you solve the case quickly. I'm prepared to help as much as I can, but I can't give you access to the will.'

'And what do Marion and Charles Koch think about all of this?'

'Well, neither of them is very happy, as you'd expect. Of course, if they killed their father then they'd be unable to inherit. But if the killer's not caught then they won't be able to inherit for five years. They're both pretty upset by that prospect.'

'But you're unwilling to change the procedure?'

'What if it turns out that in three years time it was revealed that either Marion or Charles was the killer? In those three years they could have plundered the estate and headed overseas to avoid arrest. Not that I think either of them did it, you understand.'

McEvoy nodded. It was clear that Collier was going to stick to his guns. 'Well, can you at least tell me the last time he altered his will?' he asked.

'About three months ago,' Collier conceded.

'And were you happy with the changes?'

'It was his will, Superintendent, not mine. I just acted on his behalf.'

* * *

Kelly Stringer seemed to be in her element. There were now six notice boards around the room, each covered in pieces of paper, stick-it notes and photos. Several other garda were busy at different tables. She was flitting between them giving them instructions and listening to what they'd discovered.

From where McEvoy was standing she looked positively radiant; like a different woman to that who habitually dressed years beyond her age. She was wearing a knee-length, dark green business suit, over a pale, almost translucent blouse, and low black heels. Her hair was let down, covering her shoulders.

As she moved off from the person she'd been talking to, she noticed him watching her. Her face broke into a smile and she crossed the room to join him.

'You enjoying yourself?' he asked, grinning tiredly, feeling like a teenager; nerves and lust entwining.

'You know what,' she said nodding her head, 'I am. I'm getting a real buzz out of the whole thing. For the first time, I really feel like I'm at the heart of an investigation, that I'm actually making a difference. I'm not just some routine cog, I'm... I'm the engine oil!' she laughed.

'Wait until we run out of fuel and the whole thing grinds to a halt,' McEvoy said, immediately regretting his negativity.

'We'll see. I have a good feeling about this one. There seems to be plenty to go on. Not like the Lithuanian in Trim. That seems to have already hit the wall.'

'Yeah, that seems to be going nowhere fast,' McEvoy agreed.

'I've just got this in,' she said, holding out a sheaf of paper. 'I got one of the locals to scout around on the web, see if he could find out who the Curragh internees were. He found this real geeky site that lists all of the aircraft that crash-landed on Irish soil or waters, plus their crew members. The important bit is here.' She tapped a manicured nail on the top sheet. 'A Heinkel He111H-5 crash-landed in Carlingford Lough, March 23rd 1941 after being hit by anti-aircraft fire from a British navy vessel. The crew were Oberleutnant Heinrich Brauer, Feldwebel Hans Fassbinder, Gefreiter Alois Lehrer – who died from his wounds – and Gefreiter Franz Kucken.

The three survivors were interned in the Curragh camp for the rest of the war. There is no Frank Koch on any other German plane.'

'So Frank Koch really is Franz Kucken?' McEvoy said looking up.

'And Ewa Chojnacki and Tomas Prochazka's copies of the archive files seem to confirm it,' Stringer said, smiling. 'I'm trying to find out if any of the other crew members are still alive. According to the records, Franz Kucken is originally from Freiburg, as was Adolf Kucken. It looks like Albert Koch was not who he claimed he was.'

'Jesus. And the rest of the files?'

'I've been onto the German department at the National University in Maynooth. Professor Moench is going to drive up here tomorrow morning. I'll get him to sign all the relevant confidentiality clauses and see what he makes of them.'

'Sounds good. Anything else to report?'

'No, I don't think so. We're just following up on whatever information we've got. Superintendent Galligan's been in a couple of times on fishing expeditions – making a nuisance of himself – but otherwise nothing.'

'Okay, Jesus, I'll check-in with him later. How's Tom McManus been getting on?'

'Not very well. He's had teams out all around the surrounding land and there's no sign of the missing gun or the vase fragments.'

'And Hannah Fallon?'

'Pretty much the same as last night – she's stable and on the mend. The news through the grapevine is Bishop is playing keystone cops. Half of Dublin's guards are running round chasing ghosts.'

'Well, it's about time we made a show of force. Things have gotten out of hand; the gangs think they can do what the hell they like. Look, I'm going to try and catch up on the files,' McEvoy said, bringing the conversation to a close, pleased that he hadn't overtly flirted. 'I don't think there's any need for a team meeting just now. I'll also talk to Dr John, Tom McManus and your friend Galligan.'

His phone rang. He held up a hand of apology. 'Yes?'

'Superintendent, it's James Kinneally. I think we should probably meet.'

* * *

McEvoy closed his notebook, pushed himself to his feet and crossed the hall to where Kelly Stringer was sorting through a thin pile of paper.

'Kelly, I'm going to head off, okay? Can you get hold of Barney Plunkett, Johnny Cronin and Jenny Flanagan. Tell them to meet me at nine o'clock tomorrow morning at the Costa Coffee near Argos in Blanchardstown for an hour or so to catch up on everything and sort things out. It's on the way out here and Jenny and Johnny should be able to cut across the M50 easy enough. Perhaps four heads together might make a bit of progress.'

'I'll ring them now.' Stringer turned away, heading to another desk, then swung back around, brushing her tousled hair from her face. 'If you don't mind me saying, sir, you're looking pretty frayed round the edges. Have you eaten yet? The locals say the Chinese restaurant in Athboy's pretty good. Perhaps...' she trailed off.

McEvoy nodded unsure what to say.

'Not that...' Stringer continued. 'I mean... you just look like...' she trailed off again, blushing.

'Look, Kelly...' McEvoy pulled a tight smile. 'I'm sorry. I'm on my way to a meeting with James Kinneally. Then I've got to check on how things are going in Trim, and then pick Gemma up from my sister's. Maybe some other time?' he suggested, inwardly cursing himself for not ending whatever it was that was going on, if there was anything.

Stringer nodded her head, embarrassed. 'Yes, sorry, I wasn't thinking. Maybe some other time. I'll ring the others.' She started to drift away.

McEvoy turned to one side, catching the curve of her legs below her knee-length skirt from the corner of his eyes, before heading for the door, feeling like he needed a cold shower. There was no denying that he was attracted to her. He could sense the edgy nerves whenever she was near, the butterflies in his stomach. He also knew that it would go nowhere; that it could go nowhere. He wasn't yet ready; not for the kind of relationship it might become. Not for any kind of relationship. He stepped out into the cold night air, the first spots of rain starting to fall, and headed for his car trying to push carnal thoughts of Kelly Stringer to one side and failing.

* * *

James Kinneally was sitting in the passenger seat of McEvoy's Mondeo. He appeared to be nervous, glancing around, making sure they were alone.

They were parked in the far corner of a supermarket car park on the outskirts of Trim, hidden in the shadows, away from the other cars.

'So?' McEvoy asked, staring across Kinneally at an up-turned shopping cart visible through the window.

'I… we… it's… it's about Saturday night,' Kinneally trailed off.

'What about Saturday night?'

'You have to understand that I'd like to keep this confidential.'

'This is a murder investigation, Mr Kinneally, if it's important to the case we'll do whatever's needed,' McEvoy lied. 'What is it?'

Kinneally stared out of the windscreen, his unfocussed gaze, deciding how to proceed. 'I knew this wasn't a good idea,' he said eventually.

'What wasn't?' McEvoy prompted, growing tired of Kinneally's charade.

'Meeting you like this. I'm doing this for her, though I doubt she'll thank me for it.' He turned towards McEvoy. 'Marion

D'Arcy was with me on Saturday night. We've been having an affair for the past eight months.'

'Well, that explains why you're always at her place,' McEvoy said neutrally, unable to see the dominant Marion falling for Kinneally. 'So where were you on Saturday night?'

'At her house; I stayed the night.'

'So you're withdrawing your story about staying the night in Dublin? That right?'

'Yes,' Kinneally snapped irritably. 'I've just told you, I was with Marion.'

'And I'm to believe that, since you've already lied to me once?'

'Look, I... I'm sorry about that. I was just trying to protect her.'

'By taking away her alibi?'

'By keeping our relationship secret. I didn't know that you would treat her like a suspect! It's beyond belief. The idea that she'd kill her own father is crazy!'

'From my experience, nothing is beyond belief. And she will confirm this story?'

'No, no. There's no need to ask her,' Kinneally said nervously. 'I'm telling you the truth.'

'And we need to verify it. You didn't tell her you were coming to meet me?'

Kinneally shook his head and looked down at his lap.

'So why did you come? To salve your conscience?'

Kinneally stayed silent.

'Let me guess, you came at Mark D'Arcy's request?' McEvoy suggested.

There was a slight nod of the head.

'Mark D'Arcy knew you were having an affair,' McEvoy continued, 'and he knew you were with his mother on Saturday. If he got you to confess as much then we would stop hassling her as a potential suspect. Only she wants the affair to remain secret until she either gains control of Ostara through her inheritance or through her relationship with its CEO.'

'That's... that's...' Kinneally stuttered, his anger rising again, 'slander. She doesn't want her good name dragged through the tabloid papers. I'm only recently separated. She doesn't want to be cast as a home wrecker. And she isn't. My marriage had been dead a long time; so had hers. She feels she doesn't need an alibi as she's innocent.'

'Her son feels differently?'

'Mark thinks that she's already under enough pressure. There's no point adding to that when she could be spared any additional stress.'

'He might have a point,' McEvoy conceded.

Kinneally nodded. 'So what happens now?'

'You and I both head home.'

'And the affair will remain secret?' Kinneally asked.

'I can't see any reason to tell the whole world just yet, but I can't promise it won't leak out eventually.'

'Thanks.' James Kinneally eased himself out of McEvoy's car and slipped behind the wheel of his silver Mercedes, his face pale, scanning the gloom for witnesses to the meeting.

McEvoy watched him leave the car park, turning towards Athboy, before starting his own car and heading to the exit. Kinneally might be the CEO of a large company, but he was a weak and nervous man. He wondered what Marion D'Arcy saw in him other than someone who was easy to manipulate and control; a way of hedging her bets with respect to the future of Ostara.

* * *

It was late in the evening and there had been no significant update from the team investigating the death of the supposed Lithuanian. Officers were out surveying pubs and bars in a broad sweep well beyond Trim's usual catchment area.

McEvoy eased open the door. The bedroom was cast in an orange glow from the street light seeping in round the fringes of the thin curtains. The walls were covered in posters of footballers and bands; the floor a tangle of clothes. Gemma lay facing him, her eyes closed, the quilt pulled tight under her chin, its fabric gently rising and falling. Everyday she seemed to gain more of her mother's beauty.

He eased himself into the room and perched carefully on the edge of the bed and watched her for a while. She'd made this space her own. Half her possessions were here; maybe more than half. She was certainly spending more than half her time in his sister's house.

He wanted to wake her and take her home, but what was the point? He would only be bringing her back a few hours later and long before she needed to be ready for school. He was her father and yet he barely saw her; rarely seemed to do what a parent was meant to do. He would need to be there for her on Friday; to provide comfort and support.

He'd promised he would take the day off work. Only he wasn't going to be able to make it. He would be hunting the killers of a nameless young man and a mass murderer; too busy to respect the death of his wife and look after the emotional health of his daughter. He massaged his tired eyes and levered himself standing.

Gemma stirred, rolled over, and pulled the quilt in close.

He tip-toed back to the door, closing it quietly behind him, and descended the stairs, enveloped in a sober funk. Somehow he was going to have to find a way of disengaging from work for both Gemma's and his own sake.

Caroline and Jimmy were sitting together on a black leather sofa, her back resting against his side, her legs stretched along its length. Jimmy's left arm snaked over her shoulder and rested on her inflated stomach, his right hand clutched a bottle of Czech beer.

'How is she?' Caroline asked, turning her attention away from the television and a Bruce Willis film.

'Fast asleep. I didn't wake her.'

'There's a fridge full of these things if you want one,' Jimmy said, waving the bottle without taking his eyes from the screen.

154

'I'm alright, thanks. I'd better be going. Is it okay if she stays over? I'll only be bringing her back again early tomorrow morning.'

'You know it is,' Caroline said. 'It's no bother. You look knackered, Colm. You need to look after yourself. Are you managing to eat properly?'

'Kind of,' he said, aware that all he'd had to eat since lunch time was a bar of chocolate. 'I've been thinking of getting a nanny, you know, for when the baby arrives. She can live at the house and keep an eye on Gemma.'

'She's no bother, Colm. We hardly notice she's here. Do we Jimmy?'

'What?' Jimmy muttered, his mind on the film.

'I said, we hardly notice Gemma is here.'

'Yeah.' He took a swig of his beer.

'All the same, when the baby arrives you'll have your hands full,' McEvoy said. He'd been thinking about a nanny for a while; someone to take the pressure off his sister and her partner. He'd just never got round to doing anything about it; was unsure of where to even start. There were probably agencies that took care of everything for a small fortune.

'And she'll be another pair of hands,' Caroline said. 'She's already a blessing running around for me. Stop worrying about things, will you. Get a beer and sit down.'

'About Friday,' he started, then trailed off, staying where he was, hovering by the door.

'Don't worry, we'll both be there. Jimmy's managed to swap shifts. Everything's been taken care of.'

'I'm more worried about whether I'll be there,' McEvoy muttered. 'All leave's been cancelled since Charlie Clarke decided to try and blow up Hannah Fallon and I'm up to my neck in it with these cases.'

'Surely they can give you one day off though?' Caroline said angrily. 'It's Maggie's anniversary for God's sake! You're entitled to compassionate leave. And the cases are not going anywhere; you not being there for one day isn't going to make a difference.'

'I'm entitled to whatever Tony Bishop decides,' McEvoy said, knowing that he wouldn't be pressing for leave; realising that he didn't want to be there – that he wanted the distraction of work, not the fawning sympathy of friends and family; a whole day of Maggie's death preying endlessly on his thoughts. It was bad enough now, with the long, lonely nights of insomnia, without it dragging on all day; people constantly reminding him of who and what he had lost. He didn't want to forget her, he just didn't want to end up spending the day wallowing in self-pity. 'The interests of the public come before individual officers,' he quoted.

'Bollocks,' Jimmy said, his eyes never leaving the television.

'You *have* to be there, Colm,' Caroline stressed. 'It's her anniversary, for God's sake. Gemma will need you and Ciara has gone to a lot of trouble to arrange the Mass. The whole family is travelling up. They'll want to see you, to support you.'

'I'll try and make the Mass.'

'I hope for your sake that you do. Gemma is pretty understanding, but I don't think she'd forgive you if you missed Friday. And to be honest, nor will I. You have to be there.'

'If they try and stop you, just tell them to fuck off,' Jimmy suggested helpfully.

'I could end up with a bit more time off than just Friday if I did that. And a big bloody hole in my pocket.'

'That's what the fucking unions are for.'

'You two better stop swearing when this one is born,' Caroline warned, rubbing her belly.

'Whatever,' Jimmy muttered.

'I better be going,' McEvoy said. 'I'll talk to you tomorrow. Tell Gemma I dropped in to see her.'

'I will. Look after yourself, Colm. Make sure you get something decent to eat, not a bag of chips and half a bottle of whisky.'

'I'll do my best,' he said over his shoulder as he headed for the front door. He'd follow her advice about the food, but he needed the whisky to deaden the pain and let him drift into murky darkness.

WEDNESDAY

Johnny Cronin and Barney Plunkett were already seated at a table, two large mugs placed in front of them. McEvoy nodded a greeting at them and headed to the counter, wiping droplets from his face. A front had moved in during the night bringing with it high winds and driving rain. He ordered a large mug of tea from an acne-scarred youth. Just as the steaming brew was handed to him he was joined by Jenny Flanagan.

'Jesus Christ. I've only come fifty yards and I'm soaked,' she said slightly out of breath, holding out the front of her long, black coat and gently shaking it. 'Sorry I'm a little late, I couldn't find this place; I was driving about on the other side of the shopping centre.'

'It's no bother, what do you want?'

'Espresso. Thanks.'

McEvoy paid for the coffee and instructed the youth to bring it over to the table when it was ready.

'How are things?' he asked, sitting down next to Plunkett, Flanagan taking a seat opposite him, brushing her long, brown hair off her narrow face.

'Pretty crap,' Cronin said. The same age as McEvoy, he had a full head of short, dark hair and thick black moustache. He was dressed in a tired blue suit, his tie loosely knotted. 'How about you?'

'The same,' McEvoy conceded. 'Looks as if Albert Koch was a notorious, Nazi war criminal. He spent the war in

Auschwitz and helped carry out experiments on Jewish prisoners. Wait until the media get hold of that; they'll be circling round like vultures. At least we have a couple of leads worth following, unlike the Lithuanian killed in Trim. That's going nowhere fast. How're you getting on, Barney?'

Plunkett scratched at his sandy coloured hair and massaged his neck. 'Nothing new to report,' he said referring to the Raven case. 'We're still getting reports of sightings and we're still following them up, but they all seem to be false trails. If he ever surfaces again it'll be because he wants to. We've got bugger all to go on.'

The youth delivered Flanagan's espresso and slunk away, casting them suspicious glances.

'Don't worry, he'll be back,' McEvoy responded. 'Kathy Jacobs was quite certain about that,' he said, referring to the criminal psychologist drafted in from Scotland to help on the case. 'He'll want to parade his ego and make sure people know about his genius – not that anyone is ever going to forget him in a hurry; he'll be remembered long after we're all dead.'

'In the meantime I sit in an office and push paper around and get hassled by journalists looking for insider gossip,' Plunkett moaned.

'Some would say you have the cushy number,' Cronin said. 'Plenty of guys would like that gig rather than running around the country after shadows.'

'No joy with our banknote scammer?' McEvoy interjected before Plunkett could reply.

'Nothing,' Cronin confirmed. 'If he's any sense he'll go to ground now. People know about the scam through the papers. If he does, that'll be the last we hear of him. We don't have a single lead. The guy's a ghost.'

'No luck on licence plates?' Plunkett asked.

'No. No one can agree on what car he's driving, nor can they remember the plates. And he always chooses somewhere with no CCTV, so we've no film or photos.'

'How about a photo-fit?' Flanagan asked.

'We've tried that. Each victim's produced a different face. The only thing they agree on was that he had short, dark, uncombed hair, was broad shouldered and was wearing a black, leather jacket.'

'We just have to hope that if he tries his trick again, that whoever the intended victim is contacts us in advance of any exchange,' McEvoy suggested.

'That's not what the victims want to hear,' Cronin replied.

'And what do they suggest?' Flanagan asked agitated.

'That we assign as many resources as possible to the case and catch the bastard,' Cronin said sarcastically.

'You could try setting a trap,' Plunkett suggested. 'Put a story in the paper that such-and-such is in dire straits – their business is going under or their sure-fire investment went belly-up – and see if he bites. He preys on victims, right?'

Cronin nodded his head.

'If you pose as a rich or once-rich businessman fallen on hard times he might make a pitch. How has he chosen the previous victims?'

'We've no idea. He just seemed to roll into town and cast about for a suitable fall-guy.'

'Still it might be worth a shot,' Plunkett persisted. 'Get the story into one of the dailies or some of the local papers and see what happens.'

'I'll think about it,' Cronin conceded.

'I think Barney's right, Johnny,' McEvoy said. 'Give it a go and see what happens. If nothing does, then we've lost nothing. If he bites then we can move in for the kill. God knows we deserve a bit of luck. And make sure it's near Athboy. If he does bite I don't want to have to travel to Kerry or somewhere.'

Cronin nodded his head, indicating that he'd pursue the idea.

'Jenny?' McEvoy prompted.

'Well, to continue the theme, we've hit a brick wall. We're fairly confident that the husband killed her. Actually scrap that, I know the bastard killed her. The problem is, he won't confess and we've got damn all evidence. He claims to have been in

Bansha at the time of the murders and his phone records also place him there. We have a sighting of his car near to the house but the witness can't confirm the date. We've discovered he's got a mistress, but she's a hundred per cent behind him.'

'What makes you so sure it's him?' Cronin asked.

'Woman's intuition,' Flanagan hazarded. 'It's written all over his face. He knows we've nothing to go on and his supposed grief is skin-deep at best. He couldn't care less that she's dead.'

'Have you checked the phone records for his mistress' phone?' Plunkett asked. 'Perhaps they swapped mobiles? She's in Bansha with his phone and he's at home murdering his wife. Did they ring each other that morning?'

'Twice,' Flanagan confirmed.

'Well, check with the phone company where *both* phones were. My guess is that one of the calls from her phone to his was made using the mast nearest to Kylie O'Neill's house. I take it she claims she was nowhere near there?'

'She says she was shopping in Caher.'

'So, if either of the calls was made from near to Kylie's house she has some explaining to do.'

'I can't believe we didn't think of that,' Flanagan said, obviously embarrassed. 'If you excuse me for a minute, I need to make a call.' She eased herself from her chair and headed for the door, her mobile phone already at her ear.

'It's a waste having you messing about on the Raven case,' McEvoy said bitterly to Plunkett as way of thanks. 'We all know he's well hidden at this stage. We're overstretched and we need people dealing with live cases.'

'The press and politicians will have a fit if we drop the case, even for a few days,' Plunkett warned.

'That doesn't get round the fact that we're massively overstretched. You want a cake?' he asked his companions. 'I'm starving. You better not be out of ideas, Barney,' McEvoy said rising, 'I need all the help I can get on this Lithuanian.'

* * *

Kelly Stringer had reverted to her more conservatively dressed ways, wearing a two-piece, dark blue trouser suit, flat shoes, and a plain white blouse buttoned to the neck, with her hair tied back in a pony tail. Having let McEvoy know that there had been no new developments during the morning, she directed him to a very large man, with long, grey hair and full, dark beard hunched over one of the tables, papers spread in front of him.

'Professor Moench?' Stringer prompted.

The man looked up slowly, his eyes drifting from Stringer to McEvoy.

'This is Detective Superintendent Colm McEvoy. He's in charge of the investigation into Albert Koch's death.'

Moench pushed back his chair and stood up, stretching out a massive hand. 'Superintendent,' he said with a faint trace of a German accent.

Now he was standing, McEvoy realised just how much of a giant Moench was. A couple of inches taller than McEvoy's six foot three, he was also broad and bulky, carrying a substantial stomach. His bushy beard faded to grey at the edges, and his straggly hair tumbled over the top of his brown corduroy jacket that covered a stretched red-and-blue check shirt.

'These are most interesting,' he said pointing to the table. 'Unbelievable even.'

McEvoy motioned Moench and Stringer to take seats, lowering himself down to the table. 'You think they're genuine?'

'That or extremely good forgeries.'

'And Koch, or should I say Kucken, worked in Auschwitz?'

'That's what the files indicate. I need to work on them further and the extra files being flown in from Israel will help, but I'll also need to cross-check them with the original archives to make sure they're authentic.'

'But assuming they are, Koch was a war criminal?' McEvoy prompted.

'Auschwitz was a massive complex of camps, Super-intendent. Not everyone working there was an evil sadist. Many were ordinary people caught up in an extraordinary situation. They may have witnessed the atrocities, and they might not have intervened, but they did not carry them out.'

'That doesn't exonerate them from the crimes committed there,' McEvoy said. 'They were still complicit in the genocide.'

'True, but what I'm saying is there are different levels of guilt as the trials after the war illustrated. Only a very few people were prosecuted for their part in the holocaust. If they weren't prosecuted then, why would they be now?'

'Justice?' McEvoy hazarded.

'You're an idealist, Superintendent. This is about memory and contrition. And yes, justice, but not through the courts. It is about exposing the lie at the heart of Albert Koch's life and business empire.'

'But the files suggest that Koch was more than a bystander at Auschwitz? That he took part in medical experiments and he killed people in cold blood?'

'I've only been looking at them for a couple of hours, but that seems to be the case. But as I've already said, I need to verify the authenticity of the documents before I can be sure. The material here could be an elaborate hoax. It wouldn't be the first time that forged war documents have been used to tarnish somebody's reputation. They might have taken a while to produce, but to bring down someone as rich and powerful as Albert Koch it would have been time well invested.'

'And what's your view? Are they genuine or fake?'

'I don't know.' Moench shrugged his massive shoulders. 'If they've been done properly they'd be almost perfect. The only way to find out is to check the original sources.'

'We've already checked the Irish military records for its files on Frank Koch, his brother. They've been removed along with a few others. We do know, however, that there was no Frank Koch interned in Ireland, but there was a Franz Kucken. That would tie in with copies of the documents you have. At the very least it appears that Albert Koch was Adolf Kucken.'

'And it appears that someone has started to remove files from the archives,' Moench observed.

'It's extremely unlikely that whoever it is will be able to locate all the relevant material, especially if they don't have the copies to work from. If these are genuine,' McEvoy said, gesturing at the table of documents, 'then we should know soon enough. Whatever help you need just ask, though remember, I'd like this to remain confidential for as long as possible. Last thing we need is a load of journalists joining in the hunt.'

'I think you might be underestimating the power of money and old networks,' Moench said. 'Albert Koch definitely had the first and, if he is who these files say he is, probably the second.'

'You really think he'd be able to remove all the incriminating material from the archives? He must have only known he was being investigated for a short while.'

'How long would it take to send out teams of investigators when money is not a problem? A few large holes in their evidence base would start to discredit the rest. He would claim that they'd made it all up and planted some material in certain places to make it look authentic. Most, if not all, of the witnesses are dead or very old. He brings in some clever lawyers and a good PR company and he buys himself out of trouble.'

'That sounds pretty cynical,' McEvoy said.

'I get the feeling that's usually your job,' Moench observed. 'I would call it realistic. Only a confession would have secured the truth, whatever it was, and now that will never happen. Now it's all papers, ghosts and conspiracy theories.'

* * *

He'd parked half on the pavement, half on the road. Lined up behind a heavy chain hanging between sturdy bollards were a row of Mercedes cars. Behind them was a large, glass-fronted showroom. McEvoy eased himself from his no-frills Mondeo, pulled up his collar against the driving rain, and hurried between two cars, aware that each probably cost as much his annual salary.

The small, wiry figure of Frank Koch met him at the front door, holding two green-and-white golf umbrellas. He handed one to McEvoy and forced up the other, angling it into the wind.

'Perhaps I can interest you in one of our cars, Super-intendent? I have just the thing for you – a 320CDi S class. It's just over here.' He stepped out of the shelter of the showroom and headed purposefully to the right.

For his mid-nineties, Koch was a sprightly character, danc-ing towards the row of cars, fighting the gusting wind.

McEvoy forced up his umbrella and trailed after him, trying to avoid the large puddles covering the forecourt.

'Four years old, one owner, full leather trim, satnav, digital music system. More roomy and comfortable than that thing you are driving now.' Koch came to a halt next to a large silver Mercedes.

'I'm not interested in a new car,' McEvoy replied. 'You lied to me yesterday. Your real name is Franz Kucken – we've looked up the military records. Nobody called Frank Koch was ever interned in Ireland during the war.'

'We'll give you a very good trade-in for your Ford and I'll throw in a free emergency kit,' Koch said, ignoring him. He opened the driver's door and gestured for McEvoy to get in. 'Once you've driven one of these you'll never go back. They're a different class.'

'I don't need a new car, the old one's fine,' McEvoy said, trying to keep the frustration out of his voice. 'It has four wheels and it gets me from A to B.'

'A philistine,' Koch said, closing the door. He rounded the front of the car and headed to another three spaces down the line, McEvoy trailing after him. 'Perhaps this one would suit you better? A CLK 200 Kompressor, 2 door. A coupé. More of a sport's car than the 320. You must travel a lot, Superintendent.

Why not travel in style and comfort? This car practically drives itself.'

'Weren't Mercedes vital to the German war machine?' McEvoy goaded. 'Didn't they support the Nazi party?'

'The war finished a long time ago,' Koch snapped angrily, before calming again. 'It's over. Mercedes helped rebuild the economy. Without them things would have been a lot worse.'

'You're real name is Franz Kucken and your brother was Adolf Kucken. You were originally from Frieburg.'

'My name is Frank Koch. My brother was Albert and we were from Munich.' Koch passed between the cars heading to the far end of the car park, dodging round the slicks of oil and water.

'There was no German prisoner named Frank Koch interned in the Curragh,' McEvoy persisted.

'Then the records are wrong. Find some of the other prisoners or guards, they will tell you I was there. Mary will tell you.'

'I'm not denying you were there, I'm questioning your identity,' McEvoy said.

'Perhaps a Volkswagon might be a better choice for you?' Koch said pulling to a stop in front of a racing green Passat. '1.9 TDi, ABS brakes, alloy wheels, cruise control, air conditioning.'

'You're deliberately avoiding my questions,' McEvoy said pointedly.

'That's because they are stupid questions. They are irrelevant. My brother was murdered three days ago, not over sixty years ago. You are meant to be finding his murderer, not investigating his past.'

'But what if his past is the reason for his murder?'

'Then arrest the couple who were harassing him. They were obsessed with lies as well. They were confusing my brother with somebody else, or they were after some of his money.' Koch set off towards the showroom. 'You really should think about a new car, Superintendent,' he said loudly into the wind. 'You won't buy better than a Mercedes and I'll give you a good deal.'

* * *

He stared at the rivulets of rain spilling down the windscreen. Perhaps Frank Koch was right. Perhaps Koch's history was irrelevant to his death. Whether Koch was a war criminal or not, they were meant to be finding his killer, not investigating his life; though his supposed past crimes did deserve attention and justice. His mobile phone rang, jogging him out of his trance.

'McEvoy.'

'You're meant to be giving me regular updates,' Bishop said irritably.

'I thought you had your hands full,' McEvoy replied weakly.

'I have got them full, but I still need to know what the hell's going on. What am I meant to be, a mind reader?'

'I, er, well,' McEvoy stumbled, once again put on the back foot by Bishop's management style of passive-aggressive bullying. 'We're no nearer to solving either case. A few leads with Koch, but God knows whether they'll go anywhere. It looks like he might have been a war criminal, although his life seems to have been surrounded by hundreds of rumours. We still don't know who the Lithuanian is or where he came from. At this stage, I doubt we ever will. Jenny Flanagan's convinced Kylie O'Neill was killed by her husband, but she's lacking any evidence, and Cronin seems to be chasing a ghost.'

'What do you mean, Koch might have been a war criminal?' Bishop asked, honing in on the victim most likely to attract media and political attention.

'It looks like he might have worked at Auschwitz as a chemist and was involved in a large medical experiment on Jewish concentration camp prisoners.'

'Jesus Christ. And that's why he was killed?'

'I don't know. It's one hypothesis. It looks as if it might be turning into a bit of a labyrinth case. What are the chances of getting Jim Whelan back? We need all the experience we can get.'

'None. I'm going to bring that bastard Charlie Clarke down if it's the last thing I do,' Bishop said, immediately forgetting Koch's supposed past. 'We're trying to round up members of his gang.'

'The gap will only be filled by others,' McEvoy said downheartedly.

'So what do you want us to do?' Bishop snapped. 'Nothing?'

'Get the Minister to give us more resources.'

'Stick to the policing, Colm, and the Commissioner will look after the politics. We have what we have. Just get a result and get one soon. We need something to parade in front of the media.'

'How about Charlie Clarke?'

'Charlie Clarke's a done deal,' Bishop said irritably. 'We need something else. I don't care which case; just get us some good press.'

'How's Hannah?' McEvoy asked, trying to change the subject.

'She's fine. Don't worry, Colm, I'll catch the bastards that attacked her. And they'll learn a few sharp lessons being caught,' Bishop said, meaning heads would be cracked regardless of whether they went down fighting.

'Then you'll have your good press.'

'Don't mess with me, Colm. Just get me a result.'

'I'll be taking Friday off, remember,' McEvoy warned.

'I don't think so! Not unless you get a result tomorrow.'

'It's the first anniversary of Maggie's death. There's a memorial service. I need to be there for Gemma. You were sent an invite.'

'Oh. Shit. Look, I'm sorry, Colm. I forgot,' Bishop said softening. 'I'll try to be there. I can't believe it's a year already. It seems like... well, you know.' He paused unsure what to say. 'Give your teams their heads. Any developments, I want to know, okay?'

'You'll be the first person I'll call,' McEvoy lied to the dead line.

Mickie Brehan, Colin Vickers and Kenny Clarke looked worn out and demoralised. It was difficult to appear enthusiastic when everything you did seemingly led nowhere.

'So?' McEvoy asked.

'Nothing,' Mickie Brehan said. 'Not likely to get anything on a Tuesday night. Friday or Saturday is when we might get lucky.'

'All the foreigners drink at home in any case,' Vickers added. 'Much cheaper than the pubs and you can smoke.'

'Nothing like a bit of optimism to drive things along,' McEvoy said flatly. 'Any joy with the translations, Kenny?'

'Agency's working on it; we should have them by this afternoon. We'll get some flyers made up and distribute them. A number of the papers will carry a photo and an appeal tomorrow.'

'Well, maybe that will prompt something. Concentrate on places of work for now. Leave the pubs until the weekend. Just stick at it.' His mobile phone rang. 'I better take this,' he said, standing and heading to the door. 'McEvoy.'

'It's Kelly Stringer. I think you'd better come back to Ballyglass. There's been a development.'

'What kind of development?'

'It's about that rumour of a bank robbery.'

'Remind me,' he said heading for the stairs.

'It was intimated that Koch was involved in a bank robbery in the 1950s. Kevin Townsend, one of the local guards, has been working on it. He's found newspaper reports on two bank robberies in 1955; one in Navan, the other in Virginia. A gang broke into the banks in the early hours of the morning and blew their safes. Nobody was ever charged, but he's tracked down a retired guard who worked on the fringes of the case in Navan. The banks were robbed by a gang of four. Two of the gang were thought to be Albert and Frank Koch.'

'Jesus.'

'The retired guard now lives in Mullingar. He's happy to come over to Ballyglass if it'll help.'

'Arrange a car for him. I'll be there in fifteen minutes. And see if you can track down the original case notes. They have to be on file somewhere.'

* * *

The incident room was busy with several guards working at computers or sorting through papers spread over tables. Professor Moench was still hunched over the same table, reading documents and scribbling notes onto a pad. Kevin Townsend was seated at an adjacent table, absently twirling a pen across his fingers.

Tall and thin with a narrow face framed by short black hair and sideburns, Townsend scraped back his chair and rose to his feet as McEvoy approached, nodding a nervous greeting.

'You better tell me what you know before the old boy arrives,' McEvoy said, shaking Townsend's hand before seating himself at the table, placing a styrofoam cup of piping hot coffee down in front of himself.

'I... I've... I'm Detective Garda Townsend by the way,' he said awkwardly. 'Kevin.'

'I know. I'm Detective Superintendent McEvoy. So what's the story?' McEvoy asked impatiently.

'Well, I, er... a couple of people gave statements that the victim... I mean Albert Koch... he was involved in a bank robbery. That's where he supposedly got the money to start his business.'

'I thought it was meant to be Nazi gold?'

'I, er...' Townsend stuttered, thrown off track by McEvoy's interjection.

'And did he?' McEvoy prompted.

'Did he what?'

'Did he get the money to start his business from robbing a bank?'

'Well... you see... no. But that doesn't mean he didn't take part in any bank robbery. Maybe I should start at the beginning?'

'If it'll help,' McEvoy said reaching for his coffee.

'Well, what I've been doing,' Townsend said, failing to spot McEvoy's sarcasm, 'is going through the newspapers from 1948 onwards, when Koch arrived in Ireland, trying to find any reference to him or to any robberies. Basically, I've worked my way through two of the nationals – the *Irish Times* and the *Irish Independent* – and one of the local papers, the *Meath Chronicle*, up until 1960. Koch doesn't appear in the national papers at all between 1948 and 1957. He appears in the *Meath Chronicle* first in 1952 when he bought the Breen Strong Grow fertiliser factory in Athboy from the receivers.'

Townsend passed McEvoy a printed copy of the paper. The story was in the bottom right corner of page five with the headline: 'New start for fertiliser plant.' The accompanying text was a single short column along with a picture of Albert and Frank Koch and a young Martin O'Coffey standing in front of the gates, a large shed in the background. A temporary, painted sign, 'Ostara Fertiliser', was hanging next to them on the iron work. Only O'Coffey was smiling, the Koch brothers wearing determined looks, their eyes boring into the camera lens.

McEvoy handed the sheet back.

'He only appears sporadically after that, mainly through small adverts for Ostara Fertiliser – 'Bring new life to tired soil' – until 1956 when Albert Koch and Maurice Coakley opened their first Ostara Pharmacy in Kells. In 1957, Frank Koch was bought out of Ostara by Albert and he started his own motor sales company in Navan. In 1958 Albert Koch buys The White Gallows and Martin O'Coffey the neighbouring farm.'

'And the bank robberies took place in 1955?' McEvoy said, the implications of the robberies becoming clear.

Townsend nodded, yes. 'The first one took place in Navan, Friday, February 25th, 1955. The Bank of Ireland on Canada Street was broken into in the early hours of the morning. They got in through the roof at the back of the bank, lifting off the slates and letting themselves into the attic space. They made their way down to the basement and blew the hinges off the safe using home-made gelignite.' Townsend passed McEvoy a copy of the front page of the *Irish Independent*. The story was the lead item under the imaginative headline of: 'Bank Robbed in Navan.' The picture showed a serious-faced Mr Kilbride, the manager, standing outside of the bank's imposing façade.

'They made off with just over thirty thousand old Irish pounds. I think that's about eight hundred thousand euro in today's money. Most of it would have been drawn later that day by businesses to pay their employees. The search for the thieves was headed up by Chief Superintendent Locke based in the Phoenix Park.'

'Bank robberies were the crème-de-la-crème in those days,' McEvoy observed. 'There wouldn't have been anyone below detective sergeant on the case.'

'The second robbery took place on Friday, October 21st in Virginia in Cavan. They broke into the Allied Irish Bank on the main street and again blew the safe. It was a smaller haul – just under twenty-two thousand pounds or about five hundred and ninety thousand euro in today's money.' He handed McEvoy another copy of the *Independent* with the main headline: 'Cavan Bank Theft.'

'So the total haul was the equivalent of one point four million euro in today's money?' McEvoy asked.

'It seems that way.'

'You could do a lot with that kind of money back then. Property wasn't the crazy kind of prices they are today.'

'You could do a lot with it now if you weren't in the major cities,' Townsend countered. 'You could buy half of Longford for one and half million, especially now the market's crashed.'

'And they got away with it scot-free.'

Townsend shrugged.

'I wonder what the Criminal Assets Bureau will make of all of this,' McEvoy pondered. 'If it's true, then Koch's entire business empire is founded on stolen money.'

Jimmy McVeigh was sitting on the back seat of a mini-van, his legs covered by a blue-and-green check blanket. The rain was so heavy that he would have got soaked if he'd been lifted into the Ballyglass clubhouse.

McVeigh looked his age. His face was gaunt and pale, his head bald with mottled liver spots. He wore a pair of unstylish, thick glasses over deep eye sockets, a white shirt buttoned to the neck, and a grey flannel suit jacket that had seen better days.

'The cancer nearly got me last year,' he explained matter-of-fact. 'It's back again now. I'll be dead soon – only a matter of time. I don't care this time, it can take me. I've had enough.'

'If I'd have known, I'd have come to you,' McEvoy said sympathetically. 'I didn't realise… '

'…I wanted to get out. Get a bit of fresh air. It's a good place but you're mind turns to mud,' McVeigh said, referring to the nursing home in which he now resided.

'Cancer's a terrible thing,' McEvoy said absently, McVeigh reminding him of how frail Maggie had become in her final months.

'You sound like you're speaking from experience, Colm.'

'My wife died from lung cancer a year ago this Friday,' McEvoy confessed.

'I'm sorry, son. I wouldn't wish it on anybody. Not even some of the scum I helped put away.'

'You worked on the Navan bank robbery?' McEvoy asked taking the opportunity to turn the conversation towards Albert Koch's past.

'I was just a gofer. I'd just started in the Guards; I was nineteen or twenty. Within a few hours the case had been taken over by national headquarters. A bank robbery was big news in those days. It's not like now with all the murders and drugs and armed robberies. First armed robbery didn't occur in Ireland until the early 1970s. Even then it was rare.

So Dublin sent down some hotshot – Chief Superintendent Locke. He was an arrogant gobshite; thought we were all culchie thick heads,' McVeigh said sourly. 'He was convinced from the start it was a gang from Dublin who'd driven down the country to take advantage of our poor security. He didn't think anybody local would have the brains, balls or means to pull the job off.'

'You thought differently?' McEvoy prompted.

'I didn't think anything. I was at the bottom of the pile. I just did what I was told and tried to keep my nose clean. Superintendent O'Sullivan thought otherwise. The lab people thought the gelignite was home-made. Something about the type and ratio of the chemicals; I don't know. The only people who would have had the knowledge and access to the necessary resources would have been people working in the chemical industry.'

'Hence your interest in Albert Koch?'

'Exactly. The Koch brothers weren't some clueless culchies. They'd trained and fought in the German armed forces. And Albert Koch was a skilled chemist. O'Sullivan had him pegged as a serious suspect from the start.' McVeigh winced in pain and shifted his body on the seat. 'Locke was having none of it though. There was no evidence linking Koch to the robbery and he seemingly had no motive. He had no debts and his factory was doing okay – not brilliant, but enough to stay afloat.'

'So why rob the bank then?'

'Ambition. Koch was determined to make it big. He needed the money to expand. He couldn't raise the additional capital as things stood. He was already at his credit limit. The problem was O'Sullivan couldn't pin the robbery on Koch and none of the others would talk. Locke focused his efforts on the Dublin underworld, such as it was.'

'What others?' McEvoy prompted.

'His brother, Frank, and Martin O'Coffey and Maurice Coakley.'

'And what about the second robbery?'

'We weren't involved in that. Cavan's jurisdiction, though Locke continued to head up the case. Nobody was ever charged.'

'And what happened when Koch started to spend the money – opening the Ostara Pharmacy in Kells with Coakley?'

'Nothing. O'Sullivan tried to find out where the money came from, but he got nowhere. Koch had got himself politically connected – no doubt through some of that money being stuffed into brown envelopes. We were warned off, not that O'Sullivan took much notice; he was a stubborn old bastard. But all of our evidence was circumstantial and Koch's business had picked up by then. He'd managed to negotiate some export contracts to Germany and to England. And Albert Koch was clever. He didn't buy anything outright. He put down enough for a deposit, took out loans, and laundered the haul through the books.'

'He let the money seep slowly into circulation,' McEvoy said.

'Exactly. And they all got what they wanted,' McVeigh said bitterly. 'Albert Koch, money for investment; Frank Koch, his motor sales company; Maurice Coakley, his pharmacy; and Martin O'Coffey, his farm. In some ways you have to admire their guts and patience – though that doesn't change the fact that they were common criminals. O'Sullivan was certain they did both jobs, but…' he trailed off.

'…but he couldn't prove it,' McEvoy finished.

'After a couple of years the robberies were forgotten about. O'Sullivan died of a heart attack – he was barely fifty – and Koch went from strength to strength. The only thing that remained was the rumours and those eventually seemed to die out.'

'His whole life was a lie,' McEvoy whispered, his mind wandering.

'What?' McVeigh asked.

'I said his whole life was a lie.'

'And then you die,' McVeigh replied with a crooked smile, before bending in half with pain.

174

'Do you have minute?' Jenny Flanagan asked.

'Not really, but go ahead,' McEvoy replied distractedly. He was back in the incident room waiting for his team to locate either Martin O'Coffey or Maurice Coakley.

'Barney was right – Janice Kelly's phone was in the vicinity of Kylie O'Neill's home not Caher. The two calls to Brian O'Neill's phone were made using the nearby mast. We're bringing her in for questioning.'

'Just make sure you do everything by the book. Not that… Look, take it slowly and make sure you get everything you need.'

'Don't worry; we'll make sure she hangs herself. It should be fun. She's a cocky little bitch – she thinks they've got away with it. I imagine she'll either go silent or into wild theatrics and accusations.'

'Don't let her and O'Neill meet to swap notes. Interview him at the same time or straight afterwards. Pick apart any divergences or contradictions in their stories. Listen, you don't need me to tell you what to do. Keep me updated, okay?'

'No bother. You've had a breakthrough?'

'Not in terms of catching Koch's killer, but things are developing. I'll talk to you later.' McEvoy disconnected the call.

Kelly Stringer waited for him to pocket his phone and stepped towards him. She smiled at him shyly. 'Martin O'Coffey is on his farm. He's not feeling that well – he has a cold and would prefer it if we went to him.'

'I'll go there now,' McEvoy said, starting for the door.

'There's something else.'

McEvoy turned back towards her. 'What?'

'I thought it might be useful to go back through the surveys, see what other rumours there were about Koch that might turn out to be true. I think there are a couple that might be worth investigating further.'

'Go on.'

'There's a rumour that Koch brought in a small team of builders to his farm sometime in the 1960s, probably near the start of the decade. They stayed on the farm and had no dealings with the locals. They were there for a few weeks. All the building supplies and food were shipped in. The rumour seems to be that they were German, though one person thought Dutch. Koch told people it was restoration work, but…' she trailed off.

'But what?' McEvoy prompted.

'But others thought it was something else.'

'Such as?' McEvoy asked, starting to lose patience.

'Such as a secret vault,' Stringer said, slight embarrassment in her voice, knowing that it sounded like a conspiracy theory. 'To store his Nazi gold,' she elaborated.

'Or his stolen bank money or other valuables,' McEvoy hypothesised.

'It could be what the killer was searching for?' Stringer suggested tentatively.

'Okay, get hold of George Carter and Tom McManus. We'll do another search of the place, see if we can find anything. Tell McManus to concentrate on the outbuildings, George can look after the house. What was the other rumour?'

'That Koch supplied the IRA with explosives at the start of the Troubles.'

'Jesus. This just gets better and better. Talk to Dr John and see if he can find any evidence of a link. I better go and talk to Martin O'Coffey. And while I remember, is there any news on Kinneally's apartment?'

'I'm still waiting for Harcourt Street to come back to me,' Stringer said, referring to the NBCI headquarters in central Dublin. 'I'll chase them straight away.'

* * *

The rain had eased off, but the mature beech trees were still twisting in the wind.

McEvoy was met at Martin O'Coffey's front door by his grandson, Peter. The Wellington boots were gone, replaced by battered brown shoes, but he wore the same check shirt and dirty jeans as at their last encounter in the field on Koch's farm.

'He's not well,' O'Coffey said as a greeting.

'I'm only going to be a few minutes,' McEvoy explained, not saying that he would probably be there hours if O'Coffey admitted to the bank robberies.

'Just make sure you are,' the grandson warned, widening the door and beckoning McEvoy in. 'He's an old man and I don't want any stress adding to his condition. Last thing we need is another feckin' case of pneumonia.'

'Pneumonia?' McEvoy asked, concerned. 'I was told he has the start of a cold.'

'More like the flu. I just don't want it settling in his chest. Happened a couple of years ago and it damn near killed him.' He passed McEvoy and pushed open the kitchen door.

Martin O'Coffey was standing near to a boiling kettle, a grey blanket draped over his shoulders. He turned to face the intruders. 'Tea?' he asked, his face the same colour as the blanket, his bloodshot eyes watery and rimmed red.

'No, no, you're fine,' McEvoy replied. 'I hear you're not feeling the best?'

'Been better. Peter?'

'Please.'

The room descended into silence as Martin O'Coffey made three cups of tea, shuffling back and forth between the fridge and kettle and loudly blowing his nose. He sliced a lemon in half and squeezed one half into his cup.

'Did you have the flu jab?' McEvoy asked.

'No.'

'Maybe you should get it done? It might help shift your cold and stop it developing further.'

'I'm fine,' O'Coffey replied before sniffing. 'Sit,' he instructed.

McEvoy took a seat at the kitchen table. O'Coffey joined him, his grandson moving to his cup left by the kettle.

'I wanted to talk to you in private if that's okay,' McEvoy asked filling the silence.

'I've no secrets,' O'Coffey said.

'All the same, it might be better…' McEvoy trailed off.

The old man didn't reply.

'Right, okay,' McEvoy conceded, 'but if you want Peter to leave at any point just let me know. We've been looking into Albert Koch's past. You used to be close, before you fell out over the strip of land. You used to…'

'We still want that land back,' Peter interjected. 'It's our land.'

'Peter,' O'Coffey senior warned, and then sneezed into a paper tissue.

'You used to work for him before you bought this place.'

O'Coffey stayed silent.

'How did you manage to buy it? You worked in a fertiliser factory, yet you could afford a farm.'

'I worked hard.'

'But even so, you would have needed a very large deposit and a means of paying the mortgage.'

'What's this got to do with Albert Koch's death?' Peter asked defensively.

'It's background information,' McEvoy said tartly. 'You managed to save enough on a labourer's salary to obtain a mortgage for a farm?' he asked O'Coffey senior.

'Aye.'

'You didn't have additional help?'

'What kind of help? What are you implying?' Peter said angrily.

'Look, I know you're trying to help,' McEvoy snapped, 'but I'm trying to interview your grandfather, not you.'

'And I'm making sure that you're not trying to frame him for something he didn't do' Peter responded.

'I don't frame people! I'm asking questions potentially important to the case.'

'You're asking questions about something that has nothing to do with the case! How my grandfather managed to buy this farm is his business. It has nothing to do with Albert Koch's death. How could it?'

'That's what I'm trying to establish,' McEvoy explained. 'I don't just ask random questions, however it seems to you. So,' he turned his attention back to Martin O'Coffey, 'did you have any additional help?'

'No.'

'Not from the Bank of Ireland in Navan or Allied Irish Bank in Virginia?'

O'Coffey started to cough, a wheezy, chesty rasp that ended with him spitting phlegm into the tissue.

'I think that's enough,' Peter said, moving in behind O'Coffey's back. 'My grandfather's not well, Superintendent. He needs to be in bed with a hot water bottle.'

O'Coffey stayed silent.

'I only have a couple more questions.'

'They'll have to wait.'

'Were you and Koch part of the gang that robbed the two banks in 1955?' McEvoy asked.

'No.'

'Superintendent, I must—'

'Is that how you could afford this place a couple of years later? Stolen bank money?'

'No,' O'Coffey repeated.

'That's enough,' Peter interjected. 'These are crazy accusations. Mad stuff. My grandfather bought this place fair and square. We can show you the deeds, if needed. If you want to carry on, we'll need to talk to our solicitor.'

'It's okay, I've got answers to my questions,' McEvoy said standing. 'I doubt your grandfather's going to change his story however many times I rephrase them.'

'That's because they're true,' Peter countered.

'You should get a doctor out,' McEvoy advised O'Coffey. 'Get some antibiotics to stop that settling in.'

'I warned you not to stress him out!' Peter snapped.

'No doctors,' O'Coffey said without looking up.

* * *

The rain had turned to a light drizzle, the wind easing to occasional gusts. Sitting in his car at the edge of the car park at Ballyglass GAA club McEvoy stared across the pitch to the skeleton trees in the distance. He felt certain that Frank Koch and Peter O'Coffey were wrong; somehow Albert Koch's past was intricately bound to his death. The problem was that Koch was surrounded by so many rumours and myths it was impossible to know which were true and which were fantasies. Koch could have been an ordinary chemist in the Reich and he could have amassed his fortune through his industry and initiative. Or he could have been a war criminal, a looter of gold, and a bank robber. He could have been a family man, a philanthropist and also have helped the IRA, supplying explosives that destroyed lives. He could have been any mix of these things.

He glanced at his watch and then scratched at his scalp. Gemma would still be in school. He needed to find time to spend with her. And he needed to visit Hannah Fallon again. Perhaps he would be able to get away early that evening; do whatever business was needed via the phone.

He sighed to himself, pushed open the car door, levered his tall frame out and headed to the clubhouse door. He almost collided with John Joyce as he stepped over the threshold.

'How'd you get on with Martin O'Coffey?' Joyce asked, stepping back to make room.

'As expected, he denied taking part in either robbery. The poor sod looked like death warmed up. He's trying to beat off the flu with half a lemon.'

'The old remedies are sometimes the best. Listen, there've been two developments. First, James Kinneally's story doesn't stack-up. He arrived at his apartment at,' he glanced down at his notepad, '11.41. He left again at 8.05 the next morning. Probably about the time that Albert Koch was discovered dead.'

'And he arrived alone and had no visitors?'

'And no one left with him or within two hours of him leaving.'

'So Marion D'Arcy's alibi is worth nothing and James Kinneally's in the clear for murder, but he's buggered on deliberately misleading an inquiry and he might still be an accessory?'

'Look's like it. What do you want me to do?'

'We need to question them again, see what they have to say. It should be an interesting experience as I'm not sure that Kinneally's told her yet that he's provided her with an alibi. If we make sure she doesn't know that, we can see if she plays along. And talk to Kinneally's wife; find out why they separated.'

'I'll get on it.' Joyce made to move off.

'And the second?' McEvoy prompted.

'Sugar.' Joyce stopped in his tracks. 'The husband of the bed and breakfast owned in Navan is saying that someone let themselves back into the house sometime around two o'clock in the morning on Saturday night, but he's not sure who. He just remembers being woken by the key in the door. They only had two rooms occupied, so there's a fifty-fifty chance it might have been Ewa Chojnacki and Tomas Prochazka – I'm sure I'm not saying their names correctly, but anyway. They say they were there all night, but...' Joyce trailed off.

'And you haven't managed to track down the other occupants?'

'Not yet,' Joyce shook his head. 'Mr and Mrs Murphy from Cork – paid in cash; no phone number. They were up for the races.'

'Jesus. Only thing we can do is appeal for them to come forward. In the meantime put together a full timeline of what the East Europeans say their movements were and get it checked out. If other things don't match up then it casts doubt on their story.'

'I'll get someone working on it.'

'And make sure they don't do a disappearing act.'

Joyce headed back into the incident room, making a bee-line for Kelly Stringer. McEvoy followed lethargically. Just as one line of inquiry seemed to become more promising, another took a twist. Stringer motioned at him, letting him know that she wanted a word when Joyce had finished.

* * *

Maurice Coakley walked purposefully through the large shop, in behind the counter, through the pharmacy section and into an office. He was wearing a white coat over the top of a brown, tweed suit and highly polished brogues. Neither fat nor thin, he was in good health, with ruddy cheeks, blue eyes and short grey hair that was side-parted; a pair of small, silver-framed glasses was perched precariously on the end of his nose. He took a seat behind the desk and pointed at a red upholstered chair, gesturing for McEvoy to sit.

'I've had a phone call from Martin O'Coffey,' he stated.

'So you'll know what this is about then,' McEvoy prompted.

'Not really, no. I know what you're going to ask, but it sounds to me like you're grasping at straws. We had nothing to do with those robberies. And what they have to do with finding Bertie's killer is beyond me. He was killed by an intruder, wasn't he?'

'It seems that way. The question is; what was the intruder after?'

'Whatever he could get for his next fix probably,' Coakley speculated. 'If I were you, I'd round up all the local petty criminals and drug users and shake them down. They've cost me a fortune in extra security,' Coakley said, referring to the need to protect pharmacies from theft.

'It doesn't work like that,' McEvoy explained. 'First, you can't randomly round people up and, second, we've never been able to "shake people down".'

Coakley snorted his derision. 'It happened in 1955! That old bastard O'Sullivan shook us like a man possessed. What the book says you can do and what you actually do are different things.'

'You were petty criminals.'

'We were innocent victims! He wanted to be the big shot and solve those bank robberies. He didn't care whether he got the right people or not. It's not like it's not happened. Look at the Guildford Four – they spent years in prison for crimes they didn't commit.'

'But you didn't spend any time in prison. You opened a chain of very successful shops.'

'That's because I was innocent! As were Bertie, Frank and Martin. O'Sullivan got it into his head that we were involved, but he had no evidence. None. There was none to find. He was a lunatic in a uniform; the power had gone to his head.'

'So where did the money for the first shop come from?'

'Hard work! We all spent hours at that factory, breaking our backs; working our fingers to the bone. Bertie kept it to just the four of us, that way we kept the costs down and could make better profits. He promised all of us we'd get our own businesses and he was good for his word. I worked damn hard to be able to afford this place and I worked just as hard to grow the company. There are fifty-six Ostara Pharmacies in Ireland. If it wasn't for the economic downturn, we'd have been opening nine more in the next two years. Plus we have our own brand products. Nobody is going to take that success away from me.'

'I never said I would take it away. I was questioning whether it was founded on dirty money. If you were so innocent, why did O'Sullivan take such a keen interest in you?'

'Because he was looking for scapegoats! We fitted the bill – two German brothers with military experience, one a chemist. He took two and two and made twenty-two. If you need a suspect fast, track down Johnny Foreigner. Bertie and Frank Koch were good men. They married Irish women, fathered Irish children, worked damn hard to build businesses that employed people for miles around, paid Irish taxes, and gave generously to various charities.'

'So even if they stole the money, it was a good investment?'

'If you want to look at it that way, then yes,' Coakley said tiredly. 'If they had stolen the money, which they didn't, then the banks, the state and local people got it back in spades.'

'And they got rich as well – everyone's a winner.'

'You don't seem to be listening to me, Superintendent. We never robbed those banks. Our success is built on hard work. Everything Albert Koch ever made he ploughed back into Ostara. He didn't need to rob banks; he was always saving and then investing the nest egg. He had a habit of turning pence into pounds.'

McEvoy nodded but said nothing, trying to decide how to proceed. Coakley was clearly going to keep denying any involvement in the bank robberies.

'When are you going to release Bertie's body?' Coakley asked. 'He deserves a decent send-off. You need to stop treating him as a criminal and recognise he was the victim.'

'I'll talk to the pathologist,' McEvoy replied. 'I'm sure he'll be released to the family shortly. Can you think of any reason why someone was searching Albert Koch's farm, other than petty theft?'

'No. He was an old man. He was still active, but he'd stopped making as many enemies as he used to. Doesn't mean...' He trailed off and shrugged.

'What kind of enemies?'

'People whose businesses didn't do so well under stiff competition. People he'd bought out at a bargain price. People who didn't like him muscling in on their patch. Bertie did a lot of good deeds – funded a lot of community services – but he was a ruthless business man. If there was a market to be developed or a profit to be made then he would pursue it. It wasn't something that endeared him to everyone.'

'In other words he destroyed some people's lives?'

'I wouldn't quite go that far. All's fair in business. If they had the chance they'd have done the same to him. Some people succeed, others fail. Has to be that way or there'd only be factory owners and no employees.'

'He aided the process of natural selection?' McEvoy said sarcastically.

'You can mock, Superintendent, but that's exactly what he did. We all do. What do you think you're doing when you enforce the law? You take the weak, the criminals, the low-lives and you lock them away. They sink to the bottom. The strong forge ahead. It's the same difference.'

'I don't think so,' McEvoy said uncertainly. What he did was not about evolution and survival of the fittest, it was about maintaining order. It was just that maintaining order often benefited some groups at the expense of others.

* * *

Cathal Galligan was lying in wait at Athboy garda station. 'Ah, the invisible detective,' he said sarcastically. 'Remember me? I'm trying to do the media work for this case. Only nobody's telling me what's going on.'

'You need to talk to Barry Traynor,' McEvoy suggested, referring to the press liaison officer, brushing past Galligan.

'That slick bastard's useless. He's been put out to seed. I need to know what the hell's going on. I'm being made to look like an idiot because I can't answer half the questions being asked.'

'What makes you think anyone else would be able to answer them?' McEvoy stated, stopping outside a blue door. 'If we had all the answers, Koch's murder would be solved and the killer in custody. Now, if you'll excuse me, I need to conduct an interview.' McEvoy started to enter an office in which James Kinneally and a young guard in uniform were sitting.

'The rumour going round is that Koch was a war criminal,' Galligan said. 'He worked in Auschwitz. A number of journalists are sniffing about. It's going to be all over the papers tomorrow; might even make tonight's news.'

McEvoy let the door close again, remaining in the corridor. 'I hope to God you weren't the source of that rumour, Galligan. The accusation has been levelled alright, but the evidence to substantiate it is still being examined. If the papers publish, then Ostara's lawyers will be all over them like a rash. And all over us as well. Which means all over you.'

'Don't try and pin the leak in your team on me, McEvoy,' Galligan hissed. 'I'm the messenger here, not the Trojan horse.'

'If you want to know what the progress is, I'll tell you. We are following several lines of inquiry,' he said in a South Dublin accent, mimicking a news reader. 'As yet, we do not have a main suspect. We want to thank people for their continued help. Now, I'm busy.' He pushed open the door and entered the office, leaving Galligan fuming in the corridor.

'Sorry to keep you, Mr Kinneally,' he said, sitting down on the opposite side of the desk.

'Am I under arrest, Superintendent?' Kinneally asked calmly, though his clenched hands revealed his nervousness.

'Not yet. I need to ask you some more questions.'

'What do you mean, "not yet"? I didn't kill Albert Koch.'

'I know you didn't. That doesn't mean you haven't committed an offence though, does it?'

'I don't know what this is about,' Kinneally said, shifting uneasily in his seat, 'but I want to leave. I haven't done anything wrong.'

'Except lie. You weren't with Marion D'Arcy on Saturday night. You did what you originally said. You stayed the night in your apartment in Dublin. By yourself. We have the CCTV footage from the security tapes. You arrived near to midnight and you didn't leave again until eight o'clock the next morning. Nobody else came or went either prior to your arrival or afterwards. Deliberately misleading an investigation carries a jail sentence.'

'Oh, shit,' Kinneally whispered to himself. 'I want my lawyer.'

'Oh shit, is right. If it turns out that Marion D'Arcy killed her father then you're in big trouble. And if she's relying on you for an alibi then she has a lot of explaining to do.'

'Marion D'Arcy didn't kill her father! I knew this was a bad idea. I told Mark… I mean, I thought it would… I thought…' he trailed off.

'You didn't think; that was the problem. You wanted to help Mrs D'Arcy, but instead you've landed her right in it. Even if she's innocent we're now going to have to put her through the wringer – see if your lie was needed because she herself had lied. I take it this was Mark D'Arcy's idea?'

'I'm not saying another word without my lawyer. And, unless you're going to charge me, I'm leaving,' Kinneally said, starting to rise.

'Oh, don't worry, we're going to charge you. If nothing else, we'll do you for wasting police time. I guess you'll be wanting to make a phone call,' McEvoy said standing and heading for the door. 'You might as well make yourself comfortable; you'll no doubt be here for a few more hours yet.'

* * *

'Hi, it's me. How're things?' Once again, he was sitting in his car outside Ballyglass GAA club. The sky had already faded to night, the wind still occasionally gusting, large droplets hammering onto the roof from the leafless trees. Off in the distance an orange glow revealed the location of Athboy.

'Not too bad,' Caroline said. 'What's the story?'

'The story is we're getting somewhere, but I've no idea where. It's been another long day, running from one thing to another. I'm going to hold a team meeting and try and head home. I'd thought I'd pick Gemma up and then head back to the hospital to see Hannah Fallon.'

'You could always just come here, have some dinner, and relax for a bit. Have a beer and unwind. Jimmy's hoping to watch a match later on Sky. Man U and someone. Or take Gemma out for a meal or to the cinema or something.'

'I really need to go and see Hannah. She's a good friend. I know it's a shitty double-up, but I think Gemma will want to see her again as well.'

'You're going to need to find time for family, Colm. We can fill the gap, but it's not the same.'

'I know, I know. But what can I do? I'm up to my neck in cases. The good news is, I've sorted out Friday. I'm taking the day off.'

'Well, that's a start. Look, Gemma's hovering here. I'll pass you over.'

'Dad?'

'Hiya, pumpkin. How're things?'

'Okay. Miss Cassidy wants me to appear in the school play. It's a musical. *Annie*, or something. I told her I'd think about it. She said she'd be having a word with you.'

'I take it you're not too keen on the idea?'

'Acting's for freaks. Doing the sound or lighting though would be pretty cool. They have this massive mixing deck. You can do some really spooky stuff with it. Robbie Travis did it last year and he says it's amazing. He said I can be his assistant, if I want.'

'If I talk to her, I'll tell her. Look, I'm going—'

'I was hoping, you know, that you might be a little more proactive?' Gemma interrupted. 'I really want to do this. It'll be well smart. I definitely don't want to be prancing about with all the posers on stage.'

'Right,' McEvoy said uncertainly, wondering where Robbie Travis fitted into his daughter's ambitions. Gemma was twelve going on eighteen, except in one respect – she hadn't yet gone through her teenage girl phase. He knew that at any point soon his daughter would transform into a young adult and all that would bring – hormones, rebellion, temper tantrums, make-up, clothes, smoking, binge drinking, drugs and boys. He'd broken up enough teenage parties, and arrested enough youths turned delinquent, to know how things could turn out.

'I'll talk to Miss Cassidy tomorrow,' he conceded. 'I'm thinking of going to try see Hannah again tonight. Do you want to come?'

'Only if you're not going looking like a scarecrow this time.'

'I'll make sure I'm presentable. I'm not sure what time I'll be back, but no later than seven thirty, okay?'

'I'll be ready. You are looking after yourself, aren't you, Dad? You're eating and drinking?'

'Yeah, yeah,' McEvoy lied, having missed lunch yet again. 'I'm fine. Look, I've got to go. Be good and I'll see you later.' McEvoy ended the call. Every time he spoke to his daughter it always ended with him feeling guilty. He rested his head against the steering wheel and tried to shift his mind back to the case. He'd need to ask Kelly Stringer to track down Miss Cassidy's number.

His mobile phone rang. 'Jenny?'

'They're both sticking to their story. She was shopping in Caher, he was working in Bansha. She's one cool bitch. Just answered the questions as if I was asking her about what she had for her dinner – absolutely no emotion. I'm beginning to wonder whether she did it and not the husband.'

'And what's your evidence other than the phone records?' McEvoy asked.

'Nothing, beyond the fact that she was Brian O'Neill's mistress. Her phone records place her in the vicinity of Kylie's house at the time of the murder and she had a strong motive.'

'It's all circumstantial, Jenny. Keep working at her. I'll be the bad cop. Tell her that your superiors want to charge her with first degree murder. She might serve up O'Neill to save herself. Try the same with O'Neill.'

'I'll give it a go, but I'm not promising anything.'

'And get onto Caher garda station and check out her shopping story. If she was there someone must have seen her.'

* * *

189

'Right, okay, let's make a start,' McEvoy said to the group of guards assembled in the incident room. 'Come on, let's settle down.' He waited for the room to quieten, scanning across the tired looking-faces, Galligan's scowling back.

'Right, I'm going to keep this short and sweet. You're all probably aware we now have a bit of momentum behind this case. The problem is that it all focuses on Albert Koch's life history, not his killer. The history's important, but we need to keep a focus on the murder itself. Someone was searching the house. Koch's past might provide a motive for whoever killed him, and the hanging noose tells us that whoever killed him knew something about the history of The White Gallows, but it doesn't necessarily tell us who that person might be.

'I want the alibi of everyone who came into contact with Koch in the two weeks before he died checked and double-checked. We've already had one person's alibi unravel. Three other's are looking shaky,' he said referring to the East European couple and Marion D'Arcy. 'How solid is everybody else's? I want people really pressed on this. If there are other witnesses, I want their stories corroborated. John, you're to take charge of that, okay?'

He carried on without waiting for an answer. 'Tom, George, if there is a secret compartment or room in Koch's house then I need you to find it. Draft in as many local hands as needed.

'Also a reminder. This case is difficult enough without any of its details being leaked to the media. Koch's life was surrounded by rumours, some of which might be true, others not; I don't want to see any of them printed in the papers. Or if they are, then they better not say, "According to a Garda source." The last thing we need is a slander case being taken against us. And believe me, Ostara will do it if they can.

'Anyone got anything they want to add?'

The room stayed silent.

'Right, well you all know what to do.' McEvoy glanced at his watch and grimaced. If he left in the next fifteen minutes or so, he should be able to drop in on the team in Trim and make it back to Finglas in time to pick up Gemma, assuming the traffic was free-flowing, which was a dangerous assumption.

Kelly Stringer sidled up next to him. 'We've managed to track down Marion D'Arcy. She says if you want to talk to her, then she'll meet you at her home. If you want to talk elsewhere, then you'll have to arrest her first and she'll want her lawyer present.'

McEvoy glanced at his watch again. 'Sugar,' he muttered, then more clearly, 'Tell her I'll be out to her shortly.'

* * *

Marion D'Arcy had the front door open before he had pulled to a stop. She was wearing a dark brown trouser suit over a cream blouse, a large amber pendent lying high on her chest. Her make-up was professionally applied, her fingernails copper brown. Her blonde hair had been re-dyed, covering up her grey roots.

'This is harassment, Superintendent,' she said as he rounded his car. 'I'm being harassed by you and I'm being harassed by the press. My father's died and I'm being hounded by imbeciles and blood-sucking leeches.'

'I'm sorry if it comes across that way, Mrs D'Arcy,' McEvoy said with little sympathy, 'but I'm afraid I need to ask you some more questions.'

'Down at the police station!' she snapped, referring to Stringer's original request. 'Am I now a prime suspect?'

'Not as such,' McEvoy conceded. 'Can we go inside?'

Marion D'Arcy opened the door wider and ushered McEvoy into the hall. He followed her into the living room and sat on the arm of a sofa.

'Now, what's this about?' Marion D'Arcy asked curtly, glancing at her watch, letting him know she was being little more than courteous.

'I need to check your alibi for Saturday night.'

'I've already told you, I was here all night,' she replied testily.

'Alone?'

'Yes, alone. My husband was away in France.'

'So you weren't with James Kinneally?'

'No. I mean, yes. I was with him until around ten o'clock, and then he left.'

'And where did he go?'

'Home, I presume. You'd need to ask him, Superintendent. I'm not his keeper.'

'But you are his lover?'

'What the... I... I think you should leave,' D'Arcy said haughtily, momentarily rattled. 'I've told you where I was that evening. I was here by myself. And no, I don't have any proof!'

'Given you haven't denied it, I'll take that as a yes then,' McEvoy said, staying put.

'You can take it any fucking way you want, Superintendent,' she said, losing her cool. 'You are meant to be investigating my father's death, not prying into my life.'

'Can you think of any reason why James Kinneally would state that he spent Saturday night here with you?' McEvoy asked, ignoring her ire.

'What?' she snapped, her brow furrowing, trying to fathom Kinneally's lie. 'He said that?'

'Yes.'

'Then he was lying! As I've told you, he left around ten o'clock.'

'Why would he say he was with you when he wasn't?'

'Again, you'd need to ask him. All I can tell you is that he's lying.'

'But why would he do that?' McEvoy pressed. 'Unless he either needed an alibi himself or he wanted to help protect someone who didn't have an alibi.'

'What are you suggesting? That James killed my father?' Marion said without emotion.

'It's a possibility. If he wasn't with you, where was he?'

'I've no idea, but I don't believe for a minute that he killed my father. He respected him greatly. He worked for him for years.'

192

'Well, the alternative is that he was supplying you with a false alibi. The question is why? Especially given you are denying his alibi and your alibi can't be verified.'

'Well, he… well, he obviously wanted to try and protect me,' she suggested uncertainly. 'Perhaps he wanted to try and stop you harassing me? And let's face it, that's what this is. Are you satisfied now?'

'Not really,' McEvoy said shaking his head and shifting position. 'I have one false alibi, one that can't be verified, and two supposed lovers that don't really seem that in love. You haven't once asked how he is or what's happening to him.'

'Our relationship is none of your business, Superintendent. And it's none of anybody else's either,' she said, warning him to keep the information to himself. 'I'd like you to leave now.'

'He's being held at Athboy garda station on charges of seeking to mislead an investigation and wasting police time,' McEvoy said without moving.

'He's what? You can't do that!'

'It's called the law, Mrs D'Arcy, as you well know. What was he, your insurance policy? One way or another you'd get your hands on Ostara?'

'That's it. Out!' Marion D'Arcy demanded. 'Go on, get out! I'm not answering any more of your questions. If you want to speak to me again, you'll have to speak to my lawyer.'

Reluctantly, McEvoy slid off the arm of the sofa and headed for the door. Once again he'd handled Marion D'Arcy poorly, reacting to her prickly personality and inciting her further. One thing was clear though – she didn't have an alibi for the night her father died.

He turned at the threshold. 'By the way,' he said, 'I've spoken to the pathologist. She's now happy to release your father's body for burial. If you tell me the name of your undertaker, we'll arrange for him to be picked up and transferred to their premises.'

* * *

He'd been thirty-five minutes late picking up Gemma from his sister's house. The meeting in Trim had been quick but unproductive, with no progress reported. However, the low cloud cover, infrequent street lighting, and wet, twisting and potholed roads had slowed his progress. An accident on the M50 had further delayed their progress back towards Blanchardstown and James Connolly Hospital. It had at least given them time to catch up on things and swap small talk about school and friends.

His mobile phone rang and he reluctantly answered it using the hands-free system.

'McEvoy.'

'Colm, what the fuck is going on!' Bishop snapped.

'I'm driving to see Hannah with Gemma.'

'I don't give a fuck what you're doing now, what the fuck's happening with the Koch case!'

'Can you tone down your language please, sir, I have you on hands-free,' McEvoy reasoned.

'We use fuck all the time at school,' Gemma said. 'I'm not a child.'

'I don't care,' McEvoy said. 'Anyone else swears and I'm ending this call.'

'I've just had another call from Paul Cassidy, TD for North Meath,' Bishop continued without apologising. 'He wants to know why you're treating Marion D'Arcy as a prime suspect in the death of her father when you don't have a shred of evidence.'

'I'm not treating her as a prime suspect. But she doesn't have an alibi for the night her father died and James Kinneally, the CEO of Ostara, provided her with a false one. They're having an affair, though you'd never guess it from talking to her. I had no choice but to interview her, only she's allergic to being questioned.'

'From what I've heard it's the style of questioning that's the problem, Colm. She has a lot of powerful friends – friends who could be a real pain in the backside if they wanted to be. Do you understand what I'm saying here?'

194

'Yeah, you're saying that I should treat people differently depending on their wealth,' McEvoy said facetiously.

'I'm telling you to treat people differently based on their political clout, you gombeen! Will you be smart for once; there's no point creating more grief than you have to. She's on the warpath now. And she's getting people like Cassidy to do her bloody dirty work for her. Just handle her with kid gloves,' he said, calming. 'Don't do anything to antagonise her, okay. And for God's sake, don't arrest her unless you are one hundred per cent sure she's guilty and you have cast-iron evidence.'

'I have to be able to ask her questions.'

'Look, if you need to talk to her again, talk to me first, okay? She requires diplomacy. Lots of it.' Bishop ended the call.

'What a scuzzball,' Gemma said. 'He sounds like a real langer.'

'Gemma!' McEvoy warned, thinking that Bishop didn't know diplomacy; he only knew its lesser cousin, shenanigans – political manoeuvring and shady deals. It was clear though he'd have to watch how he proceeded. That was now the second time Marion D'Arcy had used Cassidy to try and rein him in. While Cassidy was relatively small time, he could still make his life difficult. And Koch's daughter probably had more senior figures to pull in if the going got tough, along with Ostara's considerable clout.

* * *

Official visiting hours were long over by the time they'd made their way through the hospital and up to Hannah Fallon's private room. A different guard was sitting outside her door. He looked up with a bored expression as they approached, a copy of *Cosmopolitan* open on his knees.

'Catching up on a bit of reading?' McEvoy said by way of a greeting.

'Learning how the other side thinks,' the guard replied. 'Quite frankly it's scary stuff. I preferred ignorance. I'm afraid visiting hours are over.'

McEvoy pulled his badge from his pocket. 'Detective Superintendent Colm McEvoy. This is my daughter, Gemma.'

'Fair enough,' the guard said and dropped his gaze back to the magazine story on how to spot when men were cheating. 'Just remember that what these magazines say about men is rubbish,' he said, glancing back up to Gemma.

'It's alright, I know,' Gemma replied. 'They're twice as bad as the magazines say.'

The guard snorted derision and once again dropped his eyes.

McEvoy knocked gently on the door and edged it open.

The room was covered in flowers and cards, a pile of presents in one corner. Hannah was propped up by a couple of pillows. Her legs were still raised and covered by a blanket. Her hair was combed, but her face was pasty, dark crescents under her eyes. Her sister, Catherine, was sitting in the chair next to the bed, also looking exhausted. They both turned their gazes away from a small portable television to the door.

'Colm!' Hannah exclaimed tiredly. 'Come in. Jesus, I didn't expect to see you. And Gemma.'

Colm moved into the room and stood at the end of the bed, his hands on his daughter's shoulders. 'Look, we won't stay long. We just wanted to drop by and see how you were.'

'God, it's no bother. It's great you could come. Catherine said you'd come in the night it happened. I was totally out of it after the operation, so I'm afraid I don't remember – sorry. The last couple of days have been a bit of a blur to be honest. I feel like I'm an animal in a zoo, everyone dropping in to take a look and prod and poke and ask questions. I didn't realise how many people cared about me. I could open a florists,' she said gesturing at the flowers. 'And that's after I've sent half of them to other wards. Take a seat. There'll be another chair in the hall somewhere.'

'It's okay,' McEvoy said, still standing. 'We won't be long. I'm sure you need your rest. How're you feeling today?'

'Vengeful. Charlie Clarke better not show his face round here or I'll club him to death with a crutch. At least I'm going to keep one leg, though it won't win any lovely leg competitions. The doctors seem to be happy enough with it. They're going to fit me up with a prosthetic for the other one. I keep thinking it's still there. A phantom leg they call it. My head's telling me I'm wiggling my toes, my eyes are telling me there's no toes there. Once I get the new leg I should be able to walk okay after some rehabilitation.'

'At least that's something,' McEvoy muttered, unsure what to say.

'Better than I hoped for,' Hannah said. 'I thought I might end up in a wheelchair, in which case my career would be totally up the chute. I'd be able to do lab work, but the field stuff would be hopeless. I'm hoping to be back out and about in six months.'

'That's a best case scenario,' Catherine cautioned. 'It might take a little longer.'

'Six months,' Hannah reiterated. 'So, enough about me. How're things, Gemma? You managing to keep your father on the straight and narrow?'

Gemma shrugged shyly. 'I'm doing my best. He's pretty busy, so I only get to see him now and then. He needs someone to make sure he eats and drinks. He gets so wrapped up in things that he forgets.'

McEvoy felt his chest tighten with guilt and embarrassment. Realising that they might be there for some time he dropped down on the spare chair, pulling Gemma towards him so that she perched on his knee.

* * *

'Is it too late to talk?' John Joyce asked.

'Are you still out in Athboy?' McEvoy asked, stirring a cup of coffee. He'd got back from the hospital half an hour earlier and had just packed Gemma off to bed.

'I'm on my way back in to Dublin. I was following up on James Kinneally's wife. I've no idea why he left her as she seemed very pleasant to me. Open, funny, good company.'

'Money and power,' McEvoy said cynically.

'He already has money and power.'

'You can never get enough apparently. So what did she have to say for herself?'

'He left about eight months ago. She says she didn't see it coming at all. He just moved out one day – totally turned her world upside down. She thinks he was seduced by Marion D'Arcy rather than the other way around. She doesn't have a single good thing to say about her.'

'She's probably right.'

'This is the twist though. She says it took her a while to find her feet again, but that she was going to screw Kinneally for everything that he's got and also Marion D'Arcy. And she's now in a relationship with Charles Koch.'

'Kinneally's wife is dating Charles Koch?' McEvoy said incredulously.

'That's what she says. She said it started about three months since. She also says she can't believe she didn't have an affair years ago. It's really re-energised her life.'

'So James Kinneally is dating Marion D'Arcy, and Patricia Kinneally is having an affair with Charles Koch?'

'Yes.'

'And do Marion and Charles know this?'

'I presume so.'

'The lifestyles of the rich and famous,' McEvoy muttered. 'Unbelievable.'

'She says she was with Charles Koch on the night of Albert Koch's death. He stayed at her house.'

'That's not what he said. He said he spent the night by himself at his holiday cottage near to Loughcrew. I guess I need to talk to him again. Look, I'll let you get on. I'll talk to you tomorrow.' McEvoy ended the call and took a sip of his coffee. The investigation into the death of Albert Koch was full of surprises – death camps, medical experiments, secret builders, bank robberies, adoptions, and affairs. From a cynical perspective the new pairings were simply about maximising the potential return from Ostara – either through family or business inheritance. McEvoy doubted the relationships were anything to do with love or emotional commitment.

He headed to the stairs and slowly trudged up them, knowing he would now lie awake haunted by his own lost love.

THURSDAY

It was seven thirty in the morning and McEvoy was making good progress against the ribbon of vehicles heading slowly towards Dublin. He'd spent half the night lying awake, his mind refusing to stop ticking over. It was at it again; a thought was wriggling away just out of reach. They were missing something. Something obvious. They'd been so focused on finding out about Albert Koch's past they'd neglected to focus fully on his killing.

He started to run through how Koch had been found. He'd been hit on the head with a vase downstairs and then carried up and arranged in his bed. Whoever killed him was hoping that it would be mistaken for a natural death. Why else move the body? But then, why hang a noose from the White Gallows oak tree? It didn't make any sense. The rope drew attention to the fact that there'd been a visitor during the night. So the killer clearly knew the authorities wouldn't be fooled and the rope was probably a crude attempt at misdirection. It was almost certainly an improvisation, which meant that by hanging the rope from the tree the killer revealed knowledge about the history of the site. And the killer knew how to make a noose and had the strength to throw its weight over a high branch.

A yellow light lit up on the dashboard interrupting his train of thought. He was low on petrol. He cursed to himself and tried to remember how far it was to the next filling station

– hopefully not more than a couple of miles. He tried to re-muster his thoughts, but whatever insight had been hovering just out of reach had now evaporated.

After a couple of minutes he approached a garage. He pulled in, filled up the car's tank and went inside to pay. As he headed to the counter he passed a row of daily newspapers stacked up in piles. He glanced down at the headlines and pulled to a stop. Each paper led on the same story about Albert Koch.

'NAZI WAR CRIMINAL'

'OSTARA'S SECRET AUSCHWITZ PAST'

He reached down and lifted up a copy of the *Irish Sun*. The headline was, 'KILLER KOCH!' followed by, 'Exclusive: Auschwitz Torturer became Irish Billionaire!' The story was accompanied by the head shot of the young Albert Koch wearing his SS uniform and cap. He started to read.

'The billionaire tycoon, Albert Koch, 91, found murdered on Monday was, *The Sun* can exclusively reveal, an SS killer in the Auschwitz death camp. According to Yellow Star, a Jewish organisation that tracks down aging Nazis, Koch took part in the infamous Jewish Skeleton Project, removing the flesh from corpses for racial experiments.

'Koch, whose real name was Adolf Kucken, arrived in Ireland in 1948. He established Ostara Industries four years later, reputedly using looted Nazi gold. The company quick-ly grew to become one of the biggest businesses in Ireland. Wholly owned by Koch, he was rumoured to be the third rich-est person in the country at the time of his death. Story contin-ued on Pages 4 and 5.'

McEvoy didn't bother opening the paper. Instead he gath-ered up a selection of its competitors and paid at the counter.

The media and lawyers were going to be crawling all over the case now. He just hoped to God that the source of the story was Yellow Star and not the gardai. There'd be hell to pay if Galligan or another officer had leaked details of the investiga-tion. And God only knew how Marion D'Arcy, Charles and Frank Koch were going to react. They were probably apoplectic with rage and hurt, which was going to make mining them for additional information almost impossible.

He made his way back to his car, dumping the papers on the passenger seat. He pulled away from the pump, parked at the edge of the forecourt and started to work his way through the papers trying to get an assessment of how much information had been leaked.

Ten minutes later he was fairly confident that the source of the story had been Yellow Star or Professor Moench. All the information had seemingly come from documents collected by Ewa Chojnacki and Tomas Prochazka and there was no mention of the bank robbery or the supposed secret vault.

His mobile phone rang and he glanced at the screen before answering. Experience told him that when a story like this broke, all kinds of people managed to obtain his phone number, including the press.

'McEvoy.'

'Colm, tell me we are not responsible for today's newspapers,' Bishop snapped.

'I've been through most of them and it's not us. I'd say it was Yellow Star. It's all their material.'

'At least that's something. I've just had my ears warmed by Paul Cassidy again, the greasy little gobshite. Marion D'Arcy and Ostara will be taking libel cases against all the papers and she's seeking an injunction to stop them publishing any other stories claiming that her father was a Nazi war criminal. What's your take on it?'

'I don't know,' McEvoy said slowly. 'According to a professor we've bought in to look at the documents there was an Adolf Kucken who worked in Auschwitz. Proving conclusively that Albert Koch was Adolf Kucken might be more difficult though. It looks that way, but without genetic testing, and with a good set of lawyers, I think the papers are going to run into problems.'

'Good,' Bishop spat spitefully, himself a recent victim of the media's ire at the gardai's inability to stop the gangland wars and murders. 'The bastards deserve a roasting.'

'There's plenty more stories to come out,' McEvoy continued. 'It seems likely that Koch was also involved in two bank robberies in Navan and Virginia in 1955. Again there's no conclusive proof, but it looks that way. And there's no way we'll be able to keep a lid on it all, not with an army of journalists trying to sniff out a juicy story.'

'Jesus,' Bishop muttered. 'First Charlie Clarke, now this. This country's going to hell. Just try and keep a lid on things, okay? And go easy on Marion D'Arcy. She's going to be like a raging, wounded bear.' He ended the call.

McEvoy tipped his head back and stared at the car's roof, before slowly rolling it forward and starting the car. The day had barely started and yet he already wished it was nearly over.

* * *

There were a dozen journalists hanging round the entrance to Ballyglass GAA club being held at bay from the car park by two uniformed guards. McEvoy eased his car slowly through them and parked as far away from them as possible. As he levered himself out, with the day's papers tucked under his arm, the door of a gleaming, black, Audi A6, parked a few cars away, opened and a well-dressed man emerged. With his slicked back, silver hair, shiny grey suit, and long, black, woollen coat, McEvoy knew he was probably a solicitor or lawyer.

'Superintendent McEvoy?' the man asked with a North Dublin accent.

'Yes?'

'I'm John Rice.' The man rounded the car to block McEvoy's path toward the clubhouse. 'I'm Marion D'Arcy's legal adviser.' He held out his hand.

Reluctantly McEvoy accepted the offer of a handshake, noting that the man must have taken a bath in aftershave.

'You've seen the papers then,' Rice observed.

'I'm sorry about that,' McEvoy said, 'but it was nothing to do with us.'

'It's everything to do with you,' Rice said. 'You're the ones treating Albert Koch's death as suspicious. If the family doctor had been able to do his job, you wouldn't be camped out here, and everyone would be getting on with their lives.'

'Albert Koch was murdered, Mr…' McEvoy trailed off.

'Rice. John Rice,' the man repeated.

'…Mr Rice,' McEvoy finished his sentence. 'You should be talking to the papers, not me. All I want to do is catch Albert Koch's killer.' McEvoy rounded the lawyer and proceeded towards the clubhouse. A couple of the journalists started to shout across the car park, desperate to get his attention. He ignored them and kept going. There was no way he was going to talk to them directly unless he had to; not after the way he was treated by them during and after the Raven case.

'Don't worry, we are talking to the papers, superintendent,' Rice said, trailing after him. 'Damn parasites,' he said glancing over at them as a flash popped. 'I need you to put some men outside Marion D'Arcy's house. She's being hounded by them.'

'I'll see what I can do,' McEvoy offered. He pulled open the door into the clubhouse and entered. Kevin Boyle, Ostara's PR person, was waiting for him in the hallway. McEvoy pulled to a stop and turned to face Rice.

'See what you can do?' Rice said incredulously before McEvoy could speak. 'It's the least you can do. First, you treat her like a prime suspect and second you let information about the case leak to the media. She trying to organise her father's funeral for tomorrow afternoon and she's a nervous wreck. Having the media camped outside her door harassing her is a gross invasion of privacy.'

'I said, I'll see what I can do,' McEvoy stated, unable to keep the frustration out of his voice. 'I'll have men out there in the next hour. As for Mrs D'Arcy, I haven't accused her of anything. It's my job to ask questions. She doesn't like answering them. And there's no getting around the fact that she had no alibi for Saturday night and her lover, who happens to be in charge of Ostara, provided her with a false alibi. That, in anyone's book, is suspicious and demands explanation.'

Rice shook his head in frustration. 'Marion D'Arcy did not kill her father. We all know that. If you want to speak to her again then I insist that I'm present. As for James Kinneally, I've no idea why he did such a stupid thing other than he was trying to protect her from your aggressive tactics. I will do everything I can to protect my client, Superintendent. My suggestion is you start doing the same before I have to start preparing a case against you.'

'I'm quaking in my boots,' McEvoy said sarcastically. 'We have every right to question Marion D'Arcy and to explore all leads that might lead to the capture of her father's killer – if she doesn't like it, tough. Now, if you'll excuse me, I have to get on.' McEvoy turned towards where Kevin Boyle hovered.

'It won't be difficult to discredit you, Superintendent,' Rice said to his back. 'Not after how you handled the Raven case.'

McEvoy ignored him. 'Let me guess,' he said to Boyle, 'you're here about the newspapers?' The clubhouse door behind him opened and closed as Rice left.

'You have to do something to stop them printing these lies,' Boyle said, holding up three of the papers.

'Surely you have Ostara's army of lawyers for that?'

'Don't worry, they're on it, but you have to help. Superintendent Galligan's well out of his depth. He hasn't got a clue what he's doing.'

'I'll talk to Barry Traynor and get the national office to take over.'

'This needs a fully coordinated response. The international press have picked up on the story. These lies are going to be on TV screens around the world by tonight.'

'Jesus,' McEvoy muttered. This was the last thing he needed, another international media fest. He was going to have to talk to Bishop again before things got too far out of hand. 'I said I'll talk to the national office. There's nothing more I can do.'

'For God's sake,' Boyle muttered. His mobile phone rang. 'I need to get on,' he said, moving to one side. 'Can you tell Barry to contact me?'

McEvoy nodded assent and left Boyle in the corridor, entering the incident room.

* * *

He'd spent a few minutes giving Kelly Stringer instructions. She was to organise a couple of local garda to go to Marion D'Arcy's house, to get Tom McManus to step up security at The White Gallows, to track down Charles Koch and arrange for McEvoy to meet him, and to locate Ewa Chojnacki and Tomas Prochazka as soon as possible.

While Stringer busied herself with those jobs, he wandered over to where Professor Moench's massive frame was bent over a table, his long grey hair reaching down to touch the table. A giant hand was holding open a book; the other held a typed sheet of paper.

McEvoy dropped the papers on the edge of the desk.

'Have you seen these?' he asked, jabbing at the papers.

'No,' Moench answered, picking up the *Irish Sun*. 'Killer Koch!' he said aloud, looking up at McEvoy, his bushy beard containing remnants of his breakfast. 'Detective Stringer told me that the newspapers were covering the case.'

'So you're not responsible then?' McEvoy asked. 'Their source material seems to be the papers you have on the desk in front of you.'

'I haven't spoken to anyone about these papers,' Moench said offended. 'You asked me not to.'

'Not even your friends?'

'Not even my wife. And these papers have not left this room.'

206

'And are the newspapers right?' McEvoy asked without apologising for his accusations. 'Albert Koch really was Adolf Kuchen and he was involved in war crimes?'

'As I said yesterday, I need to check these papers with the original archives, but it seems that way to me. I have been investigating the Jewish Skeleton Project.' Moench turned over the book he had been reading – *Race Experiments and the Holocaust*. The cover showed a man in an SS uniform fitting measuring callipers around the shaved head of a nervous child.

'Conrad Trent,' Moench said, referring to the book's author, 'documents Adolf Kucken as a member of the Abnenebre, a kind of pseudo-academy set up by Himmler, which conducted medical experiments on Jewish prisoners. He notes that Kucken was an SS chemist working in Monowitz, part of Auschwitz, and that he was recruited there by Bruno Beger. During August 1943 Kucken travelled to the Anatomical Institute at the Strassburg Reich University where he de-fleshed the skeletons killed at the nearby Natzweiler concentration camp. There's not much more information than that, but the book proves that Kucken exists in the archives and he was involved in war atrocities. These papers,' he gestured at the table, 'match the book's evidence. Without checking properly, I'd say they are copies of the genuine files.

'Jesus,' McEvoy muttered.

'It does not prove, however, that Albert Koch was Adolf Kucken,' Moench warned.

'We know that Frank Koch was Franz Kucken,' McEvoy said. 'I'd say it all adds up.'

* * *

'It's Jenny. Do you have a minute?'

'Yeah, no bother, go on,' McEvoy instructed. He was stuck behind a tractor pulling a trailer on the gently rolling road between Athboy and Navan, slowly drifting past a procession of one-off houses on one acre plots, each house built in a different style and fronted with an assortment of walls, fences, and hedges.

'I can't decide who killed Kylie O'Neill. They've both clammed up. Neither will say anything other than to repeat their original stories. I've had the phone records checked again. His phone was definitely in Bansha. Her phone made two calls from the mast nearest to Kylie's home around the time she was murdered, though she swears blind she was in Caher. We can't find any trace of her there, nor can we in Kylie's house either.'

'So what's your hunch?'

'I think Brian O'Neill left his phone in Bansha and travelled to his wife's house carrying Janice Kelly's phone. He killed his wife and then used Janice's phone to call his own phone. Then he covered his tracks and headed back to Bansha.'

'So charge him.'

'It could equally have been Janice Kelly,' Jenny said.

'You've just said you couldn't find any trace of her at Kylie's house. He must have done it. You have enough circumstantial evidence to convince the DPP's office,' McEvoy said, referring to the Director of Public Prosecutions who decided whether there was sufficient evidence for a person to stand trial to answer a charge.

'I have no witnesses, no weapon, and no evidence to link him to the scene of the crime other than his mistress' phone was nearby and a witness statement that saw his car on the road from Bansha to the house, but who can't be sure of the day.'

'Jesus, Jenny, I have enough to be dealing with here. Can't you just get it sorted? One of the two of them did it.'

'I know that! I'm just not sure which of them. My head's telling me that he did it, but my heart's saying that she did. She's a cold-hearted bitch.'

'For God's sake,' McEvoy muttered. 'If you need to, charge them both – one for murder, one for aiding and abetting. Threaten to throw the book at them. If you want to spice things up, charge her with the murder and see how they both react to that.'

'She probably won't even blink,' Jenny said. 'I'll think about it and let you know how I get on. I'd better let you get back to your headlines.' The line went dead.

McEvoy, frustrated at the call and the slow pace of the tractor in front of him, swung out from behind the trailer. He flung the car back in, narrowly avoiding a car coming the other way. 'Jesus,' he mumbled to himself, a shiver running up his spine.

* * *

'Well?'

'They admit that Yellow Star leaked selected documents to the newspapers last night,' John Joyce replied, watching McEvoy approach the bed and breakfast.

'For God's sake! What the hell were they playing at?'

'They say it was in the public's interest to know the truth about Albert Koch before he was buried and eulogised. They didn't want all his obituaries to simply state that he was a "great fella". They want him to be remembered for what he was – a mass murderer.'

'I guess they have a point,' McEvoy conceded reluctantly. 'Come on, I better talk to them.' He brushed past Joyce and entered the hallway, turning right into the living room.

Ewa Chojnacki and Tomas Prochazka were sitting on the same floral-patterned sofa. Ewa's oval face was set in a determined pose; Tomas appeared more sheepish, his eyes downcast behind his small, round glasses.

'I suppose you're happy with today's headlines,' McEvoy asked.

'I am neither happy nor sad,' Ewa replied defiantly. 'I wish there had been no need for it, that the Nazi state had not existed, nor killed millions of innocent people for no reason other than their supposed race.'

'I know you think you've done the right thing, but you've made our job more difficult. His family and friends are going to be a lot more reluctant to talk to us now. You should have waited until we'd caught his killer.'

'We could not let him be buried as a saint,' Ewa said. 'The funeral is tomorrow. We needed to act fast.'

'Where were you between midnight and three o'clock in the morning on Sunday?' McEvoy asked, changing tack.

'We were here,' Ewa said, her face changing to one of confusion.

'There were only two sets of guests here on Saturday night. The owners said they heard someone let themselves back in at around two in the morning. The other guests said that they did not leave their room between eleven o'clock and eight the next morning,' McEvoy lied, 'so it could have only been you.'

'We were here all night. We did not leave the room also.'

'Then who let themselves in at two o'clock in the morning?' McEvoy pressed.

'I don't know, but it was not us.'

'Are you sure?'

'I am one hundred per cent positive.'

'If we discover otherwise, you will become prime suspects in Albert Koch's murder. You will have lied to us, you will have a motive, and you won't have an alibi. That will be enough for a circumstantial prosecution.'

Ewa and Tomas shared a concerned look, but neither of them ventured an answer.

'We will be investigating further your time here. If we find you have lied to us, we will be bringing you in for more questioning. In the meantime, you are not to pass any more information concerning Albert Koch's past to the media. Do you understand?'

'You think we killed Albert Koch?' Tomas asked quietly.

'I think I can't rule it out.'

'But that is stupid,' Ewa said contemptuously. 'We were seeking justice not revenge.'

'You were seeking revenge as well,' McEvoy said evenly. 'You wanted to destroy Koch's carefully constructed world.

Perhaps not by killing him, but maybe that happened by accident? You were searching his house looking for evidence and you disturbed him. A fight broke out and Albert Koch somehow ended up dead.'

'We did not break into his house,' Ewa said angrily. 'We had all the evidence we needed. And we definitely did not kill him! We were here all Saturday night.'

'We'll see,' McEvoy said, heading for the door before the couple could respond.

John Joyce joined him on the doorstep.

'That was a bit harsh,' Joyce observed.

'They deserved it,' McEvoy said. 'They shouldn't have given those documents to the media. What were they expecting; that we'd thank them for it? I meant what I said about putting them under the microscope. I want you to go over their story with a fine tooth comb. Any inconsistencies, any lies, any anything, get it checked out.'

* * *

He threaded the car past three uniformed gardai wearing luminous yellow jackets and five journalists wrapped in bulky coats, scarves and hats, and drove up past Marion D'Arcy's house to the stables, parking next to an old water trough.

He found Charles Koch cleaning out a stall. Despite the chill air he was dressed in only a check shirt, dirty jeans, and a pair of green wellington boots.

McEvoy knocked on the stable door. Koch glanced up, then went back to work, dumping a fork full of manure into a wheelbarrow.

'Do you have a minute?' McEvoy asked.

'Have you seen the papers?' Koch asked without stopping his work.

'It's nothing to do with us,' McEvoy said, slipping into the stable. 'Your father made many enemies; his past seems to have finally caught up with him.'

'Do you believe those lies?' Koch stood up straight, his posture challenging McEvoy.

'The evidence seems to point that way.'

'It's all lies! He came here to join his brother; to escape the carnage in Europe. He was a chemist for I.G. Farben in Austria. He didn't kill anyone.'

'That's not what the archive documents show.'

'Then they're wrong! And you've no right to be investigating his past. Your job is to catch his killer. Nothing else.'

'And what if his past is responsible for his death? Everything to do with your father's death seems to point to his past. And my job is to investigate anything that I think matters.'

Koch snorted derision and turned his attention back to the soiled straw.

'I wanted to talk to you about Saturday night.'

Koch stayed silent, dumping another load into the wheelbarrow.

'You told me that you stayed the night in your holiday cottage near Oldcastle.'

Koch continued to ignore McEvoy.

'According to Patricia Kinneally you spent the night with her in Kells.'

Koch paused momentarily, then continued his work.

'Why did you lie to us?'

'I didn't kill my father and there was no need to involve Patricia.'

'You're ashamed of your relationship?'

'Not in the least.' He placed the fork head on the ground and leant on the handle. 'There was simply no need to involve her.'

'No need to involve her? This isn't an optional exercise! We're talking about a murder inquiry. For all I know she's trying to provide you with a false alibi.'

'She's doing what?'

'You said you were in Oldcastle. Now you say you were in Kells. All of sudden you have a new alibi, this one with a witness.'

212

'Are you accusing me of killing my father?'

'No, I'm accusing you of lying. It makes me wonder what else you've lied about.'

'I haven't lied about anything!'

'You've just admitted to lying about where you were on Saturday night!'

Koch started to drag a fresh forkful of manure and straw together.

There was the sound of running feet across the stable yard. Francis Koch burst into the stable.

'Have you seen this?' he said agitatedly, holding up a small sheaf of paper, unaware that McEvoy was lurking in the shadows.

'Seen what?' Charles Koch said testily.

'The old man's will! It arrived in the post this morning.'

'His will?' Charles Koch said confused.

'He... he... we got practically nothing!' Francis said angrily, holding the pages out to his father.

Charles took the sheaf and started to read, forgetting that McEvoy was watching.

'You get two per cent,' Francis continued. 'Emily, Carl and myself get one per cent each. Only it's held in trust for us all. I've spoken to Mark, he got a copy as well. Emily's at work, Carl has his phone turned off. Did Marion get a copy?'

McEvoy stepped forward.

'What the hell are you doing here?' Francis snapped, spooked.

'Asking your father some questions. Can I see that?' he asked, holding out his hand.

Charles Koch ignored him, folding a sheet of paper over and scanning down the next page. He turned to the last page.

'Professor Koch?'

Charles looked up, his eyes dead. He passed the three sheets to McEvoy who cast his gaze over the typed pages.

LAST WILL AND TESTAMENT: DR ALBERT KOCH

This is the last will and testament of me Albert Koch of The White Gallows, Ballyglass, County Meath made this date, ----- ----------------, 20------. I hereby revoke all former Wills made by me and declare this to be my last Will.

I appoint Henry Collier, Esq., to be the sole executor of this my Will.

I devise and bequeath all my estate, composed of monies, shares, bonds, gilts, companies, property and other investments, whatsoever and wheresoever to the Ostara Trust. Full details of the newly formed Ostara Trust can be found in Appendix 1.

The Ostara Trust will consist, in the first instance, of the following shareholders:

Ostara Industries, 50 per cent
Marion D'Arcy (daughter) 2 per cent
Mark D'Arcy (grandson) 1 per cent
Jane D'Arcy (granddaughter) 1 per cent
Charles Koch (son) 2 per cent
Francis Koch (grandson) 1 per cent
Emily Koch (granddaughter) 1 per cent
Carl Koch (grandson) 1 per cent
Dr Gerald Astell (doctor) 0.25 per cent
Henry Collier (solicitor) 0.25 per cent
Stefan Freel (worker) 0.25 per cent
Roza Ptaszek (housekeeper) 0.25 per cent
Heidelberg University, 3 per cent (to establish an Ostara Trust endowed Chair of Chemistry, plus scholarships and visiting fellowships – see Appendix 2).
Amnesty International, 3 per cent
Yellow Star, 3 per cent
Conference on Jewish Material Claims Against Germany, 3 per cent
Hazon Yeshaya, 3 per cent
Simon Wisenthal Center, 3 per cent
Holocaust Memorial Day Trust, 3 per cent
Holocaust Educational Trust, 3 per cent
Irish Red Cross, 3 per cent

Ten Irish charities – 1 per cent each. Irish registered charities can apply to be a shareholder in Ostara Trust for a five-year period. Ten charities will be drawn randomly from those applications. See Appendix 3 for full details.

White Gallows Foundation, 3 per cent. The White Gallows house and grounds are to be converted into a centre for peace and reconciliation administered by The White Gallows Foundation. See Appendix 4 for full details.

Each shareholder will receive a yearly dividend paid in March based on the profit growth of Ostara Industries. Ostara Industries, the White Gallows Foundation, and the ten Irish charities cannot sell their shares. The remaining shareholders can sell no more than 20 per cent of their shares in any one year and other shareholders must be given first preference for purchase. The share price is dependent on the overall value of the portfolio at the time of sale as calculated by Ostara Trust's accountants. If any named party does not wish to be a shareholder in the Trust then their share shall be redistributed evenly amongst the ten Irish charity shareholders. See Appendix 5 for full details on accounting, dividends, and share price calculations.

As witness my hand the day the year first above written.
Signed:

Signed by the said testator in the presence of us, who at his request and in his presence have subscribed our names as witnesses:

Signed and address:
Frank Koch, Kilgreen, Athboy, County Meath

Signed and address:
Maurice Coakley, Laragh, Athboy, County Meath

McEvoy noted that there were no signatures on the final page, nor were there any attached appendices. Either this was a draft of a will that was never witnessed, or it was a copy of the preliminary pages of Koch's will freshly run off a laser printer. Either way he urgently needed to talk to Henry Collier to verify its authenticity. If this was Albert Koch's current will then he was as good as admitting that he'd been a Nazi war criminal. And Dr Gerald Astell had good reason to pronounce Koch's death by natural causes – a nice multi-million euro gift.

He looked up at Charles and Francis Koch. Assuming that Ostara Industries was worth one and a half billion euros, with a three per cent stake between them they were now worth approximately forty-five million euro, although only twenty per cent of that value could be accessed in any one year plus dividends, not that they seemed very happy about it.

'Now what do you think about your father's past?' McEvoy asked. 'He's giving away a good chunk of his estate to Jewish holocaust organisations.'

'This isn't my father's will,' Charles Koch said uncertainly. 'It's a hoax.'

'There's only one way to find out,' McEvoy replied. 'I'm taking this as evidence.' He headed out of the stable and started to cross the yard to his car.

Francis Koch chased after him. 'You… you can't do that!'

'Do what?'

'Take that will. I… we need it.'

'I'll give you a receipt if you want one, but I'm taking it,' McEvoy said firmly, opening his car door. 'Your grandfather was killed for something hidden in his house. Perhaps it was this?'

* * *

Generally murder cases are either solved within the first couple of days or they drag out over weeks and months. In the latter case the inquiry would slowly lumber on, either going nowhere as with the Lithuanian stabbing, or slowly and patiently starting to come together as with Kylie O'Neill. In Koch's case, the investigation was careening along, McEvoy chasing after fresh information and leads. Unfortunately, most of it was opening up new angles and potentials rather than narrowing things down, and it mostly concerned Koch's past. They were slowly uncovering who Albert Koch was, but so far this had revealed few clues as to who his killer might be.

His mobile phone rang in its holder. He jabbed at it. 'Yes?'

'Do you have a minute?' Johnny Cronin asked.

'Not really. What's the score?' McEvoy asked.

'I think we might have a bite. I've just had a phone call from a guy who saw my story in the paper and thinks he can help me out with my cash flow problems.'

'You think he's your man?'

'I think it's a strong possibility. He said if I can get hold of some cash he had a sure-fire way to double my money. He wants to meet me tomorrow morning.'

'He's either ultra confident or pretty stupid,' McEvoy observed. 'He's no idea who the hell you are, but he knows his con is pretty well known at this stage.'

'I'd say he's the confident type – friendly and conciliatory; a bit of a Jack the Lad. He knows that people are stupid and greedy. It was a long way into the conversation before he let the offer of help dangle. I said I'd think about it and get back to him this afternoon.'

'I can't do anything today or tomorrow, Johnny. I'm up to my eyes here and it's Maggie's commemoration tomorrow. I've got to take the day off. Just go ahead and meet him and set up an exchange for Saturday morning. Make sure you get some decent surveillance and see if you can find out who the hell he is.'

'Right, okay. How do you want to do Saturday morning?'

'I'll leave that to you, okay? Just keep it simple. We'll let the exchange happen, then arrest him.'

'No bother. I'll let you get back to your Nazi war criminal.'

'Feckin' papers,' McEvoy muttered. 'I'll talk to you tomorrow afternoon.'

'I thought you were off tomorrow?'

'I am. But a phone call will help break things up. If I spend all day thinking about… well, y'know. Just call, okay?' McEvoy ended the call.

Tomorrow was going to be a long day; a stressful day. Perhaps he could get away in the afternoon and attend Albert Koch's funeral. They'd have to arrange something. The press were going to be all over it, and no doubt anti-Nazi groups, and god knows who else. It would need a big operation. Galligan could look after it, but he didn't trust him to do a good job. John Joyce was competent, but if anything went wrong there would be questions about why a detective sergeant was in charge of such an event. It really needed his hand.

* * *

Henry Collier's secretary had directed McEvoy to The Darley Lodge Hotel on Athboy's main street, where Collier had hidden himself away to avoid prying journalists and curious, named beneficiaries of Koch's estate.

He'd found Collier in the hotel's bar, skulking behind a wide pillar decorated with a large mural of a Celtic serpent. In front of him was a pile of newspapers, the top one open, a half-finished cheese and ham toasted sandwich, and a near empty pint of Guinness. He was wearing the same green tweed suit and his grey hair had fallen off his bald spot and was hanging down over his ear.

Collier looked up with suspicious eyes, automatically tugging the hair back into place. 'Oh, it's you,' he said, relief in his voice. 'You wouldn't believe the morning I've had. I had to get out of the office.'

'So your secretary said. I don't think she's enjoying holding the fort very much.'

'That's what I pay her for,' Collier said without compassion. 'She should be glad she doesn't actually have to deal with them.'

'I'm not sure that's how she'd see it,' McEvoy said, feeling compelled to defend the surly, middle-aged woman who'd reluctantly pointed him towards the hotel. 'At the moment she's the only one having to deal with them.'

'Parasites.'

'The papers or the beneficiaries?'

'Both! Can you believe they've printed this rubbish?' Collier asked, jabbing at the papers. 'I knew Albert Koch for over forty years. He could be a hardnosed bastard when he wanted to be, but there's no way he took part in any medical experiments. He was a family man.'

'Nobody's saying he wasn't a family man, but the evidence doesn't look good. The papers wouldn't print this stuff if they didn't think it was true.'

'Ach!' Collier exclaimed dismissively. 'They'd print any old shite if they thought it would sell a few more papers. It's just a smear campaign. It's easy to falsify some documents and slip them into the archives. He was no more a war criminal than I was.'

'I'm not going to argue with you, but I think his lawyers are going to have their work cut out for them. And that's probably only the tip of the iceberg. Albert Koch seems to have a pretty shady past.'

'As I said, it's just a smear campaign,' Collier said indolently. 'His family's lawyers will make mincemeat of this lot.' He tapped the papers again.

'And what about the will?'

'What about it?'

McEvoy placed the will he'd taken from Francis Koch on the table. 'Is this his last will and testament?'

'I'm not at liberty to discuss his private matters until his killer is caught.'

'I'm not asking you to discuss them. I'm asking you to say whether this is his last will and testament. A simple yes or no. I can get a search warrant if you want. It might take me a few hours but I will get one.'

'Where did you get this?' Collier asked, deflecting McEvoy's question as he reluctantly picked up the papers and scanned the front page.

'Francis Koch. Apparently it's been sent to all the family members.'

'To everyone listed as a beneficiary,' Collier corrected. 'The phone hasn't stopped ringing. Parasites,' he repeated.

'And?' McEvoy prompted.

'Yes, it's the last version before he died. Or at least it looks like it.'

'And you still think he's innocent despite listing half-a-dozen Jewish war charities?'

'He was a good man, Superintendent. You might not believe that, but he was.'

'And your judgement isn't clouded by the huge fee you'll extract for being the executor or the fact that you yourself are a beneficiary?'

'My judgement's fine. You didn't know the man. I don't believe he did the things the press are saying he did. Yes, he was German, and yes, he fought in the war, and yes, he might have felt guilty about Germany carrying out the holocaust, but that doesn't mean he was an active participant. And I think they are going to find it difficult to prove that he was.' He jabbed at the papers again.

'I take it that you didn't send out the will?'

'No. I want his killer caught first so they can't benefit if they are a named beneficiary.'

'So who did send it out? Who'd have access to his will?'

'Myself and my secretary. Frank Koch and Maurice Coakley were witnesses, but they didn't read it, or get copies, they just signed it.'

'No one else?'

'No.'

'And did you type it up or did he draft it?'

'He emailed it to me. I just tweaked it.'

'He emailed it to you?'

'Yes. We did most of our correspondence via email. He adapted with the times; ran his business from home using a laptop. Without it and Stefan Freel he wouldn't have been able to carry on building and running his business empire. He could get online and monitor share prices, the property market, financial news, do whatever he needed.'

'So the draft of his will was on his laptop?' McEvoy asked, wondering where Koch's computer presently was.

'I suppose so, yes.'

'And I don't suppose you know where it is, do you?'

'It should have been in his house. In his study. It wasn't?' Collier asked, concern in his voice.

'I need to get that checked.' McEvoy had asked for the whole house to be checked for missing items. No one had mentioned a laptop. He needed to talk to George Carter. 'I'm sure it's still there,' he said, wondering if they did have it and whether anyone had had the foresight to turn the thing on and check what was on it. If they didn't have it, then whoever did had probably killed Albert Koch.

'Who had access to Koch's laptop?' he asked.

'I've no idea. Stefan Freel, Roza his housekeeper, Marion, Charles, anyone visiting the house, I don't know.'

'Jesus. Tell me about Ostara Trust,' he said, torn between finishing the discussion and ringing George Carter.

'He wanted to keep the whole group together. By putting everything inside a trust he could portion the value of the assets to individuals and groups while making sure Ostara was not divided up and sold off.'

'And who runs the Trust?'

'He made Stefan Freel the chief executive officer and James Kinneally chairman of the shareholders' board for the first five years. After that there's a procedure for appointment. It's all set out in the appendices. He wanted people he could trust to do right by Ostara Industries.'

'And what about his family?'

'What about them?'

'He gave hardly anything to them and they don't inherit Ostara outright or even run the trust.'

'I wouldn't say nine per cent of one-and-a-half billion euros is hardly anything and he didn't think they were capable of running Ostara's diverse interests. The man was a pragmatist and he wanted his legacy to continue. He did what he thought was best.'

'I don't think he needs to worry about his legacy. Everyone on the planet will know all about him shortly.'

* * *

Albert Koch's laptop had been found in the top desk drawer on Sunday and taken back to the Garda Technical Unit's lab for analysis. It had sat there untouched for the past four days. And it would probably sit there untouched for another couple more because there was no one available to boot the thing up and have a good poke around. Which meant whoever printed off Koch's will had a copy of their own. As Henry Collier had noted, that could be any one of the half-dozen people who had access to his office.

The question for now was whether the person who sent the will was also the killer? Did they actually find what they were looking for on Saturday night and now they were sharing that information? Or was it someone trying to flush the killer out into the open? Or someone playing a different game? Perhaps they were letting the world know the truth about Koch's crimes by revealing who his beneficiaries were? Perhaps they were worried that the beneficiaries would be changed after the fact to hide his criminal past?

As far as McEvoy knew, everyone who had access to the computer had benefited in some way from the will – Koch's family received modest percentage stakes, Roza ended up with a small fortune given her modest background, Stefan Freel had become the CEO of a multi-billion trust fund, and holocaust groups and charities gained access to huge finances. Of course, the person searching the house might not have been a beneficiary at all.

McEvoy tried to push the thoughts from his mind and called Colin Vickers in Trim.

'Yeah?' the boredom was evident in Vicker's voice.

'It's Colm McEvoy, any developments?'

'Nothing.'

'Is it going to be worth my time to drive over there?'

'Probably not,' Vickers said without enthusiasm. 'It's up to you.'

'I'm up to my neck here. Just keep things ticking along, okay? If there's any developments give me a ring.'

'Yeah, no bother.'

McEvoy ended the call. Vickers and the rest of the Trim team had already given up hope. Without Whelan to drive the investigation along, the whole case had ground to a halt. Vickers' idea of keeping things ticking along was probably gossiping with the local guards and slowly pushing pieces of paper around while waiting for the instruction to wind things up and to file under 'Unsolved'. He exited the hotel and headed back to his car.

* * *

Cathal Galligan was lying in wait just inside the clubhouse. He practically exploded with rage before the doors had closed. 'What the fuck's going on, McEvoy! First, I'm bypassed on the media front, now you're organising the Garda arrangements for Albert Koch's funeral. The local district is responsible for local policing. As of now, any arrangements for the funeral will be organised through my office.'

McEvoy pulled to a halt, immediately bristling at Galligan's ambush. 'Let's get one thing straight. You've been doing the media because I have better things to be doing. Only you've proven to be a complete pain in the arse. And you won't be organising the funeral arrangements. This is a murder investigation and NBCI is in charge. The funeral is part of that investigation. We'll be relying on your guards to help out, but if we tell you to stay away, you stay away.'

'Like fuck we will! You're a fuckin' gombeen, McEvoy!' Galligan ranted. 'You hear me? You think you're the big fuckin' shot coming out here lording it over us, telling us what to do, but you're wrong. This is my patch and you'll fuckin' respect me and you'll recognise our jurisdiction.'

'I hate to tell you this,' McEvoy replied, trying to suppress his anger, 'but you're clearly delusional. I'm in charge of this investigation. End. Of. Story. And if you don't like it, go and cry to your assistant commissioner or whoever the hell you've been brown-nosing.' He brushed past Galligan and headed for the incident room.

'You've picked the wrong fight,' Galligan snapped at McEvoy's back. 'You're a dead man walking.'

McEvoy ignored him and exited the passageway.

Everyone in the incident room watched him walk over to Kelly Stringer.

'I guess you all heard that?' he asked, his face flushed red.

'Bits of it,' Stringer said, smirking. She was dressed in a two-piece grey suit, over a pale yellow shirt, a small gold cross lying just below her neckline. Her hair was twisted into a knot at the back of her head, but the alluring perfume remained. 'I take it you were building bridges with the locals.'

'Torching them more like. The guy's an eejit. Does he really think we're going to organise ourselves around them?'

'He's jealous and he feels threatened by you.' Stringer paused. 'Plus he's a grade one asshole.' Her smile lit up her face.

'An asshole that's on the warpath. Two to one on, Bishop will be on the phone within the next hour. So, what's the score?' he said, trying to move the conversation along.

'I had Kevin Townsend do a bit more digging in the newspaper archives. He found this.' She opened a brown file and passed a grainy imagine to McEvoy.

'This is a photo of SS Obersturmbannführer Otto Skorzeny,' she continued reading from some notes, 'apparently one of the most famous soldiers in the German army during the Second World War.'

The photo showed a tall, broad, handsome man with dark short hair swept back from his forehead, a scar pucking his cheek. He was wearing a well-tailored dark suit and was shaking hands with a smiling, younger man. The pair was circled by a group of other men.

'He led a crack SS division. Rescued Mussolini in September 1943 from an Italian mountain top. He was captured in Austria at the end of the war and was accused of war crimes. He was cleared and in 1949, while waiting to be denazified, he escaped a holding camp and made his way to Argentina. It was rumoured that he was a senior figure in forming and controlling the escape routes for his former colleagues across the Atlantic. He turned up in Spain not long after and became a salesman for an engineering company. By the mid-1950s he was brokering engineering contracts across Europe for recovering German companies, travelling on what was called a Nansen passport – a kind of travel document for stateless people. This photo was taken in Portmarnock in 1957.'

'Is that…' McEvoy said, trailing off, his brow furrowing.

'Charles Haughey,' Stringer confirmed, naming the future leader of the country. 'And in the background?'

McEvoy's eyes traced the crowd, stopping on the serious face of Albert Koch. 'This was taken in 1957?'

'In Portmarnock,' Stringer repeated. 'Skorzeny is rumoured to have spent the night at Koch's house. He gave an interview to the *Evening Press*. He was in Ireland for a week. In June 1959 he purchased Martinstown House in Kildare and 165 acres of land, and in September 1959 he applied for permanent residency which he never received. He continued to visit Ireland and stay in the house until 1969.'

'He and Koch were friends?'

'It's possible. Skorzeny was surrounded by rumours after the war. His name is linked to several different international political scandals. He remained an unrepentant Nazi and open admirer of Hitler until his death in 1975.'

'Jesus,' McEvoy muttered. 'There was a circle of Nazi war criminals living in Ireland after the war?'

'I'm not sure about a circle, but there were at least two,' Stringer replied. 'And they had friends in high places.'

'Two was more than enough. What the hell was Haughey doing meeting Skorzeny?'

'Your guess is as good as mine, but Skorzeny was the guest of honour. Flew in in a helicopter.'

'Jesus. Tell Townsend to keep searching; see what else he can unearth. How are you getting on with the funeral arrangements?' McEvoy asked, redirecting the conversation, his gaze still fixed on the photo.

'The ceremony and burial is going to take place in Ballyglass. Church of Ireland. It's only a wee place, built to serve the Big House and family. It can seat less than one hundred and fifty. The site itself is less than an acre. They're expecting several hundred to turn up, though they think some of the VIPs will duck out now, given the papers this morning – ministers, a couple of TDs. No one wants to be associated with a war criminal. The flip side is that the papers will bring others out. It could be bedlam.'

'Have you spoken to Traffic?'

'They'll have a few teams out. The rest of it will need to be looked after by locals. We'll have a full team at the church. It's mostly going to be crowd control. Entry to the church is strictly by invitation. We're not invited.'

'I think you'll find we are. I want at least you and John Joyce in there. I'll want a full transcript of the ceremony and a detailed report on who was doing what. See if you can get in there tonight and install a couple of discrete cameras. Get one at the front pointing back at the congregation.'

'I'll see what I can do. I'll talk to George Carter.'

'And see if you can get some round the church grounds and on the approaches. The killer might decide to watch things at a distance or mingle in the crowd. What're the arrangements with the press?'

'Strictly no press in the church grounds or church. The family needed persuading to let us near the place. I ended up telling them that if we weren't then we couldn't let the funeral continue due to health and safety concerns.'

'How the hell do they think they'd keep the press away if we aren't there?' McEvoy asked, annoyed at the family's stance.

'Private security drafted in from Ostara's various plants and offices and coordinated by a specialised service.'

'Great. Just what we need. You've spoken to them?'

'Yeah, it's TM Security, Terry Macken's outfit,' Stringer said, referring to a company set up by a retired garda inspector. 'They're well used to doing rock concerts and open air events. They'll do whatever we want.'

'Well, that's something, I guess. I'll talk to Terry later. It won't stop the press getting photos in any case; they'll all have telephoto lens.'

'Just as well. If any of them came close to Marion D'Arcy she'd claw their eyes out.'

'She's been onto you?' McEvoy said, surprised.

'No. But the funeral director says, and I quote, "she's a fucking nightmare to deal with". She's been making his life hell all week.'

'Poor bastard,' McEvoy sympathised.

* * *

He was looking at a map of Ballyglass church and the area surrounding it, tracing his finger along the approach roads. Tomorrow would be chaos. The church was on a narrow lane with nowhere for more than a handful of vehicles to park. They'd have to persuade Martin O'Coffey to allow one of his fields that bordered the churchyard to be used as a temporary car park. Given the recent weather it was likely to quickly turn into a mud bath. If the guests didn't bring wellington boots their finest shoes and clothes would be ruined.

He answered his mobile phone distractedly, 'McEvoy.'

'Colm?' a female voice asked uncertainly.

'What?' McEvoy asked, turning his attention to the voice. 'Sorry, who is this?'

'Ciara,' Maggie's sister said. 'Are you okay to talk?'

'Yeah, yeah, you work away,' McEvoy said contritely, inwardly cursing himself. 'Look, I'm sorry I haven't got round to returning your call. I've been up to my neck in stuff.'

'It's okay, Caroline told me you're heading up the Albert Koch case. It seems he wasn't what he appeared to be?'

'And another couple of cases,' McEvoy said, avoiding any discussion on Koch's past. 'Everything's okay for tomorrow?' he asked, feeling guilty for his lack of help in the preparations.

'That's what I was going to ask you? I've got most things in hand. Have you had chance to draft your eulogy?'

'I've made a few notes. I'll work on them tonight.' It sounded as lame as it was.

'And you've got a clean shirt and suit?'

'I'm sure there's something in the wardrobe. I'll be fine. Don't worry, I won't make a show of myself. All my suits now fit me,' he said. After Maggie's death he'd lost a couple of stone in weight so that his clothes hung off him like a child dressing up in his father's suit. It wasn't until after the Raven case that he finally got round to buying a new wardrobe.

'And your house is ready for your parents?'

'Shit!' He'd completely forgotten about his parents coming to stay with him for the weekend. 'Look, I'll …'

'It's okay, Colm,' Ciara interrupted. 'Caroline's said she'll take care of them. They'll be staying with her tonight. Gerry, Liam, and Mary are staying in the Crowne Plaza, along with my parents,' she said, referring to McEvoy's brothers and sister. Both brothers were flying in from London with their wives and kids. Mary would be travelling up from Cork with her husband and two kids. Orla, his other sister, was not making the trip home from Toronto. She normally came only once a year, usually at Easter when she'd bring over her Canadian husband and their three kids.

'Kenny and Joe are both staying with friends,' Jennifer continued, referring to Maggie's brothers.

'Look, don't worry, Ciara, I'll be there and I'll be prepared. I'll even make sure I iron the shirt.'

'Did you order the flowers for the grave?' Ciara asked, doubt in her voice.

'Oh sh… Look, I'll get on it now. I'll have it sorted in a few minutes time. White lilies right?'

'I'll deal with it,' Ciara said firmly. 'You've enough to be worrying about. You're doing too much, Colm. You need some time for yourself.'

'Yeah, I know, but unless people stop killing each other, there's not a lot I can do. Is there anything else?'

'No, no, that's it. I just wanted to check in with you; make sure you're ready.'

'I'll never be ready, but I'll be there, don't worry. I'll try and ring you later, okay?'

'Yeah, okay. Take care of yourself, Colm.' She ended the call.

McEvoy clasped his temples between forefinger and thumb and massaged his forehead. He knew he'd let Ciara down, that he wasn't pulling his weight in organising Maggie's commemoration, but the reality was that he couldn't face into it. He hadn't made any notes for the eulogy and he had no idea what he was going to say. For some reason he thought he might wing it – speak from the heart on the spur of the moment – but on reflection that probably wasn't such a good idea. But writing a eulogy would need him to focus all his thoughts on Maggie and that always tore him apart.

'Are you okay?' Kelly Stringer asked.

McEvoy dropped his hand from his face. 'Yeah, yeah, I'm fine; just trying to deal with tomorrow.'

'You're trying to organise that as well?' Stringer said incredulously. 'Look, if you need a hand with anything…'

'No, no, you're fine,' McEvoy interrupted. 'Maggie's sister, Ciara, has everything in hand. I'm just not looking forward to it very much. I'd sooner just spend the day with Gemma than have to face all the family and friends, all of them commiserating with me.'

Stringer nodded her head not sure what to say. Eventually she said, 'Well, if you need me to help in any way, just give me a call, okay?'

'Yeah, thanks, Kelly,' he said, realising he was staring straight into her eyes. He looked away embarrassed, knowing that they had just shared some kind of a moment. 'Right, well, I better get on,' he said awkwardly, confused by his swirling emotions.

* * *

'Why the hell am I having to clear up after you?' Bishop snapped, though tiredness was evident in his voice.

'Galligan,' McEvoy stated evenly.

'The stupid bollix decided to ring me direct to ask that you be removed from the case and he be put in charge. Lucky for you he proved that he's got shit for brains. I've told him he can either do as he's told or I'll make his life fuckin' hell. My guess is he's so far up his own arse he'll try another avenue in; his divisional chief super or an assistant commissioner. Just leave him to me, okay? You've already done enough damage; last thing I need is for you to fuck things up even further. If he comes to see you, you refer him back to me. And don't let him anywhere near the press, you hear, or Koch's funeral. The eejit's a complete fuckin' liability.'

'I'll talk to Barry Traynor.'

'You do that. I'm fed up with watching your back, Colm. I don't know what you're doing, but you've got to stop pissing off the locals.'

'It's not my fault that they're self-centred eejits.'

'Well, you need to work on your eejit handling skills then. What are you doing about Koch's funeral?'

'Don't worry, everything's in hand. The press will be kept well away and the guests vetted before they can pass through an outer security cordon. We're liaising with Traffic, the locals, and a private security firm that Marion D'Arcy's organised.'

'It's complete madness that it's going ahead in the first place,' Bishop moaned. 'What the hell were you thinking about?'

'Once Elaine Jones said she was releasing the body there wasn't much I could do. It was in the family's hands.'

'You could have delayed the release. Elaine knows the score.'

'I didn't know the papers were going to go crazy. It'll be fine. We've been working on it all afternoon.'

'Which means you haven't been working on catching the killer,' Bishop snapped. 'And while we're talking about the press, I want you to take over from Galligan.'

'I don't have time to prepare for press conferences,' McEvoy said, a sinking feeling opening in his stomach. He'd been personally savaged by the media in The Raven case and was still bitter from the whole experience. At least Bishop had defended McEvoy's position, rather than conceding any ground to Galligan. 'Perhaps John Joyce could do it?' he suggested trying not to sound desperate.

'It has to be Inspector or Superintendent level,' Bishop insisted. 'This is a high profile case, not a missing cat. The public expect a senior officer to be talking to them.'

'How about Johnny Cronin?' McEvoy said grasping at straws. 'I'm not available tomorrow, remember?'

'Cronin's up to his neck with the scamming case, isn't he? Maybe it's best that you didn't do it. We want them to focus on the case, not the investigating officer. Perhaps Joyce wouldn't be a bad choice? Get them to use his doctor title – Dr John Joyce, Detective Sergeant, NBCI. That'll add some gravitas to it all; let them know that we're using an intellectual heavyweight on the case,' he said sarcastically.

'I'll tell him the good news,' McEvoy replied evenly, managing to keep his relief from his voice.

'You never know, the job might suit him,' Bishop said. He paused before continuing. 'Keep out of further trouble, Colm. I can't keep watching your back. I have enough to be doing trying to deal with Charlie Clarke's gang. We raided two houses this morning – found thirty kilos of cocaine. That's going to hurt his pocket. I'm going to keep targeting his operations until he gives up the bastards that bombed Hannah Fallon. He's either going to cooperate or he's going out of business. Don't mess up, okay?' Bishop ended the call.

McEvoy reflected that Bishop's strategy was what the gardai should be doing all the time – putting high pressure on the criminal gangs, forcing them into errors, disrupting their operations, shutting them down, and sending them to prison. It shouldn't just be a pressure tactic when particular results were required.

* * *

Martin O'Coffey had been too ill to talk to Kelly Stringer, bedridden with flu, but after a bit of persuading his grandson Peter had reluctantly agreed to let the field next to the church be used as a car park for a small fee.

McEvoy had found time to talk to Terry Macken. He'd been his usual self, full of energy and wisecracks. Whatever McEvoy wanted he was willing to accommodate as long as he still got paid the same amount and it involved no extra work. He would have forty security staff working the church. Every person attending would have their bags checked for cameras and other recording devices; these would be confiscated and held for collection until people left. There would be a one mile exclusion zone for the media.

Macken had been provided by Marion D'Arcy and Ostara Industries with a list of people who could enter the church itself. McEvoy had agreed that TM Security would still operate the outer and inner security, as long as his guards could mix amongst them and Stringer, Joyce and McManus were admitted to the church. If there was any major incident, the guards would step in and take charge. He was apprehensive about missing the event, but then maybe he would be able to sneak away from Maggie's commemoration by early afternoon. God knows he would need a break by then from the memories and platitudes.

He stood up from the table and stretched his back. Planning the policing for Albert Koch's funeral had taken up most of the afternoon. He was starting to feel that most things were now under control. Terry Macken knew what he was doing and Stringer and Joyce were competent enough.

He glanced at his watch. It was just coming up to five fifteen. He wondered how Joyce would get on with the press conference; it was due to start at the half hour. Enough time for the hacks to do a quick edit and summary for the six o'clock news. He'd tried explaining to him what it would be like now the international press were involved, but it was only through experiencing the full-on glare and the awkward and difficult questions that he'd truly know. Nothing ever really prepared you for that. He'd been through the wringer with the Raven case and had no intention of talking to a journalist again if he could help it.

His mobile phone rang. He fished it from his pocket and stared at the screen. He recognised the caller number but couldn't place it. He decided to risk it.

'McEvoy.'

'It's George Carter. You better come out to Koch's farm.'

'You've found the secret compartment?'

'We've found Hitler's fuckin' bunker! You won't believe the place. Any doubts you had about this guy being a war criminal, you can forget them. He was a bona fide Nazi fanatic. The place is like a fuckin' museum.'

'I'll be there in five minutes,' McEvoy said, bursting out of the doors into the chill air, the sky having already faded to darkness.

* * *

He'd been directed across the farmyard and out the far side to the Gallow's tree. There he was met by Tom McManus and three guards wearing large, luminous jackets, their caps pulled down tight to try and keep out the frigid air. The men were huddled together, shifting from foot to foot, their breath steaming.

'You're not going to believe this place,' McManus said directing McEvoy toward the derelict shed situated between the oak tree and the outbuildings surrounding the yard.

As they approached, McManus' torch revealed the faintest of paths. He pulled back some rusted corrugated iron and motioned McEvoy forward. It was almost pitch black inside, the pale night of the sky barely penetrating the glassless window. McManus swung his torch around the floor revealing old agricultural equipment and feed bags. There were shelves on two of the walls holding jars full of nails and old tins.

'We found this place totally by accident,' McManus continued. 'The guard searching the shed stumbled over some of the crap on the floor and grabbed at the shelf, grasping hold of this hook.' McManus took hold of the slim brass hook and tugged it downwards. He pointed his torch at the far end of the shed.

At first nothing happened, then four square feet of the floor dropped six inches and slid under the remaining dirty concrete to reveal a lighted set of stairs.

'After you,' McManus said.

McEvoy shuffled forward and descended the concrete steps. As he neared the bottom a largish room, perhaps ten feet high, forty feet in length and twenty feet wide, came into view. The wall down the left-hand side consisted of floor-to-ceiling bookcases, all overfilled with books and spiral-bound manuscripts. At their base were cardboard boxes filled with other volumes. The right-hand wall half consisted of filing cabinets, above which were framed photos, and half of floor-to-ceiling wardrobes. On the far wall, tight into the left corner was a metal ladder rising to the ceiling, to its right was a small kitchen – a

234

work surface, sink, cooker, fridge and presses. The space in the centre of the room was taken up by three, old leather-inlaid desks, piled high with books and papers, two, old office chairs, and stacked cardboard boxes leaving very little of the concrete floor visible.

'Welcome to Hitler's bunker,' George Carter repeated as a greeting.

McEvoy reached the basement floor and looked right at Carter who was sitting on the edge of the bottom part of a bunk bed. Beside him the top drawer of a bedside locker was pulled open.

'He must have just about every book ever published on the second world war in here,' Carter continued. 'You should check out the photos – Albert Koch in his finest hours. The wardrobes are full of uniforms – Wehrmacht, Luftwaffe, Navy, SS, you name it – flags, trays of military badges and other mementos.'

'Jesus,' McEvoy muttered as his eyes scanned the book-cases and boxes. The air was musty, a fine layer of dust coating everything. 'He was still a Nazi?' he asked shuffling toward the framed photos.

'He was still obsessed. As to whether he was still a Nazi, I don't know. One of those bookcases is full of stuff on what he's labelled moral philosophy and holocaust studies. He's annotated a few of them in German.'

'Perhaps we should let Professor Moench have a look at them?' McEvoy suggested looking up at the photos. All of them were printed in black and white.

Half of the photos were shots of Auschwitz – the infamous iron-work slogan 'ARBEIT MACHT FREI' (Work Brings Freedom); aerial shots of row upon row of low level huts; the chimney and cooling stacks of a factory; four emaciated men staring blankly, dressed in tatty striped clothes; three, shaven-headed men standing in a chemistry lab, glass cylinders and tubes in front of them; a clutch of children standing behind a grid of barbed wire, their faces a mix of curiosity and loss; hundreds of men, women and children disgorging from cattle trucks in a railway siding, uniformed men shunting them about; five skeleton-like figures hanging in a row from a gallows, other prisoners lined up in front of them, most of them gazing fixedly at the ground, others staring defiantly ahead.

The other half were of Koch in different situations – a couple on his own, posing in various uniforms and laboratories; the rest standing with other people in uniforms or suits. McEvoy scanned the images. The only person he recognised other than Koch himself was Heinrich Himmler. Koch was walking with him across a scarred landscape, both wearing black SS uniforms with Nazi armband. Himmler had his hands clasped behind his back, his chin jutting out, looking faintly ridiculous with his round glasses and narrow moustache, tall Aryan SS officers standing in the background.

McEvoy let his gaze stray back to the photo of the gallows. At the far end stood an SS man in his characteristic black uniform. His face was half in shadow, but it certainly looked like the young Albert Koch, or Adolf Kucken as he was then known. He moved closer to it, but it was impossible to tell. Whether it was Kucken or not, there was no denying the barbarity of the scene and the fact that Koch had been party to such crimes.

'He'd be like a child in a playpen,' Carter said, referring to Moench. 'The whole lot must be worth a fortune. He must have been collecting this stuff for years. All of the books are first editions.'

'In his will his home is to become a centre for peace and reconciliation. Perhaps all of this was to be part of the resources?' McEvoy speculated. 'Perhaps he changed his mind on things. Why else would he want this to be a reconciliation centre? Why would he have left a huge chunk of fortune to Jewish holocaust organisations and charities?'

'Doesn't get round the fact that he was a participant in the mass murder of a few million people,' Carter said flatly.

'True,' McEvoy conceded. 'But perhaps he came to recognise the madness of it all; to acknowledge his guilt and seek some atonement?'

'You don't know that,' Carter said. 'And this place wasn't exactly easy to find. It could have been hidden here for years. It might never have been found. He might not have wanted it found.'

'But what about the will?'

'What about it? That could represent the guilt of the nation, not his direct guilt.'

McEvoy didn't agree, but he didn't say anything. Instead he wandered round the desks and piles, occasionally lifting up and staring at dusty sheets of paper, most of which were in German. He reached the small kitchen area and opened the presses to find them full of tins of food. He picked up a can of peas and inspected it. Its best before date was 1994.

'It's like it's a nuclear bunker or something,' he said, more to himself than Carter. 'Where does the ladder lead to?'

'Up into the housekeeper's quarters. It comes up into the press under the sink. The kitchen there is plumbed into the same system. You'd never find the entry though unless you knew what you were looking for. The floor is still six inches thick.'

'And what about air and dampness? This must be fifteen feet underground.'

'There seems to be an air pump in the far press. The pipe must come up on the outside of the housekeeper's quarters. Probably made to look like a bathroom pipe or gutter. The walls and floor must be a few feet thick and damp-proofed. There's a small bathroom in the corner at the bottom of the stairs.'

'Did he leave any message?'

'Only the annotations he's written on things. Unless it's hidden in here somewhere.' Carter cast his hands about.

'Why would someone be looking for this place?' McEvoy asked, speculating as to why Koch's house was being searched on the night he died.

'Because it reveals Koch for who he really was? My guess is all his personal papers are in here somewhere as well. I haven't been near the filing cabinets yet. It'll take someone years to sift through it all.

'But no Nazi gold?'

'Would I tell you if there was?'

'No, but you wouldn't still be here!'

McEvoy stood in front of one of the bookcases. He scanned the titles, pulling a couple of the books off the shelf, flicking through the pages. 'Right, well, I better make a couple of phone calls. Call me if you find anything. People have been told to keep their mouths shut, right?'

'There's no way you're going to keep this a secret,' Carter warned. 'This is the biggest Aladdin's cave of all time.'

* * *

There was no news from Trim and he'd decided not to travel the few miles to the town, staying at the farm to wait for Professor Moench. He'd told Vickers that he wouldn't be available the following day either and that he was in charge until the weekend. They would have a team meeting early Saturday afternoon to go through the search protocols for that evening – the pubs would be at their busiest and more likely to be populated by immigrants out partying away some of their weekly wage, assuming they had a weekly wage. If Vickers needed anything urgently in the meantime he was to contact Jim Whelan. McEvoy doubted that Whelan would be getting a call.

As he walked around under the white gallows oak he pulled up another number. His mobile phone had seemingly become an integral part of the side of his face in the last few years. Heaven knew how his job had been done prior to its invention. It must have been a logistical nightmare. And he didn't even want to consider how much damage was being done to his brain, constantly being fried by microwaves.

'Sir?' John Joyce said.

'Well?' McEvoy asked, kicking at wet leaves.

'Bloody terrifying,' Joyce said, the adrenalin still in his voice. 'I know you said it would be like the Spanish inquisition, but I didn't realise you meant it literally. There must have been over fifty of them there plus TV cameras and photographers. You'd think I was Albert Koch the way they were questioning us.'

'You have information they want,' he said flatly, 'unless you give it to them they'll quiz you like you committed the murder yourself.'

'Well, they seemed pretty pissed off at the end. I told them feck all and so did Kevin Boyle. He tried to read them the riot act but they just railroaded right over him. He's threatened to sue them all if they continued to report that Koch was a Nazi. That really set them off. What they really want is to talk to Koch's family and Ewa Chojnacki and Tomas Prochazka. I made sure they were unavailable as you suggested – moved them to a new hotel. They weren't happy with the move and they're not happy at not being able to follow up today's papers in person.'

'Tough,' McEvoy said without sympathy.

'The media are probably just going to make stuff up. They were asking all kinds of questions; fishing for anything that might make a headline.'

'As long as you didn't give them one,' McEvoy warned.

'I stuck to the script. Barry Traynor wants me to do a one-on-one with Paul Reynolds,' Joyce said, referring to the crime reporter for RTE, the Irish national broadcaster, 'in twenty minutes' time for the nine o'clock news – which is kind of exciting and scary at the same time. My wife's told half the country. Oh yeah, and they want to know if they can get exclusive access to the church tomorrow?'

'Not a chance,' McEvoy said kicking at a stick. 'The family have said strictly no press.'

'Barry seems to think it might be a good idea. Let just one in to get pictures for everyone else.'

'Well he needs to talk to Marion D'Arcy. My guess is she'll tell them to go to hell.'

'Well that's her prerogative, but if she doesn't, then they're all going to flock there and try and find a way in.'

'Probably will regardless,' McEvoy observed. 'They want to dig for dirt and I doubt they trust RTE to get it for them.'

He saw the large, looming figure of Professor Moench being led from the farmyard towards him by a uniformed guard. 'Look, I've got to go. We've discovered Koch's secret vault. It's full of Nazi memorabilia and books about the Second World War. It's unbelievable stuff. And keep that to yourself, okay?' McEvoy said, cursing inwardly for telling Joyce. 'Last thing we need is that splashed across the feckin' papers. We'll have every Nazi treasure hunter on the planet swarming round here.'

'Don't worry, I won't say a thing.'

'Good. I'll talk to you later. I want to talk you through tomorrow. It'll be a big day for you and Kelly. We've done all the plans and Terry Macken knows what he's doing, but I'm relying on you to keep the whole thing on track. Don't say anything stupid to RTE, okay.'

McEvoy ended the call. There was no getting around the fact that he was going to need to be at Koch's funeral; partly for his sanity and partly in case anything untoward happened. He couldn't take the risk of leaving a detective sergeant in charge of things, especially when he was also trying to do the job of dealing with the press. Terry Macken had operational experience but lacked authority now he'd retired. And there was no way he was leaving Galligan in charge – an incident would be guaranteed. The real question was how he was going to ease himself away from Maggie's commemoration without seeming like a callous fool.

He turned to greet Professor Moench. 'If you thought the Yellow Star files were interesting, wait 'till you see this.' He led Moench to the derelict shed and down into the bunker. 'If there's any confession in here, or any confirmation of Koch's real identity, we need to find it.'

* * *

He passed the exit to Finglas and continued along the M50, the city lit up in orange to his right, the faint silhouette of the Wicklow Mountains beyond. He'd spent another couple of hours rooting through Koch's secret bunker, but hadn't found anything that revealed very much more about Koch than he already knew.

Professor Moench had spent the time browsing the books and papers, unsure where to make a start. He was in equal parts fascinated and appalled. At times he had been very animated, becoming angry and shouting in German as he read Koch's annotations in the margins of some of the books. They seemed to confirm that Koch had been present at some of the events discussed, including the Jewish Skeleton Project. In places Koch had made corrections to some of the authors' speculation and filled out missing details. From a volume of Primo Levi's, *If This is a Man*, it was clear that Koch had known Levi, who'd been a slave chemist in Monowitz.

After an hour or so the professor announced that he needed some air and had disappeared up into the cold night. He had returned some twenty minutes later, his long, grey hair framing a determined face. All he'd said as way of explanation for his short absence was, 'This man was a fuckin' monster. A fuckin' *ungeheuer*!'

McEvoy knew that by staying on in the bunker he had become isolated from the world, his mobile phone redundant inside the thick subterranean walls. He was just killing time, putting off having to head home to see his parents and Maggie's family; to prepare for the following day.

He continued to Collinstown cemetery, parking near to the wrought-iron gates. He headed for the entrance as a plane roared in low to land at Dublin airport. He levered himself up and over the fence and headed for Maggie's grave. This was how he wanted to commemorate her, the two of them together, not in a service with tens of other people, half of them strangers.

He didn't need to articulate his thoughts in a eulogy to know how much he missed her. He remembered her every day.

He barely slept because he couldn't cope with the empty space in the bed beside him. Their daughter was the spitting image of her mother – every time he looked at her, Maggie stared back; her joy for life replicated in Gemma's personality.

He crouched down and placed his right hand on the grave, the stress of the last few days washing over him, making him feel nauseous. He whispered a greeting and started to tell her about how he was getting on.

FRIDAY

'Dad! Dad! Wake up!'

McEvoy slowly became aware of Gemma's insistent pleas, her hand shaking his shoulder. He could barely remember such a deep sleep.

'We're late!' Gemma snapped.

'Jesus.' He slowly twisted his legs off the bed and sat up. A pile of scribbled notes and an empty glass reeking of whiskey were sitting on the bedside locker. 'What's the time?'

'Ten to nine. The service starts at ten.'

'Oh, shit,' he mumbled. 'You look… pretty,' he hazarded, unsure whether twelve year olds were pretty or beautiful – at what stage girls became young adults.

Gemma was wearing a dark green, velvet dress over a black polo neck top and thick black tights, her hair held back off her face by a velvet band studded with fake diamonds.

'Colm, do you have a clean shirt?' Maggie's sister called from the landing.

'Yeah, yeah, it's all under control,' he answered back, not sure whether there was one in the wardrobe. 'I'd better have a shower,' he said to Gemma, easing himself up.

'You need to hurry,' Ciara warned, anxiety in her voice. 'We can't keep everyone waiting. There's a funeral in the church at eleven.'

'I'll put the kettle on,' Gemma said. 'Do you want toast or cereal?'

'I don't think we've got time for that, pumpkin,' he said rising to his feet and trudging to the door.

'You have to eat, Dad. Look at you, you're like a stick insect,' she chided.

'Toast then. Thanks.'

McEvoy slipped off his pyjamas and stared at himself in the mirror. Gemma was right. He had wasted away to six foot three of skin and bones. He'd lost three stone in weight since Maggie had become ill and then died. He just couldn't seem to muster much of an appetite and, as his daughter kept telling him, he got so wrapped up in his work that he forgot to sustain himself.

He showered and shaved. The piping hot water at least made him feel clean, washing the whiskey sweat away, but his head felt dull and weighty, unable to focus. He dressed hurriedly, putting on a cream shirt, a black tie and a dark blue suit. He grabbed his piles of notes from the bedside locker and headed downstairs.

Ciara was waiting in the hallway. 'Jesus, Colm, are you okay?' she said taken aback at his pale and gaunt appearance.

'Yeah, yeah, I'm fine. I just forgot to set the alarm clock. Look, I'm sorry, about last night. This case is taking up all my time. I guess we better get going.'

'Your toast, Dad!' Gemma cajoled from the kitchen doorway.

'I can eat it on the way. Come on, let's get this over with. Not that… you know what I mean.'

* * *

The day was unseasonably mild for November, a blue sky dotted with light grey clouds. McEvoy tugged down the sleeves on his suit and cast a nervous glance across the car park at the side of Finglas church. Gemma and Ciara had disappeared towards the church entrance the moment they arrived, leaving him stranded. He'd used the opportunity to briefly check in with

Kelly Stringer. Everything seemed to be in hand for Koch's funeral later that day.

He reluctantly headed off towards the front of the church feeling decidedly out of place. Around him other cars and guests were arriving; people Maggie and himself knew from work or through Gemma's friends. They nodded and half-heartedly waved but seemed cautious about approaching him. He nodded back, but made no effort to go and talk to them.

He rounded the corner and practically walked into Caroline and Hannah Fallon's sister, Catherine. Behind them the entrance to the church was busy with people starting to file in.

'Jesus!' McEvoy exclaimed, rising up on his toes, managing to stop his forward momentum.

'Can I have a quick word, Colm?' Catherine asked, sharing a conspiratorial look with Caroline. She took him by the arm and walked him back round the corner of the church. 'Look, I know this is probably a terrible faux pas,' she said, speaking quickly, 'but Hannah has money on you disappearing the minute this ends and you're so busy that no time is a good time. Plus, I've got to get back down to Nenagh tomorrow – Gerry's probably got the kids eating nothing but take-aways. Anyway, I've been talking to Caroline and Gemma. You know I was at school with Caroline? We were wondering whether it would be okay for Hannah to, y'know, to move into your house when she gets out of hospital?

'She doesn't want to go back to her house. Not after those creeps put the pipe bomb through the door. She's going to put it on the market as soon as it's patched up and redecorated. But she can't come and stay with me as she needs to go to rehab in Dublin, and I can't come and stay up here all the time because of the kids. I mean, I'll be back up whenever I can; I just can't be up here all the time.

'She won't be back in work for at least four months, probably six or more. She can be there for when Gemma gets out of school and just help out. What do you think? She'll be like a housesitter stroke babysitter.'

'I…' McEvoy trailed off, dumbstruck.

'Look, you don't need to answer now,' Catherine continued hurriedly, 'I just wanted to put it out there.'

'But where would she sleep?' McEvoy muttered, trying to compute Catherine's request; trying to deal with its inappropriateness given the event they were about to attend. 'Will she be able to manage the stairs?'

'Caroline thought you could put a bed in the dining room. You don't use it apparently.'

'I… right.'

Ciara rounded the corner, her face pulled tight in a pained look. 'Colm! Come on! We're starting in five minutes.' She disappeared back out of view.

'So, what do you think?' Catherine pressed.

'I… yeah, whatever,' McEvoy said dazed, unsure of himself, unable and unwilling to think through the request. 'I'll talk to Gemma.'

'Excellent. Thanks, Colm.' She steered him back round to the front of the church and gave a guilty looking Caroline a surreptitious thumbs up.

* * *

Maggie's family were in the first row; her mother, father, sister and brother, along with their kids. McEvoy was sitting behind them, Gemma jammed tight into his side at the end of the pew. On his right were his mother and father, then his brothers and sister. Immediately behind them were aunts, uncles and cousins from both sides of the family. They'd all shaken his hand when he'd entered the church, pulling tight smiles, nodding their condolences, whispering kind words.

He tugged his mobile from his pocket and glanced at the screen. No new messages. Nervous, he swivelled round and looked behind him. The massive church was a third full at best. It had been almost full on their wedding day and to the rafters at Maggie's funeral. He recognised most of the faces, even if he couldn't place many of them in his befuddled state. Halfway back was Gemma's teacher and three rows of kids from her class at school. He spotted Tony Bishop entering the church and taking a seat near to the door ready for a quick getaway. Barney Plunkett was sitting a few rows ahead accompanied by his wife; Hannah Fallon's sister in the row in front.

He wasn't sure what he felt about having Hannah move into the house. She was a good colleague and had been one of Maggie's friends, but it would still be an intrusion into the household. In some ways it would be a blessing, especially with regards to looking after Gemma given the ridiculous hours he was working and Caroline's pregnancy, but it would also set the tongue of every guard in the city wagging. He could live with that as long as she wasn't expecting more. More simply wasn't an option.

He shook his head. He couldn't believe, on this of all days, that he agreed to Hannah moving in; that he was worrying about what people might think. He felt his heart fill with guilt and remorse. He turned back to face the altar and glanced at his watch. They were ten minutes late starting. His stomach was knotting with nerves.

He pulled his notes from his pocket and scanned through them quickly. They were nothing more than random thoughts scribbled after too much whiskey. He had no idea what he was going to say. He had no idea what was going to happen. He'd left everything to Ciara to organise. Gemma jabbed him in the ribs. He looked up.

A priest had materialised from somewhere. He was speaking but McEvoy could barely hear what he was saying. All he wanted was to get out of there; for the floor to swallow him whole. His shirt felt tight around his neck.

Everyone slipped forward off the pews. He followed, miming the prayer, then slid back up onto the pew. The priest said a few more words, then they were on their feet singing a hymn. He'd barely come to church since he was a child; funerals and weddings were the only times he took part in a service. It was familiar but strange; a weird echo of a ritual mostly forgotten. Everyone sat again.

Gemma slipped from his side and headed to a lectern at the front of the church. She started to tell the congregation why she thought Maggie had been the best mother in the world.

He could feel the tears roll down his cheeks. She looked so vulnerable and yet so strong up there; young and yet older than her years. He heard someone behind him sucking in air as they cried. This is why he didn't want to be here, it would be like this all day; people reminding him of what was no more; endless hours of wallowing in grief.

His mother tapped his thigh and handed him a tissue. The phone in his pocket started to vibrate. He ignored it and dabbed at his cheeks. He smiled weakly at Gemma as she returned to her seat and took her hand, squeezing it gently.

Next Ciara went up and read a gospel and then there was another hymn. Then he was easing his way past Gemma and walking towards the lectern.

He turned to face his friends and family. Nearly everyone was gazing at him, a few had their heads bowed, many were wiping tears from their eyes. His mobile phone started to vibrate again. He pulled his tattered notes from his pocket, staring down at them, but not seeing the writing.

Eventually he looked up.

'Look, I'm sorry but I don't have a speech prepared; just these useless notes.' He held up a handful of crumpled paper. 'To be truthful I didn't want to face up to the task of writing it. I thought, you know, that I could just stand here and tell you what Maggie was like. I mean, I spent over twenty years of my life with her. We had a beautiful child together. I should have lots to say, right? Lots of memories, anecdotes, funny stories; things that would tell you all what a wonderful, funny, beautiful woman she was. But you all know that already. Anybody who ever knew her, knows that. Which is why we all miss her so much. I know I'll be spending the rest of my life with her. I talk to her everyday and there isn't a minute when I don't think about her. I'm sorry, Ciara, I know you went to a lot of trouble organising this. I should have put some more effort in, but the truth is, I commemorate her everyday. I always will.'

McEvoy leant against the lectern for a couple of seconds looking lost then walked back to his seat, his gaze directed at his feet, too embarrassed to look at Maggie's family or his own. He felt like a fool. Had acted like a fool. His mobile phone vibrated in his pocket.

He squeezed in past Gemma. His mother placed her hand on his knee and squeezed. He could hear her sobbing. A couple of hands patted his back. Maggie's mother turned back towards him and offered a weak smile, her face tear-stained. He looked down at his hands too ashamed to hold her eyes.

The priest continued to drone on. As they rose for another hymn he couldn't resist pulling his phone discretely from his pocket. He'd two missed calls and had three new messages – two telling him to ring his answering service and one from John Joyce.

'Peter O'Coffey dead. Ring when get chance. JJ'

McEvoy slipped the phone back into his pocket and wondered how much longer the ceremony would last and how he might be able to slip away with the minimum of fuss. He was looking for an excuse to avoid the rest of the day – the endless reminiscing, the cold soup and sandwiches at a local hotel, limp handshakes of condolences – but not another death. He couldn't help speculating as to how O'Coffey had died and who his killer was. Gemma broke his thoughts, tugging him back down as the hymn ended.

* * *

It was ten to eleven before McEvoy and the rest of his and Maggie's family had managed to exit the church. The next set of people were milling around the entrance awaiting the arrival of the hearse. Bishop had long gone and most of the others had already set off to the local hotel where the reception was being held. The two families were standing together, chatting, reluctant to follow.

Starting to feel impatient, McEvoy pulled Maggie's sister to one side. 'Look, Ciara, I need to head off,' he said apologetically. 'There's been another death.'

'Jesus, Colm, you can't go just yet,' she complained. 'It's barely eleven o'clock. There are people here who want to say hello; catch up with you. Can't someone else deal with it?'

'Not really, no. The victim is Albert Koch's great nephew. I need to get out there and find out what the hell's happening. Koch's funeral's this afternoon and half the world's press are going to try and gatecrash it.'

'And what about Gemma? And Maggie?'

'I've already told Gemma and she's fine with it. Besides, she has all of you to look after for the rest of the day. And, as for Maggie, as I said in the church I commemorate her every day. Nobody misses her more than I do. Don't worry, I'll be back as soon as I can.'

'This isn't good enough, Colm!' she whispered harshly. 'You promised you'd take the day off. You can't just keep abandoning your family for work.'

'Look, Ciara, this isn't the time or place, okay?' McEvoy tried to say as reasonably as he could. 'I can't just walk away from my job like other people. I'm always on call regardless of what's going on in my personal life. If someone gets murdered, I have to go and investigate.'

'Well, perhaps it's time you walked away and got a job where you can spend more time with your daughter,' Ciara said angrily.

'I spend as much time with her as I can,' McEvoy said defensively. 'If I walk away I still need to work, we'll still need a wage coming into the house. And if I leave the guards there's no going back. I'm a bit long in the tooth to try and train for a new career.'

'I'm not asking you to give up the guards, but maybe you could transfer to something that'll give you more time for Gemma.'

'Look, Ciara, I appreciate your concerns and I promise we'll talk about it again, but I need to go. I'm sorry.' He walked away from his sister-in-law over to where Gemma stood with his parents. He crouched down to her. 'I'll be back later, okay, pumpkin. Try and behave yourself.'

She nodded her head. 'I'll do my best.'

McEvoy placed his hand on her hair and pulled a weak smile. He levered himself back up. 'Look, I'm sorry,' he said to his parents. He twisted on his heels and headed for his car. He felt a mixture of guilt and relief and the slow surge of adrenalin. Ciara was right, he did need to find more time for Gemma, but he also needed his work. It was a conundrum he'd think about once he'd reduced his current caseload.

* * *

He drove most of the way to Ballyglass with the blue lights hidden behind his radiator grill blazing. He'd managed to do the journey in forty minutes. John Joyce had informed him that Peter O'Coffey had been found shortly after nine-thirty by a freelance photographer trying to scout out a possible route to somewhere with a good view of Ballyglass Church. He was lying on the slope down into a dry ditch on the boundary between O'Coffey's and Koch's farms. The initial impression was that it was suicide. He'd blown his brains out with an old pistol, possibly the one missing from The White Gallows, and in his other hand he clutched a scrawled note that said, 'I did it. I'm sorry.'

McEvoy pulled to a stop behind a marked Garda car and stepped out into a light breeze, the sky now threatening rain. Over the hedge to his left he could see activity down across a field in the row of trees forming its boundary. Above him he could hear the chopping of rotor blades. He looked up to see a news helicopter circling high overhead. He hoped that Joyce had made sure the body was covered.

He hurried along the roadway, passing three more parked

cars including the state pathologist's van, to a gate guarded by a uniformed guard.

'Detective Superintendent McEvoy,' he announced, showing his identification.

'You might want to change your shoes, sir,' the guard said, glancing down at his own muddied trousers and boots. 'It's all churned up where the cattle have been.'

McEvoy stared at the gateway entrance and then across the field. 'Shit,' he muttered to himself and headed back to the car and his wellington boots. He couldn't afford to keep replacing suits.

'Technical have asked that you follow the markers in, sir,' the guard instructed when he returned.

'Thanks.'

McEvoy eased his way through the mud in the gateway and then out across the field in a path running parallel to the ditch, passing the figures working amongst the trees, before cutting back diagonally towards them. As he neared he could see that the trees were on the near side of a deep, dry ditch, barbed wire strung between them. Tom McManus and John Joyce were standing on his side of the barbed wire fence watching him approach.

He greeted them both and peered down into the cutting. On the far bank, Peter O'Coffey was lying with his head near to the bottom of the ditch, a dark stain spreading out from under it. He was wearing a green wax jacket, blue jeans and dark grey wellington boots. An old pistol rested amongst the fallen leaves an inch or two from his right hand. It looked as if he'd stood or knelt at the top of the ditch, pulled the trigger, and then slumped forward into the crevice. Thankfully, the tree canopy was protecting the site from the prying eyes of the news helicopter.

George Carter, dressed in a white boiler suit, was standing at the top of the ditch watching Elaine Jones ease herself down next to O'Coffey's head. For a couple of minutes she inspected him, gently lifting his chin so she could see his face. Off in the field on the far side, Chloe Pollard was working her way back towards a gateway.

252

'Well?' McEvoy asked.

'Ah, Colm,' Elaine Jones said peering through the hawthorns. 'I'm sorry to drag you away from Maggie's commemoration, and I'm sorry I wasn't there. I seriously doubt this was a suicide. The bullet passed through his temple and then out just below his left cheek bone.' She tapped her face, mimicking her description. 'The angle's all wrong. He was shot from slightly behind and above. Almost impossible to shoot yourself like that. I'd say he was kneeling down on the edge of the ditch and was then executed.'

'Executed?'

'That's what it looks like to me.'

'And the note in his hand?'

'God knows,' Carter replied. 'He either killed Koch and this is revenge, or someone is trying to hoodwink us into thinking he killed him.'

'Either way, we have a killer out there,' McEvoy observed.

'We think O'Coffey came in through that gateway over there,' Carter said, pointing to where Chloe Pollard was presently standing. 'The photographer who found him came in through the gate up at the road and worked his way down the line of the ditch. We've roped off your side just in case whoever killed him headed out your way. I'm trying to limit access this side to preserve whatever evidence there is in here, though tweedle dum and tweedle dee there have marched around in their size twelves messing things up.'

'We've said we were sorry, didn't we,' Joyce said, peeved. 'We had to get down to the body. He might have been alive.'

'After he'd been shot in the head?' Carter said sarcastically. 'I'd say whoever killed him had to drag him forward a little to stop his feet being visible from the field. We'll see what else we can find. Footprints, hairs, whatever.'

'Right. Well, I'd better leave you to it. Get that gun prioritised for ballistics analysis. Elaine, can you give me a call as soon as you've had chance to do the autopsy?'

'It'll be a few hours, Colm. George and Chloe need to finish up here, then we'll take the body in to Navan.'

'That's fine.' McEvoy turned to Joyce and McManus. 'Has his family been told yet?'

'A couple of uniforms went to see his wife half an hour ago,' McManus said, grateful that it wasn't him who'd had to go to break the news.

'Okay, good. Right, John, you'd better get yourself ready to do a bit of media work. Man found dead. Single gun shot to the head. We're treating it as suspicious. No other details just yet and no further questions. Then get over to Ballyglass Church and give Kelly a hand.'

'You're going to let the funeral go ahead?' Joyce asked.

'I don't think we have a choice at this stage. Tom, you'd better come with me. We need to talk to his wife.'

* * *

The uniformed guard stationed outside of Peter O'Coffey's bungalow directed them up to Martin O'Coffey's farmhouse. There they were let into the hall by another guard. They found Peter O'Coffey's wife in the kitchen chopping vegetables. She was a plain faced, broad-shouldered woman in her late thirties with shoulder-length, brown hair, wearing a grey fleece jacket, blue jeans and white runners.

'Mrs O'Coffey?' McEvoy asked.

She looked up from the chopping board, a hard, determined set to her jaw.

'I'm Detective Superintendent Colm McEvoy and this is Sergeant Tom McManus. We're very sorry about the death of your husband.'

She nodded her head and went back to slicing carrots.

'We need to ask you some questions.'

'I need to finish preparing this soup. The old man's got a bad case of flu.'

'Perhaps the soup can wait a while,' McEvoy suggested.

'I can answer your questions while I work,' she said, without looking up. 'I don't have time to stop. After I've done this, I have a farm to look after, then I have to go and collect the kids from school. They don't know yet. What do you want to know?'

McEvoy and McManus shared a quizzical look. O'Coffey's widow seemed remarkably blasé about her husband's death.

'Do you have any idea why someone might have killed your husband?' McEvoy asked.

She stopped chopping and looked up. 'Killed him? I was told he committed suicide. They said there was a note.'

'That's what it looked like at first, but the pathologist thinks he was probably shot by someone else.'

She cut a few more slices of celery and then pulled a kitchen chair out and sat down heavily. 'I thought the stupid fucker had taken the easy way out, leaving us to pick up the pieces.'

'You thought suicide was likely?'

'We... things have not been easy for the past year or so.' She clutched and pulled her hair, closing her eyes. 'All while the rest of the country was getting rich, we were struggling to survive. It's been worse than ever recently. If it wasn't for the subsidies we'd have gone under years ago and we owe the bank a small fortune.' She covered her face with both hands, speaking through the heels of her hands. 'He said he would make it okay. He said he knew how to get the money. When I... I thought he'd done it so we'd get the insurance money.' She started to cry.

McEvoy sent McManus off to get some tissues and after a couple of minutes of comforting she'd regained her composure.

'The note found in his hand said, "I did it. I'm sorry." Do you know what that refers to?' McEvoy asked.

She shook her head no.

'Do you know where your husband was Saturday night?'

'Drinking with that idiot, Francie Koch, in Athboy. They'd meet up most Saturday nights for a blow out.'

'What time did he get back?'

'It must have been gone two o'clock. I'd gone to bed a couple of hours before. Him and Francie were like brothers – best friends since school. I thought he was a wee gobshite. He thought he was god's gift to the world. I don't think he liked me very much either.'

'Did he say where he was until two o'clock?'

'Drinking with Francie. That's all he said.'

'But you didn't tell us that.'

'It's bad enough we were on our last legs without him going to prison for some drunken accident! What the hell would I do then? What would the kids do? And Martin? We'd definitely lose the farm.'

McEvoy shook his head. She'd lied for her husband, despite the fact that he might have killed a man. Somehow she'd managed to justify any doubts she had for the sake of the children and farm. He didn't have the heart to tell her that probably the only reason they had a farm in the first place was because Koch and Martin O'Coffey had robbed two banks. When that came out he wasn't sure what would happen.

'You think your husband might have killed Albert Koch?' he asked.

'I'm not saying he did it! I asked him and he said no and that was enough for me.'

'But you had some doubts?'

'I've said enough. I shouldn't have said anything.' She stood back up and moved to the chopping board.

'Mrs O'Coffey, someone's just killed your husband. It might be the same person that killed Albert Koch, or it might be someone else. Do you think your husband was there when Albert Koch died?'

She stopped chopping, but didn't look up. 'Look, Peter and Francie were always creeping round Albert Koch's farm. They were both obsessed with finding his mythical gold. They were searching for some hidden vault. Complete baloney, but they were obsessed. They'd been looking for it since they were kids. Peter thought that if he could find it he could save the farm. Francie just wanted to be rich.'

McEvoy remembered that Roza had once found Francie searching Koch's bedroom. Perhaps the pair of them had got drunk and decided to sneak round The White Gallows in the early hours trying to find the rumoured secret vault when they disturbed the old man, then accidentally killed him and tried to cover their tracks by placing him back in bed. Given their intoxication, taking the gun and hanging the noose from the tree might have made sense.

'So you thought that maybe he'd been sneaking around again?' McEvoy asked.

'I thought it might have been possible,' she conceded. 'He told me that he'd come straight back home after the pub. He swore blind he hadn't been near to Koch's place.'

'But you thought otherwise?'

She ignored him, chopping the vegetables.

'Mrs O'Coffey,' McEvoy prompted.

'Yes.'

'Was he at Koch's farm?'

'I don't know. Probably. He was in a hell of a state when he got back,' she said without looking up. 'Usually he's drunk, but this time he was just hyper.'

'And he was with Francie?'

'He was always with feckin' Francie.'

An idea started to form in McEvoy's mind. 'How do you think Peter was going to raise the money to save the farm?'

'I've no idea, but he seemed pretty confident. Peter always had some scheme or another. Some sure-fired way to lose more money.'

'How about if Peter was trying to blackmail Francie?' McEvoy suggested. 'Perhaps Francie killed Albert Koch? Francie's now quite rich from his grandfather's estate.'

'You think Francie killed Peter? You're mad! They were like brothers. There's no way Francie killed Peter.'

'Brothers fall out with one another,' McEvoy suggested.

'Especially when one of them gains everything and the other is about to lose it all.'

'No,' she said quite emphatically. 'I don't believe it. Francie's a cocky little bollix, but I can't believe that he'd kill Peter in cold blood.'

'Well, if Francie didn't kill Peter,' McEvoy said, doubt in his voice, 'the question is, who did?'

* * *

'Well?' McEvoy asked, now they were back in his car.

'Francie and O'Coffey killed Koch – accidental or not – then Francie killed O'Coffey.'

'Seems that way,' McEvoy conceded. 'She didn't want her husband in prison, but I guess she would have preferred it to him being dead. If it was an accident the worst they would have got was manslaughter, might even have been ruled an accidental death with the right judge and jury.'

'I doubt that's how they would have seen it,' McManus said. 'They probably thought they'd get done for murder. It's not like they called an ambulance or tried to save him. They carried him upstairs, took the gun, tried to set up a diversion, and left him to die.'

'True. Right, well, we probably haven't got enough time to bring Francie in before the funeral. We'll let him attend his grandfather's service and then pick him up afterwards. In the meantime, find out if anyone has taken a full statement from the photographer that found the body.'

'I'm on it,' McManus said, easing himself back out of the car.

McEvoy turned the ignition and started to head towards Ballyglass Church. A few moments later his mobile phone rang.

'McEvoy.'

'It's Johnny Cronin. You told me to give you a ring. Is now a good time?'

'Now's fine. What's the story?' McEvoy asked, a bit of lightness back in his voice, confident they were about to wrap up the Koch killing. Shooting Peter O'Coffey had been a pretty dumb thing to do. But then so had been searching The White Gallows in the dead of the night.

'I met with our scam artist fifteen minutes ago,' Cronin replied. 'He's a border's man who thinks he's a bit of a charmer. My guess is Monaghan, maybe Cavan. He spins a very smooth line about scratching each other's back. For fifty thousand clean notes he's willing to trade me one hundred thousand in used ones. He wasn't shy at hinting where it came from. And he didn't mind letting me know what would happen if the guards turned up.

'I've set up the exchange tomorrow morning at ten o'clock in Clonmellon. It's just down the road from you. I have someone running his licence plate through the computer at the minute, but my guess is it'll probably turn out to be false. Hopefully we can track him home.'

'Right, okay. I'll try and be there. We might have this Koch case wrapped up by tonight.'

'You have someone in the frame for it? I heard you have another body?'

'Peter O'Coffey. Shot in the head this morning. I'm just on my way to pick up the prime suspect – his so-called best friend. Family and friends. I'm telling you, Johnny, you're better off sticking to strangers.'

* * *

Terry Macken's outfit had managed to put down metal matting to create a basic road grid to stop the soft ground instantly churning to mud. McEvoy parked on the grass and walked back up to the road and the short distance to the church, his path guided by luminous jacketed security guards. High in the sky a hovering news helicopter droned as it slowly circled, filming the scene below.

The small church was surrounded by a low stone wall that enclosed the old cemetery. Most of the gravestones looked ancient, with only a handful of new ones dotted amongst them. In one corner was a set of old, family crypts, their roofs turfed over, steps leading down to bolted doors. At seemingly random locations were narrow yew trees and the occasional lone pine. To the left of the church was a freshly dug grave, the soil mounded to one side. At evenly spaced intervals along the perimeter were security guards. Except for the helicopter there was no sign of any media presence.

The church itself was compact with tall, thin stained glass windows, and a small spike of a spire. A fairly sizable crowd had already started to gather at its entrance, though not as many as McEvoy had been expecting. Some were queuing to enter, others just milling around, shaking hands and chatting. Two speakers were pinned above the door piping out the organ music from inside.

McEvoy spotted Terry Macken standing to one side with Kelly Stringer, keeping a discreet eye on things. He was dressed in a well-tailored black woollen coat over a smart, grey business suit, a small earpiece pushed into his right ear, a narrow microphone extending across his cheek. He looked calm and collected, his grey hair cut short, eyes alert, his face full of colour. Kelly Stringer looked stunning in a two-piece, black suit, the skirt ending just above stocking-clad knees, her hair worn down. A black mackintosh coat hung on her shoulders. In contrast to Macken, her face wore a concerned look, worried about how the afternoon would unfold.

'Jesus, Colm, you look like shit,' Macken said, humour in his voice, as McEvoy approached.

'Well, at least it matches how I feel. You look like you're doing well for yourself. I take it business is booming?'

'I can't complain. Next gig after this is The Rolling Stones. Then Radiohead. If you want any tickets just let me know, okay? And if you ever want a change of scene I can always use seasoned pros, y'know what I mean?'

'Well, I…' McEvoy stuttered unsure what to say, especially after his dressing-down that morning by Ciara.

'That kid of yours doing alright?' Macken continued.

'Yeah, yeah, she's grand.'

'And this morning went okay? I was sorry to hear about Maggie, Colm. Shit happens, y'know.'

There was an awkward pause, no one sure what to say.

'We've set it up as you asked,' Stringer said to fill the silence, 'a far outer perimeter and another around the church. Dr John is already in the church. It must be pretty full in there. I'll go in when the hearse and family arrive.'

'Good. And no trouble?'

'Not really,' she continued. 'Some people who think they should have been invited but weren't. Some people pissed off they couldn't bring their cameras and mobile phones into the church. Some press trying to bluff their way in. There's a small anti-Nazi demo on the road out of Athboy, a dozen or so but they're mostly behaving themselves.'

'I guess there's a neat symmetry to it all,' Macken said. 'Albert Koch's killer topping himself on the morning of his funeral. I guess he couldn't live with himself.'

'Peter O'Coffey didn't kill himself,' McEvoy said solemnly. 'More like executed. Once this is all over, we need to talk to Francis Koch. He's not to slip away, okay?'

'Executed?' Macken said, confused. 'He blew his own brains out is what we were told.'

'That's not what Elaine Jones thinks. Someone blew his brains out for him. And O'Coffey's wife said that her husband arrived home gone two in the morning the night Albert Koch died, all hyper. She thinks he was probably snooping round the farm with Francie Koch looking for buried treasure. If O'Coffey…'

'Jesus. What the…?' Macken's attention had been diverted to a scene at the entrance to the church. Two of his security men and a plain clothes officer were wrestling with a man. 'Sorry, Colm, I need to deal with this.'

261

Macken set off for the door, McEvoy trailing behind.

Stefan Freel had been jostled to one side and pinned to the church wall. His face was flushed with anger.

'I'm sorry, Sir,' Macken said in a neutral voice. 'The church is very small and the family have given strict instructions as to who can and can't go inside. You can pay your respects from outside.'

'This is ridiculous, I was Albert Koch's...' Freel searched for the right word, 'assistant. I'm the new CEO of the Ostara Trust.' He spotted McEvoy. 'Superintendent?'

'It's okay, let him go,' McEvoy instructed. 'Let's have a look at that list?'

One of the security men passed it to him.

'My mother said she does not want him in the church,' said a man in his late thirties stepping forward. 'Mark D'Arcy.' He held out his hand.

'Ah, the man who makes false alibis,' McEvoy said sarcastically, ignoring D'Arcy's proffered hand. 'A funeral, Mr D'Arcy, is not the place to take petty revenges. Mr Freel was your grandfather's right-hand man for a number of years. He probably spent more time with him than anyone else. He has the right to pay his last respects.'

'The family doesn't want him in the church.'

'Are you sure that's wise given he's now in charge of the Ostara Trust?' McEvoy cautioned. 'You should be building bridges not burning them,' he suggested, the irony of his advice not lost on him.

'We'll see about the Ostara Trust. He's not coming in,' D'Arcy repeated.

'Mr Freel?' McEvoy said.

'Fuck them!' Freel snapped angrily. 'I'll stay out here. You've just made a big mistake, Mark. As the superintendent's just warned, you really don't want me as an enemy. I was your grandfather's apprentice. I've learned every lesson he had to teach about how to fuck people over.' Freel wandered to one side, challenging the stares of onlookers.

262

'Jesus,' Macken muttered.

'Here we go,' McEvoy said as a hearse pulled up at the church gates, two black cars pulling up behind it.

The crowd started to part. Mark D'Arcy headed for the cars and Kelly Stringer slipped into the church.

Marion D'Arcy stepped from the first car dressed from head to toe in black, her face covered with a net veil, followed by a man McEvoy took to be her husband. Next followed Charles Koch, followed by a beautiful young woman that McEvoy instinctively knew was Jane D'Arcy given her resemblance to her mother.

From the second car emerged Frank Koch and his wife Mary, Francis Koch looking pale and frayed, and a woman McEvoy didn't recognise but guessed was Francis' sister, Emily, and then his brother, Carl.

Collectively the group were worth about one hundred and thirty-five million euro, plus whatever Frank Koch's motor sales empire was worth. Somehow, McEvoy thought, that wouldn't be enough for them. Marion D'Arcy and her family wanted it all. They didn't care about Albert Koch's criminal past or how he'd built his business empire. They just wanted to get their hands on what they saw as rightfully theirs. Stefan Freel would have his work cut out to maintain the Ostara Trust as set out by Koch in his will. No doubt the family already had a team of lawyers poring over the small print trying to find ways of contesting the division of spoils.

Charles, Francis and Carl Koch and Mark D'Arcy moved to the hearse, lifting the plain oak coffin clear of the long car and up onto their shoulders, each pair clasping each other's jackets to provide a stable base. In step, they headed for the church entrance, the waiting mourners bowing their heads or crossing themselves forgetting they were attending an old Protestant church. Behind them trailed Marion D'Arcy, her head held high, her wrist threaded through her husband's arm, followed by Frank Koch and Mary, then Jane D'Arcy and Emily Koch. They entered the church and the old wooden doors closed behind them, the security guards stepping across to block any further access.

McEvoy half-thought about sneaking in, but couldn't face a second church service in one day. It would be enough to hear it on the loud speakers. Plus he could deal with any situation that arose outside given Stringer and Joyce were trapped inside. Instead he walked to the church gate and leant against the cold stone. The wind had started to pick up and the sky was darkening as a front moved in from the west. If they were lucky the ceremony would be over before the first drops fell.

* * *

He pressed his neck further down into the collar of his coat and tipped a fragile umbrella into the wind to try and fend off the driving rain, wondering if he should give the nicotine patches another try.

Anyone who had listened to the service on the speakers would have thought that Albert Koch was a saint – a loving family man, caring employer, generous philanthropist – rather than a mass murderer, bank robber and ruthless businessman. The editing of the truth was as audacious as it was crude.

The congregation were now all huddled under multi-coloured umbrellas surrounding Albert Koch's final resting place. McEvoy couldn't see what was happening at the graveside or hear what was being said but he didn't care. His only concern was to make sure that Francis Koch didn't disappear.

After a few more minutes the crowd started to break up. A dozen or so headed for the gate almost immediately, either desperate to get out of the wind and rain or to beat the inevitable traffic jam as everyone tried to leave together. Most hung around in small groups and swapped small talk, taking it in turns to sidle over to the grieving family and say a few words of condolence.

Eventually the churchyard started to empty. Maurice Coakley and Henry Collier left together, looking suitably

264

sombre. Dr Astell was deep in conversation with another elderly gentleman. James Kinneally looked like a broken man, but his wife Patricia, leaving separately, looked like the cat who'd got the cream. Stefan Freel strode out with determination in his eyes, nodding an acknowledgement at McEvoy. Roza Ptaszek looked pale and drawn, clinging onto the arm of her boyfriend, Janek. McEvoy knew from Tom McManus that she felt conflicted by her inheritance given the revelations about Koch's past and was trying to decide if she could accept. She'd lost several family members in the death camps that dotted Poland during the war and now thought of Koch's riches as blood money. He nodded a greeting at her, but she just tightened the grip on her boyfriend's arm and lowered her face.

The family were the last to leave. Marion D'Arcy swept past McEvoy as if he were invisible. Frank Koch gave him a fierce glare, but his wife smiled weakly. Everyone else trouped out with their heads bowed. Francie Koch was the last person in the group. He was without an umbrella and was soaked through.

McEvoy stretched out his hand. 'I'm sorry, Francis, we need a word.'

Francie drew to a stop but didn't say anything. His face was pale, his eyes unfocussed and puffy from crying.

'We need to ask you some questions about Peter O'Coffey. I'd like you to come with us to Athboy garda station.'

Francie visibly blanched at the mention of O'Coffey's name, but stayed silent.

McEvoy took hold of his elbow and started to guide him through the gate. Joyce and Stringer were positioned on the narrow road, standing in front of the hearse. A garda car to escort Francis Koch to the station was waiting out of immediate sight in O'Coffey's field. High above them the news helicopter circled the churchyard, fighting the wind to stay in place.

Charles Koch appeared in front of McEvoy blocking their passage.

'What the hell is going on?' he demanded.

'I'm sorry, Professor Koch, but we're taking your son in

for questioning about the deaths of your father and Peter O'Coffey.'

'But that's ridiculous!' Charles snapped.

'I didn't kill Peter,' Francis mumbled.

'See?' his father said angrily. 'He says he didn't kill them.'

'He said he didn't kill Peter O'Coffey. He said nothing about his grandfather.'

'He didn't kill him either!'

Marion D'Arcy joined her brother. 'What the hell is going on?' she demanded.

'We're taking your nephew in for questioning.'

'No, no. That's not happening,' she warned. 'We've had to put up with all... with all this,' she said, sweeping her hand in an arc, referring to the security. 'He's coming to the reception and that's it.'

The garda car pulled up on the far side of the hearse.

McEvoy tried to move forward, speaking at the same time. 'I'm sorry, Mrs D'Arcy, but that's not your decision to make. Another of your relatives was found murdered this morning and I want to discuss his death and your father's with your nephew.'

'He's just told you that he didn't do it,' Charles Koch spat, continuing to block McEvoy's path. 'Francis, say something!'

'Look, I'm very sorry,' McEvoy said, trying to keep his frustration in check, 'but I'm investigating two murders. If I want to question your son, that's what I'm going to do.'

Terry Macken, John Joyce, and the driver and his partner from the garda car eased Charles Koch and the other family members to one side, allowing McEvoy to pass through to the waiting car with a passive Francis Koch.

'You're going to pay for this,' Marion D'Arcy warned. 'We have powerful friends. You'll be lucky to keep your job.'

'You work away, Mrs D'Arcy. My family thinks I could do with a career change.' McEvoy opened the garda car door and eased Francis into the back seat. 'And besides,' he said turning round, 'I doubt your many powerful friends will be in a hurry to help you now your father's past is coming to light.'

'Why you...'

Terry Macken blocked Marion D'Arcy's path as she launched herself at McEvoy, her eyes blazing with hate and anger.

'You're finished. Do you hear, finished,' she screamed. 'Francis, do not say a word until my lawyer arrives. Nothing. Do you hear me? Nothing!'

McEvoy slammed the car door shut. The driver climbed in, his partner rounded the car and got in the back seat, keeping Francis Koch company.

McEvoy slapped the roof of the car and it pulled away. He headed back along the laneway to retrieve his own car. He wondered how prophetic Marion D'Arcy's words would be. Taking Francis from the funeral was not ideal, but he couldn't take the risk that he might slip away afterwards.

* * *

They were in the same room in which James Kinneally had been interviewed. Francie Koch was sitting slumped on an old plastic, grey chair, looking like a drowned rat, his hair plastered to his head. McEvoy was sitting on the opposite side of a cheap table, its Formica top scratched and punctured. Tom McManus was standing by the door, leaning against it.

So far Francie had refused to say anything.

'The way I see it, Francis, is this,' McEvoy said. 'Peter O'Coffey and yourself were making your way back from Athboy, drunk as lords, when you decided to go on a treasure hunt. You let yourself into your grandfather's house and you started to search for his supposed stash of Nazi gold. Only you disturbed the old man who then came downstairs, armed with his old gun, to see what was going on. One of you hit him on the head – knocked him clean out. Then you carried him back upstairs and fled, hanging a rope from the oak tree to divert attention from yourselves.'

Francie stayed silent, staring down at his interlocked fingers, his thumbs picking at one another.

'You probably weren't expecting him to die – just wake up with a bad headache. But the blow was too hard and he had a massive stroke. Or perhaps he died while you were there and that's why you hung the rope? Either way, you killed him. So now you're in the frame for murder, but you're also about to inherit a fortune. Only Peter O'Coffey isn't going to receive anything and he's in massive financial trouble, so he asks you for money in exchange for silence. If he's going down, he'll take you with him. So you arrange to meet him at the edge of his farm. You bring your grandfather's gun and you try to reason with him, but he won't listen, so you shoot him in the head and try and make it look like he's committed suicide; that he'd killed your grandfather and couldn't live with himself.'

Francie continued to stare at his hands.

'So, how did I do?' McEvoy asked. 'Did I get everything right? Or most of it right? Or…?'

'I didn't kill Peter O'Coffey,' Francie mumbled.

'But you did kill your grandfather?' McEvoy pressed.

Francie stayed silent.

'If you didn't kill Peter, Francie, then someone else did. Which means you're probably next… Look, Francie, you're not helping yourself. At the moment you're looking at two life sentences for murder. You'll spend a minimum of twenty years in a prison cell you'll be sharing with some messed-up psycho. It'll be a living hell.'

Francie briefly glanced up, then back to his hands.

'If you've got a good lawyer, you might be able to get the death of your grandfather turned to manslaughter. Might even get it ruled as accidental death. Who knows? If that happens you might only end up with a suspended sentence – a couple of years max. But Peter,' McEvoy shook his head, 'that was cold blooded murder. A gun to his head, blowing out his brains. No way you're going to be able to wriggle out of that one, even if you've got the best lawyer money can buy.'

'I *didn't* kill Peter,' Francie stated firmly.

'And your grandfather?... We will find forensic evidence linking you to the murder. One of your hairs or some fibres from your clothes in your grandfather's bed, or on his pyjamas, or on the rope. We have casts of all the footprints at the base of the gallow's tree. My guess is they'll match yours and Peter's. We know that you left the pub together on Saturday night; that you didn't get home until gone two in the morning.'

'We were just talking.'

'You went on one of your adventures to find your grandfather's secret vault of Nazi gold.' McEvoy could see the guilt and shame eating Francie up inside. If Koch was going to confess it would be soon. 'Francie?'

'We didn't mean to kill him,' Francie whispered on cue. 'It was an accident.'

'You didn't mean to kill who, Francie?' McEvoy pressed.

'My grandfather,' Francie snapped. 'We were drunk. We thought we'd have a bit of a nose around. We knew Roza was with her boyfriend in town. As we neared the farm we spotted that East European bitch's car parked in on a track, hidden in from the road. We figured they were probably looking for the same thing as we were. I don't know. It just made us more keen to get into the house itself, maybe catch them snooping around – see if they knew something we didn't. They'd been a fuckin' pain, going round asking questions, making crazy accusations. Only we never saw them.' He snorted a laugh to himself.

'We started to search the place, but we were making too much noise. The whole thing was ridiculous, the pair of us stumbling round drunk. After a few minutes the old fool woke up. We heard him creeping about upstairs, but we didn't think he'd come down. By the time we heard him on the stairs we didn't have time to get out. He came into the room holding a gun. I... I mean, Peter, panicked, hit him on the head with the vase. He dropped to the floor like a sack of potatoes. I couldn't believe it. He just slumped down.'

'And?' McEvoy prompted.

'And we got out of there. We just left him lying where he was. We figured he'd come round and call the guards. Peter had the idea of throwing a noose over the tree. He thought that maybe it might point the finger at the East Europeans – we knew they were there somewhere. Given their stupid accusations they had a motive for breaking and entering; for hanging the rope.'

'You left him there?' McEvoy said, his brow furrowed. 'You didn't take him back upstairs to his bed?'

'No, no. We left him where he fell.'

'And you didn't clean up the vase or take the gun?'

'No. We got out of there. That must have been the East Europeans unless he came round and did that himself.'

'And then what?'

Francie shrugged. 'We swore each other to secrecy and we both went home.'

'That's it? You just hoped that it would go away?'

'We thought he would come round or Roza would find him.'

'You left an old man to die.'

'We didn't know he was going to die, did we! We didn't mean to kill him! It was an accident.'

'And you seriously expect us to believe that this East European couple were there as well? Don't you think that's a bit of a coincidence?'

'They were there,' Francie whined.

'But you didn't see them.'

'But their car was there. We saw it.'

'And why didn't you say anything over the next couple of days?'

'Because we… because we couldn't,' Francis said limply.

'So why did you kill Peter then? You fell out with one another?'

'I *didn't* kill Peter! We were friends. We've been friends since we were kids. We were second cousins. Why would I kill Peter?'

'Because you'd inherited a fortune and he was about to lose his family farm. He wanted money for silence.'

Francie stared down at his hands.

'He did ask you for money,' McEvoy prompted.

'Yes. I said I'd give it to him – enough to clear his debts.'

'But he wanted more?'

'Yes! But that didn't mean I killed him!'

'How much more?'

'Half. He wanted half. I told him I couldn't give him half; that the money was tied up in a trust. He didn't believe me. He said he needed the money soon or the bank would seek to sell the farm to recoup their debts. He said that if he went down, he would take me with him. I told him I'd cover the debts to save the farm, but I couldn't do anything else for a while.'

'And?'

'And he stormed off. He said he needed more than that. That he would find another way.'

'What way?'

'I don't know. I told him to wait until after the funeral and we'd try and sort it out then, but there was no reasoning with him. I just hoped he wasn't going to do anything stupid like go to you or the press. I thought that if you hadn't worked out it was us within a couple of days we'd probably be okay. You'd keep digging for a while and then it would all die down.'

'And instead he did something more stupid. Stupid enough to get himself killed. If you didn't do it, Francis, who did?'

'I don't know.'

'You've got no ideas at all?'

'No. Maybe the East European couple? They seem to be obsessed with bringing our family down.'

'You really think that they killed him?'

Francie shrugged. 'I don't know. What happens now?'

'You sit here and try and work out who killed Peter O'Coffey, we go outside and try and work out what we're going to charge you with.'

271

McEvoy stopped the recorder and pushed himself back from the table and headed for the door. He followed McManus out and down the corridor. 'Well?' he asked.

'I think it's probably as he told it.'

McEvoy nodded. His discomfort at his interpretation of the murder scene had resurfaced. The reason the hanging rope had made little sense was because there had been two attempts at a cover-up – one by Francie Koch and Peter O'Coffey, the other by whoever had taken Albert Koch's body back upstairs to his bed. Neither of them knew about the other's crude attempt. 'And the East European couple?' he asked. 'Do you think they were there?'

'Possibly. I don't know. I don't think Francie killed Peter O'Coffey though.'

'Why not?'

'He seems too in shock. Too afraid for himself.'

'So who the hell did kill Peter O'Coffey then?'

Before he could continue, the door to the garda station burst open and John Rice, Marion D'Arcy's lawyer, barrelled in. 'Where is he?' he commanded.

'You're too late,' McEvoy said, pulling a tight smile. 'He's just confessed to killing his grandfather.'

'We'll see about that,' Rice snapped. 'He's confused. He's just buried him for God's sake! I need to see him.'

'He's down the hall. Tom, can you show Mr Rice the way.'

'What have you charged him with?' Rice demanded.

'Nothing yet. I'm thinking about it. The minimum will be manslaughter. You have ten minutes before I return. Do you want coffee?'

'Tea. White. No sugar. And make it twenty minutes.'

* * *

Thirty minutes later and John Rice had still not emerged from the interview room. McEvoy had used the time to make some initial notes and to have quick chats with Tony Bishop and John Joyce.

272

A large group of journalists had gathered outside Athboy garda station demanding to know what was happening. Joyce was working with Barry Traynor to prepare a short statement confirming that the man who had died earlier that day was Peter O'Coffey, one of Albert Koch's neighbours; he had been killed by a shot to the head and a man was being held for questioning in connection with the deaths of Albert Koch and Peter O'Coffey.

He'd also spoken very briefly to Jenny Flanagan. Given the evidence to date, she hadn't been able to decide whether it was Brian O'Neill or his mistress that had killed Kylie O'Neill, so she had released both of them without charge late the previous evening. She'd instructed them that they were not to leave the locality. She had spent the day canvassing the area again, while a forensic team combed the O'Neill family house and surrounding land for evidence that would identify which one was the killer and who was the accomplice. She sounded frustrated, but hopeful. If they didn't discover anything else she would try to persuade the Director of Public Prosecution's Office to proceed with a case against Brian O'Neill based almost entirely on circumstantial evidence.

McEvoy looked up from his notebook as McManus approached.

'After y'man comes out, we'll charge Francie, then go and talk to the East Europeans and see what they have to say for themselves,' McEvoy said. 'I can't see them tidying up after Francie and Peter – they'd have nothing to gain from it. So, the question is, who benefited most from making Koch's death look natural? It has to be a member of his family, right? They knew Ewa and Tomas were asking questions and the last thing they wanted was a murder investigation that raked over and exposed his past.'

'Marion D'Arcy,' McManus said. 'She has no alibi and was insistent that he died in his sleep. She'd even got the doctor to go along with it.'

'And it probably would have worked if Roza hadn't discovered the body first and called us,' McEvoy said, nodding his head in agreement.

'Do you want us to go and collect her?'

'No, no. We don't have any firm evidence yet. If we jump in too soon her hotshot lawyer will be all over us and she'll totally clam up. Let's see if George Carter can come up with something from either site first; we'll go and talk to Ewa and Tomas. Come on, hotshot's twenty minutes are long up.'

McEvoy headed back along the corridor, knocked on the door and gently eased it open.

John Rice had pulled a chair round to Francie's side of the table. He snapped his head round at McEvoy's interruption. 'Five more minutes,' he barked.

'Okay, okay,' McEvoy backed out into the corridor and leant on the wall opposite. 'Touchy bastard.'

Three minutes later John Rice left the interview room. 'I want my client released immediately with no charge,' he demanded. 'He made his statement under duress and he withdraws it in its entirety.'

'He confessed to killing his grandfather,' McEvoy said patiently. 'He was searching the house with Peter O'Coffey when they disturbed him. They cracked him on the head and left him to die.'

'He admits to being on the farm and searching for a secret vault, but he swears he did not kill his grandfather. Perhaps that was Peter O'Coffey. He can't say and you can't prove otherwise.'

'I thought you just said he withdraws his confession in its entirety,' McEvoy said, an amused hint to his voice.

'Don't try and mess with me, Superintendent,' Rice growled. 'You were questioning him without legal representation present at a time of deep emotional distress. That confession will stand up in court for half a second and you know it. You have no evidence linking my client to the death of Albert Koch.'

'Except that he confessed in front of two officers and on the record. He hadn't asked for legal representation and he didn't object to us recording the conversation. We were simply asking him some questions. He confessed to killing his grandfather and he vehemently denied killing Peter O'Coffey. That's good enough for me.'

'Well, it isn't good enough for me. I want him released immediately.'

'Well, that isn't going to happen. I'm about to charge him with murder.'

'Murder! That's... Look, Superintendent, we both know that charge's not going to stick. At the absolute worst what he supposedly confessed to was manslaughter. And we both know that I'll make sure that doesn't stick either. Either you come up with some concrete evidence or you let him go.'

'He smashed a vase on his grandfather's head and then left him to die, trying to divert suspicion from himself by throwing a noose over the gallows tree. He could have called the emergency services. He could have stayed and looked after him. Instead he fled. The killing itself might not have been premeditated, but everything that came afterwards was done to deliberately try and cover his tracks and ensure that Albert Koch died. I'm charging him.'

McEvoy stepped past Rice and back into the interview room, Rice and McManus trailing.

'You're making a big mistake, Superintendent,' Rice warned. 'You're just wasting everybody's time and costing the taxpayer money.'

'Says you, who bleeds the taxpayer dry every time he goes to court!' McEvoy snapped back.

* * *

His mood had soured since tangling with Marion D'Arcy's lawyer. He knew that John Rice was probably right. Unless they could find some convincing evidence that Francie Koch had smashed the vase over his grandfather's head, he was likely to be set free. The confession would be picked apart and enough reasonable doubt cast to make any prosecution unlikely. The best they might achieve would be a conviction for accessory to manslaughter, assuming they could make it stick that Peter O'Coffey had killed the old man. And his wife's lawyers would probably do their best to cast doubt on that.

He pulled up outside of Kells Garda Station and climbed out, Tom McManus clambering from the passenger side. Ewa Chojnacki and Tomas Prochazka had been collected from their hotel and were waiting for him inside.

Cathal Galligan was lurking at the entrance. 'You've got a fuckin' nerve coming here,' he barked at McEvoy, blocking his path.

'Stop acting like a child and get out of the way,' McEvoy demanded, not in the mood for Galligan's games.

Tom McManus took a step backwards, unsure of the situation. The duty officer looked on amused from behind a counter.

'This is my station, McEvoy, and things will be done my way. If you want to interview anyone here, I want to be present.'

'Like hell you will, now get out of the way before I make a couple of phone calls.'

Galligan held his ground, his eyes blazing.

'I'm not going to fight with you, Galligan, but I will bring the world down around your ears.'

After a few moments Galligan stood to one side having come partially to his senses. He kept his head held high, his eyes boring into McEvoy. 'This isn't over yet,' he warned. 'And you're history,' he said to McManus.

McEvoy bundled past Galligan and let McManus overtake him to show the way.

'What an eejit,' McEvoy snapped. 'Don't worry about him,' he said to McManus' back. 'If anyone's history round here it's him. He's a dinosaur.'

McManus stopped outside of a dark blue door. 'They're in here.'

McEvoy knocked gently and then entered. The guard who'd been keeping Ewa and Tomas company nodded at him.

276

'Detective Superintendent Colm McEvoy. Thanks for babysitting them.' McEvoy held open the door and the guard passed through. 'We meet again,' he said to the couple.

'Why have you brought us here?' Ewa asked, standing up. 'We've done nothing wrong.'

'You lied to us,' McEvoy replied, sitting down.

'Lied? We told you the truth,' Ewa said collapsing to her chair again, casting a nervous glance at McManus who had stayed standing by the door. 'Your newspapers all believe us.'

'You lied to us about where you were on the night Albert Koch died. You were at his farm. It *was* you the bed and breakfast owner heard returning in the middle of the night.'

'No.'

'We have two witnesses that saw your car parked near to the farm at two o'clock in the morning. One of them is now dead. The other admitted to accidentally killing Dr Koch. You were there and I need to know what you saw.'

'You are arresting us?' Ewa asked, her face crumpling with concern.

'That depends. You lied to us, now we need the truth. Why were you at the farm?'

Ewa shared a look with Tomas before gathering herself. 'We were looking for Adolf Kucken's secret vault. He was an avid collector of Holocaust and Nazi memorabilia. It would be a valuable find and it would confirm that Koch was Kucken and that he was a war criminal. It probably held other papers that we have not been able to locate.'

'How did you know about the vault?'

'There were the rumours and he had to be hiding his collection somewhere. We knew that Roza wouldn't be there on Saturday night, so it was a good time to explore.'

'And did you find it?'

'No.'

'But you did see two other people searching the house?'

'No.'

'You saw nobody?'

'We saw a Mercedes car arrive as we were leaving. It pulled into the drive and parked.'

'And did you see who got out?' McEvoy asked, aware that Marion D'Arcy drove a Mercedes.

'No. Nobody got out. We didn't want to be seen there, so we climbed over a fence and cut across a field to the road.'

'Tomas?' McEvoy prompted the silent Slovakian.

'It is true. We saw no one.'

'And you didn't enter the house?'

'No,' Ewa answered. 'We looked in the yard and outbuildings. We thought it was a more likely hiding place. We heard movement in the house, so we decided to leave.'

'But you didn't see who was in the house?' McEvoy pressed.

'No. It was dark and we did not want to be seen. We left.'

'And that's when you saw the car arrive?'

'Yes.'

'And could you see into the car? Could you see who was behind the wheel?'

'No, they were in darkness.'

'There were two occupants?'

'Just a driver.'

'And what colour was the car?'

'I don't know. Something dark – black or blue.'

'So, I want to get this straight,' McEvoy said. 'You were at The White Gallows. You heard someone moving about the house. You saw a car arrive with a single occupant and park, but nobody get out. The next day you hear that Albert Koch was killed during the night and you decided not to tell us any of this?'

'We were afraid you would think that we killed him. We had a very strong possible motive.'

'So you decided to lie to us?'

'The important thing was Adolf Kucken was dead and that the world heard the truth about him.'

278

'The important thing was that a murder had been committed and you withheld useful information! There are other forms of justice than death! Because of you another person has been murdered! You do realise that, don't you?'

Ewa and Tomas did not reply. Tomas continued to stare down at the floor. Ewa stared at the plain, cream wall.

'You've nothing to say?' McEvoy pressed.

'We're sorry,' Ewa said quietly.

'Tell that to his wife and children,' McEvoy said, rising to his feet. He headed to the door.

'What will happen to us now?' Ewa asked meekly.

'Nothing. You will stay here and write out a full statement. Sergeant McManus will wait for you to complete it and then escort you back to your hotel. You will stay there for the time being.' He opened the door and started to exit, then turned. 'You were right by the way. There was a vault and it was full of Nazi memorabilia.'

'Can we see it?' Ewa said, regaining some of her confidence.

'No,' McEvoy said, closing the door behind him.

* * *

It was just gone seven thirty by the time he entered Ballyglass clubhouse. The incident room was quiet, only Kelly Stringer and a couple of guards present. Stringer was talking to one of her colleagues, a wide smile across her face. She was wearing the same outfit as at the cemetery, though she had pulled her hair back into a ponytail. The guard said something and she laughed, her whole face lighting up. She really was quite beautiful, McEvoy thought, turning away embarrassed at the thought.

He turned his attention to a table on which was spread out that morning's newspapers.

The *Irish Sun* led with, 'SECRET NAZI VAULT'.

The *Irish Times* with, 'KOCH LEAVES OSTARA TO HOLOCAUST CHARITIES.'

He flicked through them quickly. They had all led with stories about either Koch's past, the secret vault, or details of Koch's will. Tomorrow's headlines would all be about the murder of Peter O'Coffey and Koch's funeral. And the media pressure would ratchet up again, keen to further expose Koch's past and to speculate on who murdered him and O'Coffey. He hoped that John Joyce was up to the task because if he wasn't then they would eat him alive.

'Sir?' Stringer said from his side. 'I didn't see you come in.'

McEvoy turned to face her. 'I didn't want to disturb Romeo there. Is he taking you anywhere nice?'

'I...' Stringer started to blush. 'We were just talking about the case. I... He... there was...'

'Don't worry, I'm only codding you. Jesus, Kelly, look at the colour of you! Not that I'd blame him for trying, you look fantastic in that suit.' McEvoy felt himself start to blush. 'Not that I...' he trailed off.

'Not that you what?' Stringer asked, her hand rising and tangling with her hair.

'Nothing,' McEvoy said embarrassed. 'How are things,' he asked, trying to change the direction of the conversation, confused by his feelings of desire, guilt and shame.

'Not too bad,' she said, lowering her arm and her gaze. 'The funeral seemed to go okay except for the ending. There didn't seem to be too many people. It took a while to calm the family down when you took Francie away, but they eventually left for the reception at Marion D'Arcy's house.'

'Any news from George Carter or The White Gallows?'

'George has headed back to Dublin to work on the site material. Professor Moench left the farm about an hour ago; he's going to come back tomorrow morning. He's says that Koch seems to have had some kind of conversion over many years – he came to recognise his crimes and the Nazi regime for what they were.'

'I'm sure that will please his thousands of victims,' McEvoy said sarcastically.

'At least he saw the error in his ways; changed his will so that their descendents would get some kind of compensation.'

'Yeah, sorry, Kelly – it's been a long day. I'm heading home shortly. The reason I popped in was to ask you to organise some discreet surveillance of Marion D'Arcy. She was at her father's house the night he died. I think Peter O'Coffey tried to blackmail her and she decided to cut her losses, though keep that to yourself for now, okay? I don't want to see that in tomorrow's papers.' He jabbed at the table.

'I want to see if George can place her at the site before we bring her in for questioning,' he continued. 'It needs to be discreet, okay? If she finds out about it, she and her hotshot lawyer will be shouting the place down.'

'I'll get on it now,' she started to turn away from him.

'And Kelly?'

'Yes?'

'Nothing,' he said embarrassed, losing his nerve. 'I'll talk to you tomorrow morning.'

* * *

The traffic back into Dublin had been light and he'd made it to Collinstown cemetery in just under an hour. On the way he'd spoken to Elaine Jones, the state pathologist. She confirmed that Peter O'Coffey had died from a single gunshot to the temple sometime between six and eight that morning. O'Coffey had probably been kneeling, the shooter standing, the gun barrel pressed tight against the skin. The shot had entered high on the right temple, passed through the frontal lobe and out just above the upper left molars. She was confident that he would have died almost instantaneously, though McEvoy doubted that would be any consolation to O'Coffey's wife and children.

Maggie's grave was covered in fresh flowers. His white lilies were placed at the base of her headstone. Next to them an arrangement spelt out the word, 'Mammy'. McEvoy felt the tears prick and role down his cheeks.

He stood there silently for five minutes in the rain and wind, his aborted flirting with Kelly Stringer weighing heavy on his heart and mind.

'I'm sorry,' he eventually muttered. 'I'd better go find our daughter. I love you.'

He crouched down, reached through the flowers, and touched the ground, then headed reluctantly back to his car.

Ten minutes later he pulled up a few doors down from Caroline's house. He eased himself slowly from the car and trudged to the front door. It sounded as if a party was going on inside – lots of voices talking and bursts of laughter. After a few moments hesitation he pressed the door bell.

The door was opened by Jimmy, a can of lager grasped in one hand, his face alive with humour.

'Colm! Come in, come in. Jesus, bud, you look like fuckin' shite. You want a beer?'

'You got any whiskey?' McEvoy asked, stepping into the warm house, shaking off his wet coat.

'Is the pope a fuckin' Catholic. What do you want – Powers, Bushmills, Jameson?'

'Whatever's open. And make it a large one, thanks.'

'No bother, bud. A large one coming up.'

McEvoy watched Jimmy stagger down the hall towards the kitchen and then pushed open the door to the living room.

Crammed into the room and spilling into the knocked-through dining space beyond were his own and Maggie's families – their parents, siblings, and nephews and nieces – all chatting and laughing, holding glasses of wine, beer, whiskey or soft drinks. Three albums of family photos were laid open on a coffee table.

'Dad!' Gemma shrieked, noticing him standing in the doorway. She clambered up from the floor and launched herself at him.

He wrapped an arm around her and held her in place, her arms ringing his neck.

'There you go, bud,' Jimmy said, handing him a tumbler of whiskey, brushing past him into the room. 'Get that down yer.'

'Colm!' his mother shouted, well oiled with red wine. 'You look like a drowned rat! Come in, come in.'

Everyone in the room either said his name or raised their glass. He felt his sombre mood start to lift. These weren't people simply mourning the passing of a loved one, they were celebrating the life of a wonderful person. They were remembering the good times – the laughs, the jokes, the stupid stories and anecdotes, the light Maggie brought into their lives – and the bonds that continued to bind them as family and friends. Suddenly he felt relaxed; the weight of his grief and the pressures of work lifting temporarily from his shoulders.

'Look, you're on the telly again,' Gemma said, pointing at the screen in the corner of the room.

It was tuned to Sky News, the sound turned off. The picture was an aerial view of O'Coffey's farm, five small figures dotted on either side of a row of trees. It then swapped to an aerial view of Ballyglass Church and then to a hearse and two black cars passing a cameraman on a laneway.

'Can we turn that damn thing off?' McEvoy asked, stepping into the room. He took a sip of the whiskey, letting it trickle down his throat, warming his body.

SATURDAY

He rolled over and fumbled for his mobile phone. His head felt thick, his mouth fuzzy. He'd made it home through the wind and rain at a little after two o'clock in the morning, inured against the elements by a whiskey armour. Gemma had long since fallen asleep so he'd left her to stay with his sister.

'Yeah?' he grumbled into the phone.

'It's George Carter. You left a message for me to ring you first thing.'

'Right.' McEvoy slowly pushed himself up in the bed and glanced at the alarm clock – 7:48.

'Are you okay?'

'Hangover,' McEvoy muttered, massaging his eyes. 'I had a few too many last night.'

'Do you want me to ring you back later?'

'No, no, it's fine. I wanted to know if you'd got anywhere with the Peter O'Coffey site?'

'Jesus, give us a chance. He only died yesterday. We're going to start work on it in the lab this morning.'

'I need to know if Marion D'Arcy can be placed there – any footprints her size, whether there are Mercedes tyre treads on the road, any hair samples, whatever. I'm going to go and talk to her later this morning and any concrete evidence would help.'

'You don't want a lot then,' Carter said sarcastically. 'Tuesday's more likely.'

'I'd prefer this morning. I want to keep this thing moving. If she did kill O'Coffey, then the longer we leave it the more chance she has of getting rid of any evidence and to put in place a cast-iron alibi.'

'Can't you just go with what you've got?' Carter pleaded.

'I'd prefer something a little more concrete, George. All I have is a strong hunch and a witness statement from two people that Marion D'Arcy's lawyer will argue have good reason to point the finger of suspicion at her. He's a slick bastard.'

'The best we're going to be able to do are footprints. Whoever killed him had to have left some prints, the place was a quagmire. I'll get on it when we get in.'

'I'll be with Johnny Cronin until eleven or so, hopefully arresting our banknote scammer. I'll call you after that.' McEvoy ended the call and swung his legs out of the bed. He had a bright spot of pain throbbing just behind his forehead, his eyes aching with tiredness. He slowly levered himself upright and headed for the shower. Once he'd washed and dressed he'd source some aspirin and coffee, then walk back to Caroline's to pick up his car and head off to Clonmellon.

* * *

He'd made reasonably good time from Dublin, aware the whole way that he was probably still over the alcohol limit. As he neared Clonmellon, a small village fives miles beyond Athboy, located on the road from Mullingar to Kells, he had spoken briefly to Kelly Stringer who confirmed that Marion D'Arcy had not left her house since the funeral reception.

As he drove into the village the road doubled in width, one half forming ample parking for the small businesses and old houses that lined the street. He pulled to a stop opposite a pub and turned the engine off. He tipped his head back and closed his eyes. The stresses of the week and the previous night's drinking had caught up with him. All he wanted to do was curl up under a warm duvet and sleep for twelve hours. There was a gentle tap at the window. He tilted his head and opened his right eye. Johnny Cronin stared back grim faced.

McEvoy pushed open the door and levered himself out. The wind was still gusting but the rain had now stopped, patches of blue sky appearing to the west. 'Well?' he asked.

'You look like shit,' Cronin replied. He was dressed in a black leather jacket, blue jeans and white runners.

'That's funny, because George Carter thought I sounded like it too. Too much whiskey, too little sleep.'

'It went okay yesterday?'

'Yesterday went fine. I'm just glad I don't have to do it again anytime soon. So, who is he?'

'No idea. The plates were false and we lost him in the back roads of Cavan.'

'Jesus, Johnny. How're you going to do this?'

'We've agreed to meet in front of the market yard,' Cronin said pointing a little way along the road to where a high set of black, iron railings ran along the street, their length broken by a tall set of gates, a green sign hanging from one of the stone pillars. 'I wait there in my car. He turns up in his. We swap the money and then I grab him.'

'That simple, hey?'

'The simpler, the better.'

'And what about back-up?'

'I have two guys ready to box him in. He gives me the money and they top and tail him.'

'And what do you want me to do?'

'Nothing. Sit and watch. Twiddle your thumbs.'

'And what if he's got a gun or back-up of his own?'

'He's a one man operation and I doubt he's got a gun; it's not his style. If he has then we let him go and follow him. He won't get far; we've got the locals primed. We'll corner him and call in armed response. Happy?'

'It's your show,' McEvoy said, rubbing at his face trying to massage some life into it.

McEvoy had moved his car a little further along the street, making sure he had a good view of the market yard. He'd spent the twenty minutes before the bank scammer was due to arrive catching up on the morning's headlines.

The *Irish Sun* led with 'EXECUTED!'

The *Independent* with the not quite accurate, 'MAN EXECUTED AT NAZI FUNERAL.'

The *Irish Times* with, 'RELATION OF NAZI WAR CRIMINAL SHOT DEAD.'

Johnny Cronin was pacing back and forth at the side of his silver Volkswagen Passat, glancing nervously at his watch every few seconds.

Twenty minutes late a black Mercedes pulled up near to Cronin's car, facing the opposite direction. Cronin approached, appearing edgy, and leaned down to the driver's window. After a few seconds he returned to his own car, tugging an Aldi shopping bag from the back seat. He glanced around him, then pulled a wad of notes from the bag and passed them through the Mercedes window.

A couple of seconds later Cronin raised the bag to the window and opened it wide, revealing its contents. A hand snaked out, grabbed a handle and the car shot forwards yanking the bag from Cronin's grasp. As the car raced back onto the main road the bag disappeared through the driver's window. A green Opel Vectra pulled away from the kerb and tried to block its path, but the Mercedes veered around it; a red Renault Megane started to do a U-turn and then braked hard to avoid an oncoming SUV, whose driver blared her horn loudly.

'Shit!' McEvoy muttered as he watched Cronin scramble into his car and set off in pursuit. He turned the ignition, switched on the blue emergency lights and followed. He really didn't have time for this kind of caper.

* * *

The scammer had made it as far as Crossakeel before he over-steered trying to take a right-hand turn onto a narrow lane, seeking to lose his pursuers before they realised he'd left the main road. The car skidded sideways across a short verge through a wooden fence and into a ditch. He was scrambling from his car, tugging the Aldi bag free when the first pursuing car arrived, blue lights flashing behind its radiator grill. He thought about running, then raised his hands and pulled a wry smile, waiting to be arrested.

Johnny Cronin arrived a few moments later followed by McEvoy.

'Had to give it a try,' the scammer said, shrugging his shoulders.

'For fuck's sake, you could have killed someone,' Cronin snapped.

'I didn't though, did I?'

'Except for Gerald Staunton,' McEvoy said, drawing level with Cronin's shoulder. 'Remember him? He's the guy you stole fifty thousand from and he topped himself a few days later.'

'I didn't know the loser was suicidal,' the scammer said, becoming more serious. 'You can't blame that on me. He'd have done it in any case.'

'You pushed him over the edge, you stupid fucker,' Cronin said. 'He'd lost everything once you'd robbed him of what little he had left. He hadn't just lost his business, he'd lost his dignity. He couldn't see any way back.'

'Don't try and pin his death on me,' the scammer said, starting to lose his cool. 'He was prepared to break the law to keep his business going. He was quite happy to try and double his money. He knew the money was stolen. I was offering him a way out.'

'So now you were his knight in shining armour?' Cronin snapped. 'You didn't even give him the stolen money! You left him high and dry. You preyed on people's desperation.'

'I couldn't give them the stolen money, could I?' The

scammer smiled weakly. 'I didn't have it. Gullible people will believe anything. I just dangled the temptation in front of them.'

'For God's sake,' McEvoy muttered. 'How much have you made pulling this stunt?'

'Now that would be telling.'

'A couple of hundred thousand?' McEvoy pressed. 'More?'

The scammer simply shrugged his shoulders.

McEvoy pulled Cronin to one side. 'Arrogant bastard. Look, I'm going to leave you to charge him and sort this out.' He gestured at the stricken Mercedes. 'I need to get back to the Koch case. Hopefully we can wrap that up today as well. Next time, make sure the bad guy gets out of the car before giving him the money!' He turned and hurried back to his car before Cronin could reply.

* * *

Yet again he was parked up outside Ballyglass clubhouse. The surge of adrenaline from the brief car chase had dissipated and he was back to feeling sluggish and tense. He pulled up a number on his mobile.

'Carter,' said a distracted voice.

'George, it's Colm McEvoy. You got anything for me yet?'

'No. We've been looking through the photos and the casts we made, but unless she has at least size nine feet she wasn't there.'

'There must be something,' McEvoy said confused. 'Perhaps she worked her way down the ditch? It was fairly dry, wasn't it?'

'Yeah, but she still would have had to get to the field. I think you're looking for a man.'

'It has to be her,' McEvoy muttered. 'It was her Mercedes at The White Gallows the night her father died. She was the one who insisted that he'd died a natural death and persuaded the doctor to lie for her. She had no alibi for her whereabouts and she'd previously been caught sneaking round her father's house by the housekeeper and Stefan Freel.'

'Perhaps she had hired help?' Carter suggested. 'She could afford it. Or perhaps she's working with someone? An accomplice?'

'James Kinneally, perhaps,' McEvoy speculated. 'He's like a big puppy dog around her.'

'And he'd kill someone in cold blood for her, would he?'

'Yeah, you're right. Probably not,' McEvoy conceded.

'If I had to put my money on anyone,' Carter said, 'I'd put it on Stefan Freel. He seems like a cold-hearted bastard to me.'

McEvoy agreed that Freel was shallow and self-conceited, but Marion D'Arcy seemed more likely. She was at The White Gallows the night her father died and she had a hell of a temper. Carter might not have yet found any forensic evidence to link her to O'Coffey's murder, but it wasn't hard to imagine her forcing her nephew to his knees and pulling the trigger.

'Look, George, I better go, okay?' he said drawing a close to the exchange. 'I need to go and talk to Marion D'Arcy.'

McEvoy ended the call before Carter could reply. He eased himself out of the car and headed into the clubhouse.

Kelly Stringer looked radiant in a smart, grey suit and white blouse, three buttons open to reveal a tiny gold cross resting on her pale pink skin. Her hair was down and she smelled of the same perfume as earlier in the week.

'What's the latest on Marion D'Arcy?' McEvoy asked as businesslike as he could, wanting to avoid any more awkward moments.

'She's still in her house. Her daughter left about an hour ago, but her husband and son are still there. So's her brother, Charles. Are you okay? You don't look too good.'

'I'm fine,' he said, more brusquely than he intended. 'Where's Tom McManus?'

'Out at The White Gallows with Professor Moench.'

'Can you tell him to meet me at Marion D'Arcy's house in ten minutes? And tell the surveillance team that I'm on my way there as well. I think it's time to ask Mrs D'Arcy some difficult questions, don't you? She either killed Peter O'Coffey, or she had someone do it for her. And find out where Stefan Freel is as well, will you? I might want to talk to him later.'

* * *

Tom McManus was parked just inside the gates to Marion D'Arcy's estate. Out on the road was a small gaggle of journalists waiting for the Koch family to emerge and face their questions. McEvoy swept in past two uniformed guards and drove up to the front of the house, parking in the shadow of the portico. McManus pulled in behind him. A marked garda car coasted to a stop a few yards further back.

'I want to make this quick,' McEvoy said to McManus as they headed to the front door. 'We'll bring her in for questioning; I want to make sure her answers are formally recorded. This charade's gone on long enough.' He rapped hard on the door.

A few moments later it was opened by Mark D'Arcy. 'What do you want?' he asked gruffly. 'Time for our daily harassment, is it?'

'I'm here to talk to your mother,' McEvoy replied tersely. 'Can we come in please?'

'No,' D'Arcy said firmly. 'She's already told you that she's not prepared to talk to you again.'

'That's not her choice to make, is it? We're investigating a double homicide. That gives us the right to talk to whoever we want – including your mother.'

'I thought Francie has been charged with the murder of my grandfather?' D'Arcy said, his face creasing in confusion, still not giving way.

'He has, now get out of the way,' McEvoy snapped, pushing open the door and stepping into the large hallway.

'But… you think my mother killed Peter O'Coffey?' D'Arcy said incredulously, trailing after McEvoy. 'That's ridiculous.'

'Where is your mother?' McEvoy demanded, his temper starting to fray. 'Do we need to charge round the place like bulls in a china shop or are you going to go and find her?'

'I'm here, Superintendent,' Marion D'Arcy said, descending the stairs. She was wearing a green waterproof coat over a dark brown polo-neck jumper, tight cream jodhpurs, and knee-length riding boots. She looked tired and drawn; her hair was un-styled, her face free of make-up. 'I'm just about to take one of the horses out for a canter.'

'I'm afraid not,' McEvoy said firmly, 'we need you to come to Athboy garda station to answer some questions.'

'About what?'

'About the night your father died and the death of Peter O'Coffey.'

'This is a joke, right?' Marion asked as she reached the bottom of the stairs. 'We've been through all this already. Several times. I was here the night my father died and I didn't kill Peter O'Coffey. End of story.'

'We have new evidence. I need you to come to Athboy garda station so we can interview you formally,' McEvoy insisted.

'Superintendent, I really think—' Mark D'Arcy started.

'I'm talking to your mother,' McEvoy interrupted, 'not you. As far as I'm aware this has nothing to do with you.'

'I… it's… it's got everything to do with me,' D'Arcy stuttered. 'You're harassing this family. If you…'

'Mark!' Marion D'Arcy snapped, silencing her son. She turned her attention back to McEvoy. 'If you want to continue this ridiculous charade I'll answer any questions you want, but it'll be done here and with my lawyer present.'

'I'm afraid not,' McEvoy said as evenly as he could, trying to suppress his bubbling anger. 'If you don't want to come voluntarily I have a garda car waiting outside.'

'Are you threatening to arrest me?' Marion mocked a laugh. 'With what? Being related to the two victims? I hope to God you know what you're doing, Superintendent, because despite the slander in the papers this family still has powerful friends. And we will sue for damages.'

'I know exactly what I'm doing,' McEvoy persisted, aware that he had little concrete evidence on which to arrest Marion D'Arcy except the sighting of her car by two people known to hold a grudge against her. 'So, are you coming voluntarily or am I going to have to arrest you?'

'On what charges?'

'Failing to cooperate in a garda investigation, seeking to pervert the course of justice, conspiracy to murder, they'll do to be going on with.'

'That's a joke, right?' Marion snapped angrily.

'No, it's not a joke, Mrs D'Arcy,' McEvoy said firmly. 'I'm deadly serious.'

'Well, you're going to have to arrest me.'

'Mother!' Mark D'Arcy warned. 'I really think you should—'
She cut him off with a glare.

'Fine,' McEvoy said. 'Tom, go and get those two outside while I charge Mrs D'Arcy.'

'Mark, call John Rice and tell him to get to Athboy garda station as soon as possible,' Marion D'Arcy instructed. 'And get onto your Uncle Frank, he'll know what to do. You're making a big mistake, Superintendent. I had nothing to do with either death.'

* * *

He was pacing the corridor, anxious to make a start. Now that his anger had dissipated he was starting to worry that he'd been too hasty.

Marion D'Arcy had left her house with her head held high and had seemingly welcomed the flashing cameras of the media as they passed through her gates, staring from the back window of the garda car defiantly. Since arriving in Athboy she'd sat imperially in an interview room waiting for John Rice to arrive. Her confidence was unsettling.

His mobile phone rang. 'McEvoy.'

'You better know what the hell you're doing, Colm,' Bishop snapped. 'I've just had the Minister for Justice on the phone, warming my ear. He didn't take kindly to having to deal with, and I quote, "this shit", on a Saturday. I take it that you have forensics or witnesses that link Marion D'Arcy to both murders?'

'I... er,' McEvoy stuttered, 'not exactly. We have some circumstantial evidence.'

'You *are* messing with me, Colm, aren't you? You do know who we're dealing with here, don't you? Someone who can get the ear of the Minister within fifteen minutes of being arrested! The family might be under the media spotlight for supposed past crimes, but they still wield a lot of power.'

'She's... she's involved in all of this,' McEvoy said weakly. 'I know she is.'

'You *know* she is! Why couldn't you have waited until you had some solid evidence? Are you a complete idiot?'

'I...'

'Now you've got her there, you'd better question her. But unless she confesses and signs a sworn statement, you're to let her go and then you stay well away from her. Do you hear me? You don't go near her again until you have incontrovertible evidence that she was involved in either killing. And stay away from the rest of her family as well. I don't believe you sometimes. Jesus.'

'I'll...'

'I've got to go. We still haven't found those bastards who tried to blow-up Hannah Fallon. Try and use a bit of cop-on, will you?' Bishop ended the call.

McEvoy tipped his head back and stared at the magnolia-painted ceiling. Whatever confidence he'd had this morning had now vanished entirely. The chances of Marion D'Arcy confessing were slim to none. And the chances of linking her directly to either murder had the same odds. He'd probably just made an enormous mistake. He closed his eyes, his exhaustion washing over him.

His mobile phone rang again. He tipped his head forward and looked at the screen before answering.

'John?'

'The media have gone bananas,' John Joyce said. 'They want to know why you've arrested Marion D'Arcy.'

McEvoy felt his heart sinking. 'Tell them that we've simply brought her in for questioning – she's helping us with our enquiries. No charges have been made,' he replied, thinking of the following day's newspaper headlines.

'I thought you'd arrested her?' Joyce said confused.

'We're still making our minds up,' McEvoy hedged.

'So you've not arrested her then?'

'Listen, John,' McEvoy said, regaining some composure, 'we did arrest her, okay; it was the only way to get her to come in, but we haven't yet questioned her. Just hold off on telling the media anything until we've questioned her and either let her go or formally charged her with an offence. We need to be careful about how all of this is reported.'

'You want me to say nothing?' Joyce said incredulously, aware of the pressure the media were putting on the press liaison team.

'For an hour or so. Until then, she's helping us with our enquiries.' McEvoy ended the call. Things seemed to be going from bad to worse. What should have been a moment of triumph had somehow turned into a rear-guard action.

* * *

Marion D'Arcy was whispering to John Rice when McEvoy entered the room with Tom McManus. She stopped what she was saying and stared at him with contempt.

'Right, we'll make a start, shall we?' McEvoy said as confidently as he could, sitting down.

McManus fiddled with the digital recorder and McEvoy listed the date, time and people present.

'I demand to know why you have arrested my client,

Superintendent?' John Rice said before McEvoy could ask his first question.

'Because she wouldn't answer our questions, she's lied to us, she's tried to alter the course of an investigation, and I believe she might have conspired in the murder of Peter O'Coffey.'

'You believe?'

'Yes, I believe,' McEvoy said, starting to regain some confidence. 'That's why we're here; so she can answer our questions.'

'So this is a fishing expedition?' Rice said sarcastically.

'No, this is a murder investigation,' McEvoy said firmly, 'and I need to ask Mrs D'Arcy some questions.'

'I've instructed my client to say nothing until you've provided conclusive evidence to substantiate your claims. Unless you can do so we will be exercising our prerogative to leave.'

McEvoy sighed audibly. 'Okay, let's play it your way,' he conceded, moving his gaze to Marion D'Arcy. 'I'll tell you how I see it and you can tell me whether I'm right. If I'm not satisfied with your answers, I'll keep asking questions. If you don't want to answer them, fine; we'll let the DPP decide whether charges are to be pressed.'

Neither D'Arcy or Rice replied.

'This is what I think happened. You drove to The White Gallows in the early hours of Sunday morning. You parked just inside the gateway then you made your way to the house. Given that Roza was staying with her boyfriend, your plan was to take advantage of her absence to search the place. My guess is you were after the latest copy of your father's will. When you let yourself in, you found your father lying either unconscious or dead in the library. Instead of panicking or calling for an ambulance, you carried your father upstairs and placed him back in his bed. Then you went back downstairs and tidied up, picking up the vase fragments and taking the gun. You probably even searched for whatever it was that you were looking for. How am I doing so far?'

'You're crazy,' Marion D'Arcy said dismissively.

John Rice placed a hand on her arm silencing her.

'You then left the house, went back to your car and drove home. The next morning you planned to return to the farm before Roza got back from Athboy, only she got there first and called the guards. You organised Dr Astell to attend to your father and persuaded him to declare that your father had passed away in his sleep. Given that Dr Astell was a major beneficiary of your father's will there might well have been some kind of prior agreement. Your father probably wanted to ensure he had a nice, quiet death; unlike the thousands he killed during the war. He didn't want anyone looking at his life too carefully in case people discovered the truth about his past. You knew that two members of Yellow Star had been sneaking about the place asking questions and you wanted to try and keep things as quiet as possible. I'm still on track?'

Marion D'Arcy was staring at him with contempt, but stayed silent.

'Three witnesses saw you arrive at your father's farm. Peter O'Coffey was making his way home after killing your father and hanging the noose as a diversion. As you know, Peter had serious financial problems and was on the verge of losing his grandfather's farm. Only he wasn't listed as a beneficiary in your father's will like Francis. At first he tried to blackmail Francie, his co-killer, but he'd no ready cash to give him. Angry and desperate he decided to try the person he'd seen arriving at the farm as he was leaving. After all, they had something to hide. They'd been at the house and they'd tried to pass the murder off as a natural death. Rather than accede to Peter's wishes you instead decided to kill him with your father's gun, seeking to make it look like suicide. At the very least it would look like Francie had killed him. You met him at the border between the two farms, made him write out a short note, and then blew his brains out.'

McEvoy sat back in his chair. It all fitted together. He'd regained his composure.

Marion D'Arcy glared at him angrily but remained silent.

'And why would my client have done such a thing?' John Rice asked.

'Deep insecurity,' McEvoy replied. 'She'd been adopted by Albert Koch when he married her mother. She knew that the will had been recently altered and she wanted to make sure she was still a beneficiary; that she would still inherit what she saw as her share of Ostara Industries. She killed or had Peter O'Coffey killed to ensure his silence. She probably didn't realise he had his own guilt to protect.'

'So now she had Peter O'Coffey killed?' Rice said, seizing the opening.

'No. Yes.' McEvoy said, floundering. 'I'm not yet sure.'

'You're not sure? You're accusing my client of killing a man in cold blood and you're not even sure if it was her that killed him? This isn't evidence, Superintendent, its speculation!'

'Mrs D'Arcy was at her father's house in the early hours of Saturday night,' McEvoy repeated again, feeling uneasy.

'And my client insists that she wasn't. So, what's your evidence that she was there? One of your supposed witnesses is dead!'

'She was seen by Ewa Chojnacki and Tomas Prochazka pulling into the gateway.'

'Those two scandal-mongers!' Rice exploded. 'You can't trust anything those two family wreckers say! Jesus, they're hardly impartial witnesses, are they? They're out to try and destroy the Koch family.'

'Nevertheless, they saw Mrs D'Arcy's dark blue Mercedes arrive at the farm. And Mrs D'Arcy cannot account for where she was on the night of his death,' McEvoy persisted.

'That's it?' Rice said dismissively. 'That's your evidence? Two unreliable witnesses who have an unsubstantiated vendetta against my client's family, and the lack of an alibi because she was by herself?'

'I don't drive a Mercedes,' Marion said, her face creased in a puzzled expression. 'I drive a Range...' she trailed off.

McEvoy felt his heart skip a beat. He was doomed. 'But I saw it parked in front of your father's house when I first arrived there. A dark blue Mercedes. And I saw the same one parked outside the front of your house on Monday morning.'

Marion stayed silent.

'You don't own a dark blue Mercedes?' McEvoy pressed, drowning slowly. He should have got the registration plate checked before he rushed in. He was so tired and stretched and keen to wrap the case up that he'd made an elementary mistake. He was going to be hung out to dry by Tony Bishop and what was more he deserved it.

Marion D'Arcy glanced nervously towards John Rice, a realisation opening in her own mind, and in that moment McEvoy gained fresh hope. She knew whose car it was.

'If it wasn't your car, whose car is it?' he asked urgently. 'James Kinneally's? … Stefan Freel's?'

She stayed silent, giving him a disdainful look.

A thought started to emerge inside his mind. 'Your brother's?'

She cast her glare down at her hands.

'It was your brother's,' McEvoy said as an accusation. 'You borrowed his car. Oh, sweet… It was your brother's car,' he stated, the penny finally dropping.

McEvoy pushed back his chair and headed for the door. Charles Koch had been at his father's house in the early hours of Sunday morning. Just as James Kinneally had lied for Marion D'Arcy, Patricia Kinneally had lied for Charles Koch. O'Coffey had tried to blackmail Charles like he had his son. His reward was a bullet to the head. He turned at the door. 'Where's your brother now? Mrs D'Arcy?'

Marion D'Arcy raised her eyes and stared fiercely at McEvoy but stayed silent.

McEvoy shook his head in frustration and headed from the room. He took a couple of steps and returned to the doorway. 'We're not finished yet. I'll be back shortly.'

'I'm sorry, Superintendent, but we are,' Rice said firmly. 'You have no reason to continue to hold my client.'

'Fine, but you might as well make yourself comfortable, Mr Rice, because as soon as I find her brother, I'll be bringing him here for questioning.'

'You'll be wasting your time, Superintendent. You have no evidence against him either, just the sighting of a car which could have belonged to anyone.'

* * *

There were no journalists left at the gates of Marion D'Arcy's house. McEvoy sped up to the house still furious with himself.

He leapt from the car, rushed to the front door, knocked loudly and waited. There was no response. He knocked again but there was no sign of life. He walked quickly to the side of the house and headed towards the stables. The horses in the neighbouring field stared at him with mild curiosity before lowering their heads back to the lush grass. A dark blue Mercedes was parked at the entrance to the stable yard.

The car was empty and so was the yard. A couple of horses watched his progress round the stables from their stalls. One of them neighed loudly.

As he started to make his way out of the far side of the yard Charles Koch came into view a hundred yards away approaching on horseback. The horse was walking sedately, breath snorting in clouds from its nose, Koch gently rolling from side to side.

'I've been told to expect you,' Koch said as he neared. 'My lawyer tells me not to say a word until he's present.'

'Shit,' McEvoy muttered to himself. He could feel any hope of wrapping the case up in the next couple of days starting to slip away. And unless they could find forensic evidence on Koch himself or his clothes – traces of cordite or blood or mud – they were in trouble. Everything else rested on circumstantial evidence that John Rice would systematically shred or cast doubt on. Even if they could prove that Patricia Kinneally had provided a false alibi for the night Koch's father died it wouldn't be enough for a safe conviction – it wouldn't prove that Koch had killed Peter O'Coffey.

Koch passed McEvoy and made his way into the yard. He dismounted slowly and gracefully.

'I need to ask you some questions,' McEvoy said, more in hope than actual expectation of answers.

Koch stayed silent tugging at the girdle strap that kept the saddle in place.

'Why did you go to your father's house in the early hours of Sunday morning?'

'I didn't.' Koch pulled the saddle free and hung it on an open doorway. Steam rose from the horse's sweaty back.

'Your car was seen arriving at two o'clock in the morning.'

'It wasn't my car.' Koch moved back to the horse and started to work on the bridle.

McEvoy shifted his feet and decided to try another line of questions. 'Why did you kill Peter O'Coffey?'

'First you try and frame my son for murder and now me?' Koch said evenly, lifting the bridle over the horse's ears and slipping the bit from its mouth. 'Why would I kill Peter O'Coffey?'

'He was blackmailing you,' McEvoy said without confidence.

'Blackmailing me! Why would he want to do that?' Koch draped the bridle over the saddle and took a brush hanging from a nail.

'Because he knew that your son had killed your father and he was desperate for money to save his farm.'

'My son did not kill my father, Superintendent. Peter did, and it was an accident. The last few days have been a nightmare because of that accident.' Koch started to brush the horse's coat.

'Is that why you killed him?'

'I've already told you. I didn't kill him!'

'You drive a dark blue Mercedes that was seen arriving at your father's farm at two o'clock in the morning the night he died.'

'I don't think so, Superintendent. I was at Patricia Kinneally's house.'

'About which you've already lied. Why should we believe you now?'

Koch stopped brushing the horse, turning to face McEvoy. 'Because it's the truth. Do you know how many people own dark blue Mercedes around here? That's why my uncle is a very rich man. And how do you know it was dark blue in any case? At two o'clock in the morning it could have been any dark colour – black, blue, green, red. They'd have all looked the same.'

'So whose car do you think it was,' McEvoy asked sarcastically.

'I don't know. How about Stefan Freel? He drives a black Mercedes 320. Or…' Koch trailed off.

'Or who?' McEvoy prompted.

'Nobody.'

'Nobody,' McEvoy repeated, aware that Koch was right; the car at The White Gallows that night could have belonged to any number of people. 'This isn't over yet,' he said weakly. 'I'll be getting in a forensic team to go over your car. If they find any evidence that you were near to where Peter O'Coffey was killed…' He petered off, reluctant to make the threat.

'You won't find anything, Superintendent. I didn't kill Peter,' Koch reaffirmed.

* * *

Stefan Freel dropped his tall, thin frame down heavily onto the leather chair behind his desk and pointed to a seat with one hand, the other scratching the side of his prominent nose.

McEvoy sat where directed and crossed his right leg over his left. 'Working on a Saturday?'

'I work every day and now there's even more to do. Establishing Ostara Trust demands time. I was back in work immediately after the funeral.'

'You didn't go on to Marion D'Arcy's house afterwards then?' McEvoy asked, acknowledging the little love lost between the pair.

'She wouldn't let me into the church; I'd say the chances of getting into her house were zero.' Freel shrugged. 'That's okay; Dr Koch wouldn't have wanted the fuss. If the tables were turned and we were burying Marion he would have been back working before the first sod hit the coffin lid.'

'No point letting grief get in the way of making money,' McEvoy said sarcastically.

'You may mock, Superintendent, but money makes the world go round. Grief is just a distraction. Why waste time on the dead when life is for living?'

'Clearly you've never loved anyone,' McEvoy said bitterly.

'Perhaps not, but I'm not sure I've missed anything.'

McEvoy shook his head sadly. Freel's emotional depth was skin deep. He might have material wealth and wield a certain amount of power but he knew nothing of the finer things in life, like love. 'You own a black Mercedes 320?' he asked getting to the point of the interview.

'Yes.'

'It was seen parked outside The White Gallows at two o'clock in the morning, the night Albert Koch died.'

'I don't think so, Superintendent,' Freel said with an amused smile. 'Not unless it was stolen from Dublin Airport. It was parked in Area J in the long term car park Friday and Saturday night. I'm sure their surveillance cameras will confirm that. Besides I thought Francie Koch has confessed to his grandfather's death?'

'He's confessed to leaving him for dead. Someone else carried him back up to his bed and left him to die.'

'Well, it wasn't me, I was in London completing a deal.'

'You won't mind then if we re-check your story?' McEvoy said without conviction.

'You can check it as many times as you like, but I have several witnesses. I had dinner at an investment banker's

Thames-side apartment on Saturday night and I stayed in the Dorchester.'

'And what about the car parked at Dr Koch's house?' McEvoy asked.

'What about it? I've already told you that mine was at Dublin Airport.'

'I meant, whose car could it have been if it wasn't yours?'

'I… I'm not sure. Both Charles Koch and Mark D'Arcy drive Mercedes. So does Francie Koch.'

'Mark D'Arcy?' McEvoy said, remembering Charles Koch's, 'Nobody'.

'He has a dark green E240.'

'And what about Francie?'

'A gold one. I'm not sure of the model.'

McEvoy stared past Freel into space. He needed to talk to Mark D'Arcy.

* * *

'George? How are you getting on with those Mercedes?'

'I'm not. I don't think whoever killed Peter O'Coffey drove to the field. I think they rode there. I've just been back up to the murder site. There are horse prints in the mud at the gate. We could try matching the shoe prints to the horses at Marion D'Arcy's stables. It's only about a mile and a half as the crow flies from her house to where we found the body.'

'And what about car tracks?' McEvoy asked.

'I think the horse prints are a better angle,' Carter persisted. 'The footprints and the horse prints overlap – sometimes a foot-print on top of the horse's, sometimes the other way round. They *had* to have been made yesterday morning; any other time and that wouldn't have been possible. Do you see? It would have been one or the other unless he passed by as the murder was happening. I didn't think anything of it until I saw the stables out here. And a horse hasn't passed by since we found the body; I've checked with the poor bastard who's guarding the place.'

'So you think that whoever killed O'Coffey had to have got there by horse?'

'I'm ninety-nine per cent certain.'

'Right, okay, start with the horses of Charles Koch, Francis Koch, and Mark D'Arcy.'

'Which ones are they?'

'Koch's is the middle stable on the right-hand side as you enter the yard; a big, brown, brute of a thing with white nose markings. I wouldn't go in there on your own,' McEvoy warned. 'Francie's is next door. I don't know about Mark D'Arcy's. There was a stable girl there the first time I paid a visit, perhaps she'll be able to help you?'

'I'll track her down and don't worry, we'll get some casts and do some comparisons. I'll also send someone back out to the laneway to see if we can follow the trail back.'

'Thanks. Give me a call as soon as you've got something.'

'You'll be the first to hear.'

* * *

McEvoy was back at Marion D'Arcy's house, sitting in the living room where he'd first interviewed her nearly a week previously. Opposite sat an exhausted looking Mark D'Arcy.

'You drive a dark green Mercedes E240?' McEvoy asked.

'Yes,' D'Arcy replied tetchily.

'Can you account for its movements last Saturday night?'

'Yes. It was in Galway. What is this, Superintendent, am I now a suspect? I thought my cousin has already confessed?'

'A dark coloured Mercedes was seen arriving at your grandfather's house at two o'clock in the morning the night he died,' McEvoy said, ignoring D'Arcy's assertion.

'Well, it wasn't mine.'

'You were in Galway,' McEvoy restated.

'Yes. And I have plenty of witnesses who can confirm that.'

'How long does it take to drive here from Galway. Two hours? At that time of night, maybe less. You could drive here and be back in Galway before six o'clock and nobody would be any the wiser.'

'Are you serious? You really think I drove all the way back to my grandfather's place? For what?'

'I don't know. You tell me.'

'I didn't drive back. Jesus!'

'Do you ride your mother's horses?' McEvoy asked, changing tack.

'Occasionally,' D'Arcy said slowly.

'Did you take one out yesterday morning?'

'No. I was making preparations for my grandfather's funeral.'

'So you definitely didn't go for an early morning ride?'

'No. I've just told you. You actually think I killed Peter O'Coffey,' D'Arcy stated anger rising in his voice.

'I think it's a possibility,' McEvoy replied. 'You own a dark green Mercedes and you ride a horse.'

'So does half of North Meath! Talk about wild accusations. Jesus Christ!'

'Our forensics teams are presently comparing horse prints found where Peter O'Coffey was murdered with the horses in the stables.'

'That's nice for them,' D'Arcy said sarcastically. 'Do they have a warrant? Even if one of our horses was up there it doesn't mean I was riding it!'

'We have footprints as well,' McEvoy stated.

'You're welcome to take a cast of my shoes,' D'Arcy lifted his leg towards McEvoy.

'So who was out riding yesterday morning?' McEvoy asked ignoring the proffered foot.

'I've no idea. As I said, I was too busy making sure all the arrangements were in place for my grandfather's funeral. Something that you did your best to ruin.'

'By arresting his killer?' McEvoy said, arching his eyebrows. 'I would have thought the family would have been pleased that we'd caught the person responsible for his death.'

'Pleased? Are you taking some perverse pleasure out of this fucking nightmare? My grandfather's been accidentally killed by my cousin and my second cousin has been murdered, and your three prime suspects seem to be my mother, my uncle and myself! There's absolutely nothing to be pleased about. I was with my car in Galway on Saturday night and I did not go out riding yesterday morning. I have plenty of witnesses for both occasions!'

'Don't worry, we'll be following up with all of them,' McEvoy offered weakly.

* * *

He was standing on the back steps of Athboy garda station trying to marshal his thoughts. It was no use; his mind kept drifting back to how he'd managed to make a total mess of the day so far, ignoring procedure and stumbling from one potential perpetrator to another. Clutching at straws was no way for an experienced officer to conduct an investigation. There was every possibility that he'd done immense damage to any case that they might build as the inquiry plodded on.

Bishop was going to crucify him. Not only had he acted unprofessionally, he'd ignored his warning, interviewing both Charles Koch and Mark D'Arcy without his approval. The only thing that might salvage things was a critical breakthrough, but he wasn't holding his breath.

He massaged his temples and rubbed his right eye with the heel of his hand, trying to exorcise the tiredness from his face. He needed to slow down, take his time over things; stick to established procedures and try and repair whatever damage had been done.

So far they'd managed to ascertain that Marion D'Arcy and her daughter Jane, Charles Koch and his son Carl, and Frank Koch, had all been out riding at some point on Friday morning. All of them owned or had access to a dark coloured Mercedes. They were all refusing to cooperate with the investigation and

McEvoy couldn't blame them, given his form in the last few hours.

As soon as his chat with Mark D'Arcy was over he'd pulled George Carter out of the stables and started the process of trying to obtain a formal search warrant. He wasn't hopeful that they'd be back any time soon; John Rice's skills and Marion D'Arcy's political clout would see to that. And whatever they had was probably going to be inadmissible in court. It had been a dumb thing to do in the first place.

He cursed at himself, scratched at his scalp and sucked down a lungful of fresh air trying to imagine it swirling with nicotine-laced smoke. What he needed right now was a miracle. Or at least a lucky break. Something. Anything.

His mobile phone rang.

* * *

McEvoy strode nervously down the corridor towards the interview room. According to George Carter's analysis of the material he'd managed to collect during his unauthorised search, the person waiting inside was Peter O'Coffey's killer. One half of his brain was warning caution, the other saw possibilities of redemption; a last chance to try and prise open the case before it descended into a legal and political quagmire that would drag on for weeks, if not years; an opportunity to save himself from a dressing-down and possible disciplinary procedures. He'd already broken half a dozen rules, one last roll of the dice could hardly do more harm.

He opened the door to the interview room and took a seat opposite Charles Koch. John Rice sat to his left; a uniformed officer hovered uncomfortably in the corner of the room. McEvoy turned on the recorder, listed out the formalities and turned his attention to Koch.

'A few more questions, Professor Koch,' he said evenly, smiling weakly. 'The horse you were riding this morning, is it yours?'

'My client is not prepared to answer any questions until we have a full explanation as to why he's been brought here,' Rice interceded.

'It's okay, John,' Koch said, placing his hand on Rice's wrist. 'I'm happy to answer any questions the Superintendent has. The sooner this is over, the sooner we can leave. The answer to your question is that it is my sister's horse. All the horses there are.'

'But you ride it?'

'You saw me riding it.'

'And you're the only one who rides it?'

'No, no. The stable girl takes it out occasionally. Sometimes Francis. Perhaps Marion.'

'But you were the only one who has ridden it recently?'

McEvoy could see the concern start to grow in Koch's eyes.

'Yes,' Koch answered more hesitantly. 'I don't know,' he said backtracking. 'Someone else might have.'

'But you were riding the horse yesterday morning?'

'Yes,' Koch answered slowly, knowing the stable girl had seen him leave.

'So the only way its footprints could have been found at the gateway to the field in which Peter O'Coffey died was if you had been there?'

'I regularly ride past that field, Superintendent; it's part of a circuit I make. The prints there could have been there for some time.'

'So you passed that gateway yesterday morning then?' McEvoy asked calmly. If Koch answered yes, then he could be placed at the crime scene at approximately the time of the murder. If he answered no then he would be caught in his own lie. If he refused to answer he was as good as admitting his guilt.

Koch's face betrayed his inner conflict. 'No,' he eventually muttered, shaking his head.

'So that was a "No"?' McEvoy pressed.

'I... er.' Koch glanced left at his lawyer. The colour had drained from his face.

'My client does not wish to answer that question,' Rice said firmly.

'He's already given an answer to the question. I'm asking him to confirm it.'

'My client wishes to withdraw his answer, Superintendent. He didn't understand the question.'

'As the recording will testify, Mr Rice, the question was a very simple one and your client gave a straight answer. He said, "No"; meaning that he did not ride past the gateway yesterday morning.'

'My client is withdrawing his answer,' Rice insisted.

'Look, it was a very simple question,' McEvoy repeated. 'I don't understand what the problem is. All I did was ask him whether he rode past the gateway to the field in which Mr O'Coffey was found dead yesterday morning. Surely he can remember what he did only yesterday? If the answer is "no", then he couldn't have killed Peter O'Coffey. Surely that's the answer that you want him to give?'

'You're trying to play games, Superintendent. My client does not wish to answer.'

'Is that what you think the problem is? Is playing games the preserve of lawyers only? You're not even giving your client the chance to confirm the answer to a simple yes or no question. You're answering for him. He's already answered "no". I'm asking him to confirm his answer. If the answer is in fact yes, then he was at the scene of a murder at the time that it approximately occurred. If the answer is no then...' McEvoy shrugged.

'No,' Koch said panicking. 'The answer is...'

'We are not prepared to answer any more questions until I have consulted with my client,' Rice interrupted quickly. 'Privately.'

'That was the wrong answer, Professor Koch,' McEvoy said with satisfaction. 'You see, we *know* that you were there yesterday morning. The killer's footprints had been over-stamped by your horse's. You've not had chance to return since, so it could only have happened when you were there meeting Mr O'Coffey. By answering no you've caught yourself in a lie. Juries don't like lies. But they do like concrete, forensic evidence.'

'I demand some time to talk to my client,' John Rice snapped.

'Okay, I did ride past the field but it was empty,' Koch conceded.

'Charles,' Rice warned.

'I never met Peter O'Coffey,' Koch finished.

'But surely you'd have seen him in the field if your horse's hoof prints were over the top of the killers?'

'I didn't look into the field,' Koch said pulling an amused smirk. 'And who's to say I was passing at the time of the murder? It could have occurred either before or after I went by.'

'And yet your horse's hoof prints are scattered all over the gateway as if he'd been tied up there.'

Koch stayed silent.

'And the killer's footprints were mixed in with your horse's. In fact, some of his prints were over the horse's and vice versa. The only way that could have happened is if whoever the killer is got off and on the horse. Which means you are the killer, Professor Koch. You killed Peter O'Coffey.'

Koch cast his gaze down to his hands and stayed silent.

'Superintendent, I'd like to consult with my client,' Rice said firmly but lacking his usual edge.

'Absolutely,' McEvoy said standing, feeling a swell of confidence in his chest. 'We will find additional forensics to place you at the scene, Professor Koch – traces of cordite or blood or mud on your clothes and shoes or on your horse or his tack.'

As McEvoy reached the door, Koch cleared his throat. 'I didn't intend to kill him, Superintendent,' he said calmly.

'Pardon?' McEvoy said startled, turning back to face him.

'I said, I didn't intend to kill him…'

'Charles, I strongly advise you to…'

Koch placed a hand on Rice's sleeve to silence him.

'They have all the evidence they need, John. As the Superintendent says, they'll find more. Why fight it? Murder seems to be in our nature – first my father, then my son and now...' He shrugged. 'We've all taken another person's life.'

'Charles, I really think that you...' Rice persisted.

'John, it's over,' Koch said more harshly. 'Even your brilliance isn't going to get me out of this.'

'You shot Peter O'Coffey,' McEvoy prompted, sitting back down at the table, amazed at Koch's change in attitude.

'He wouldn't listen to reason; he wanted too much for Francie's freedom.'

'So you decided to silence him?'

'It was the only way,' Koch said neutrally. 'I tried to make it look like suicide. I obviously failed. He *had* been involved in the death of my father. Do you know what I was thinking when I made him kneel down in the mud? Nothing. My mind was a complete blank. I could have been peeling potatoes. I knew then how my father could have killed all those people. They were nothing to him. They were just potatoes.'

Koch stopped and McEvoy stayed silent waiting for him to continue. John Rice had folded his arms, tipped his head back and was staring at the blistered paint on the ceiling, obviously fuming at his client's foolishness.

'He begged me for his life, you know. Begged. It was pathetic. We both knew that if I let him walk away he would come running to you. He wouldn't have accepted a single payment; he would have kept coming back for more. It was bad enough that those Yellow Star scum and the press wanted to try and destroy us - we expected that; but someone we took in and helped? We rescued his great aunt from shame and poverty and took on her daughter as one of our own. We gave his grandfather work and helped him establish their farm and that's how he tried to repay us? I thought I would feel remorse afterwards, but I felt nothing. Nothing then, nothing now. I guess I am my father's son.'

'And you were at your father's house on Saturday night?' McEvoy prompted.

'I thought I'd have the place to myself given Roza was away for the evening. It seems I wasn't the only one.'

'You found your father in the library?'

'I thought he was just unconscious at first. I carried him up to his bed and then went to look for his attackers. I assumed it was those two yids who'd been making trouble, asking their stupid questions. When I returned he was dead. My father knew that someone might come one day to kill him. He didn't want any publicity. He looked like he'd just passed away in his sleep so I tidied up the house and left. I told Marion in the morning. She was to look after the funeral arrangements.'

'Only Roza had called the guards,' McEvoy stated.

'I'd forgotten that Roza might return early in the morning. Marion was apoplectic.' Koch smiled to himself. 'She always had a short fuse.'

'Why were you there? In the middle of the night?'

'His will.' He shook his head slowly. 'I was looking for his will. I knew that he'd altered it. I was afraid of what he'd done. He seemed to have become a changed man in recent months; he'd become more… distant; introspective. He was losing his mind and God knows what he'd done. I needed to check for myself and it seems I was right to be worried. A few months ago and he'd never have made a will like that. What a mess.'

'And did you find it? Was it you that sent it around to everyone?'

'Me? No, no. My guess is that was Stefan Freel stirring things up. He was the one with the most to gain. He'll have wanted it in the public domain before Henry Collier produced the old will instead.'

'And Francis?' McEvoy prompted.

'I didn't know Francis and Peter had killed my father until I met Peter yesterday morning. I should have known it was them. They were obsessed with finding the vault. They'd been searching for the rumoured hoard of hidden Nazi gold since they were children. They were obsessed by it.'

'You knew about the vault?'

'I was there when it was built. I discovered a way in not long after. It was my playground; my library. I helped him build it up over the years. It's probably one of the best private collections in the world,' he said proudly and paused. 'I knew all about my father's past, Superintendent. He never confided in me, but we both knew I knew. The evidence was all around me.'

'And you weren't appalled by it? That he'd helped kill thousands of people?'

'He was a product of his time and culture,' Koch said evenly. 'He'd been taught to hate the Jews with a passion. They all were – Hitler's generation. He did what the regime required him to do.'

'So he was just following orders?'

'Yes.'

'Even if those orders were to murder innocent people?'

'They weren't innocent. Not to the Nazis. They were the enemy; the reason that Germany had been on its knees. They were the parasites that were sucking away the good life.'

'So an entire race deserved to be wiped from the face of the earth?'

'He didn't invent the final solution, Superintendent.'

'But he did help enact it. He did take part in the Jewish Skeleton Project. He was more than a guard at Auschwitz. And what about the underground museum? Why collect all that memorabilia?'

'The war affected my father deeply. It haunted him constantly that Germany lost and surrendered unconditionally. That all the cities were flattened. Everything destroyed. That the country was split in two. He was a believer in National Socialism – he felt it was his duty to preserve the past; to collect material so that he could try and understand how it all went wrong. Every spare moment he spent reading from his library.'

'So why did you help him?'

'I was his son, why wouldn't I have helped him?'

314

John Rice tipped his head forward and shook it gently.

'Because he was a war criminal. You knew, yet you did nothing about it.'

'He acted under orders. It was war. Awful things happen during a war.'

'He killed numerous people in cold blood, many of them fellow Germans.'

'They'd been sentenced to death.'

'By who? There was no trial, no judge, no jury! They were innocent victims who'd been rounded up, put on a train and taken to a monstrosity of a place to be killed and incinerated – wiped from the face of the Earth.'

'He did what he needed to do to survive and to try and help his country win the war.'

'If he loved his country so much, why did he come to Ireland? Why didn't he stay in Germany after the war and help to rebuild it?'

'You know why,' Koch said calmly, picking at a fingernail. 'He would have been persecuted and possibly executed as a scapegoat for Hitler's madness. My father did not start the war, nor did he order the killing of the Jews. He was an ordinary German caught up in extraordinary times.'

'He could have taken a different path.'

'You think people had choices? People did what they were told.'

'I thought you said he was a believer in National Socialism? He was a follower, an instigator, not some passive puppet; he actively sought to realise Hitler's vision.'

Koch snorted derision. 'Now you're just trying to twist my words. My father did his duty, nothing more, nothing less.'

'And what about your father's will? It seems as if he changed his mind. It suggests that he saw himself guilty of a significant crime. After all, he left a fortune to Holocaust charities.'

Koch shook his head slowly. 'The family will be contesting the will. He was an old man; he'd started to become confused. He was losing his mind.'

'Or gaining it,' McEvoy parried. 'Along with a conscience.'

'Ostara Industries was not built on the back of the Holocaust! My father built it by himself through hard work and vision. We owe the Jews nothing. You hear, nothing!'

McEvoy slowly shook his head. 'Ostara Industries was founded on money stolen from two banks in 1955.'

'Now you're just being facile. You'll never meet a man who worked as hard as my father. Never. Why would he rob a bank?'

'Why would he kill innocent people?'

'They weren't innocent! There's no such thing as innocence – only degrees of guilt.'

McEvoy sighed. It didn't matter what he said, Charles Koch would always be an apologist for his father. There was a remote possibility that Koch was simply following orders during the war, but that didn't negate the criminality of the acts. Yellow Star's evidence though suggested that he'd been a proactive participant. He'd murdered several, powerless people and participated in genocide, taking an active role in the Jewish Skeleton Project of the Abnenebre. His actions were indefensible however much his son protested.

But then what did he expect of Charles Koch? He had murdered Peter O'Coffey, one of his own family, in cold blood rather than share the family's riches to buy his silence and Francie's freedom. He'd described the murder as the equivalent to peeling a potato – Peter O'Coffey and millions of Jews reduced to inanimate vegetables; entities devoid of family and friends, of feelings and emotions, of rights and entitlements. The Koch dynasty had little to do with family – bonds of shared compassion, forgiveness and hope, rather it was about the ruthless pursuit of industry, power and legacy. Perhaps Albert Koch had begun to realise this as he neared the end of his life? Had come to understand that his victims were as human as he was; were more human than he was given the blood on his hands. His will certainly demonstrated a profound change of view, but it was too late for his kin – they were already set in his image.

316

McEvoy felt an over-powering desire to leave the room and call Gemma. Like Albert Koch he'd let work become his dominant focus; an emotional crutch in place of his family. He'd even left the memorial service held for his beloved wife, abandoning his daughter on a day when she needed him most. What kind of father was he becoming? What kind of daughter was he raising? Gemma was everything, and yet that was barely reflected in how he was conducting his life.

* * *

McEvoy had left Charles Koch to consult with a deflated and disillusioned John Rice and had headed to a small office to call home. As he withdrew his mobile it rang and, instinctively, he answered it.

'McEvoy.'

'What the fuck is going on, Colm?' Bishop snapped. 'Are you congenitally predisposed to go off the rails in the middle of an investigation? First, the Raven case, now this! Arresting Marion D'Arcy on a hunch. A fuckin' hunch that turns out not to be true! She's livid and she's on the war path. For the second time in a day I've had that bollix, O'Reilly, on the phone,' Bishop said, referring to the Minister for Justice. 'He wants to know what the fuck is going on, and so do I. I've enough to be dealing with, without wandering around after you clearing up your fuck-ups. Well? What have you got to say for yourself?'

'Look, I'm sorry,' McEvoy muttered, a dark, sinking feeling folding over him. 'I—'

'Sorry! Is that it? Not only have you probably fucked up any case you were building, but Marion D'Arcy is almost certainly going to throw the book at us. And she'll no doubt win. It won't matter a damn that her father was a war criminal. Do realise how damaging that will be? Not only will we have to pay her damages, but our reputation will be in tatters. Please tell me that you haven't arrested any more of that goddamn family.'

'Well, I…'

'Oh Jesus, Colm. Which one?'

'Charles Koch. He's…'

'The brother? Which bit of "do not talk to any of the family before talking to me" do you not understand?' Bishop raged. 'What is this, double your money? Let him go and stay well away from them. All of them. If you so much as want to look at them, you're going to have to argue your case with me first. And it'll have to be a fuckin' good case. Am I making myself clear here?'

'Charles Koch has just confessed to the murder of Peter O'Coffey,' McEvoy said quietly, aware that Bishop had every right to be apoplectic with him.

'He's done what?' Bishop queried, the wind instantly dropping from his sails.

'He's confessed to the shooting of Peter O'Coffey. Once we've got a search warrant, I'm confident we'll get all the forensic evidence we'll need for a successful prosecution.'

'Charles Koch has confessed to the murder of Peter O'Coffey?' Bishop repeated, unable to keep the disbelief from his voice.

'Perhaps you might be able to tell the Minister?' McEvoy suggested.

'Don't get fuckin' smart with me, Colm! You're still in the shit. Right up to your scrawny neck. I want to see a report by the end of the day.'

'Sir.'

'And Colm?'

'Yes?'

'I hope for your sake that he doesn't withdraw that confession.' The line went dead.

McEvoy dropped heavily into a chair and clasped the bridge of his nose before massaging his forehead. He had an overwhelming desire for a whiskey and a smoke. He dialled Caroline's number.

It was answered on the second ring. 'Hello?'

'Caroline, it's Colm, is Gemma there?'

'She's out the back with Mam and Dad. Is everything okay? You don't sound too good.'

'Everything's fine. I've just arrested Peter O'Coffey's killer.'

'Let me guess, Albert Koch's daughter? She looks like a hard-faced bitch to me.'

'The son, but keep that to yourself, okay; we've not told the media yet. I'm telling you sis, never trust family, they're deadly.'

'What makes you think I trust any of you? Even if I do know how far I can throw you. I'll just get Gemma for you.'

The line went quiet for a few moments. McEvoy closed his eyes and massaged them through his lids.

'Dad?'

'Hiya, pumpkin.'

'Have you managed to eat anything? I bet you haven't.'

'Not for a while, but I'll get something in a minute. Look, I'm hoping to finish up here in the next couple of hours. I was thinking that maybe we could go out for a Chinese tonight? You, me, Caroline, Jimmy, and your grandparents.'

'Jimmy's working a late shift tonight.'

'Well, the rest of us can go. No expense spared. And to-morrow morning I thought we could go for a walk along Dollymount Strand.'

'Have we won the lotto? Two trips in two days?'

'Oi, cheeky. I'll be back by seven at the latest, okay? I just have to wrap some things up here first. Can you ask Aunt Caroline to book a table for eight o'clock?'

'You're not going to be smelling of manure again, are you?'

'What? No! That's only happened the once, hasn't it?'

'Yeah, but it still happened. It was embarrassing.'

'Well, I won't be stinking of manure tonight, okay? Look, I better be getting on; the sooner I finish here, the sooner I can come home. Make sure you behave yourself until then. I love you.'

'I love you too, Dad. Are you okay? You kind of sound a bit weird.'

'I'm fine,' he lied. 'I'm just... We've just made an arrest. Things are a little chaotic right now. I'll see you soon.'

He ended the call and leant back in the chair, tipping his head back and closing his eyes, waves of tiredness and regret washing over him.

* * *

He wandered to the front desk and glanced out onto the street. The press were crowding the road and pavement ever hopeful of a new headline. John Joyce and Barry Traynor were feverishly working up a press release to announce the arrest of Charles Koch for the murder of Peter O'Coffey.

A few cameras flashed in the low winter light, the congregation starting to part and surge. Frank Koch bustled through the journalists and up to the station door. McEvoy pushed it open and instructed the guard outside to let him in.

'I've come for my nephew,' Koch demanded.

'Your nephew's going to prison for a long time,' McEvoy said wearily. 'He's confessed to the murder of Peter O'Coffey.'

'We both know that's nonsense!' Koch snapped harshly. 'He's not going anywhere. You don't have a case.'

'I'm afraid we do.'

'You're living in hope, Superintendent. We both know you are out to try and ruin our family. This has become a vendetta for you!'

'Then you'll be pleased to know that I'm recommending that the investigation into the two bank robberies you did with your brother in 1955 are re-opened and the file passed to the Criminal Assets Bureau,' McEvoy said losing patience with the old man. 'We'll also be sorting through the contents of your brother's vault to see what other secrets it holds. We might even look into the disappearance of records from the military archives, Gefreiter Franz Kucken.'

320

Frank Koch's face flushed red. '*Sie bumsendes schwein! Ich sehe sie in der hölle!*' He turned on his heels and left the station cannoning into the waiting crowd.

'He doesn't seem to like you very much,' Kelly Stringer said from behind him.

'The feeling's mutual,' McEvoy replied, turning to face her.

'I hear that Charles Koch has confessed to Peter O'Coffey's murder.' She smiled, her eyes crinkling with delight.

'He seemed to take some kind of perverse pleasure that both he and his son had inherited his father's capacity to sow death. Somehow they've proven their worth.'

'They've proven their sickness. I thought... I thought perhaps we could... y'know, maybe go out and celebrate?' Kelly muttered, her hand buried in her hair. 'If you're not, that is—'

'I'm sorry, Kelly,' McEvoy interrupted, aware of his desire but unable to realise it, 'but I can't. I need to finish up here and then go home. I've been neglecting things of late. I'm taking Gemma out this evening.' He glanced away, a hollow gap opening in his stomach.

'That's... that's okay,' Kelly said blushing. 'Maybe some other time.' She started to move reluctantly away.

'Some other time,' McEvoy repeated, watching her retreat, aware that he'd done nothing to sever whatever strange, unrealised bond existed between them.

* * *

He'd already spoken to Jenny Flanagan, telling her that the earliest he would be able to travel down to Tipperary would be Tuesday. Hopefully she might have made some progress by then, but it seemed as if the case was heading into a quagmire. Ultimately closing the investigation would probably hinge on fresh forensic evidence, a new witness, or the view of the DPP's office. Sometimes that was just the way it turned out; a discordant song that muddled through to a tuneless fade-out.

He ended his phone call with Colin Vickers and leant back in the uncomfortable, plastic chair, tipping it up onto two legs. He'd told Vickers that he wouldn't be attending the late afternoon team meeting in Trim and that he should continue running the case in his absence. Saturday night represented their best chance of identifying the man found stabbed to death on the banks of the River Boyne the previous Saturday night. The pubs would be packed with young people spending their hard-earned cash; alcohol and guilt perhaps freeing some otherwise silent or forgetful tongues.

He wasn't holding his breath. They hadn't had a single solid lead since the body had been discovered. They didn't even know if he was indeed Lithuanian. Deep down he suspected that the man would never be identified and his killers never caught. Unsolved murders were becoming increasingly common, especially with respect to gangland killings and random acts of violence.

Which reminded him – he needed to think about how he was going to accommodate Hannah Fallon once she left hospital. He would need to move a bed downstairs and reorganize the living space. He'd talk to Gemma about it this evening; he knew she'd have her own ideas as to how to set things up. It would be strange to have a woman living in the house once again. He wasn't sure if it was a good thing or not – wasn't sure what he thought – only time would tell.

He glanced at his watch and sighed, tipping the chair forward. He pulled a piece of paper towards himself, clicking the top of a pen to reveal its nib, and started to write. After a few moments he stopped. Bishop could wait for his report. He had more important things to be doing late on a Saturday afternoon; things that he'd been neglecting for too long. He pushed back his chair and headed purposefully for the door.

Acknowledgements

I had the idea for this book while attending a Klaus Tschira sponsored workshop in Carl Bosch's villa on the outskirts of Heidelberg. Many thanks to Heike Jöns, Christiane Marxhausen, Peter Meusburger and Edgar Wunder for their invitation to attend and their hospitality. Cian O'Callaghan, John Driscoll, Brendan Bartley, Cora Collins and Mervyn Kitchin read through a draft and made useful comments. John McElligott, a former Detective Superintendent with the National Bureau of Criminal Investigation, answered all of my questions with good humour, read through a draft, and gave excellent advice. Sean O'Riain kindly copyedited the proofs.

The following books proved useful in providing information about IG Farben, Monowitz, the Ahnenerbe, the Jewish Skeleton Project, and Skorzeny's time in Ireland.

Hayes, Peter. (2001) *Industry and Ideology: IG Farben in the Nazi Era.* Cambridge University Press: Cambridge.

Pringle, Heather. (2006) *The Master Plan: Himmler's Scholars and the Holocaust.* Hyperion: New York.

O'Neill, Terence. (2008) *Hitler's Irishmen.* Mercier Press: Dublin.

Details on all the planes that crashed or landed on Irish soil or waters can be found at: http://www.csn.ul.ie/~dan/war/crashes.htm